Eye of the Moonrat

By Trevor H. Cooley

Map By: Michael Patty

To Jeannette; the love of my life, my eternal companion, and first true editor.

Without your support and encouragement, I may never have written this story down.

The Bowl of Souls Series:

Book One: **EYE of the MOONRAT**

Novella : **HILT'S PRIDE**

Book Two: **MESSENGER of the DARK PROPHET**

Book Three: **HUNT of the BANDHAM**

Book Four: **The WAR of STARDEON** *Upcoming*

Book Five: **MOTHER of the MOONRAT** *Upcoming*

Table of Contents

The Thunder People
Jack's Rest
Trafalgan Mountains
Academy
Reneul
Wobble
Pinewood
Dark Forest
Sampo
Silvertree Elves
Mage School
Tinny Woods
Fandine River
N
W
E
S
Wide River
Maloroo

Prologue

"*If you had only followed my instructions in the first place, you would have had your prize weeks ago*," said the sultry female voice.

"Yes-yes. So you say," Ewzad Vriil replied with a frown. He didn't want it to come to that.

"*I have never led you wrong, Master.*" Her tone was petulant as always. "*Why do you find these particular requirements so difficult?*"

"Shut up!" he snapped and unclenched his hand from the wrinkled orb in his pocket, severing their connection. He wiped the hand on the front of his gold-embroidered jacket in distaste. She may never have steered him wrong, but she only obeyed him because she had to.

Ewzad leaned against the dark altar at the rear of the cave and sent his limited magical energies out to probe the chamber walls for the thousandth time. Nothing. He had been searching for weeks, but still could not find the compartment he knew was hidden there.

The interior of the cave was moist and cool. The light from a dozen torches bathed the chamber in a flickering light. His servants standing guard at the entrance exchanged nervous glances as Ewzad Vriil began to pace back and forth. No one liked to be around the nobleman when he became angry. Horrible things could happen.

Fortunately for them, Ewzad's anger didn't have time to build into a full fury. He noticed a large servant pause at the chamber's entrance. The man knelt and waited to be acknowledged.

Ewzad continued pacing. He didn't make all the servants kneel, but this man had bad knees and it amused Ewzad to make him kneel for as long as possible. Sometimes he waited for hours before letting him stand. Tonight however, he was expecting a guest. He only waited a few agonizing minutes before barking out, "What is it? Speak!"

The servant cleared his throat. "Master, Captain Blem has arrived. He wishes to see you."

"Fine-fine. Let him in, then! Hurry-hurry!" Despite his earlier reluctance to follow the voice's instructions, excitement had replaced the frustration in Ewzad's eyes. The servant disappeared and returned a few moments later with the captain. Ewzad put on a grin as his friend came into view.

"Yes! Finally, Blem my friend, you arrive!"

Blem looked much as Ewzad remembered. He was a large, bulky man and despite his lowered status, still dressed in the finery one might expect from minor nobility. His intimidating presence had been very useful to Ewzad during their younger days.

The large man entered the chamber with a smile that faded as Ewzad came into view. He paused just outside the passageway and stared as if seeing someone different than the old friend he had expected.

Ewzad knew why Blem stared. He had heard the servant's whispers of late. His fine clothes were rumpled, his hair oily. Sure, he hadn't bathed in a long time, but what did it matter? There was important work to be done. The servant's screams had assured him that they would not whisper those things again.

"Well, come on in, Blem. You do have it, yes? Please tell me you do."

The captain shrugged a sack from his shoulder and pulled out a thin box made of dark wood. "I hope that it's worth it. I was nearly caught while retrieving this for you."

Ewzad rushed forward and snatched the box away. He turned it over in his hands, searching for the proof he needed. The top of the box was inlaid with jewel-encrusted runes, the most prominent being a chaotic mix of the symbols for water and fire. Ewzad's grin widened. A steam rune, this was indeed the prize he needed.

"Yes!" he crooned in glee.

Blem frowned. "Did you hear what I said, Ewzad? Three of

my men were killed. I barely escaped with my life!"

"Oh dear!" Ewzad said with a sympathetic pout. He placed an arm around Blem's shoulders in what he thought was a consoling way. "It is good that you survived, old friend. Yes-yes, it is. You see, I still need your help." He led Blem towards the rear of the chamber.

"So . . . what is this place, anyway?" Blem asked, eying the room and in particular, the dark altar with distaste.

"This, my friend, is the hiding place of the Rings of Stardeon. They are the means to regaining our former place in the kingdom."

"Well I don't see anything. Where are they?"

"They are hidden, dear Blem. Oh yes, hidden well. But you have brought me the key." Ewzad opened the box and pulled out a dagger made of dark steel. The blade was encrusted in what looked like rust at first glance, but on a closer inspection appeared to be dried blood. Deep red jewels glimmered on the hilt. "Yes-yes-yes. This is the key."

"Alright. So how does it work, then?" Blem watched his old friend warily. Ewzad had always spoken in a unique manner, but the way he was talking now went beyond mere eccentricity.

"Do you see the altar there?"

"Yeah." As Blem looked closer, he saw that the surface of the altar glistened with a scarlet wetness. He took a step back. "Ewzad . . . why the blood?"

Ewzad laughed at his friend's discomfort. "Oh, don't worry, Blem. It was just a goblin or two. They grow thick in the hills around here. It's part of the ceremony that opens the tomb, you see."

If only it had been as easy as killing a few goblins. The books said that a sacrifice had to be performed on the altar to open the tomb, but he had tried several times to open it with no results. Paying heed to the female voice was the only way he had found the proper instructions.

"Do you see the lock, Blem?"

"No." The large man leaned forward. "What lock?"

"It's right in the center of the altar," Ewzad said, licking his lips. "A slot where the dagger goes."

Blem leaned over further, squinting his eyes. Ewzad lunged forward and plunged the jeweled dagger deep into his friend's back. Blem jerked and turned around.

"What?" A rivulet of blood ran down the captain's chin. He stared at Ewzad, with shock-filled eyes. "Why? Why did you do that?"

"Oh, I am truly sorry, Blem. I am. But it had to be this way, you see. Yes, for the tomb to open I needed to use that dagger. And it had to be an old friend . . . my old dear friend."

The dagger pulsed with energy and a swirl of darkness leeched from its hilt. A bellow of pain pierced Blem's bloody lips. He arched his back, clawed at the dagger handle, but could not reach it.

Ewzad shoved his friend forward onto the altar and with some difficulty held him there as he thrashed. Blem's screams built in intensity. Ewzad ignored him. His eyes scanned the room, searching for proof that the voice had been correct about the ceremony.

A crack sprouted on the north wall of the cave. Several other cracks appeared and stretched to join it, forming a jagged square. A block of stone slowly pushed out of the wall and fell onto the ground with a thud.

Ewzad left his dying friend, grabbed a torch from the wall and rushed forward to peer into the hole. He trembled as he reached inside. His hands gripped the jeweled box that contained the artifact and removed it from its tomb.

"Finally it's mine. Oh yes-yes!" He cradled it to his chest, not noticing that his old friend's dying screams had faded. "No one will dare deny me now, oh no!"

He gripped the box with both hands and slowly lifted the lid. The box opened to reveal his treasure nestled inside. Two sets of five rings, one for each finger, linked together with golden chains. Oh how the rings gleamed in the torch light.

Ewzad reached his hand inside the box. As his fingers touched gold, he heard a new voice in his mind. Unlike the other one, this was darker and most definitely male.

"***Ewzad Vriil, You Are Mine.***"

*　　　　　　*　　　　　　*

The ancient man traversed the peaks of the mountain, his feet touching ground that no human eyes but his own had ever seen. It was a savage place. Beasts with wicked teeth watched the man and hungry stomachs growled, but they did not attack. They were not allowed.

He staggered, but did not fall.

The ancient man was weary. He had fasted many days and nights seeking communion with his master. He had a feeling that an event was coming, something that could change the face of the land.

He came upon a sheer cliff and walked along the base of it. Soon he found the familiar jagged staircase. He had built it with his own hands over a thousand years ago. As he had countless times before, the ancient man climbed the stairs to the top of the highest peak. Now he lay exhausted and prayed, waiting for his eyes to be opened.

It came abruptly. A warmth settled over him and all weariness and hunger left his body. The world unfolded before his eyes and he saw what had been set in motion; what would be and what may be. He noted the most likely progression of events. Many decisions faced him. The ancient man sighed as the vision ended.

"I see, Master."

As he descended the mountain, the man thirsted. He paused near a large boulder and struck the surface with the palm of his hand.

A spurt of water shot forth from the rock. The ancient man drank his fill and moved on.

The water continued to flow. The spurt became a brook, trickling down mountain paths, carving into the rock. The brook became a mountain stream. The stream emptied into a pond. The pond became a lake. Grass grew. Flowers bloomed. Life came to a barren land.

Changes of this magnitude often followed the actions of the Prophet.

Chapter One

The noise of the crowd faded to a buzz in Justan's mind. He saw the opening he had been waiting for. With a cry of triumph, he thrust in with his right sword, but with a flick of his opponent's wrist, the opening was closed. The parry knocked his sword out wide, leaving him open for attack.

His opponent didn't take the opening, but darted forward, leading with his large shield. It was just enough to block Justan's view of his sword arm. Justan scrambled back, waving both swords in a feeble attempt to block the attack he knew was coming.

His opponent timed it with perfection, whipping his sword over the top of his shield. Justan didn't see the strike coming. The attack might have ended the fight, but he stumbled over his own feet and fell. The blade missed his skin by a hairsbreadth. The audience gasped.

It was a sweltering day, but despite the heat, the arena was packed with thousands of spectators. All of them were screaming and cheering on their favorites. This was the final day of the Battle Academy entrance exams and the excitement had risen to a fever pitch. The layers of bleachers seemed to tower above the combatants as if at any moment the crowd could topple on top of them. For many trainees, their last battle in the arena today could decide whether they would enter the prestigious school or lapse into obscurity. The pressure was suffocating.

Justan landed on his back, knocking up a cloud of fine dirt that clung to the sweat pouring off of his body. He rolled to the side and sent his left sword slashing at the legs of his opponent. The man saw it coming and jumped aside. As the crowd roared, Justan wondered why his opponent wasn't sweating.

Justan rose to one shaky knee, but before he could stand, his opponent leapt forward again and stood over him. The man's sword darted in from every angle around the large shield. Justan kept both of his swords working above him in a clumsy attempt to turn aside the attacks. Somehow he was able to keep his opponent's sword from drawing blood.

Something was amiss. He was facing a skilled student of the Battle Academy. The man could have cut him open with any of the strikes, but he continued to allow Justan to turn them aside. Was he toying with him?

"Come on trainee, you gotta do better than that," the student said, his voice just loud enough for Justan to hear. Justan looked over the shield into the man's eyes and saw nothing but boredom. The student rolled his eyes in disgust. "By the gods man, this is the tests," the man spat. "You trying to embarrass your father?"

With a roar, Justan leapt up, launching his shoulder into the shield. The man's eyes widened in surprise and he fell back a few steps, giving Justan time to attack.

He hacked at the man in a fury, pounding strikes off the shield, aiming for any bit of flesh he could see around it. He could feel the crowd tense up in anticipation, but through his anger, Justan knew it was useless. The man was too good.

The student continued to parry his strikes with ease, but now Justan saw his eyes flash with irritation. He slammed Justan's weapons aside with the shield and followed through with a thrust of his sword. The blade pierced through the gaping hole in Justan's defenses.

Justan felt steel bite into the flesh of his shoulder. He fell to his knees. The fight was over. First blood had been drawn.

The great horn blew signaling an end of the match and the crowd erupted into applause. Mages ran across the field to tend to Justan's wound. Without bothering to pull his blood drenched shirt aside, they laid their hands directly over the wounded shoulder.

Justan stared at the ground, so numb he barely registered the familiar tingling energies of the magic knitting his flesh back together. When they were finished, he didn't take the customary bow to the crowd, but instead strode back to the side of the arena where the other trainees sat awaiting their turn.

Without looking up, he gave the swords back to the

armorer and headed to his seat. As he sat down, he thought he saw a few sneers, but most of his fellow trainees ignored him. None of them offered any conciliatory words. Justan didn't care. He hadn't made any friends over the last year, but he hadn't been in the Training School to make friends. The only thing he ever wanted was to become a great warrior.

Not that it mattered now.

Justan didn't see how the council would let him enter the academy after this year's round of tests. He had done much better this year than the last, but his bad scores in archery and hand-to-hand fighting had forced him into a precarious position.

He didn't watch as the other trainees tested. He sat with his head in his hands, dread boiling in his stomach. Final scores would not be announced until the end of the day at the Battle Academy, but Justan knew he had fallen short. All of his years of training and it had come to this. What was he going to do?

When the final horn blew, Justan left his seat and exited at the far side of the arena from where his parents would be waiting for him. He wasn't ready to face his father.

Sure, his father would congratulate him for doing his best and pat him on the back, but Justan knew that there would be disappointment lurking behind his father's smile. No matter how hard he tried to hide it, how could Faldon the Fierce, the greatest warrior in the Dremaldrian Battle Academy not be disappointed in a worthless son?

"Justan, wait!"

How had she arrived so quickly through the crowds? She must have left her seat in the arena early. Justan reluctantly forced his feet to slow down so that his mother could catch up.

He looked back and saw her making her way through the press of people. His mother, Darlan, was still young at first glance, but gray hairs had crept into her red curls of late. People always spoke of her beauty, but Justan saw the worry lines that creased her eyes and forehead after years of wondering if her husband would return from battle. She hadn't liked her son following in his footsteps.

"Justan, sweetie, I am so sorry," she said and embraced him. The scent of lavender filled his nostrils. He stiffened, but bore the embarrassment, not wanting to hurt her. She pulled back and looked at him with concern. “Are you okay?”

“Am I okay? I failed, mother. You saw it.”

“Actually, I didn’t see it. You know I can’t look when you are fighting. Your father told me what happened afterwards.” Justan scowled in response, and she squeezed him again. “But it may be okay, they won’t announce the results until this evening. You did really good in the strategy test.”

“I always do well in the strategy tests.” His scores had been the best the Training School had seen in years. He had even defeated several of his teachers in the battle games.

“Well, maybe it will be enough this time,” she said.

Justan grit his teeth. “It won’t be, mother. Why would they want me? I can’t fight!”

“That’s not so!” she scolded, rubbing his arm. “Of course you can. I have never met anyone as determined as you. Why, you have been training all your life.”

It was true. He had grown up in the shadow of the Battle Academy and his first memories were of watching his father train in the backyard. He spent his childhood dreaming up war campaigns and fighting invisible monsters with a wooden sword.

He used to sneak over and watch the trainees practice, imitating their movements. On his fifteenth birthday, Justan entered the Training School himself, eager to show everyone that he was going to be as great a warrior as his father. What's more, he was determined to do it on his own. He saved up his own money to buy a pair of used swords and set out to prove that he could succeed.

Justan shook his head. “It doesn’t matter. I still fail. It doesn’t make sense. I have memorized every sword form, studied every great warrior. By all rights, I should excel, but my body betrays me at every turn!”

“Sweetie, you are still growing. Why your father-”

“I’m seventeen!”

His father had a spectacular musculature that brought fear into his opponents, but no matter what Justan did, he couldn’t get muscle to grow on his thin frame. He exercised twice as much as the other trainees and still he tired before most of them.

The worst part for Justan was sparring. He knew the proper stances and techniques. His mind could instantly point out his opponent's weaknesses. But his limbs would not move as he told them. He lost almost every fight.

Darlan's face fell. "I understand your frustration. Justan . . . you know your father and I are proud of how hard you have worked. But maybe this isn't what you are meant to do. You have so many other talents. If you could just try something else . . ."

"Just stop! You have never wanted me to be a warrior anyway." She didn't refute him.

"Honey, you know I just want you to be happy . . ."

"No you don't! Not really!" Justan winced at the hurt in her eyes. "Look, I'm sorry. I'm not angry at you, I just . . ."

Justan realized that people were staring.

"Mother, I'll talk to you more about it later. I just need to be alone, okay?" Without waiting for an answer, he turned and left.

His mother meant well, but he had been down this road before. After he failed Training School the first time, his parents had forced him to apprentice with a scholar, hoping he would enjoy putting his mental talents to use. Justan hated it. After only two weeks painstakingly transcribing soup recipes for a crusty old house chef, he quit and immediately reapplied to the Training School.

He started the second year determined not to fail again. He focused on his studies, practiced harder than ever before. He spent no time away from his training. To avoid distractions, he stayed away from the other students, even the teachers when possible. At the end of the year he had shown some improvement, but it hadn't mattered. After everything he had done, it still wasn't enough.

Justan forced away tears and pushed his way through the crowd with his head down. One man wearing a bright white mage robe grabbed his shoulder as he passed by. The man opened his mouth to say something, but Justan scowled into the man's face and jerked his shoulder free.

He took a couple steps before he realized something familiar about the man. He had seen the man in the white robe around the training grounds several times watching him practice. Justan turned back, but the man was gone. Justan shrugged and continued on his way. He needed a place to think.

He wandered into the training grounds. It was a patchwork of open fields and fenced in areas where the trainees toiled to develop their bodies and hone their skills. They would be deserted now that the tests were over. His mind churned. He had blown his chance at entering the Academy. What was he going to do?

Justan sat on an empty bench near the archery range and ran his hands through his short dark hair. He could leave home, travel to another kingdom perhaps. There were other warrior schools, other training programs. None of them were as good as the Battle Academy, but there was nothing he could do about that. If they didn't work out, he could join a king's army, maybe climb up the ranks and make a name for himself that way. One day he could come back to his father with his head held high, having proven that he was a great warrior.

Justan heard footsteps and whispers. He paused in his thoughts and looked around. The sounds stopped. He didn't see anyone. He got up and slowly walked away from the archery range. There was movement in the trees behind him and he began thinking that it might have been a bad idea to leave the arena crowds.

He knew better than to linger alone like this. Some of the other trainees had taken to bullying him. Perhaps it was because they didn't like the way he kept to himself. Perhaps they resented him because of his father or maybe they just did it because they could. He didn't understand their motivations, but he had learned to stay away from them.

Justan picked up his pace. The footsteps followed. He headed back toward the arena thinking that he could lose them in the crowd, but by the time he got there most of the people were gone and he was sure that his followers were still right behind him.

He reached over his shoulders to pull his swords, but his sheaths were empty. Justan swore. He had left the training swords with the armorer and his own swords were at home.

He ran toward the shopping district on the border of the Training School. There were bound to be plenty of places to hide there. Besides, the crowd might discourage his pursuers from making a scene.

He dodged around vendors and passers-by until he found a narrow alleyway. He ducked inside and waited for his pursuers to pass. He hugged the old brick wall, careful not to make a sound. After a few seconds, he saw two men sneak past. He didn't recognize the big man, but the smaller one was Kenn Dollie, a buffoon who fancied himself Academy material.

Justan had fallen into trouble with Kenn when he defeated him in the strategy test earlier in the week. Ever since then, Kenn had given him grief whenever possible. So far Justan had been able to ignore the little man, but this time it looked like he meant business. Both men carried clubs.

"Why now?" Justan moaned under his breath.

He backed into the alleyway a little further to ensure that they did not see him. Just when he thought that it was okay to leave, the large man's beefy head peeked around the entrance. Justan groaned.

"Kenn! He's in here!" the man shouted. Justan put on a disarming smile.

"Good day. What a great testing week we had this year. Did you see that last fight?" He took a casual step forward.

The large brute squeezed his bulk into the alleyway and tapped the end of the wooden club in his palm. "My friend wants to talk to you."

"Maybe later. I'm quite busy right now." He took another step forward. "So, if you'll excuse me . . ." The man blinked, but he didn't move. Justan sighed and turned to run the other way.

"Justan, Justan," Kenn said as he entered the alley from the other end, cutting off his escape. "Don't try to talk your way out of this. You're not going anywhere."

Kenn crept forward, his club pointed at Justan as if it were a sword. "You embarrassed me in the strategy test."

"Come on, Kenn. It was the tests. I had to beat you," Justan explained, though he had to admit to himself that he had indeed gone further than needed to win. At the time, he felt that he had no choice. It wasn't personal. With his other test scores running so low, he needed to show just how good he was. He had shown no mercy. Kenn had looked like a fool.

Kenn smirked. "We both know that you had it in for me,

Justan. You could have just beat me, but you had to make me look bad. Well you know what?" Kenn whacked his club against the alley wall. "Now it's my turn to beat you and make you look bad. What do you think, Benjo?"

"I-I don't know, Kenn," the large man said, a hesitant look on his face. "I want to start Training School this year and I don't need any trouble. Besides, I don't even know the guy."

"Benjo's right, Kenn," Justan agreed. "No one wants any trouble."

Kenn scowled. "No one's gonna hassle you about it, Benjo. This is a warrior training school. They expect this stuff to happen. Besides, you were there, he failed the last test. He's a nobody now." Benjo still looked hesitant. "Benjo, remember when we were little and that kid, Floot made fun of you in front of the girls? Well this guy is just like Floot. He thinks he's better than everybody else."

"No!" Justan protested. "Benjo, hear me out. I would neve-." Justan ducked just in time to avoid Benjo's club, which took a chunk of mortar out of the wall above his head.

He backed up a few steps and licked his lips, his eyes darting along the alley looking for an escape. There was none. Instead, Justan put on a disarming smile and walked calmly towards Kenn.

"Hey, I'm sorry about what happened. You are right. I beat you harder than I had to, but it wasn't personal. I'll make it up to you. I can show you show you how to defeat those moves I made."

Kenn shook his head to let Justan know that he wasn't backing off.

"Come on, Kenn I'm trying to apologize." He extended his hand and stepped a bit closer. Kenn's guard dropped slightly.

Justan shoved the smaller man aside and sprinted for the safety of the street, but his escape was short lived. Benjo's meaty hand grabbed the sword sheaths strapped to Justan's back, jerking him to a stop. The large man pulled Justan in and wrapped two heavy arms around his torso, holding him tight. Justan struggled until he realized that the man was too strong, then snapped his head back, smashing Benjo's nose.

The big man yelped in pain and Justan broke free. He saw

Kenn's swing coming and tried to dodge out of the way, but he wasn't fast enough. He caught the club square in his chest.

He sputtered, the air blasted from his lungs. Benjo's large hands grasped him from behind and threw him into the hard alley wall. Justan stumbled and saw Kenn's club coming in again. He blocked it painfully with his forearm and started to take a swing at Kenn's face, but Benjo's foot caught Justan in the stomach. He crumpled to his hands and knees, gasping. His vision blurred.

Justan swore under his breath. Why did it always come down to this? Why couldn't his body be quicker or stronger?

He gritted his teeth, waiting for the next blow to land, but none came. There was a shout and a couple of thuds. A hand grabbed him by the collar. He was lifted to his feet.

"Are you alright?" asked a feminine voice.

Justan was more than a little confused. He shook his head to clear his vision and saw a striking woman standing before him. She was tall, perhaps a bit taller than he was. Her skin was deeply tanned, and her long hair raven black. The woman's piercing green eyes were staring right into his.

"Hello?" She spoke with a thick accent that Justan could not quite place. "Shake it off, boy! I know they did not hit you that hard."

Justan looked down, surprised to see Kenn and Benjo on the ground behind her. Both men were unconscious, big red welts swelling up on the sides of their heads. He looked back at the woman again, his jaw dropping.

She was wearing tanned leather pants and a short-sleeved shirt covered with a dark green breastplate made of some kind of hardened animal hide. Framing her face were intricately woven braids tied at the ends with colorful green ribbons. In one hand she held a quarterstaff that was as long as she was tall, made with a strange featureless gray material. Her other hand was still holding Justan up by the scruff of his neck.

"I'm fine. I'm fine," he replied, reaching back to extract himself from her grip. He took one step away from her and steadied himself against the alley wall, doing his best to ignore his pounding head. "Who are you?"

A frown appeared on her fair face. "That is not for you to

ask, boy."

"Boy?" She didn't appear to be much older than he was. Justan winced as he realized that he was being rude. She had rescued him after all, though needing to be saved by a woman stung his pride. "I'm sorry. I guess I should thank you. I mean . . . thank you very much."

"That is better," the woman said. She turned and walked away, stepping over the two unconscious men. Justan was tempted to follow her, but his head throbbed. He decided that he had better go home.

Justan's headache eased as he walked and he decided that his ribs didn't hurt enough to be broken. A big nasty bruise was showing up on his forearm though, and he could feel a scrape on his forehead from when Benjo threw him against the wall. He hoped his parents wouldn't notice: he didn't want to have to explain the fight on top of everything else.

The crowds were thinning. He stopped at the fountain in the middle of the market and examined his reflection in the cool water. His dark hair was disheveled and his clothes covered in dirt from the arena and the alley floor. He slicked his hair back with water from the fountain, wiped off the dirt as best as he could, and continued on his way. He felt defeated for the second time that day. His day wasn't over.

He wandered into the neighborhood where he had grown up. Sturdy homes built by sturdy folk lined the street. Tiny tidy gardens filled the space between them. Children chased each other and squealed.

They could have lived anywhere in the city now, but Darlan preferred their old home. Even though it had been fixed up and contained all the conveniences available, the building still looked much like it did as Justan grew up.

It was a two-story log-frame building with a wood shingle roof. Flowers lined the front of the house. Darlan had made it a warm and inviting place. Even now, Justan could smell the aroma of his mother's muffins wafting down the street.

His father was standing in the doorway with arms folded when Justan arrived. Justan gulped. How long had he been waiting?

"Do you want to talk about it now?" Faldon asked, as usual getting right to the point.

"Not really," Justan said.

"Suit yourself, then. It can wait." He wasn't one to push things on his son, which was one of his most redeeming qualities as far as Justan was concerned. Faldon shoved a warm sweetmuffin under Justan's nose. "Eat quickly. We need to get down to the Academy. I just heard that they're going to read out scores early this year."

"Why? They always wait until the end of the day."

Faldon shrugged. "You would think that with my position on the council, I would learn about such things in advance. But no one told me about it until Tad sent a runner ten minutes ago."

Justan walked into the front room, sat down on a padded bench, and took a bite out of his sweetmuffin.

"I don't want to go," he mumbled.

"What?" his mother said as she entered the room already dressed in her best clothes.

"I failed!" Justan snapped. "We all know what the Training Council is going to say. I'm not getting in to the Academy and all of the other trainees know it. The only reason for me to go is to stand there and be humiliated!"

Justan's mother sat on the bench beside him. "When did you start caring what anyone else thought?"

Justan didn't answer.

"Look, Justan," Faldon said. "You turned seventeen last week. You're a man now. I've considered you a man for two years. And until now I thought that you were acting like one."

Justan sat sullenly and took another bite of his sweetmuffin. "I still don't want to go."

Faldon snorted. "You are going with me to the council hall with everyone else. You will stand there and be gracious to those who are admitted into the Academy. Then you'll come home and we'll talk about what you are going to do next. Now get ready!"

"Fine!" Justan stomped into his bedroom and began changing into clean clothes.

"Fine," he said again to himself. He would go and bear this humiliation, but if his father thought that he was going to change the direction of his life now, he was wrong. Justan grabbed his swords and strapped them on.

By the time he returned to the front room, Justan was already weighing options in his mind. He grabbed another sweetmuffin and followed his parents out the door.

Chapter Two

They didn't speak much as they walked. A heavy sense of dread settled around Justan's heart as he and his parents made their way towards the Battle Academy. Countless times, Justan had imagined standing before the council and accepting their invitation to join the Academy. Now those dreams were ashes. He would be dismissed out of hand.

Soon the walls of the Academy loomed overhead. Justan's father nodded to guards at the gate. They recognized Faldon the Fierce right away and let the family enter.

The Dremaldrian Battle Academy began as a fort. The Kingdom of Dremaldria had always been beset by the goblinoids, trolls, and ogres that lived in the untamed wilds on its eastern border. During the dark times, these creatures constantly raided the kingdom. The king commissioned a fort to be built at the border of the kingdom to prevent these raids and protect the populace. Over the years, it became a mighty encampment for Dremaldria's vast border patrols.

The design of the fort wasn't anything special. It was larger than most, but there were many forts similar to this elsewhere in the lands. What made this fortress famous was the sheer skill of the warriors trained there.

Over the decades of constant raids and skirmishes, they developed their training program into the best in the known lands. Thousands of lives were saved by the skills of these men, and the raids upon human lands decreased.

During the War of the Dark Prophet, the fort was besieged several times by the Dark Prophet's armies. Each time, the soldiers were able to burst forth from the protective walls and use their superior training to overcome the armies surrounding them. By the time the war was over and the Dark Prophet had been destroyed by the true Prophet and his companions, the fort's reputation had grown to the point that men traveled from kingdoms all around, seeking to be trained by these warriors.

The influx of would-be warriors made it necessary to weed out the talent, and eventually the school was split in two. The original battle school stayed inside the fort and became the Dremaldrian Battle Academy, while the grounds behind the fort became the Training School.

Now, though the Kingdom kept an obligatory seat on the council, the Academy was an independent institution. They continued to protect the borders, but also contracted out trainers and soldiers to many different kingdoms and peoples. Graduating from the Academy was one of the highest honors a warrior could receive and any graduate could make a comfortable living by contracting with the Academy or seeking his fortunes elsewhere.

Few people who were not students, nobles, or treasured guests were allowed to enter the walls of the Academy itself. Even Justan had only been inside three times in his life: twice to be present as his father received great honors, and once the previous year when he stood before the Training School Council after having failed entrance into the Academy the first time.

In his previous visits, Justan had been excited, asking his father questions and generally making a fool of himself. This time, he walked in silence to what would be, to him, the chopping block. His father tried to lighten the mood with a joke and his mother whispered words of encouragement, but to no avail.

Justan trudged, head down, as they passed the various training areas and buildings where the finest warriors in the lands learned their trade. He didn't look up until they reached the council building in the center of the Academy. There standing in front of the large doors, towered the carved statues of great warriors from the past that endlessly watched over the students at the Academy. In his mind's eye, they were staring down upon him with deep disapproval.

Justan and his parents walked through the great doors of the council building and were greeted by nods of admission from the student guards at their posts. They passed through a long, high-ceilinged foyer where the stone walls were decorated by weapons and tapestries depicting great battles. In the past when Justan had walked through this foyer, he had envisioned those marvelous weapons in his own hands. He had imagined wading through the battles in the tapestries, cutting swaths through evil monster hordes, and saving maidens from the dragons and orcs who dotted the landscape. But this time, every battle in the tapestries was one in which he would never participate and every weapon on those walls was a dagger in his heart.

The council hall was the center hub of the Academy. This was the area where students were addressed, judgments were made and large functions were held. The room was large and spacious, the curving walls designed to carry the voices of the council throughout the hall. No matter how large the gathering, the students standing at the rear could hear just as clearly as those in the front.

“That's strange.” Justan’s mother paused just inside the doors of the council hall. “Where is everyone?”

His mother’s comment shook Justan from his reverie. He lifted his head and looked around. Now that he thought about it, the walk to the council hall had been strangely quiet. The last time he was here, many trainees and their families had been packed in this hall awaiting their final scores. This time the hall was empty.

A raised dais dominated the far end of the hall. There were ten seats on that dais, one for each council member. Usually the final test scores for the trainees were announced by the members of the Training School Council, but their familiar faces weren’t present. Instead, sitting on the dais were nine members of the Battle Academy Council.

Apart from Justan’s father, they were the most respected men in the Battle Academy. These were the men who taught the most feared and admired warriors in the land. Faldon had spoken of these men with great respect, and Justan had dreamed of being in their classes all his life.

Justan's body broke out in a cold sweat. His legs went numb. What was going on? With his father standing beside him, the entire council was present. For what possible reason would the Battle Academy Council have him brought here alone?

He looked up at his father for some hint of what misery was to befall him, but Faldon stared straight forward, not giving anything away. Justan wanted to turn around and leave but Faldon grabbed his arm and pulled him forward to stand before Tad the Cunning, head teacher of tactics at the Academy.

Each member of the council had an equal say in matters, but being the most quick witted and fleet of tongue, Tad was the voice of the council to the outside world. He was a tall, imposing man with intense eyes, gray hair, and a single scar across his brow. There were many rumors of how that scar had come to be, and Justan had often wondered in the past. But at that moment, all he saw was his executioner, grim faced and menacing.

"I will make this quick, for the members of this council are very busy and have much more to attend to before the night is over," Tad began. "Justan, son of Faldon the Fierce, we have watched you with interest this year as you went through the various skill tests. We have seen your intuitive strategic skills and have determined that given time, there would be few who could match you.

"I doubt that there are many teachers in this Academy who have not heard of how you beat Oz the Dagger in the strategic games earlier this year," he added. There were many nods and appreciative chuckles in the council at this. "You are very possibly the most driven individual we have ever had the opportunity to observe. Even when you fail, you fail with determination."

Justan gulped. A glimmer of hope began to flicker in his mind.

Tad continued, "You have great potential if you can hone your skills as a leader. However, you have shown too little skill in the physical tests. Your foibles in the armed combat and hand-to-hand tests have become legendary. No warrior, especially a student of this school, would follow you into battle at your current level of physical prowess, thus making your strategic talents worthless in the field. You cannot be a good leader if your men don't respect you."

The flickering glimmer of hope vanished.

"We have deliberated hard on what to do with you. After your perfect score in the strategy test we had all but decided to offer you an invitation to join the Academy, but the score you received in the weapons combat test today left you short." Tad sighed. "The rules are explicit in this. We cannot allow you to enter the Academy at this time."

Justan stood numb. What was the point of all this? Was this his father's idea? Did his father think that he would take his failure easier if the entire Academy Council threw it in his face?

Tad continued, "However, Justan son of Faldon the Fierce, we hate to let someone of your potential go. We have consulted the rules on this matter and even though it is customary that applicants are passed over after having failed the final exams twice, there is nothing in the law books that specifies the number of times one can enter the Training School. In fact, though it has been a long time, this exception has been made before in the past."

Justan's heart thundered. His mother grabbed his shoulder in excitement and he struggled not to shout in joy.

"You . . . you are serious?" he sputtered. "You are really giving me another chance?"

Tad raised a hand, his stare serious.

"Justan, you must hear me out before agreeing to this. Realizing the nature of this huge exception, we have adjusted the regular procedures. If we allow you a third year in the training school, understand that this will not be an easy task. If you are to become a student of the Academy, many of the freedoms you have enjoyed these past years as a trainee will be gone."

"Yes, sir," Justan said.

"You will eat, sleep, and bathe at the Training School. You will not be allowed to visit any friends or family. You will not go to holiday celebrations. You will not even leave the grounds unless required to by a teacher or to attend a test of skill.

"You will work harder and be judged harsher than ever before. In short, you will belong to us. If you fail the tests again next year, there will not be another chance. This council will meet again after next year's final exams. We will then decide the direction your life will take."

"What do you mean?" Justan's mother blurted. "You will decide what exactly?"

Tad lifted a scroll from behind the podium. "This contract spells out all the details. Justan will obey our ruling and follow the path we give him at that time, no matter the direction. Even if we decide to make him a laborer building rock walls near the border, our decision will be final. He will be bound by this contract to follow that decision." His gaze shifted back to Justan.

"Finally, I must tell you the reason that we asked your parents to bring you here alone today. We did not want to offer this rare of an exception in front of the whole city unless you agreed. Even though the conditions in your contract are strict, there will be cries of 'unfair,' especially considering who your father is. You have until this weekend to decide." He handed the contract down to Justan. "Tell no one about this unless it is made official."

Tad turned and began speaking to other members of the council.

Justan looked down at the contract. He didn't need to read the words. If he couldn't pass the tests after a third year of Training School, he didn't deserve to be a warrior anyway.

Faldon clapped his back in congratulation and Justan's elation soured a bit. His father had shown no surprise during Tad's speech. He had known all along what was about to happen. Had he pulled in favors to get this done?

It was an unsettling thought. Would he be betraying his own conscience to accept this offer? Was he admitting that he could not succeed without his father's intervention?

Then again, this was his decision to make. They weren't forcing it upon him. Surely it wouldn't be so bad to accept that offer of help just this once. After all, he still had to complete the training on his own. Once he had passed the tests and entered the Academy, it would all be worth it.

"Your Honor!" Justan said. Tad looked back down upon him. "I don't need to wait. I wish to sign the contracts now."

"I mean . . ." Justan forced himself to calm his voice. "I accept your most generous offer."

Tad the Cunning laughed. "Somehow your eagerness doesn't surprise me. Very well, you will report to the Training School immediately. A guard will escort you to the barracks where you will await further instructions."

Justan hadn't expected to report to the Training School so soon. There were several days before the new training classes began. He opened his mouth to ask why, but decided against it.

Things were going too well for him to complain.

He took a quick moment to hug his mother and shake his father's hand. Then a guard came and led him away.

They left the Academy and headed through the streets of Reneul to the Training School grounds, where the guard deposited him at the barracks. When Justan asked the man what he was supposed to do, the guard told him that it did not matter as long as he didn't leave the training grounds. He wasn't to take a footstep outside the grounds in any direction unless ordered by the council itself.

Justan picked a bunk, but he couldn't sit down. He was too excited to rest. Besides, it was light out for another couple of hours yet. There was still time to train. He had a year to prepare to take the tests again, but he couldn't wait to get started. Justan left the barracks and walked to the practice field.

He did some stretching exercises and worked through the hand-to-hand combat forms. There was a twinge in the shoulder the mages had repaired and his bruises throbbed, but it wasn't too bad after his body loosened up a bit. He was just starting to sweat when he noticed someone standing near the edge of the barracks, watching him.

It was the woman who had helped him in the alley. She leaned on her staff and shook her head as she watched his movements. She mumbled something that he couldn't quite make out and strode across the practice field towards him. She approached in a smooth gait that fitted a warrior much better than a woman, and stopped in front of him.

She frowned. "This will take some effort."

"What do you mean?" Justan asked. "What are you doing here?"

"I have been sent here to make sure that you do not fail the tests again next year."

"What? Thank you for the help with Benjo and Kenn and all. I appreciate it. I really do. But I can't accept your help."

She didn't seem fazed. "Students are allowed to tutor with accomplished warriors in their spare time. I have been told that you have not taken advantage of this in the past."

"I have never wanted to take advantage of that," Justan

replied.

“You will now.”

“But I don’t need a tutor. I am going to do this on my own. I have to. I . . .” Justan’s eyes narrowed. “Wait, who sent you? Was it my father?”

“I was approached by certain members of the council, including your father, yes. And they say that you have signed a contract to do as they wish. If you do not accept this training, they will close your opportunity. In fact, if you do not let me help you, you are to be removed from the Training School.”

“I don’t think so,” Justan said. “They didn’t say anything about a tutor.”

“Here is the official document.” She reached into a pouch on her belt and pulled forth a sealed letter. “I was instructed to give it to you if you refused.”

Justan looked at the letter as if it was a viper. The council did not trust him. They didn’t think that he could handle it on his own. A true warrior needed no one else. Justan almost quit right there.

“How could my father do this to me?”

“Perhaps he wants you to succeed,” the woman replied. “Perhaps this is more of a chance than you deserve. How badly do you want to join the Academy? Is this just a game to you?”

“Keep the letter.” Justan looked into her eyes. “If I have to let you watch over me like a child, then so be it. I have to do this. But I will do this my way. I will not be led around by the nose for everyone to see.”

She shook her head, her gaze uncompromising. “Whether you pass or fail will be your choice, that much is true. I cannot do it for you. But when you are training with me, make no mistake, I am in charge. You will listen to me and train the way I tell you to. If you will not listen, then I will leave and you will not be allowed to enter the Academy. I have the final say in this. Do you understand?”

Justan‘s face grew red with anger, but she was right. There was nothing he could do about it. His back stiffened. That didn’t mean he was going to make it easy for her.

“Yes I do understand.” He bowed to her with a flourish.

"When do you want me to start, your highness?"

"You will not refer to me in that manner," she grunted. "But since you sound so eager, we will start now. Select your weapon of choice. Let us see what you can do."

She watched as Justan crossed to the nearby training closet. He rummaged through it, pulled two wooden practice swords out and turned to her.

"You fight with two swords?" she asked. "That seems a little advanced for a trainee."

"That's my style." Justan twirled them in his hands. "I have always fought with two. I am nearly as good with my left hand as with my right."

"Nearly as good is not nearly good enough," she replied with a half-grin and hefted her strange gray staff. "Come, let us see how bad you really are."

She twirled the staff over her head twice and started toward him. Justan could see that she was good just by the way she moved. She attacked, moving on the balls of her feet with lithe graceful movements that were more catlike than human. Her whole body flowed in perfect balance, whipping her staff about in a whirring blur.

Justan's arms could not keep up with her graceful motions. Before he registered the first hit, he had already been tapped on the arm, knee and wrist, knocking the sword out of his left hand. He bent to pick up his sword, only to get whopped twice on the back of the head.

Justan came at her with quick slicing attacks using both swords. He poured all of his concentration into the task, but she was too good. He could see the small openings she left, but his arms couldn't keep up with her parries.

Justan's last clumsy attack came with both swords up high. She batted his weapons aside, spun around, extended the staff, and swung low. The staff caught Justan behind the knees, launching him into the air. He landed on his back in the dirt.

She leaned over him, her face expressionless. She wasn't even breathing heavy.

"For now, you will work with one sword. Once you have mastered that, you can try two." She reached a hand out to help

Justan up, but he ignored her and got to his feet.

Justan groaned. His body ached all over and the blows to his head had re-ignited the headache that had started with the alley fight. However, he was not about to be cowed. He cast one of the practice swords aside and stood facing her.

"Okay, but before we start again, my lady, what is your name?" he asked

She snorted. "When you have earned the right to know my name, I will tell you. In fact, you have not even earned the right to be called by your own name. Until you have, I will call you by whatever name I wish."

She twirled her quarterstaff back and forth, her staff making a whirring noise. Justan gritted his teeth and went into defensive posture.

"Fine, but if you don't tell me your name, what am I supposed to call you? Staff lady?"

"You will call me Ma'am," she replied and came at him.

Chapter Three

The next morning, Justan was awakened by a sharp pain in his side.

"Wake up, boy. It's time for your run," the warrior woman said, poking him with the staff again.

"Run?" Justan opened his eyes to find that it was still dark outside the barrack windows. He tried to sit up, but his body cried out in painful protest. He collapsed back on his cot. "Not now. Come back later."

"You. Will. Get. Up. Now!" she commanded, punctuating each syllable with a kick at the legs of his cot.

With her last word the cot collapsed, spilling Justan onto the cold floor. Thankfully, his blankets came down with him, strategically covering his nakedness. He vowed to sleep in his clothes from that time forward.

"If you are not outside and running in five minutes, you will be getting up an hour earlier tomorrow." With that, she spun on her heels and walked out of the barracks.

Justan cursed under his breath and forced his aching body to stand. He was glad that the other trainees had not been there to see this. They were due to arrive in a few days, and he wasn't looking forward to their jeers as they watched this woman order him around.

The chill fall air had Justan shivering as he left the barracks and joined her outside. She raised one eyebrow at his discomfort.

"The first lap around the training grounds should warm you up. You will run four this morning."

"Four laps? That's over five miles!" His usual routine was two. Justan toned down his voice. "Look, Miss, I am still aching from yesterday. Besides, don't I get breakfast first?"

"Once again, you will call me Ma'am," she said. "Five laps,

then. Shall we go for six?"

Justan shook his head and tried to hide his frustration. "No, Ma'am."

"You can eat after you run. Now go!"

Justan forced a smile and bowed. "Yes Ma'am."

He trotted off despite his body's protests. The first lap was agony, but once he got going, the aches and pains faded. He breathed in the crisp morning air. Surprisingly, he felt pretty good. That is, he felt good until the end of the second lap. His lungs burned and his legs wobbled, but he kept going. Justan nearly collapsed halfway through the fourth. The mystery woman must have known, because she started running beside him. She barked at him every time he thought of slowing.

By the time he started the fifth lap, Justan hated her. He was determined to prove that he was stronger than she thought he was, but that determination was hard to keep up. When he reached the end of the lap, he collapsed at her feet, no longer caring what she thought.

The sun was just peeking over the horizon when Ma'am dragged an exhausted Justan to the mess hall, located next to the barracks. He wondered if any of the cooking staff would be in that morning since the rest of the trainees hadn't arrived yet. From the way the sleepy-eyed cook glared at Ma'am as he ladled a heap of porridge into their bowls, Justan suspected that she had dragged the man down to the kitchens herself.

"Eggs, Mark!" she snapped. "I told you to make the boy three eggs!"

"Alright, Ma'am, alright. I'll make 'em right away," the cook said, then mumbled something about double pay. It irritated Justan that she had no problem calling the cook by his first name.

Justan spent the rest of the day at the mystery woman's beck and call, performing various tasks and exercises while her hawk-like green eyes watched him. She worked him long into the night and he collapsed on to his cot as tired as he had been the night before.

The next day, Justan awakened to yet another grueling five lap run. Afterwards, while he devoured his breakfast, she set forth some rules.

“Training classes start soon,” Ma'am said. “However, I have spoken with your teachers and canceled most of them.”

Justan winced. He had been looking forward to classes starting again, if only to have some time away from this woman. Where did she get the time to speak with his teachers anyway? She was with him all day and into the night. Did she ever sleep?

“There is no need for you to take hand-to-hand combat or swordplay, for I will be taking over your training in those areas. Also, with the extensive conditioning routines I will be teaching you, there will be no need to exercise with the other trainees.”

“What about strategy class?”

“I spoke with Oz the Dagger and he informed me that he didn't want you in the class.”

“What? Why? That’s my favorite class!”

“He feels you have learned everything he could possible teach you. He also said that other trainees should have the opportunity to win once in a while.” A rare smile twitched at the corner of her mouth. “You will, however, continue to take archery.”

“Why archery?” It was his least favorite class, mostly because of the teacher, Mad Jon.

“I use a sling. It is better for you to learn the bow from an archer.”

Justan wanted to argue that she was trying to teach him swords with her staff, but their conversation was interrupted as a steady stream of early arrived trainees entered the mess hall to eat. When Kenn and Benjo reached the food line, Justan dropped his fork. The Training Council must have granted Kenn a second year. Justan groaned. This was the last thing he needed.

The days flew by and Justan’s new taskmaster remained a mystery. She was with him from the moment he awoke to the moment he fell asleep, yet he never learned anything new about her. He called her Ma’am and she called him Boy. To his dismay, he caught himself thinking of her as if Ma’am was her real name.

Kenn teased Justan relentlessly about her, saying things like, “Look, everyone. Here comes Justan the Great, home from a long day of being beat up by that wild woman!”

Justan was usually so tired by the time he entered the

barracks, it was easy to ignore Kenn and fall to sleep. Everyone else left Justan alone for the most part. But Ma'am would drag him out of bed so early and send him to sleep so late that the other trainees began complaining to the teachers. Justan was soon assigned his own room in a separate outbuilding. It wasn't anything special, just a single room with a cot, a chest, and a door. But the solitude was welcome.

His least favorite part of the day was the morning run. He had never enjoyed running. When he was a child, Justan had developed an awkward gait. The other kids always teased him about it. Ma'am tried to force him to run correctly, but in this area her efforts were fruitless. When Justan concentrated on running properly, it only slowed him down. Eventually she just let it go, mumbling something about how running like that might be helpful if he needed to dodge arrows.

Over the past two years at the training school, Justan had forced himself to endure the run so that he would be prepared for the stamina test, but no matter how much he pushed himself, it never seemed to get any easier. It was as if his body refused to improve.

Ma'am however, took things to a new level. She pushed him and pushed him until he wondered if she was trying to kill him. For the first few weeks he gasped and sputtered when his run was over. Then, to his surprise, it got easier. His running improved until he could finish four laps around the training grounds without keeling over. As soon as she saw that improvement, Ma'am increased his laps.

Ma'am employed a stringent conditioning program to put some muscle on Justan's narrow frame. For breakfast each morning, she hounded the cooks into serving him more and more meat and less grain. She then worked him through countless exercises, many of them quite strange.

Some days, she would find a large gnarled tree on the grounds and force him to climb it over and over again. On other days, she would tie one end of a rope to a post and twirl the other end, making Justan jump over and over every time the rope neared his feet. She even spent one morning a week having him carry large rocks around from place to place.

Most of the time Justan didn't understand the point of these exercises, but they seemed to be effective. Every time she taught him a new one, he awoke the next morning with soreness in muscles he never knew he had.

His afternoons were spent in the practice arena. Ma'am sparred with him constantly, teaching him in both armed and hand-to-hand combat. Despite her lithe frame, she was a strong woman. With her quick, graceful movements, she pummeled him back and forth across the field without mercy.

Her training style was all action. She didn't waste time lecturing. Often, she started hand-to-hand combat by using the same throw on him over and over until he figured out how to counter it. The only encouragement she would give was the occasional, "Come on, Boy, figure this out."

Ma'am sparred against him using every implement in the training closet for variety, but her favorite weapon was her staff. How he hated the staff. It looked unimpressive upon first glance but Justan soon learned it had amazing qualities.

Ma'am could change the shape and texture of the staff with but a thought. She could make the wood soft as if padded, or as hard as cold steel. Sometimes the tip of the staff would flatten out and become pointed like a spear or form a razor sharp edge like a halberd. But it didn't matter how she used it. With that staff in her hands, she was undefeatable.

With dogged determination, Justan analyzed the way she moved and tried to anticipate her parries and attacks. To his amazement, though his movements still seemed clumsy, he began to move faster and more accurately. By the time she finally let him use two swords again, he had to admit that he was better. This was something he had not been able to say in the course of his personal training throughout the years.

Just as he was gaining confidence, the lessons grew even harsher.

One day, when sparring, Ma'am introduced a new technique.

"Today I will disarm you," she stated.

Justan gripped his sword hilts and went into his defensive stance. With a whir of her staff, both of his swords flew through the air and he found himself staring stupidly at the empty hands in front of him. "How did you do that?"

"Again."

Justan picked up his swords and turned to face her. She was already on the attack. With two quick taps, the swords fell to the dirt.

"Again."

Justan's face reddened. He kept an eye on her as he picked up the swords this time. She moved suddenly. Two quick taps.

"Again."

Justan's thumbs throbbed, but he did as she asked. He willed his hands to an iron grip. Fully prepared, he watched her come. The swords flew away just as before, but this time it hurt much worse. He yelped and shook his hands in pain.

"Gah! Would you stop it, Ma'am? Let me get ready!"

"Again," she replied.

The pattern continued until his wrists and hands became so bruised and swollen that he found it hard to grip the sword at all. Then she moved on to something else. She didn't say anything about it again until the following day, when she announced her intention to disarm him again.

Justan tried to shrug off the multitude of minor humiliations he endured each day, but they piled up on him. Countless times, he felt like throwing his practice sword in her face and leaving, but every time he felt despair overwhelming him, he looked into Ma'am's piercing green eyes and refused to give in. Her tactics would have defeated the spirits of most men, but Justan refused to be like other men. He could not allow her to make him throw his dreams away.

Soon winter arrived, bringing harsh winds and stinging snow. Training continued at an even harsher pace. Justan's lungs burned in the cold air and at times his fingers grew so numb that he couldn't even tell when he had dropped his sword. Ma'am looked uncomfortable wearing winter leathers, but she never let up.

One cold morning after breakfast, Ma'am skipped the normal workout regimen and dragged him through calf-deep snow to the archery range. It was located on one of the few wooded areas on the grounds. Just enough trees had been cleared to make room for the long practice lanes that were marked off with colored rocks.

Targets were placed at various distances, some of them barely visible in the snow.

She handed him a bow and a quiver of arrows from the training closet. Wisps of steam fled from her lips as she spoke.

"Your archery teacher has informed me that you have not shown improvement." She pointed him towards a target. "Shoot." Justan focused, pulled back, and let an arrow fly just to watch it land in the snow in front of the target.

"Again."

His next arrow flew to the side.

She grasped his shoulder and turned him to face her. Her green eyes bored into his. "Why is there no improvement?"

"I don't know," Justan replied. He kept his voice calm and didn't avert his gaze, though his frustration was building.

"That is not a satisfactory answer. Mad Jon is considered to be the best teacher in the Training School. Can you explain to me why, when you have studied under him for years and the other trainees have only been here a few months, you are still his worst student?"

"He is a horrible teacher! All he does is spout philosophical garbage. That does not make the arrow hit the target."

"Are you not willing to try?"

"I am, Ma'am. I mean, I do!" Justan's bottom lip quivered and he turned away. "It's no use."

"No use?" Ma'am gripped her staff until her knuckles were white. "What nonsense is this?"

"I said there's no use!" Justan growled. "I try and I try but nothing . . ." he trailed off at Ma'am's disapproving glare. Suddenly, it was more than he could stand.

"Listen to me! I know how to shoot. I have studied every book the school has on the subject. Every time I stand in front of the target I calculate the correct trajectory. I factor in the strength of my pull along with the wind resistance. Every factor is accounted for. Every shot that I let go should hit the mark. It should! It's unexplainable, yet I have never given up. I shoot arrow after arrow until my fingers bleed and I still don't get any better!"

The anger faded from Ma'am's eyes, replaced by something Justan could not identify. A moment passed before she spoke. “Keep shooting,” she stated, and walked away.

Twenty minutes later, she returned with a strange person at her side.

There were several different humanoid races in the lands. Humans, dwarves, elves and gnomes were the most common. Justan had seen members of each race come through the city of Reneul at one time or another, but the individual that accompanied Ma’am was unlike any he had ever seen.

He was slight of frame and had pointed ears like an elf. However unlike other elves, his hair was short and stubbly while his skin was dark and leathery and hung loose on his frame. Despite the cold chill of winter, the elf was barefoot and wore only a loincloth. A small pack was slung over one skinny shoulder, while a bow and quiver was slung over the other.

The strange elf conferred with Ma'am in an odd language filled with clicks and whistles. His eyes then settled on Justan. The elf walked up at Justan and sized him up, poking him several times to get him to move this way or that. Justan did as directed, but looked at Ma'am questioningly.

The elf made a few clicking noises and Ma’am nodded at Justan to keep shooting. Something about the elf prompted him to try his best. He concentrated as hard as he ever had, but it didn’t help.

The elf watched Justan fire a few arrows before stopping him. He lifted Justan’s arm and felt his muscles, then ran one hand across Justan’s chest until it lay over his heart. A few seconds passed, then he leaned in and pressed his ear against Justan’s chest. After a moment, the elf snorted. He blew a long stream of angry sounding clicks and whistles Ma'am's way, and stormed off into the trees.

Ma’am shouted something after the disappearing elf. She looked at Justan in exasperation. “What do you give me to work with, Boy?”

“Who was that?” Justan asked. Ma'am threw him a stern look and Justan re-worded his question. “I’m not asking his name. I'm just curious. What kind of elf is he? I have never seen anyone like him.”

She looked at Justan thoughtfully, as if trying to decide

whether or not to tell him.

"He is an ancient; one of the first-born. He is one deserving of the utmost respect," she said. "He says that you have a good body and soul for the arrow."

"Really?" A smile crept up the corners of his lips.

Ma'am shook her head before he got too excited. "He also said that though your heart knows what to do, you have learned to shoot completely wrong. Your mind is at war with your soul and that you are too stubborn to learn the correct way."

The smile faded, replaced by a frown. "How could he possibly know anything about me?"

Ma'am sighed.

"Just keep practicing," she said, and Justan did. But there was still no improvement.

Chapter Four

Eventually the air grew warmer. The snow melted. Green leaves sprouted on the trees and the smells of spring filled the air. But more than just the seasons were changing.

More often than not Justan was wide-awake before Ma'am banged on his door. The morning runs went from exhausting to invigorating. He even began looking forward to them. By the time summer began, he was running ten laps.

As Justan's skills increased, so did Ma'am's signs of approval. Every once in a while she would actually say, "Good", or on a rare occasion, flash a smile. Justan lived for these moments. He found himself trying to please her. He worked even harder than before, something he would never have thought possible.

He had often wondered why he hadn't improved while training on his own. As his training with Ma'am progressed, he started to realize that all those years, he had set limits for himself without knowing it. His inner frustration had cut him short. By taking away his freedom, Ma'am wasn't trying to crush his spirit. She was pushing him beyond his own preconceived notions of his limitations.

Two weeks before the first day of tests, horrible news rocked the Kingdom of Dremaldria. King John Muldroomon had died in his sleep. A month long time of mourning was declared. The council was forced to push testing week back two weeks. To Justan's relief, he had extra time to prepare.

That morning Ma'am showed up at Justan's room with a strange package wrapped in coarse brown paper. It was long and thin, tied with a golden string.

"What is this for?" Justan asked.

Ma'am smiled as she handed the package to him. "It is your

birthday, Justan, son of Faldon the Fierce."

"My birthday?" Justan laughed. "You're right. Wow, I never would have remembered if you hadn't told me." The fact that she knew about it made him wonder how often she spoke to his father. Then it hit him.

"Whoa, wait a minute. . . You just said my name! What did I do?" His mind whirled. "Is this because of my birthday?" The smile remained on her face, something which he found oddly unnerving. She was his stern taskmaster, the iron woman, firm and unyielding. Yet here she was, smiling at him. She looked . . . well, beautiful.

"You have earned that right, Justan. You have shown marked improvement and I am pleased. So is the council. Everyone is pleased by your progress."

Justan would normally be annoyed by the interference of the council and his father, but at this moment it couldn't touch him. For once in his life, he felt proud.

"So, Ma'am," he said, lightness in his heart. "What am I to call you now?"

A bit of the familiar sternness re-entered her eyes.

"You will continue to address me as you have been. The small amount of respect you have earned will not lessen your duties. I fully expect you to continue to improve." Justan wasn't fazed by the rebuke. He broke into a grin that she couldn't help but return. Ma'am shook her head. "Enough of this babble. Open your gift so that we can get back to your training."

Justan sat down on his bed and untied the golden string. He pulled the paper apart to find a magnificent bow. It was light and well balanced. Intricate shallow carvings curved along its length. His eyes widened. This bow was made of the same gray material as Ma'am's staff.

"What, why . . .?" he sputtered. "Ma'am, it's beautiful. Where did this come from?"

"This bow was made by Yntri Yni. The weapon master of my kingdom."

Justan again wondered where she found the time to arrange everything when she was with him training all day. "Wait, was he the elf that visited us on the archery range?"

"Yes. He was passing through on the way back from his yearly pilgrimage and he owed me a favor." Ma'am leaned forward, her eyes blazing and intense. "This is a Jharro bow, made from the wood of the sacred trees of Yntri Yni's people."

Justan tightened his grip on the weapon. It felt warm to the touch.

Ma'am continued, "Every Jharro weapon bonds to the mind of its master. It will respond to your life force, become an extension of you."

Justan sat for a moment in silence, focusing on the feel of the weapon in his hand. It felt good. He handed the bow back to her. "I am not ready. When it comes to marksmanship, any extension of me couldn't hit a mist bronto."

"With this you would. Yntri Yni told me that it would fix your problem. However, you would not be allowed to use it in the tests, as it is a magical weapon."

Justan thought for a moment. "I am sorry, Ma'am. I cannot accept this gift now. This is an item of great value. My inadequacy would cheapen it. Besides, how can I ever learn to shoot properly if I depend on the powers of a magical weapon? No, it is best that I wait until I can do it justice."

Justan saw approval in Ma'am's eyes.

"Spoken wisely. If you wait until you become stronger, it will be an even more powerful weapon in your hand." She wrapped the bow back into the brown paper, then gave him a pointed look. "I wasn't going to let you have it now anyway. This is to be an incentive to you. Strive to be worthy of it. I will hold it until you are ready."

"Thank you, Ma'am. I will," Justan said, feeling a little foolish. Of course she wouldn't let any part of his training be easy.

She walked to the door. "Come, Justan. You are running twelve laps today. Quickly now or I will start calling you 'Boy' again."

Justan grinned and sped out of the door. He had never been so excited about the run.

The summer faded quickly. On the day the tests would have normally started, Justan woke and was ready to go before

Ma'am arrived. Just as he was about to leave, Justan was surprised by a knock on his door. Ma'am never knocked.

He opened to door to see a short balding man wearing a courier's smock.

"Good morning," the man yawned. "You Justan, son of Faldon the Fierce?"

"Yes."

"I was instructed to give this to you by a very rude young lady that has no respect for proper business hours." He held out a sealed letter.

"Yeah, I'm sorry about that. It's her way." Justan took the letter and started to open it. The courier left his hand out expectantly. "Oh, right." Justan rummaged in his pouch and gave the man what he supposed was a fair tip for delivering the letter.

The man sighed as he looked down at the coins Justan had deposited in his hand. "Typical. Good day sir."

Justan read the letter. Ma'am said he had the morning to himself. She didn't say where she was going; just that she had something to attend to.

Justan frowned. What was she up to? It would probably result in some painful new form of training. He wondered what he should do with his morning of freedom.

For a moment he fantasized about going back to sleep, but only for a moment. He didn't have time to rest. He only had a few precious days left before the tests began. Besides, if Ma'am saw that he hadn't done anything productive, whatever she was planning would be a lot worse.

Grumbling, he started his run. He ran eight laps and headed to the archery range. It was the area of his training that most weighed on his mind. He wanted to be worthy of Ma'am's gift.

Arriving at the range, he thought back to what Mad Jon had taught in archery class. Everyone said he was a great teacher, but Justan couldn't take his lessons seriously. The man was full of ridiculous sayings like, "Clear your mind of everything but a single flame. Imagine that your target is that flame . . ." and so on. The other trainees always looked so ridiculous standing there slack-jawed, sometimes with their eyes closed, sometimes humming, trying to conjure up a campfire in their mind.

Justan had never bothered with it. Archery was like any other form of combat, all it took was practice. Shoot the bow enough, learn to factor in all the variables, and the arrow would strike true.

Justan stopped at that thought. He chuckled at himself. Who was he kidding? All the slack-jawed trainees in those classes still had better results than him.

He sat back and thought for a moment. What could it hurt to try? He looked around to make sure no one was watching him. There were only a couple other trainees at the range. Most people were still eating breakfast and archery classes wouldn't start for another couple of hours.

He fit an arrow to the string and looked at the target. He tried to imagine this "flame" that his teacher had talked about, but he couldn't focus. He almost laughed aloud. It was too silly of a notion. He couldn't see a flame. All he saw was a target.

But there was something else. One day he had tried to explain to Mad Jon how his calculations should work. Mad Jon had told him, "Your problem is that you aren't shooting at the target. You shoot at everything else but the target. You can't shoot the wind. You can't shoot trajectories. Forget those things for now. They become instinct later. Just shoot the target!"

Mad John's statement had seemed simple minded at the time, but Justan shrugged and brought the bow up. He sighted the target and let loose without thinking. The arrow sailed true, but landed right in front of the target. He shook his head and tried it again. Clearing his mind of frustration, Justan pulled the string back to his ear, sighted the target and let everything else blur. He released. The arrow struck the edge of the target. Justan's eyebrows rose in surprise.

Maybe that was just a fluke. Perhaps not. The strange old elf had told Ma'am that his heart was warring with his mind. What if Mad Jon had been right? What if the problem was that he focused too much on his calculations?

He sighted the target again and drew back the bow. He emptied his mind of calculations and doubts and focused only on the center of the target. It felt so foreign, but he was determined. He let his arms aim on instinct alone. He released the arrow and held his breath as it soared. It struck just shy of the middle of the target. A shout escaped his lips.

Ma'am showed up at the archery range after midday meal. "Justan, I have been looking for you all around the training grounds. It is a good thing you leave such obvious tracks."

"Ma'am, look at this! I'm starting to see what Mad Jon was trying to say," Justan interrupted. He let loose an arrow that missed the target by a foot.

"Wait! Let me calm down." He took a deep breath, pulled back on the string and let another arrow fly. This one stuck into the top of the target. "See, I can do it now!"

He shot two more. One struck the center. Justan giggled and went to collect his arrows.

"It took you long enough!" Ma'am shouted after him. It was as if she had expected this result. "Now put the bow away and follow me. Let us see if you have suddenly learned to swing a sword." As she turned and walked toward the practice field, Ma'am couldn't conceal her smile.

Justan grimaced and put the equipment away. What horrific training session had she been putting together all morning? As it turned out, she had something new in mind this day.

The practice arena was set up much like the larger arena in the city, but without the towering bleachers. The large round area was fenced in and consisted of weapons closets and three large rings where in the combatants could fight.

When Justan arrived, still bubbling over his new discoveries in archery, he found Ma'am standing there with an unfamiliar man.

The man was an imposing figure, as tall as Justan, but very muscular. His face looked as though carved from marble with a strong jaw and a cleft chin. He was dressed for travel with trail worn boots and a long well used cloak on his back. The hilts of two swords protruded from his hips.

The man gestured with one hand as he spoke to Ma'am and Justan gasped. There was a rune on the back of the man's right hand. A warrior rune.

This man was a named warrior.

The man glided over to Justan and reached out his hand, "I

am Hilt. Pleased to meet you, Son of Faldon."

Justan clasped his hand. It gave him chills. He imagined he could feel the power restrained in this man.

"I am honored, Sir Hilt," Justan replied. And indeed he was.

Very few named warriors existed. This was a man who had reached the pinnacle of fighting prowess. To become named, a warrior must be completely at peace with himself and fully cognizant of his own ability. Justan had grown up near the premier battle school in the known human lands, and this was the first such warrior he had met in person.

"Please, just call me Hilt," the man said with an easy smile on his face.

Justan wanted to say more. He wanted to ask the man a thousand questions, but he found it difficult to get his lips to move.

"The Bowl of Souls," he blurted.

"Yes?" Hilt chuckled. "What about it?"

Justan's face turned red. "I-I'm . . . It's just that I can't believe I'm standing in front of someone who has been there. Been named I mean."

When a warrior felt that he had achieved perfection, he traveled to the Mage School in the southern part of Dremaldria, where the Bowl of Souls was kept. It was said that the Bowl of Souls had the power to read a warrior's heart. All he had to do was dip his weapon into the waters of the bowl and if he was found worthy, a rune would appear on his right hand and he would be given his true name. If a warrior was not found worthy, nothing would happen. He would never be given a second chance.

"I'm sorry," Justan said lamely.

Hilt smiled and patted him on the shoulder. "I understand that you fight with two swords."

"Yes!" Justan said, shifting from foot to foot. "I have practiced all my life. I'm not very good," he admitted. "But then again I have mainly taught myself."

"That's not necessarily a bad thing, Justan," Hilt said. "Practicing by oneself is to be encouraged. The only way you will ever be able to truly master the blades is by learning your own strengths. However, practicing alone is useless without a solid base of experience. I have met many men who are self-taught and they all have weaknesses caused by lack of interaction. Believe me, it is far better to learn from others. If not, you have to learn by trial and error, and that is a hard way to grow."

Hilt stepped into the role of teacher as if it was the most natural thing in the world. Justan, who could not get over the presence of this man, hung on his every word. Ma'am stood to the side, gauging Justan's response. She nodded with approval.

"I came here to watch the testing, and to conduct some business with the Academy, but with the delay over your king's death, I'm available to spar with you for the next few weeks." Hilt smiled. "That is, if you're willing."

Justan almost fell over. "Yes! Yes of course, sir!"

Hilt nodded. "Very well. I will meet you here at noon bell every day and teach you the forms. With that knowledge, you will be better able to train on your own. With the proper forms you will learn how your body responds to movement. You will learn better control and coordination."

Hilt drew his blades from the sheathes at his waist. "Watch," he said, and started into what seemed to be an intricate dance, his blades whirling in complex patterns. His body spun and leapt into the air. It left Justan breathless. Watching this man was to see the epitome of what he wanted to become played out before his eyes. Hilt's familiarity and confidence with his weapons, his complete mastery of his body and every movement. These were the things that Justan had longed for all of his life.

Hilt stopped so abruptly that Justan didn't see him put his swords away. The man wasn't even breathing hard. "That was a two blade sword form, one of the more complex ones. Of course I don't expect you to learn that one right away, but it wouldn't hurt to have some impressive sword forms in your arsenal for the tests, now would it?" He took one look at Justan's eager expression and laughed. "Shall we begin?"

Justan jumped in immediately. He would have been thrilled to be trained by any dual blade master, but one who was named? He could not believe his luck. It did not occur to him until later that his father had most likely paid the man a handsome sum to do it. But, Justan didn't care. As far as he was concerned, it was the greatest gift his father could have given him.

The last days before the Training School tests flew by. Justan spent more and more time training with the bow and sparring with Hilt. This meant he spent less time with Ma'am. Strangely, Justan found that he missed that time.

Justan learned the sword forms Hilt taught him as best as he could. Hilt could be stern when Justan started to tire, but he showed infinite patience with the young man's ineptitude.

The man was as big a mystery as Ma'am. He didn't spend time talking about his past, but Justan had the impression that Hilt was from a distant kingdom. There was the slight accent that Justan couldn't place, and he had a flair about him that convinced Justan Hilt was more than just a warrior, maybe even nobility.

Under Hilt's tutelage, Justan felt better about his ability to fight with two blades. Though he had a ways to go before he would consider himself a competent fighter, Justan was gaining more confidence in his chances to get into the Battle Academy.

Justan was unaware of the forces arrayed against him.

Chapter Five

Testing week consisted of five final exams, one test on each day. The week started with the test of stamina, followed by distance weapons, hand-to-hand combat, strategy, and ending with armed combat. Each of the tests during the week was worth up to five points, and a trainee had to earn at least fifteen points to be accepted into the Battle Academy. It wasn't easy. Each year, less than a third of the trainees passed.

The week of testing was a huge event for the Kingdom of Dremaldria and the City of Reneul in particular. The city spent months preparing for the influx of people. Businesses often made as much money in that single week as the rest of the year combined.

People from all over the kingdom flocked to Reneul to watch the tests of endurance and skill. Some came to support family members, others came just for the spectacle of it all, but by the time the first day of testing arrived, the streets were clogged with spectators.

This year, with the King's death causing the tests to be postponed, many spectators had come early and been caught unprepared for the delay. The city's population was expanded for longer than planned. The extra food and supplies stocked for the crowd were soon exhausted. To add to the problems, controversy and discontent hung thick in the air.

The King's son, Prince Andre Muldroomon, threw out his father's staff of advisors and replaced them with his own friends, who were known among the populace as a bunch of rowdies and thugs. The people understood that this was the way of kings and successions, but the people held a particular dislike for Prince Andre's main new advisor, Ewzad Vriil, a man who had been banished by the prince's father.

These factors combined to create a problem hitherto unseen in the orderly streets of Reneul. Tempers ran high. Bar room brawls spilled into the crowded streets. One day things got so out of hand that students from the Battle Academy were called out to help the city police put down a ten-block skirmish. When the first day of testing finally arrived, the Training School was surrounded by the most raucous crowd seen in decades. Everyone needed a spectacle to relieve frustrations.

This year, they were going to get one.

Justan had been placed in the first group of students testing each morning throughout the week. It was the time slot dreaded by most of the trainees. Minds were still clouded from sleep and reactions were not at their peak. Justan finally had a reason to be glad that Ma'am got him up so early every morning.

He awoke the day of the stamina test full of energy and excitement. He dressed quickly and ran to the kitchens. He was careful to eat very little. He had been a victim of eating a big breakfast before the stamina trial his first year and learned his lesson while emptying his stomach on the side of the trail.

Ma'am was waiting outside for Justan when he left the mess hall. She looked almost as excited as he was. "Justan, did you eat a light breakfast?"

"Taken care of."

"Make sure to stretch out your legs before the run."

"I know."

Ma'am sighed. She looked jittery and anxious. "I feel like I am the one running today. Listen to me, Justan. I will be waiting at the midway point with some water. Pace yourself. I hear that they have changed some things this year."

"Really?" There hadn't been a course change in the stamina test in years. "What's different?"

"I have only heard rumors, but I am sure that you will be told about it before you start."

"I am ready Ma'am," he said. "Don't worry. I won't fail you."

"Justan, you could not fail me. Not in this. I know you better than that." She smacked his back. "Now go. Do not be late."

It was fall now and Justan found the crisp wind invigorating. The leaves had begun to turn on the trees. Some of them had fallen, leaving the landscape littered with orange and red.

Justan smiled as he made his way to the test site. It was nice to have Ma'am clucking over him like a mother hen. It meant she cared. In fact, it made Justan feel so good that he became nervous. And he wasn't sure why.

At first he had seen her as a stern taskmaster and a fierce enemy. Later on he knew her to be his friend. But lately he had begun to notice a beautiful, feminine side of her that made him want to please her all the more. Why did that frighten him so?

Justan shoved the thoughts away. He didn't have the luxury of examining his feelings today. He focused back on the task ahead of him.

The stamina test was held on the north end of the training grounds in the hills that bordered the city. They were called the Scralag Hills; so named because of the ghost that was said to haunt the area.

Justan arrived at the start site before most of the other trainees. He stretched and warmed up until the rest of them arrived. Justan watched the motley group of fifty trainees as they gathered and chatted with excitement. He didn't know much about those he was competing against. He had spent so little time with the other trainees that year that he recognized few of their faces.

Then he saw Benjo. Why did he have to be here?

At least Kenn hadn't drawn the first round as well. Neither of them was much trouble alone; it was when they got together that they caused problems. Not that it mattered much. He didn't think that they would try anything during the testing. There were too many people around. The testing week rules stated that anyone caught cheating would be expelled and lose any opportunity to enter the Battle Academy.

Soon hundreds of spectators were crowded around the starting line and many others were heading up the trail for different vantage points. The crowd created a lot of noise laughing and talking to each other as they waited for the test to begin.

Swift Kendyl, the endurance trainer for the school, soon appeared and raised his arms to call for silence. Kendyl was a wiry man who always seemed full of energy. The story of how he had earned the nickname of Swift Kendyl was legendary.

After Kendyl graduated from the Academy, his first assignment was as a standard bearer for the Brasbeck Army. One day a huge dragon swooped down from the sky and began breathing fire all over his fellow soldiers. As the legend goes, Kendyl sprinted up the dragon's tail, across its back and thrust the pointed end of the Brasbeck standard into the beast's eye. By the time the dragon knew what hit it, Kendyl had already run back down its tail to safety. The dragon roared in pain and flew away, leaving most of the humans alive.

Justan was pretty sure that the story was exaggerated. He had asked about it once, but Kendyl would never confirm or deny the events.

When the crowd finally quieted, Swift Kendyl spoke. He addressed the trainees, but he made sure that his voice was loud enough that the spectators could hear.

"Welcome to day one of the Dremaldrian Battle Academy Training Exams!" The crowd erupted into applause. "To be a student in the Battle Academy, you must have the strength and endurance necessary for the long march. The trail this year has been changed to better represent the conditions a soldier might run into.

"The course is fifteen miles long. Be sure to keep an eye on the colored stones that mark the trail. The stones change color every mile, making it possible for you to keep track of your progress. As in the past, the first four miles run along the edge of the Scralag Hills. But this year the trail veers through the center of the hills. During this stretch of the trail-."

"Sir!" A trainee held his hand up.

"What is it, Zaid?" Swift Kendyl did not like being interrupted.

"Um, Sir, won't that take us into the territory of the Scralag?"

Swift Kendyl chuckled. "There have been no sightings of the Scralag for years." His face gained a mysterious expression and he looked toward the spectators. "But yes."

Murmurs ran through the crowd.

It was obvious to Justan that Swift Kendyl was pandering to the crowd, but he still didn't like the development. He knew the tales of the Scralag, but that wasn't what bothered him. Several kids he knew had been injured climbing those hills when he was a child. The area was treacherous, full of ravines and loose sharp rocks. It was as if the hills themselves were falling apart.

Swift Kendyl cleared his throat. "As I was saying, during that five mile stretch, no spectators are allowed. You will be by yourselves until you come out of the hills. The final six miles of the course weave back around to the starting gate.

"As you all know, there are five available points in the test today. The key to getting the best score is to keep moving. A mage will be keeping track of your movement along the trail. Anyone who stops to rest along the way will be docked one point. The rest of the points will be awarded according to how long it takes you to finish the course.

"Finally, there is to be no contact between students. If any of you pushes or shoves another trainee, you could be disqualified. It is best that you don't even speak to each other. There is no need. This is not a competition. You will be judged on your individual performance only. Any questions?"

There were none.

The trainees were brought to the starting line. The hornsman blew a clear note and a mage sent a fireball arcing into the air. The test had begun.

Pandemonium erupted. Spectators crowded in on either side of the trail, all of them cheering for their favorites or just screaming in general. A lot of pent up energy was released.

The first mile of the trail was lined with dark blue rocks. Justan started at a quick but steady pace, his awkward strides in perfect rhythm. The crowd's noise was intrusive, but he kept telling himself over and over, this is just like any other run.

But it wasn't. The trail ran through long stretches of muddy ground and curved over steep hills that sapped the strength from his legs. As the stones lining the trail turned from blue, to green, to yellow, he saw many other trainees slowing down.

Justan smiled. In years past, he was the one slowing down. Ma'am's bizarre conditioning routines were helping him just as much as the morning runs.

Then the rocks that marked the path changed to a deep red. Guards stood along the sides of the trail, stoically forbidding any spectators to pass. The trail took a sharp turn, heading deep into the crumbing hills of the Scralag's territory.

Soon the sounds of the raucous crowd faded in the distance. The silence made the trail seem ominous. The already cool autumn air quickly dropped a few degrees. Justan shivered. He was sure that the Scralag was just a tale told to keep the children out of the dangerous hills, but he couldn't help but take comfort in the fact that he wasn't running alone.

The rocky path soon turned into loose slate that shifted about under the runners' feet. As the miles crept by, the constant rise and fall of the trail and the stress of concentrating on the shifting footing took their toll. Justan felt as if his feet were weighted with lead. Several of the trainees had stopped to rest.

As the trail curved up and around the side of a particularly large hill, the slope on the right became steeper. The path narrowed in a forbidding way. The trail became so narrow that the trainees were forced to run single file. The gaps between runners widened.

Three miles into the Scralag's territory, Justan found himself running alone for the first time. The only sound he could hear was the crunching of his own feet in the loose rock as he laboriously wound his way along the side of the large hill. The narrow trail wove around a large boulder.

Out of nowhere strong hands grasped Justan's shoulders, jerking him to a stop. A harsh voice whispered from behind him.

"Kenn says hello," Benjo said. He had picked a good spot to lay in wait. It was the only section of the trail where no one would be around to witness his actions. Before Justan could react, Benjo shoved him off of the edge.

Justan tumbled down the steep side of the hill, scattering sharp rocks everywhere. His body careened toward a cluster of boulders at the bottom. He tried to slow his descent, but only succeeded in scraping up his arms and legs.

Time slowed down for Justan. It was as though he were outside of his body watching everything happening in slow motion. Strangely, he felt calm. Was he going to die? Was this it?

Justan's torso slammed into a boulder at the bottom of the ravine, bringing him to a jarring stop. It was a moment before he could breathe again. When he did, his ribs screamed out in pain.

Justan lay still for a moment and took slow breaths, running his hands over his side. He decided that though his ribs might be cracked, they weren't broken. He searched himself over for other injuries, hoping that he would still be able to finish the race. He was covered in cuts and bruises, but none were too serious.

He winced in pain as he stood on shaky legs. He looked back up the side of the ravine shocked to see that the trail was only a couple hundred feet up. It seemed like he had fallen forever. Benjo wasn't there anymore. He must have run on as soon as Justan fell down the slope.

The air grew cold. An icy breeze blew from the large cluster of boulders behind him. With effort, Justan ignored the dread that filled his stomach. He started to climb back up the hill.

A hissing whisper screeched out from behind him. The hairs on the back of his neck stood on end. Justan slowly turned. A ghastly figure was standing between the boulders.

The Scralag stood ten feet tall with skin a sickly white. Its long, thin arms nearly touched the ground, its hands tipped in long black claws. Cold radiated from its body, turning the air about it into a frosty mist.

Justan didn't dare breathe. The Scralag swayed for a moment as if disoriented. Its skeletal, noseless head searching back and forth.

The Scralag's beady red eyes latched onto Justan and its thin lips pulled back into a hideous smile, revealing a gaping maw full of sharp, curving teeth. Justan wanted to scream, wanted to run, wanted to do anything, but he couldn't. He didn't know if it was a spell or his own fear that immobilized him, but he was frozen in place.

The Scralag took several shuffling steps toward him, but did not immediately attack. Instead, it put its shoulder to the largest of the boulders and tilted it back. It pulled something from underneath the boulder and moved silently toward Justan. Mist trailed behind it like a shroud. Then it was right beside him, pressing a small, ancient-looking book into his hand.

Justan stood still, frozen with an icy fear as the Scralag reached up with one claw and traced something on his chest. Its touch burned like fire. The Scralag began chanting in a strange wheezing language, a white-tipped blue tongue visible between its wicked teeth. The eerie chanting reached a crescendo. It lunged forward. Its razor teeth snapped shut an inch from Justan's face.

Justan wasn't paralyzed anymore. With a primal scream, he shoved the Scralag away and scrambled up the hill, oblivious to the sharp rocks slicing his hands and legs. He was up to the trail before he knew it.

Justan sprinted full-speed away from the creature. He knew was right behind him, its claws ready to tear him apart.

He ran harder than he had ever run before. Soon he was out of the Scralag's territory. The waiting spectators were shocked to see Justan sprinting along the path, covered in contusions. He flew past stunned trainees without looking back. He didn't even notice passing Benjo. Justan ran for two straight miles before his beat up body caught up with his fear.

He slowed a little. His side began to ache with each ragged breath and he remembered his cracked ribs. Every bruise and twinge let itself known. Justan came to a halt, gasping for air. He looked down at his hands and saw frost clinging where he had touched the creature. A familiar voice rang out from within the spectators.

"Justan!" Ma'am rushed over to him. "By the gods, Justan, what happened to you?" Justan lurched and she helped steady him as she looked over his wounds.

"I fell."

"I can see that." She handed him some water. "Some of these cuts are deep. Is anything broken?" He shook his head. "Well, despite 'falling' you have actually made good time. So far you have lost only the one point for stopping."

Justan smiled at Ma'am. He wanted to unload on the woman who had become his mentor and friend, to tell her about his frightening experience, but he had to move on. He wouldn't get another chance to run this course.

Justan drank some water and stepped away from her, feeling a little bit steadier. "Well, no more wasting time, then." He started to stumble off when he noticed an uncomfortable lump in his back.

He reached back to find something stuffed in the back of his pants. It was the book that the Scralag had given him. He must have tucked it back there at some point during his escape. He handed the book to Ma'am

"Hold this for me. I'll explain later." There was puzzlement in her eyes, but she took the book without question and prodded him forward.

"Get moving!"

Justan staggered on. He tried to find a steady pace. His mad sprint had made up for the time lost in the fall. Now he just had to be steady and get his body back into a rhythm.

The stones lining the trail were yellow at this point, meaning that he still had five miles to go. Five miles! He felt like he had already raced twenty. He focused his mind and tried to ignore the pain that accompanied each jolting step and each intake of breath.

He stumbled out of the hills to more rousing applause from the spectators and the pain began to fade. Justan found that his reservoir of adrenaline wasn't empty quite yet. He had three miles to go and he had caught a second wind.

As the pain retreated, Justan's thoughts turned toward his experience. The Scralag's visage flashed through his mind. It was actually real. He had stood not two feet from it. Its icy hand had touched him. The memory brought back a trace of fear. The Scralag had touched him and it . . . it had given him a book. Why would a ghost give him a book? What was in it?

He was still mulling over this mystery, not paying enough attention, when he stepped into a depression in the road. His foot rolled within his boot. Something gave way inside his ankle and Justan crashed to the rocky ground. The crowd gasped.

The shock of the fall re-ignited the pains in his body. He lay in the dirt breathing heavily and moaned for a moment. Bitter thoughts ran through his mind. How was this possible? How could one person have so much bad luck in a single day?

Justan forced himself to stand. There was still a mile left to go. His ankle screamed with each step and fresh blood dripped from a new gash in his forehead, but still he stumbled on. The last mile stretched before him as if it would never end. Every step forward seemed a step back.

The ankle slowed him down greatly, but as the finish line came into view, Justan noticed a few runners nodding to him respectfully as they passed. Several trainees kept pace with him in case he fell again.

Justan lifted his head. His body didn't hurt so badly anymore. He wiped some blood out of his eye with the back of his hand and ran on.

Before Justan knew it, he was in front of the finish line. A huge crowd cheered. Many of them shouted his name. Ma'am was there, waiting with several teachers.

The moment he stepped over the line, people swarmed forward. His vision swam. Ma'am was speaking to him, but he couldn't understand what she was saying. He felt hands grasping him.

The world went black.

Chapter Six

When Justan's vision cleared, he was laying on a pile of blankets in the Judges Tent. He looked up and saw a crowd of people staring down at him. Ma'am, Hilt and several of the teachers from the school were there. In fact, the whole training council was present. Swift Kendyl held a very frightened-looking Benjo Plunk in place by the scruff of his neck.

A mage was brought in to the tent to heal Justan's wounds. Soon he felt the probing tingle of a healing spell moving through his body. The mage smiled down at him. "It's not too bad, kid. You have a few cracked ribs, a sprained ankle and enough abrasions that it looks like you got in a fight with a swamp cat, but don't worry. This shouldn't take too long." Justan could feel the ache in his ribs cease and his wounds began to close.

Everyone started asking questions at once. Justan was trying to decide which one to answer when the healer cried out.

"What's this?"

The mage pulled up Justan's shirt. The room went silent. There was a frost-encrusted scar on his chest in the shape of a circle with a jagged line drawn through it.

"It's a frost rune!" the mage said. "How did you get it?"

Justan, stared at the scar open mouthed, looked up into the stunned faces above him and stammered. "I-it was the Scralag. When I fell off the trail, it was there, waiting. It . . . drew this on me, I guess. What is it? What does it mean?"

The mage stared at the rune and shook his head. "I don't know." He traced his finger along the rune, mumbling a spell. "At least it isn't hurting you in any way I can see."

"Well, can you take it off?" Justan asked.

The mage closed his eyes and concentrated. "I can't. I'm afraid that you are stuck with it for now. Maybe you should have a full wizard look at it. There are some wizards at the Mage School that have experience with this kind of thing."

Ma'am reached down and helped Justan get to his feet. He felt exhausted from the healing, but at least nothing hurt anymore. Everyone began asking questions again. Justan answered them as best as he could, though for some reason he didn't understand, he didn't mention the book that the Scralag gave to him.

When Swift Kendyl asked him why he fell, Justan looked straight at Benjo. The large man turned away, his face red.

"I don't know," Justan said. "Perhaps I slipped. Perhaps it was the Scralag. All I remember is passing a big boulder in the road. The next thing I knew, I was tumbling down the slope."

Benjo's shoulders slumped in relief. Swift Kendyl looked at the big man with a frown, but with Justan's history of clumsiness, he didn't push the point. The council determined then and there to change the course of the Stamina Test. Swift Kendyl raced out to direct the runners around the Scralag's territory.

Later that day, the point totals were announced. Justan received three points for his efforts. He refused to be bitter about it. He had done as well as he ever had in the stamina test. Besides, considering all that had happened to him during the run, he was fortunate to have received the points he did.

The story of his encounter with the famed ghost had spread through the training grounds like wildfire. The other trainees swarmed around Justan, asking about the Scralag. When he was finally able to get away from all the prying questions, he found Ma'am and Hilt talking together near the archery range.

Hilt saw Justan approaching and smiled. "Justan! What a day for you, eh? Have you grown tired of all the attention yet?"

Justan thought about it for a moment. "It's strange. Everyone is acting like I am this hero. But, it's not like I fell and met the Scralag on purpose. It doesn't feel quite right."

"That's how it should always feel, Justan," Hilt said. "Being a hero isn't as fun as it seems. If you listen to the praises of others too much, you'll start believing them. That's when 'heroes' make mistakes, and that's when 'heroes' get killed. Remember the way you feel today, because if you go in the direction your dreams are pointing you, you will find this kind of praise everywhere you go." Hilt clasped Justan's shoulder. "Well, I have things to do. I will be watching again tomorrow."

He turned, bowed to Ma'am, "Miss," and walked towards the city.

Justan watched the warrior go and scratched his head. "Wait! Sir Hilt!"

"Just Hilt, Justan. You don't need to call me sir."

"I must ask you." Now that Justan had stopped Hilt, he wasn't quite sure how to phrase his question. "Um, how do you . . . know . . . so much? You don't seem that old. I mean, you're definitely younger than my father, and yet you seem to know everything there is to know about being a warrior."

Hilt laughed. "Like I told you before, Justan. All knowledge does not have to come from experience. Look at yourself. I understand that you defeated Oz the Dagger in strategy class. Does this mean that you know more about tactics than him?"

"No," Justan admitted.

"And don't assume that I am a better fighter than your father just because I have this rune on my hand. Being named has nothing to do with a person's skill level."

"But only the greatest warriors are named."

"Ah, but what makes a warrior great? Is it skill? Is it experience? Is it accomplishment?"

Justan's brow furrowed. "Okay . . . I'm confused."

Hilt chuckled again. "Becoming named has nothing to do with any of those things. There is only one requirement. Do you wish to know what it is?"

Justan nodded.

"I can only tell you one thing and that is this. You must know who you are."

"Know who I am," Justan repeated.

"That's right. Now I really must go," Hilt said and strode back towards the city.

"Did you understand any of that, Ma'am?" Justan asked.

"I do not know enough about it, Justan," she said. "I had not heard of this naming ritual until I came to the Academy. No warrior among my people has ever made the journey to the Bowl of Souls."

Justan smiled. “Maybe you’ll be the first.”

Ma’am gave him a wry look and pulled the Scralag’s book from a pouch at her belt. She looked at him expectantly.

He took the book from her and turned it over in his hands, looking closely at it for the first time. The book was very old, the leather binding faded and cracked. The front cover was torn in half. Justan could just make out the letters “BO” and what looked like an “A”, but that letter was torn in half with the rest of the cover. He looked up at Ma’am.

“Have you read any of it?” he asked.

“Of course not,” she said.

“I have no idea why it gave the book to me. I have been thinking about it all afternoon, but . . . Honestly, I am afraid to open it. What if it’s something bad?”

“My people believe that when a spirit has great need, it will seek out someone who can help,” Ma'am said. “Sometimes they give us gifts to help them.”

Justan thought it over. “So you think that it gave this to me because it needs something?”

“Perhaps.” She shrugged.

“Like what? What would a ghost need?”

“There are many different kinds of spirits and not all of them are evil,” Ma’am said. “You can feel an evil spirit’s presence. Did it feel evil to you?”

“It looked like the scariest thing you could imagine, but,” Justan thought back to his experience. How had it felt? It was a hard thing to quantify. He had been terrified, but now that he thought it over, the Scralag hadn’t necessarily felt evil. Just dangerous. “No . . . no I don’t think so. But what would it want?”

“I do not know. After you told the council your story, Hilt went out to the place you described on the trail. He found the boulders and searched around them, but there was no sign of the creature.” She gestured at the book. “Perhaps your answers are in there.”

Justan ran his fingers over the cover again. He opened it and leafed through the pages. They were hand-written in dark ink. Though the book looked weathered and dirty on the outside, the pages inside looked clean, hardly damaged at all.

It was written in the common tongue and Justan tried to read it, but after the first word, his vision blurred. He felt disoriented. He looked away and his vision returned. Ma'am looked at him, concern in her eyes. He tried to read it again, but this time the disorientation was so violent that he felt sick to his stomach. He shut the book. "Maybe I'm not supposed to read this."

"What is wrong?" Ma'am asked.

"I can't get past the first word. I think there is a spell on it."

"What is the first word?"

"The," Justan replied. Ma'am frowned. "What? Do you want to try reading it?"

Ma'am refused and again she seemed offended that he'd asked. Justan thought that odd, but he had more pressing things on his mind. He ran a hand under his shirt and traced the scar. It was still covered in frost. Why had the Scralag marked him? What did it need?

Justan shook off the nagging questions.

"I don't have the time to figure this out right now." His focus had to be on scoring as many points as possible in the tests this week. He could worry about the Scralag after he was accepted into the Academy. Surely there were experts there who could help him. Justan looked at the archery range. "I'd like to get in some practice before I go back."

Ma'am smiled. "You may earn that bow, yet."

Later while Justan was shooting, Ma'am confronted him, "You did not really 'fall' did you?"

"Yes, I really did fall," Justan said. "I just had some help, that's all." He let loose and the arrow hit near the center. Justan found that lately he was hitting near or in the center most of the time. His skill was improving rapidly and it scared him to think of how much his stubbornness had been holding him back. If only he had been willing to listen to Mad Jon's teachings in the past, he wouldn't have needed this extra year.

"It was Benjo," Ma'am stated, interrupting his reverie. Justan nodded. "Why did you not tell Swift Kendyl about this when he asked?"

"I can handle Benjo and Kenn by myself," he said automatically. Then he smiled and shook his head. "I get the impression that Benjo doesn't hate me like Kenn does. I think he's just used to doing whatever Kenn tells him. The truth is I figured that having Benjo on my side might help me the next time I run into those two." He turned back to his shooting.

"You are wise beyond your years, Justan son of Faldon the Fierce." Ma'am said with what he took to be sarcasm. He didn't see the growing respect in her eyes.

Under her breath, she added, "Do you realize how much you have grown?"

Justan didn't hear her. He was focused on the target.

Chapter Seven

Justan awoke from a deep dreamless sleep. It was still pitch black in his room and his body ached from the rigors of the day before. He tried to go back to sleep, but after tossing and turning for a while, he laid in the darkness with his eyes wide open, fingering the frosty scar on his chest. The experience of the day before replayed in his mind.

He sat up. Why was there no moonlight? There had been a full moon the night before. He stood and moved to his one small window. He pressed his face against the glass, but he couldn't see anything outside.

Justan opened the door and winced as bright light flooded the room. The sun was well over the horizon.

"Oh no," he moaned.

He was supposed to be in the first group of students in the distance weapons test that day. If he was late, he would forfeit any points!

With a yelp, he threw his clothes on and scampered outside. No wonder he overslept. Someone had draped a thick woolen blanket over his window and piled dirt around the base of the door.

Justan sprinted across the training grounds, pushing through the crowds of spectators until he reached the archery range. He arrived just as Mad Jon was about to explain the rules for the day's test.

Justan breathed a sigh of relief. He had made it there just in time. However that didn't curb his anger. It had to have been Kenn. He was going to have to do something about the man soon. He could take his problem to the training council, but he didn't have any real proof. Not yet.

Mad Jon began explaining the rules, flashing a stern look at the nearly tardy Justan. The number of points received in the ranged weapons test was determined by a mark system. Each target was painted with three consecutively smaller rings. The outermost ring was worth one mark; the next ring worth two, and the small circle in the center was worth three marks. There were six rounds of shooting and their five best shots would count, making a possible fifteen marks.

The results for each round would be posted on a large board hung near the spectator's gallery. Only those trainees who scored fourteen or fifteen marks would receive the full five test points.

Justan was the first trainee in his group to shoot. He walked to his assigned target and took up the bow that was provided. The school used a standard issue bow for all training throughout the year, so he was familiar with its feel.

The crowd was lined up behind the archers, cheering for their favorites. The story of what had happened to him in the stamina test the day before must have spread through the spectators. The section behind Justan was particularly loud.

Justan fit an arrow to his bow and pulled back. He concentrated on the target and pushed everything else aside, the sounds of the crowd, the other archers; he let all of it blur. It was as if the natural order of things, all of the little factors that he used to worry about, were relayed to his subconscious. As he let go, Justan knew that the arrow would fly true. And it did. The arrow struck quivering in the center of the target. Justan raised his bow in the air and shouted with glee.

The world crashed back in on him in the form of the crowd's roar. The sound was nearly deafening. Justan looked back in surprise. When it came to the spectators, he was used to disappointed silence. It was a nice change.

On his next turn, he was able to reproduce the same focus and struck the center again. His third shot was just as successful and the crowd around his shooting spot had grown even bigger. The other trainees in his group looked back at him with irritation.

Elated, Justan walked back with the other trainees to await his next turn. He couldn't believe it. Nine marks in three shots. If he kept this up, he could earn five points in this event. The only test he had ever received five points in was the strategy exam.

"Hey Justan."

He turned to see Kenn Dollie smirking petulantly, his wiry arms folded in front of his chest.

"What are you doing here, Kenn?"

Kenn knew that he wasn't supposed to mingle with the other trainees during the archery test. Kenn specialized in throwing daggers. Thrown weapons specialists didn't test until later in the day.

"I hear you barely made it in today," Kenn said with a sneer. "Wild night?"

"Go away, Kenn."

"So that wild lady been teaching you to shoot?"

Justan sighed.

"Yes, Kenn, as a matter of fact she has." He pointed Ma'am out in the crowd. "Why don't you go ask her for a lesson?"

"Ooh, yes. I like 'em wild! You think she'd go for me?" Kenn licked his lips. "I could show her a thing or two."

Justan laughed out loud at the idea. "Sure, I think she would go for you, Kenn. In fact, why don't you walk over to her and put it just that way? She likes the dirty talk," he jeered, trying to keep a straight face.

Kenn fixed him with an evil glare and said in a voice that sent a chill down Justan's spine, "Maybe she won't have a choice." He slinked into the crowd.

Justan had to force himself not to chase the man down and throttle him. He knew that Kenn wouldn't dare try anything. He was too afraid of Ma'am. Besides, she could take care of herself. Still, Justan could not get rid of the sinking feeling that Kenn's remark had left in his chest.

As he arrived in place to take his fourth shot, Justan was still fuming. He turned to glance at Ma'am and saw Kenn in the crowd, standing near her. The skinny man smiled and made an obscene gesture. Justan knew that Kenn was just trying to break his concentration. He forced himself to calm down.

Justan raised his bow and tried to achieve the same level of focus he had earlier in the day. He trained his sight on the center of the target, but he was not able to get rid of the anger that was stuck like a dagger in his mind.

He let loose and the arrow flew wide of the mark, barely sticking into the outer edge of the target. A disappointed moan came from the crowd. Justan let the bow fall to his side, furious at Kenn, but even more furious at himself for letting Kenn's comment get under his skin. Luckily, he was allowed to let the worst shot go, which meant that he still had a chance to receive the full five points in the test.

He had to get his emotions under control. Why did Kenn's remark unnerve him so? Justan didn't have to wonder long, for as he walked back to wait for his next shot, Kenn was standing at Ma'am's shoulder, grinning from ear to ear.

Kenn motioned to her. The man was about six inches shorter than Ma'am and the crowd was so loud that she had to bend down a bit to hear what he said. Kenn, with that evil sneer of his, whispered in her ear. To Justan's horror she smiled back at Kenn and leaned in close, as if to kiss him.

So quickly that Justan could barely see it, Ma'am threw an elbow into Kenn's face, flattening his nose. Then while Kenn was still stunned from the unexpected attack, she planted one end of her staff firmly between his legs, shifted her feet, and launched Kenn out of the crowd. The greasy little man soared over the fence to land on his rear right in front of Mad Jon.

Mad Jon frowned down at the man. "Kenn Dollie? Get off the field. You're not allowed out here until the final session." Kenn groaned. One hand tried to stem the flow of blood pouring from his nose. "Do you hear me, Dollie?"

"It's not my fault, Sir. It was that wild woman! She-"

"She?" Mad Jon asked, one eyebrow raised.

A wave of laughter rippled through the crowd. Ma'am turned back to watch the contest, her face beet red. Justan shot her a cheerful wave, but only received a glare in return. He had no idea what Kenn had said, but Justan was glad that he had never thought to make any advances on her himself.

Mad Jon escorted Kenn off of the field. The smaller man limped off, shooting glares at all the laughing spectators.

During his fifth shot, Justan was still chuckling inwardly and his focus again suffered. The arrow hit the line between the center and the inner ring, giving him two marks. Now his last shot had to be perfect to get full marks on the test.

As he waited for his final shot, Justan tried to calm himself. He had so much energy he was getting jitters. The wait seemed to go on forever.

When the time finally came, Justan's hands were shaking. He fitted the arrow to the bow and closed his eyes. He tried to push everything away. The nervousness and tension went down with a struggle, but the noise of the crowd was pushing in on his consciousness. They were chanting his name. The noise pounded in his mind rhythmically. Justan embraced the noise and opened his eyes.

He raised his bow. The crowd hushed. He felt a wave of calm come over him. Justan could feel the spectators willing him to succeed. It seemed as if the target was just two feet in front of him. He released. The arrow buried itself deeply into the center of the target.

The crowd erupted.

Justan stood in stunned astonishment. What had just happened? How had he done that? Could he do it again?

He pushed the questions away. Five points for the day, an achievement he had never dared dream he would receive in the archery exam! He had to see Ma'am.

Justan scanned the crowd and his eyes caught someone else instead. It was the man in the white robe who always seemed to be studying him. The man's dark eyes bored into Justan as if he could see into his soul.

Justan pushed his way through the spectators, determined to speak with this man and find out who he was. But the people crowded in shouting congratulations and wanting to shake his hand. It wasn't long before Justan lost sight of the man.

Later that day, he met up with Ma'am to go over some last-minute preparation for the next day's hand-to-hand combat test. She had a fearsome glare in her eyes. Evidently she was still angry over what had happened earlier with Kenn.

Justan was sure that she was taking some of her anger out on him during the training. At one point she had him in a particularly nasty choke hold and Justan squealed, "Ma'am, remember I got five points in the test today!"

She looked down at him with his face going blue and for a moment he saw her eyes soften. Ever so briefly he saw that beautiful smile curl her lips.

"Yes, Justan, you did well," she said. Then she swept his feet out from under him, dropping Justan to the ground. "If that dradatchi had not accosted me, I would be in a good mood!"

Justan had no idea what a dradatchi was, but even though he lay in the dust, gasping for air, he started to laugh.

Chapter Eight

The man in the white robe was striking. The whiteness of the hair that hung heavy about his shoulders stood out in stark contrast to dark eyebrows and a black beard that was trimmed short and neat. He stood with hands clasped in front of him, holding onto his walking stick. He spoke calmly, but there was such confidence in his voice that each phrase sounded like a command.

The Battle Academy council members, led by Faldon the Fierce, looked down upon him from their raised dais. He could tell by the sternness of their facial expressions that they were not pleased with his arguments.

Faldon the Fierce was the first to voice his displeasure. "This was not our agreement, Ambassador. The boy shows great improvement. It looks like he will pass the tests easily this year. I am afraid that we will have to allow him entrance into the Academy."

The man in white responded, "We understand the council's position on this matter and we too are pleased to see the young man succeed. However it would be unfair to him if he were not allowed to reach his potential. His encounter with the Scralag is a great example of why he is so special. He was born with a rare gift, and I am sure that the council would not want to deny him that."

Faldon bristled as the ambassador emphasized the word council. Before he could respond, Tad the Cunning stood and placed a calming hand on Faldon's shoulder.

"Ambassador, the testing is not yet finished. We shall make our decision once the week is over." There were several nods of agreement. Tad smiled. "Until then, enjoy yourself. Have a good time at the celebrations. Who knows, perhaps you will find someone else with potential." Tad then gestured to the door.

With a slight bow, the man in the white robe turned and left.

As soon as the heavy door shut behind the man, Faldon turned to the rest of the council.

"My son won't agree to this. He scored a five in the archery test today. Five! He is finally reaching his dreams. We can't give in to their requests. They may be powerful allies, but we can't take this opportunity away from Justan. Not if he actually succeeds!"

Sabre Vlad the swordsmanship teacher spoke next. "Faldon, we know. We've all watched Justan grow since he was a boy. We won't allow politics to interfere with the promises we made him."

Another voice came from the back of the room. "Have you considered that the ambassador may be right?" The man who had spoken moved out from behind the tapestry where he had been concealed during the meeting. He walked before the council. "I beg your forgiveness for my stealth. I know that it was not my place to listen. I saw Ambassador Valtrek in the crowd watching Justan and followed him here."

The council members looked down at the man in shock. The only one not surprised by his appearance was the leader of the Assassin School, Hugh the Shadow, who nodded at the man appreciatively.

Faldon the Fierce rose to his feet. "You're right it's not your place, Sir Hilt!"

"Once again, I did not intend to listen in on a private meeting," Hilt said. "And I do apologize. However, since I have heard, I believe I have something of importance to add."

Faldon seemed about to respond again, but Tad the Cunning gestured for Hilt to continue.

"I have been training with Justan for the last two weeks, and you are right about his desire to accomplish his goals. But you must also know that his dreams sell him short.

"I have seen much of his character and I know that there is more out there for Justan than simply being an academy graduate. For Justan to reach his full potential he needs to learn who he truly is. He will not do that by following the path he wants to travel. Unfortunately, I must leave tonight and I will not be able to watch him pass the final tests, as I know he will. But I owe him this much. I plead with you to do for Justan what is truly best for him." Without another word, Hilt bowed and took his leave.

The council's argument raged into the night.

The Training School's arena was located in the center of the training grounds. It was a large round field with seating for over five thousand spectators on terraced benches. In the center of the field were several rings marked in white stones where the trainees would compete in the hand-to-hand combat test.

The arena was rarely filled to capacity. Aside from testing week, it was mainly used for practice and occasional exhibitions. But on this day, not only was the arena filled, it was overflowing. More than a thousand spectators could not find seats and stood outside of the arena straining to hear what was going on.

The hand-to-hand combat test was a crowd favorite. In the stamina and ranged weapon tests the trainees only competed against themselves. In this test the stakes were higher. Each trainee faced off against an experienced academy student.

Justan sat in the section with the other trainees, shifting his feet and wiping his sweaty palms on the legs of his pants as he waited his turn. He hadn't been looking forward to this test. After archery, hand-to-hand combat had always been his worst subject.

He tried to tell himself that he had done well enough in the first two tests. This one didn't matter as much. He didn't have to score very high. He could just do his best and that would be okay. But these thoughts didn't sit well. He felt the weight of the eyes of many spectators resting upon him and he knew that they were expecting him to do something amazing.

Justan took a slow deep breath and focused on all that Ma'am had taught him in the past year. It wasn't very likely that he would face anyone that was as good as she was. With that thought, he loosened up a little. Perhaps he wouldn't do so badly after all. By the time it was his turn to step into the arena he felt much more confident about his chances.

When Justan heard his name announced, he stepped away from the other students and walked onto the arena floor. As he stepped into his assigned ring, the crowd applauded. Standing in the huge arena full of people, he felt small. He supposed that the crowds had been nearly as big in the other tests, but now it was different. They towered above him on the benches, chanting his name.

The judges called Justan's opponent forward. He was an academy student named Jobar da Org. Justan didn't know much about the man except that he hailed from Narlin, an oceanside country far to the south. By the way that Jobar carried himself, Justan could tell that he was a formidable opponent.

Jobar entered the ring with confident strides. He took off his shirt and flexed his muscles, displaying bronzed skin covered in intricate tattoos for the crowd. Jobar was much shorter than Justan, but built like a dwarf, with a tough thick body and bulging muscles.

Justan took one look at the man's physique and decided to keep his own shirt on. Though he was in better shape than he had ever been before, Justan still only considered himself of average build. He would have to rely on talents other than his strength to win against this man. In this first section of the test, he would be on offense while his opponent could only use defensive moves. His stomach began to flutter again.

The hornsman blew a short note. Justan started in at his opponent. He began with a series of kicks that Jobar easily blocked. Frustrated, he went into several jabs and short kicks, trying to find the man's weaknesses. There were none that Justan could see. Jobar was very smooth with his blocks and parries. Justan took a deep breath and stalked around Jobar, feeling out his strategy.

He came in with a high kick that Ma'am would have been proud of. Jobar picked it off with one thick forearm. Justan grabbed the arm and tried to throw him, but the man simply twisted out of his grasp.

Justan was running out of time. The hornsman could blow a note at any time to end the match. Jobar da Org was just too good. He was a man who practiced with the Academy's skilled instructors and students every day. He knew all the moves.

And that might be his weakness, Justan thought. Jobar was used to fighting people with Academy training, but how long had it been since Jobar fought someone who had no training?

Justan yelled and went at the man's face. He threw clumsy punch after clumsy punch. Jobar easily blocked them, though he looked confused. While still throwing ugly punches, Justan hooked his right foot behind Jobar's left. Then instead of punching again as the man expected, he grasped Jobar's blocking arm and shoved.

Jobar fell off balance. As he swung his left foot around to regain his stance, Justan shoved him again. Jobar stumbled out of the ring. The crowd roared. The judges shrugged. It hadn't exactly been a finesse move, but it worked.

On the way back to their seats, Jobar glowered at Justan. "That won't happen again, trainee. Next time it's my turn."

As Justan sat with the other trainees to await the next section, he tried to ignore Jobar's penetrating glare. The man's eyes didn't leave him once while the other trainees competed. By the time Justan's name was called again, he knew that he was going to pay for that last move. In this section of the test, Jobar would be on offense while Justan could only use defensive moves.

Sure enough, as soon as the hornsman blew, Jobar came at Justan with a vengeance. He threw heavy punches and kicks that bruised Justan's arms when he tried to block. Jobar stepped back and circled, smiling as Justan rubbed his sore arms.

Justan prepared himself for the next attack. He knew that it was going to hurt. But he didn't understand how quick Jobar could be until the man came at him.

Jobar spit out a sudden flurry of punches that slipped through Justan's defenses, smashing him twice in the face. While Justan was still dazed, Jobar sent a foot into his stomach. Justan curled over in pain. He couldn't breathe. It felt like he had been beaten with a hammer.

Jobar's next move happened so fast that Justan barely registered it. With a grunt, Jobar grabbed an arm and a leg with his viselike hands. He swung Justan up over his head, turned, and hurled him outside the ring. Justan struck the ground with an audible thud. The crowd moaned in sympathy.

A mage rushed over to heal Justan's bleeding nose and bruises. When the mage had finished, Justan stood and walked back to his seat. The crowd peppered him with cheers of encouragement, but Justan wasn't feeling it.

The last section was normally the most brutal fight. Each combatant could use both offensive and defensive moves. The healers would be busy today.

Justan waited as the other trainees were trounced by their academy opponents. It was a rare thing for a trainee to win in this round. The judges were more concerned with how a trainee fought than if he won. Most of the trainees went into the arena just determined not to look bad. That attitude had always turned Justan's stomach. It was not the way a true warrior would approach a battle.

Justan heard Jobar laugh as one of the younger trainees was tossed through the air. He frowned. He didn't know how he was going to do it, but he absolutely had to beat this man. Jobar noticed Justan watching him and tried to stare him down. Justan matched him glare for glare. The powerful man only kept eye contact for a short time before breaking away with a chuckle.

Justan could see that the man wasn't cowed. Jobar knew that he could beat him. He had taken his measure on the field. But Jobar didn't understand how determined Justan could be.

Justan examined his opponent closer. Was there anything he could use to his advantage? Justan took mental notes. The man had short hair, nothing to grab onto. He did have one big earring. The man was extremely fit and had no old injuries that Justan could see. But wait, perhaps there was. At second glance, Justan saw a large scar running across the top of Jobar's left foot. When the judges called out his name, a wicked grin was plastered on Justan's face.

Jobar scowled at him as he approached. "What are you smiling at, trainee? Don't you know that I will break you to pieces?"

Justan's grin became a little less wicked.

As they entered the circle, a roar of anticipation leapt from the spectators. When Jobar shouted out and flexed his muscles for the crowd, Justan played his first card. He took his own shirt off. The crowd gasped. But they weren't looking at his physique. Jobar stared in surprise at the frost-encrusted rune that sparkled on Justan's chest.

"A gift from the Scralag," Justan remarked.

The fierceness went out of Jobar's eyes. Everyone had heard rumors of his encounters with the ghost during the stamina test.

Justan was hoping that this revelation would unnerve the man enough to give him an opening.

Indeed, Jobar did not immediately go on the offensive this time, giving Justan the opportunity to start his plans. With a battle cry he charged at the man, swinging all of his weight behind a powerful uppercut. Jobar caught his incoming fist in one thick hand. He twisted, immobilizing Justan's arm, bending him at the waist. This was a basic hold and Ma'am had taught him how to get out of it, but Justan instead took advantage of Jobar's closeness. He stomped on the top of Jobar's scarred foot.

Jobar growled and reversed his grip, bringing Justan's arm up behind his back. Then Jobar snaked his other arm under Justan's armpit, up and around the back of Justan's neck, leaving Justan's free arm extended in the air. This should have left Justan with no effective way to attack. But Justan reached back with his extended arm and hooked one finger through Jobar's earring.

"Don't you dare!" Jobar hissed. He wrenched Justan's arm up even further. Justan could feel his shoulder slowly working its way out of its socket.

In desperation, he stomped on Jobar's scarred foot again. The man grunted and wrenched his arm further. Justan yanked frantically on Jobar's earring. He stomped Jobar's foot yet again. The man roared in pain and shoved Justan away.

With a resounding pop, Justan's socket left his shoulder. He cried out with the pain, but refused to give in. He turned to face his opponent again. It was at that point that he realized he still had Jobar's earring attached to his finger.

Jobar limped toward him with one hand holding his bloody ear. Though Jobar winced with each step, Justan could see murder in his eyes. With his one arm dangling at a weird angle, Justan knew that he was doomed.

For a moment he considered stepping out of the circle to end the match. But he couldn't make himself do it. Instead, he did what no one expected. He attacked before his opponent could.

Justan leapt into the air as if to kick at Jobar's head. Jobar raised an arm to block the move, but instead of extending the kick, Justan's leg shot down. All of his weight and momentum was focused on his heel as it caved in the top of Jobar's scarred foot with a sickening crunch.

Jobar forgot about anything else but the searing pain. With a roar, he pushed Justan away and dropped to the ground, cradling his ruined foot.

Jobar's shove landed on Justan's dislocated shoulder. Justan stumbled and sank to his knees with the shooting pain. His thoughts blurred. He nearly passed out. The hornsman blew to end the match with both combatants incapacitated.

Chapter Nine

Everyone eagerly awaited the announcement of point totals later in the day. Justan was nervous. He wasn't sure how his odd display would be judged.

Hand-to-hand combat was supposed to be a beautiful thing to watch, full of acrobatics and harmonious control of the body. There had been nothing poetic about Justan's fight. It had played out with all the charm of a bar room brawl. He tried to win the only way he could. But he hadn't exactly won. It was more of a draw. And he had made an enemy.

That old wound of Jobar's had taken a lot of work for the mages to heal and even then, they said that it would never be quite the same. Justan felt a little guilty about taking advantage of Jobar's old injury like that. He didn't hold any ill will toward the man after all. He was still mulling it over that evening when Ma'am met him by the archery range.

"Justan, they have posted the results. You received three points today!" she said. "This gives you a total of eleven points so far. You could have the fifteen points you need tomorrow before you even take the final test."

Justan smiled and nodded. This was great news. He had never expected to get this far so quickly. But his excitement was tempered by the guilt that had been plaguing him.

"So, what did you think of my performance today?" he asked. Ma'am looked into his eyes and somehow he sensed that she knew the question that was really behind those words.

"It was not pretty." She stood with her arms crossed, but a slight smile curled the corners of her lips. "But real fighting rarely is. The way that you fought showed that you knew your deficiencies. Not too long ago you would have fought the way you had been taught and lost." She patted him on the shoulder. "Do not be too concerned about your opponent. I know Jobar. The man needed a little humility. He will be a smarter fighter because of the lesson you taught him today." Then with a mischievous whisper she added, "The other students have started calling him Jobar Three Lobe."

Justan laughed, finally relaxing a bit. Ma'am always seemed to know the right thing to say to either make him feel better, or push him so that he would become better.

"Well tomorrow is my strongest event. I have received five points in the strategy test every year." Suddenly he felt very tired. He had worked so hard for so long. But now that he was finally here, now that victory was in his sight, he felt that something was missing.

He forced a smile on his face. "I hope the council is proud."

Her eyes sparkled. "I am sure that they will be tomorrow. And they will not be the only ones. Sir Hilt left something for you." She pulled out a long leather bundle that Justan hadn't noticed before. "He asked me to give you this. He had to leave last night."

Justan stood. "He did? But why?"

"He would only say that he had business to attend to." She untied the straps that held the bundle together and unrolled it so that Justan could see the contents.

Two shining swords lay nestled inside the leather wrapping. They were each around three feet long and very well made. The grips were worn, but the swords were highly polished and well cared for.

When Justan picked them up, he could immediately tell that they had excellent balance. He twirled them with his wrists. The swords fit him perfectly. "I can't believe it," he whispered.

"Sir Hilt said that they are his practice swords," Ma'am said. "He wanted me to tell you that you could use them until you found better ones."

"He is wrong," Justan said. "They are wonderful."

"He also left you this." She handed him a piece of parchment.

Justan took it with a bit of sadness. He wondered why his teacher needed to leave so suddenly. He opened the letter and read,

> *Justan,*
>
> *I am sorry that I will not be able to be there at your moment of victory. Ever since I saw your determination the first day we trained, I knew that you would succeed. It takes a rare person to push forward the way that you have.*
>
> *This inner drive you possess is a great strength, but I fear it is also your weakness. I will try to explain what I believe has held you back.*
>
> *From what I have seen in the last two weeks, you have developed a belief that in order to be truly great, you must succeed without the help of others. You have been isolating yourself in order to achieve your goals. This is folly. Any man that starts out with an attitude like that is destined to fail. Justan, you must trust in others. It is crucial if you want to reach your potential. You simply cannot do it alone.*
>
> *I would also warn you to be aware that your goals may drag you short of your potential. I sense far greater possibilities within you than you can see.*
>
> *I will be watching your progress with interest, my friend. I am sure that our paths will cross again. Until then, Justan, it has been a pleasure.*
>
> *Hilt*

Justan read the letter over several times. Finally, he folded the letter and put it in his pouch. Justan turned to Ma'am.

"There is something I must tell you." He told her everything he had been holding back, starting with the reason that Kenn hated him. He told her about the heavy blanket that had been placed over his window in the night and the remarks Kenn made to him at the archery. He had kept these things to himself, determined that he could handle anything Kenn dished up on his own. But there was too much riding on the next two days of testing. Kenn might try something else.

Ma'am was not happy. She flushed a deep red when he stammered out what Kenn said about her at the archery range. When he finished, she shook her head.

"It doesn't matter now. Benjo and Kenn have been expelled from the Training School."

"What? How?"

"The instructors were aware of Kenn's hatred of you. Swift Kendyl had his suspicions about your fall in the stamina test despite your story. After witnessing Kenn's actions during the archery exam, he decided to keep an eye on them. Early this morning he caught Kenn and Benjo trying to sneak into your room."

"Okay, I can understand them getting in trouble, but expelled?" It didn't make sense. Pranks were fairly common at the school and the teachers tended to turn a blind eye to them, though they were frowned upon during test week.

"Normally you would be right, but Swift Kendyl found a sleeping potion in Kenn's possession. We have no idea where they got it. It was a powerful and rare potion, nothing a person would use in a simple prank. It was enough evidence to show that they were trying to sabotage your chances for today's test. Expelling them was not a hard decision. The teachers never liked those two anyway."

"I'm surprised that I didn't hear about this earlier."

"I asked that the teachers not announce it until after the test," Ma'am said. "I did not want to break your concentration."

Justan frowned as something else occurred to him. "Ma'am, testing time is still a public event. Kenn and Benjo may be expelled from the Training School but that doesn't prevent them from entering the grounds as spectators. What's to keep them from trying something again?"

"Do not be concerned. Those two are more trouble for themselves than anyone else. They will not try anything again. They are most likely too busy wondering where their next meal is going to come from to worry about you." Justan tried to smile, but found that he couldn't. She placed a hand on his shoulder. "If it would help you feel better, I can make sure that someone watches your room for the last two nights of the tests."

Justan's mouth dropped in horror at the suggestion. Ma'am nodded.

"I thought not." She pushed him towards his room. "Go. Sleep. You have been healed twice in one day. I am surprised that you are still standing. I will wake you in the morning and make sure that nothing impedes you in the exam. Now go."

When Justan finally got to bed, he didn't think that he would be able to sleep. There was too much running around in his mind. But Ma'am was right. His body overrode his mind and he slept the whole night through.

Justan awoke to the early morning glow entering through his one small window. At first he was startled, but he realized that it wasn't bright enough to be full daylight yet. He stretched and washed in the washbasin, letting the cold water wake him up completely. He put on his clothes and started for the door, deciding to take a quick run before breakfast.

As he shut the door behind him, something caught the corner of his eye. He turned to see a small bag tacked to his door. He looked around but didn't see anyone nearby. He opened the bag to see a familiar green ribbon and a folded piece of paper.

His heart dropped. He quickly unfolded the piece of paper. There was a brief note: *Don't worry, I've only taken her shopping. Remember, I like 'em wild.*

Justan swallowed. Kenn abducting Ma'am? On the surface it was a ludicrous idea. Sure, she hadn't been there to wake him as she had promised, but Justan couldn't imagine anyone catching her unawares, much less someone as inept as Kenn. What finally convinced him was the ribbon.

He remembered a time during practice when one of her ribbons fell out of her hair. When he had tried to pick it up, she had smacked his hand so hard, it hurt for days. Ma'am would not have let it out of her sight.

He held the ribbon carefully in his hands. The note said he had taken her shopping. His hands clenched into fists. Justan strapped on his new swords and ran towards the Training Market.

That's where Kenn had to have taken her. Justan didn't know what he was looking for, but he didn't care.

He searched up and down the streets, pushing past crowds and vendors looking to make deals. Where would they be? Kenn obviously couldn't hold her hostage out in the open.

Justan was well known by now. Many people in the market called out his name as he passed by. He politely nodded, but didn't speak to anyone. He didn't have time for any delays. The strategy test would start in about two hours.

After traversing the length of the Training Market several times, Justan hesitated at the city border. Reneul seemed to loom over him. The only place left to search was the Reneul Market, in the city. But it was off limits. He had signed a contract stating that he would not leave the training grounds this year. If he was caught leaving with all these witnesses, his contract would be forfeit and he would not be able to enter the academy. Perhaps that was what Kenn was trying to get him to do. Perhaps they were watching him, just waiting for him to step over the line so that they could call the guards.

A year ago, Justan would not have hesitated. He would have gone back to take the test. Taking this kind of chance would have been unacceptable to the old Justan. But he had changed. Some things were more important than the tests. The memory of Kenn's sickening smile directed at Ma'am convinced him. Ignoring the watchful eyes of the passers-by, he stepped into the city.

He searched up and down the market street of Reneul looking for any sign of them. Time grew short. He knew that if he were to search any longer, he would miss the test and the last year of training would go to waste. He could lose any chance he had of entering the academy. All the people who helped him this year would have done so in vain. Ma'am, Hilt . . .

Justan came to a stop so fast he stumbled. He had been ignoring Hilt's words from the night before. It was ridiculous to think that he could find them in the city all by himself! Why hadn't he gone and found Swift Kendyl or Oz the Dagger and told them of the situation? The vision in his mind of himself as 'the hero saving the day' that had overridden his common sense. The thought that his indulging such a selfish notion could hurt Ma'am was something he could not bear.

He had to get back. Justan's heart beat madly in his chest as he sprinted back to the Training School. His only thoughts were of reaching someone in authority to help. He made his way back to the Training Market and began once more pushing his way through the crowd.

Then something stopped him dead in his tracks. There was another green ribbon. This one tacked to the gnarled wooden door of an old storeroom that looked like it hadn't been used in some time.

Without thinking, Justan pulled his swords. He charged the door and kicked it in. He darted inside and caught a quick glimpse of Kenn standing over an unconscious Ma'am before something wet splashed him in the face. He blacked out.

Justan slowly became aware of muffled voices. He couldn't move at all. He couldn't feel his body. The only thing he could feel was his eyelids and they felt like they were glued shut. The voices got louder. He strained to hear what was being said.

"The test is over. He missed it. Now let's get out of here. We didn't have much of that stuff left when I hit him and I don't know how long they're going to sleep." It was Benjo's voice.

Kenn's greasy voice came out in response. "Yeah, yeah. The test may be over . . . but I don't think that's enough."

"Come on, Kenn. Let's go." Benjo was starting to sound worried.

"I don't think so." Kenn must have seen Justan's eyelids twitch, because he kicked him in the ribs. "Wake up, Justan! I want you to see something."

Justan's eyes fluttered open. He could see somewhat, but the edges of his vision were clouded over. His head felt like it had been stuffed with cotton. He still couldn't move his limbs.

"Why?" he croaked.

"Why what, Justan?"

"Why . . . this?" Was all he could squeeze out.

"Because you are everything I hate in this world!" Kenn snarled. "You think you are so much better than everybody else just because your daddy makes sure you get all the breaks." He kicked Justan again, harder this time. "Now because of you, I am out of the school! My one chance to get ahead in life and a spoiled boy takes me down."

"I didn't do this to you, Kenn," Justan coughed. The kick had hurt that time, but he was starting to get some of his movement back. "You did this to yourself."

Kenn ignored him. "At first I thought that you would get away with it and I'd be stuck on the street while you got into the Battle Academy!" His voice reached a feverish pitch. "Luckily I was able to get another potion from that old guy in town. Now you are out of it, too!"

Justan was starting to think that Kenn was insane.

Kenn pulled a dagger from a sheath at his belt and walked over to Ma'am, who was still unconscious on the floor. He pulled her head back by her hair and placed the knife against her throat. A giggle burst from his throat.

"Maybe I should take care of the wild lady." Kenn's voice was off kilter. "One of her main goals in life seems to be to humiliate me."

Suddenly Justan's limbs didn't seem so heavy. He lurched to his feet, but Benjo grabbed him tight.

"You know, though. I do like them wild. What do you think, Justan? You think she would like it?" Kenn ran his unshaven cheek against hers and grinned an evil grin. His voice lowered and became husky. "Yes, I think she would."

"I will kill you!" Justan promised.

Kenn pressed the tip of his knife harder at Ma'am's throat, causing a bead of blood to form.

"Kenn, I-I don't like this," Benjo stammered.

"Hold him still! I want him to watch this."

Justan thought he saw Ma'am's eyelids flutter.

"No!" Benjo said. "You're going too far!" His grip around Justan lessened.

"Shut up and hold him!" Kenn hissed. "I'm going to enjoy this." He put the knife down and lifted Ma'am's head from the floor. He fumbled with the fastenings on Ma'am's clothes with one hand. He ran his tongue along her cheek.

What happened next was a blur. Benjo released Justan. He stumbled toward Kenn, but before he got there, it was already over.

With a roar, Ma'am bit into the side of Kenn's face. Her fist shot out and caught him in the throat. Kenn clutched at his face and throat, gasping for air. Ma'am was already on her feet. She kicked him over and over. Kenn stopped moving.

Justan tried to pull her away. She grabbed his wrist and threw him to the side. He waited for a moment, but when it didn't look like she was going to stop, he tried again.

This time he was able to grasp Ma'am around the waist. He lifted her away, still kicking at the air. He looked around for Benjo, but the man was gone. The door to the room was ajar.

"Enough, Ma'am! It's over." Kenn was unmoving, his eyes rolled back into his head, his body bruised and broken from the beating. "He's not worth it."

Ma'am continued to struggle in his arms. "In my land, he would die for even thinking of what he was about to do!"

"Well not here," Justan said, though he wasn't completely sure that Kenn was still alive. "Let the council take care of him."

He held her close until she stopped struggling. For a moment, her arms reached around him and held him back. He thought she began to sob. It didn't last long.

"Fine!" She pushed him away. "Fine. We will call the guard to take him away."

They didn't have to wait long. One met them at the door. People in the market had heard the ruckus. Ma'am stormed outside while Justan tried to answer the guard's questions. Soon another guard came and Justan watched as they took Kenn's still form away. Kenn was still breathing, but barely. If the man didn't die from the beating Ma'am had given him, he would probably wish he were dead by the time the council got through with him.

Justan joined Ma'am on the street outside. He was shaken by her appearance. She looked disheveled and upset, fingering her hair and pacing back and forth. She wiped the cheek where Kenn had licked her over and over with a piece of cloth.

Justan stared at her, wanting to help, wanting to hold her close and tell her it was okay. But that wasn't what she would want. He dug into his pocket and handed her the green ribbons that Kenn had taken. She snatched them from his hands and quickly weaved them back into her hair. As she did so, she seemed to regain some of her composure.

"You're bleeding." Justan pointed to her throat, where the tip of Kenn's knife had pierced her skin.

She reached towards the wound but her hand stopped short of touching it. "It's nothing," she said, but her fingers were trembling.

A guard found their weapons inside. Justan retrieved them and handed the gray staff to Ma'am. She gripped the staff so tightly that Justan could hear the wood creak.

Ma'am seemed to take strength from the feel of her staff in her hands. By the time they started walking toward the Training Council Chambers, she seemed to be back to normal. They walked for a moment in silence before Justan spoke.

"How did it happen?"

Ma'am didn't look at him as she answered. "I was keeping watch outside of your room when I saw the two of them creeping along in the dark. When I approached them, that oily little goblin splashed me with something."

"I'm sorry Ma'am, I-."

"What we need to worry about now, Justan, is the fact that you missed the test today."

"It's over. Isn't it?" He hung his head. "Kenn won. They won't let me take the test again. I finally had the chance of my life and he took it from me."

Ma'am stopped and turned to face him. Her voice was matter of fact, "What do you mean, Justan? All you need is four points."

"Four points." Justan blinked. The thought hadn't occurred to him. He had never before received more than two points in the armed combat test. Sure, he had improved over the last year, but four points? It was impossible. Wasn't it? Justan steeled himself.

"I have no choice. I will just have to do it, won't I, Ma'am?"

Ma'am reached out and grabbed Justan's shoulders. Her striking green eyes pierced his.

"My name is Jhonate bin Leeths."

With one squeeze to Justan's shoulders, she turned and walked on toward the Training Council Tent. Justan stood stunned for a moment, then rushed after her. Suddenly, to Justan, nothing seemed impossible anymore.

Chapter Ten

Jhonate stood in front of the training council and explained in clipped sentences how she had allowed herself to become trapped by someone as incompetent as Kenn. Despite the serious nature of the subject, as Justan watched her a slight grin etched his cheek.

She had told him her name.

He had never heard a name quite like it. What did it mean? There were many different naming traditions in the various human kingdoms and Justan knew about a lot of them, but Jhonate was exotic. He knew nothing of where she was from. She avoided the subject every time he brought it up. He had figured out early on that wherever she did come from, a person's name was given great meaning. He wondered if he was now allowed to call her by her name or if he was just allowed to know it.

When she finished her tale, the council gathered together and conferred. After a couple of minutes, Oz the Dagger stepped forward.

"Jhonate, daughter of Xedrion bin Leeths, we have determined that you are not at fault here."

At fault? Justan wondered. Jhonate hadn't done anything wrong. She had been the victim.

"However," Oz continued. "You should not have taken it upon yourself to guard the boy last night. You should have let the proper authorities know if you had any suspicions of sabotage in the tests. In your contract, you promised to report everything of importance that happened during the training of this trainee. That you did not report the previous attempts on Justan is completely irresponsible."

Jhonate stared down at that statement, her face a mask of embarrassment.

"But, seeing as you are an Academy student and not directly under our jurisdiction, we must defer judgment in this case to the Battle Academy Council. You should expect to hear from them soon."

Justan's eyebrows rose. Jhonate was an Academy student? How was that possible? There hadn't been a new female academy student in years. One had to graduate from the Training School to enter and Justan knew that he would have heard of any female training student that passed the entrance exams. A few women had tried that he could remember, but none had succeeded.

Then again, it made some sense. In the beginning Justan had thought his father was using her as a spy to keep track of him. Now he understood that she had no choice. One of her responsibilities as a student would have been to report his progress to her superiors.

Still, the label of student seemed to diminish her somehow. Justan had always seen her as being something more. Now he didn't know what to think.

He shrugged the thoughts away. It didn't matter. She had become his closest friend. That was the important thing. He watched as Jhonate stiffly walked back to stand beside him, glaring at the ground.

"Justan, son of Faldon the Fierce, step before the council," Oz commanded. "Now please tell us what in the world you were thinking?"

"Well, first of all, sir, let me say that this wasn't Jho-, uh," Was he supposed to say her name or not? "It wasn't her fault, sir. I asked her to keep quiet about Kenn and Benjo. I was worried that things would get worse if they got in trouble."

"We have already commented on her case, Justan. We are discussing you now. Tell us what happened this morning."

Justan told his side of the story, leaving out the part where he left the training grounds and went into the city. He didn't want to hang himself.

When he was finished, the council conferred again. This time they spoke for much longer, some of them quite animated. Justan glanced at Jhonate. She continued to stand with her head down, deep in thought.

Oz the Dagger stepped forth again. His face betrayed no emotion. "Justan, son of Faldon the Fierce, we have come to a decision. You have been in this Training School for three years. You have learned by now that a real warrior does not run blindly into battle. You should have informed the council as soon as you realized that she had been taken. It is possible that we would have found them and you would not have missed the strategy test.

"The fact that you rushed into such a situation knowing what was at stake was both irresponsible and selfish. It is time that you grew up and figured out that your decisions affect others, not just yourself. Kenn could have been successful in his attack on Jhonate. What would you have done then?"

Justan felt Jhonate's hand press down on his shoulder for support, but he could not bear to look at her. The council was right. His ego had led to all of this.

"Considering your actions today, we cannot let you retake the strategy test. The rules are clear in this matter and you haven't provided an adequate excuse for us to make an exception. However, son of Faldon, you will not be expelled from the school. You will be allowed to compete in the Armed Combat test tomorrow."

Oz smiled reluctantly. "You have made great strides this year and we have been thrilled to see your improvement. You still have a chance to enter the academy with a strong performance tomorrow. I for one will be watching with interest."

A guard escorted Justan and Jhonate out. Though the news was better than it could have been, Justan left with a heavy heart.

Jhonate stood in front of him and pointed towards the practice field. "Come, there is not much daylight left. You need to get one more good practice in before tomorrow."

Justan turned away. "Why would you even want to be around me? All that happened to you today was my fault."

Jhonate grabbed Justan by the arm and spun him around to face her. "Have you learned nothing? Do you still think that everything revolves around you?"

"Huh? Well, n-no."

"Evidently you do, because you act as if I had no choice in my actions." She glared at him, her eyes simmering. "Understand me now. I did what I wanted to do. You did not make me do anything that I would not have done on my own."

"I didn't mean that! I- I . . ." Justan sighed. "Look, if I hadn't made Kenn and Benjo angry, then they wouldn't have taken you. If I had told the council what was going on in the first place then none of this would have happened." She shook her head at him again, but before she could speak, he continued, "I should not have come after you alone. The council was right. I acted so selfi-"

Jhonate clamped her hand over his mouth. "No more! Kenn and Benjo made their own decisions. You did what you had to do. As for the rest, you came after me even though you knew you would miss the test. What you did was not selfish. You acted nobly, Justan. Stupidly yes, but nobly."

She released his mouth. "The council was right about one thing, though. You need to grow up and concentrate on tomorrow. Come, we are short of time."

Justan's head spun. "Uh, yes Ma'am."

Jhonate pressed her index finger against his lips. There was a sudden softness in her eyes he was not expecting. "Do not call me that any longer," she said. She turned and headed toward the practice field.

"Yes . . . Jhonate." The name felt strange coming out of his mouth. He liked it.

Neither of them saw the man in the white robe enter the council tent behind them.

The crowd at the arena the next day was the largest ever recorded. The tale of what had happened to Justan the day before during the strategy test had traveled throughout the city. Once an underdog, Justan had been elevated from a person of interest to a star. Everyone was rooting for him, and all knew the stakes. To make four points in the close combat exam was a difficult task for any trainee, especially for Justan who had been stuck in the same situation the year before. The gambling houses were overwhelmed with bets and the guards had their hands full with crowds of people lined up outside, trying to get in.

Justan sat with the other trainees. Everyone nervously awaited their turn in the packed area. They were all frightened, and for good reason. Each one would be facing an experienced student from the academy with real weapons. Most likely they would lose, and most likely it would be painful. The mages would treat the wounds right away, but even the healing process wasn't pleasant.

The mages at the field that day were some of the best. The Mage School in southern Dremaldria had a contract with the Battle Academy. They supplied healers for the academy and in return, the academy sent guards for the Mage School's grounds. They always sent up an extra group of healing specialists for the tests.

The agreement was absolutely necessary in order to heal the often-serious injuries that would result. The rules specified that no one was to strike a fatal blow, but in reality it was a hard request to make of fighters in the heat of battle. There had been deaths in the past. Justan remembered the last time that a trainee had died in the arena.

His name was Bennsen Landrey. He had been quite the expert with his unique two-dagger style. In fact, he had been so good that his year as a trainee was considered a formality. Bennsen's opponent was a skilled student named Rudfen Groaz. His weapon of choice was the spiked mace and shield.

During the final combat section of the test, Bennsen made a fatal error. He ducked down to avoid an attack, perhaps trying to score some blood on Rudfen's leg. Unfortunately, one of the spikes on the Rudfen's mace drove through the back of Bennsen's skull. His death was instant. There was nothing the mages could do.

They say that Rudfen had never been quite the same after that. He eventually left the academy and never returned. Bennsen had been the first man Rudfen had ever killed. The rules changed quickly after that. No blows to the head were allowed.

The worst wound Justan had received was during his first year taking the test. While trying to parry, he had directed his opponent's sword right into his belly. Without the mages he would have most likely died. It was the first time he had known that a healing could hurt so much.

Despite the possibility of injury and the tension filling the air from the other trainees, Justan wasn't nervous. He was eager. He looked forward to putting his newly learned skills to the test.

Justan sat back and waited for his turn at the offensive

section of the test. And waited, and waited. Surprisingly, all the other trainees finished, and his name still hadn't been called. The crowd was restless. Some of them were beginning to boo. Justan realized that the judges had held him until last to draw out suspense for the crowd.

The final academy student entered the ring. The crowd oohed. He was Qenzic, son of Sabre Vlad. His father was the swordsmanship teacher at the Battle Academy and a member of the council. Qenzic's weapon of choice was the longsword. He was quite well known for his prowess with it. The only armor he wore was a small metal shield on his left arm.

Justan's name was finally called. Qenzic nodded at him carefully. Justan had earned a very unpredictable reputation this year. None of the academy students had wanted to be the one to fight him.

When Justan entered the ring, the crowd roared. The two fighters could feel the thousands of eyes focused on them. Both broke into a sweat.

Justan knew that Qenzic was the superior swordsman. His only advantage was that fighters using two swords were uncommon. It was unlikely that Qenzic had faced someone with that style before.

The crowd was so loud that the combatants barely heard the horn blow.

Justan only had a short period of time to make an impression with the judges. He dove at Qenzic, sending his swords out in fluid strokes. The man parried every attack with ease. Any strike that got past his sword was blocked by his shield. It was obvious that Justan wasn't going to win using conventional means, so he improvised.

Instead of bringing his swords in with complementing strikes, Justan used a technique that Hilt had shown him once. He assailed his opponent in a random pattern, a chaotic blend of slices and thrusts. At Justan's level of skill, this attack style was too dangerous to use in a real battle. It left too many holes in his defense. But since Qenzic couldn't fight back, Justan felt it was worth a try.

At first Qenzic was able to block the moves with ease, but

Justan kept on. Time grew short. He had to draw blood soon. Then Qenzic began hesitating. Even though Justan's attacks were sloppy, the student was having a hard time anticipating the next strike.

Justan finished his plan with a flourish. Suddenly, out of the chaos, he struck in with a perfectly timed double thrust, extending both of his swords evenly spaced. His opponent was not expecting this standard move after such a bizarre series of attacks.

Qenzic blocked the right blade with his shield. But Justan's left blade slipped passed Qenzic's sword and sliced the underside of his forearm. It wasn't a very deep cut, but it didn't need to be. It was first blood.

The hornsman blew. Justan was given a standing ovation by the crowd. The judges chuckled, having expected something bizarre from Justan.

Qenzic swore and threw down his shield. He glared at Justan as he allowed the mages to tend to his arm. As Justan walked back towards his seat, he did not see Qenzic's glare transform into a smile. The Academy student had come up with a plan.

Justan arrived at his seat and was bombarded by congratulations from the other trainees. At first he was giddy. After all, he had drawn first blood against the son of the swordsmanship teacher at the academy. Then he remembered that he too was the son of someone on the council, the man who had given Qenzic's father the job, in fact.

In all actuality he had nothing to gloat about. He had barely won the match. If this test ended up anything like the close combat test, Qenzic would come out to teach him a lesson during the defensive section. Justan wasn't looking forward to the experience.

The defensive section was a rough one for the trainees. The academy students felt like they had something to prove this year. Very few of the trainees were able to hold their own against them, and Justan winced while watching trainee after trainee get brutalized by their academy opponents. His own turn came all too quickly.

The hornsman blew and Justan walked to the circle. The crowd roared again but this time it didn't seem to affect him as much. His attention was focused across the ring at his opponent. Qenzic adjusted the small shield on his left arm and smiled at him.

Justan wondered why the man kept his shield on. Most combatants took their armor off when it was time to be on offense so that it wouldn't slow them down. Justan did not wear any armor. His style demanded freedom of movement. He supposed that he should wear some light bracers, maybe even a fine chain mail if he could one day afford it. Unfortunately it was too late for any of that.

Qenzic didn't attack in a rush. Instead, he sauntered over to Justan and casually took a swipe at him. It was such a slow swing that Justan easily blocked it with one of his swords. The man continued at a slow pace. He took measured swings that Justan easily blocked.

There were some boos from the crowd. The judges looked at each other and shrugged. Justan didn't like this. The man had something up his sleeve and it wouldn't be pleasant. The series of slow attacks went on until Justan was sure that time would be up. It happened just as the judges were about to signal the hornsman.

Qenzic lunged forward. He swung his shield at Justan's head with such force that Justan had to put both of his swords up to deflect it. Qenzic's long sword cut in right behind the shield. He could have struck Justan anywhere, but he had a lesson to teach.

Justan tried to intercept the strike with his right blade. His sword went spinning through the air. The spectators gasped.

Justan stared vacantly as his sword hit the ground. There was blood on the hilt. He brought his hand up to his face. Three of his fingers were missing. Justan flexed the thumb and forefinger that remained. Something about it struck him as funny. Distantly, he knew that he was in shock.

The mages arrived quickly and picked his fingers up off the ground. Justan stood stunned as they used complex spells to reattach the severed digits. What bothered him wasn't that he had lost his fingers, though that was an unpleasant experience that he would never like to repeat. He had been outwitted. That hadn't happened to him in a long time. Oh, Justan had been beaten, and frequently. But that had always been because of lack of experience or skill on his part. This time his opponent had beaten him with his mind.

He recognized another one of his faults at that moment. It was arrogance. He had been so sure that he was smarter than Qenzic that he had let his guard down. As the truth struck him, he started laughing. The healers looked at him with concern, not understanding the source of his mirth. Once he had complete movement in his hand again, the mages allowed him to return to his seat.

Justan once again watched the other trainees as he waited for his turn at the final part of the test. An odd sense of peace settled over him. He saw himself in a new light yet again. It seemed as if he were finding more faults in himself every day. This was quite discouraging, but at the same time, every time he rooted one of them out, he became better. He would learn from this moment. He would not let his guard down like that again.

He wondered how the judges were grading him so far. It couldn't be good after that last match. He would have to do everything right this time, or all was lost. He had to win the final match.

By the time the other trainees finished, the air was electric. The energy in the crowd had been building for hours. When the hornsman finally called Justan and Qenzic out, the sound was deafening. Here was the match that they had all been waiting for.

Justan and Qenzic stepped out into what would become one of the biggest spectacles in Training School history. Fights broke out outside the arena once people realized that it had started. The guards were hard pressed to keep order.

When Justan looked into Qenzic's eyes, he could see that Qenzic expected to see a man shaken. Losing digits is not pleasant. Instead, Justan showed him someone composed, someone who looked into his eyes without trepidation. He bowed, giving Qenzic credit for defeating him in their previous battle. Qenzic bowed back and it began.

Neither of them rushed in. They circled each other, taking measure. A hasty attack was not an advantage in this part of the contest. In this battle there was no time limit. The first fighter to draw blood three times would win.

Justan twirled his swords back and forth with his wrists,

testing the movement in his reattached fingers. The crowd was a constant cacophony that he muted down to a dull roar in his mind. The hair rose on the back of his neck. Somehow he knew that something special was about to happen.

They came at each other. Steel rang against steel. Qenzic took the offensive. He delved deep into his lifetime of study to mete out intricate strikes that Justan was hard pressed to counter.

Justan fought as he had never fought before. Though Qenzic was by far the better swordsman, the entire stadium was behind Justan. It was just the boost Justan needed, as if part of him was reaching out and harnessing the energy being given off by the crowd to use for focus and control over his usually rebellious body. His muscles tingled and he pressed on. The crowd went crazy.

The battle became an unnerving mix of grace and brutality. The standard battle forms that the men had been trained with were soon cast aside. Both men went off instinct. Blurring attack after blurring attack was meted out and parried. It was a whirlwind of movement that seemed as if it might never end. But eventually there was a slip.

Justan bounced off of a hard parry and twirled around to deal out a swift slice. Qenzic brought his shield up, but it was just a little too low for a proper block. Justan's sword skipped off the top of the shield to score him across the nose.

The horn blew, though it could barely be heard over the crowd. The healers rushed in to tend to Qenzic's wound.

Justan could not believe it. He had drawn first blood. He had actually struck the first blow against an accomplished swordsman. He wasn't able to hide his grin. But the fight wasn't over. The healers were soon finished and the men came at one another again.

Their energy had not abated one bit. Each spectacular attack was defeated by an even more spectacular block or parry. Thus it went, back and forth, until both had their swords tangled up high. Qenzic lifted his leg and kicked Justan away.

Justan stumbled backwards. His right foot touched just outside the ring. That was counted as blood drawn. The crowd moaned. The healers came to check for wounds.

"What's going on Justan?" Qenzic said. Justan saw a

respect in Qenzic's countenance that hadn't been there before. "Were you holding back in the first two parts of the test?"

"I'm just as surprised as you are." Justan replied with a smile.

Qenzic looked nervous. They both knew he had gotten lucky with that kick. They were too evenly matched. To make things worse, while he was breathing heavily, Justan hopped from one foot to the other, full of energy.

The mages stepped back and he started forward. For the first time, it seemed Qenzic wasn't sure how this was going to end.

The fight was on, a crazy whirlwind of steel and flesh. Justan fought as he had never before thought possible. He summoned forth strength and control as if he had grabbed it from the very air. The crowd's excitement buzzed in his veins. He felt that he could do almost anything.

Justan completed attacks that he had only dreamed of. His swords skipped off of Qenzic's shield and sword in a blur. Sparks flew. Several times, Justan saw an opening in Qenzic's defenses, but couldn't take advantage of it without striking a possibly fatal blow.

The battle went on and on for what seemed like hours to the two men, though in reality it was closer to twenty minutes. The quickness of the combat built with the crowd's voices rising to a crescendo. Justan felt as if he was going to pop with so much energy.

Then without warning, the energy tapered off. The battle slowed down. The combatants came to realize that the hornsman had been blowing furiously for some time.

Both men stared at each other in shock. What had just happened? Was one of them bleeding? Actually, they were both covered in blood from several small nicks and cuts that neither had noticed. They didn't know who had just won, but both of them knew they had just fought the fight of their lives.

One of the judges raised a hand until silence slowly settled over the crowd. The match was called a draw. There was pandemonium.

This was a story that would be told for years to come. Everyone at the arena that day would talk about the time that

Justan, son of Faldon the Fierce, had battled Qenzic, son of Sabre Vlad, to a draw in one of the most amazing fights ever seen at the Training School exams.

The combatants leaned on each other for support as they waited for the mages. There was no animosity between them, just true respect. They were met by healers with water, which both drank lustily. Once their many small wounds had been healed, they went before the scorers' table. They bowed to the judges, and to their surprise, the judges bowed back.

The moment was almost broken for Justan, though. The man in the white robe sat right beside the Judge's table staring at him, shock in his eyes.

Jhonate waited for him underneath the arena, beaming. She reached out to clasp his shoulder, but he leaned in and embraced her instead. Tears streamed from his eyes. She returned his embrace. When they broke apart, both were laughing.

Justan knew he had done it. All of his work had finally paid off. He would be accepted to the Battle Academy. It was one of the happiest moments of his life.

Chapter Eleven

Justan and Jhonate left the arena for the kitchen. Justan was physically tired, but still mentally energized from the high that his battle had left him in.

"Ma' . . . er, Jhonate?"

"Yes, oh mighty warrior Justan," she replied with mock gravity.

"There is something I don't understand," he began, but stopped to think for a second. They got in line for the food and he continued, "Something happened in the arena today that should have been impossible. We both know I'm not that good. This afternoon, it was like . . . I could do anything! Time seemed to slow down for me . . ."

He shook his head with embarrassment. "I am having a hard time describing it. It was as if I borrowed the strength from everybody in the arena and used it in the fight."

Jhonate nodded. "You fought today as I have never seen a man fight before. You may have battled beyond your ability today, but this is not so strange. Men have been known to do that on the battlefield."

Justan smiled. "Perhaps you're right. But even so, I still think that there is more to what happened today than that."

"I believe that what we saw today was a glimpse of your potential, Justan. You have it in you to be a great warrior. I have known this from the very beginning. Lately you have begun removing the blocks within you that have been holding you back."

They got their plates and as they went to sit down, realized that all of the trainees in the room were staring at them. Someone started clapping. Soon, everyone had joined in.

Justan's face went red. He had come from a crowd of thousands calling his name, but somehow this was more personal. For years he had felt like he didn't belong with the other trainees.

Now they were treating him like he was a hero.

He thanked them and tried to smile, but after a few minutes he had to get out of there. He couldn't eat with all of those people watching him. Justan and Jhonate left, leaving their plates mostly untouched.

As they walked away from the kitchen, an academy guard ran up to them. He spoke to Justan.

"Here you are. I have been looking for you all over the training grounds. The council wishes to speak with you."

"Uh . . . alright," Justan said in surprise. "But would it be okay if my trainer came along?"

The guard looked at her and nodded, but as Justan and Jhonate started toward the council tent, the guard stopped them again.

"Not the Training School Council." He pointed towards the towering walls of the academy. "Come, this way."

Justan was taken aback. He had expected the Academy council to want to see him sooner or later because of his contract, but not this soon.

As they walked, Justan developed a frightening theory. Somehow they might have found out that he had gone into the city while looking for Jhonate. Since his contract was with the Academy and not the Training School, his discipline would be under their jurisdiction. His heart went cold in his chest.

Jhonate seemed to know what he was thinking. She put her hand on his shoulder. "All may not be as it seems. Do not worry. The council will explain when we get there." For all of the comfort in her voice, her eyes looked worried, too.

They crossed through the barracks and classrooms. People shouted to Justan and he waived back politely, but he wasn't enjoying the attention. They navigated the bustle of the Training Market in the fading daylight and Justan stopped at the city line. They would have to pass through the city to enter the main entrance of the Academy.

"Wait, I can't leave the Training School grounds until the final scores are announced. It's part of my contract."

The guard knew this was coming, for he handed Justan a note. "The council is making an exception."

Justan glanced at the note. It was indeed authority for him to pass. He handed it to Jhonate, but she declined to read it. He knew that it was silly, but he had hoped for a second that he would be able to stall for a while. He was enjoying being able to savor his victory and wanted to hold on to that feeling for a while longer. When they reached the gates, his father was waiting for him.

As always, Faldon the Fierce was a striking figure. He stood at about the same height as Justan and his hair was the same dark color, though there were some streaks of gray. Faldon was superbly muscled. This night he wore a blue vest over a short-sleeved chain mail shirt. Strapped over his back was the famous two-handed sword that he had named The Monarch. Faldon's deeds with that blade were at the center of many legends, but he had never explained how he had come to possess it.

Justan had not seen Faldon since he had signed his third-year contract a year ago. He hadn't realized how long that year had been until he saw his father's welcome smile. Justan felt a lump in his throat. For all of his bitterness about his father's influence in his training, he truly loved the man.

"Father," he said stiffly. His father embraced him. To his surprise, Faldon the Fierce, the most respected man in the Academy, began to cry.

He pulled back. "My son. I was there today. It was magnificent. You were everything I knew you could be!" Justan was staggered. He had never seen his father this proud of him. He started to tear up, too.

"Where is mother?"

"When I told her you were coming home tonight, she was so excited that she rushed home to get your room ready. Don't worry. We will go see her right after the meeting."

Jhonate took this emotional scene as her cue to leave, but Faldon stopped her. "Please, Jhonate. Come with us. You are his teacher. You have earned the right to be here."

"Thank you, sir," she said and smiled at Justan. He grinned back. It looked like this summons to the council wasn't a thing to be feared after all.

As always, the inside of the Battle Academy was a stirring sight. In the light of the fading sunset, the exquisite craftsmanship on every building glowed with an orange hue. The atmosphere was completed by the students moving from place to place with purpose, each one with a warrior's stride.

But the grandness of the surroundings did not reach Justan's thoughts that evening any more than it had the last time he was there. His father's presence, though comforting, puzzled Justan.

"Father, why did you meet me at the entrance rather than waiting for me in the council hall?"

Faldon looked uncomfortable answering the question. "The rest of the council voted me out on this one. They said I am too biased to be a good judge in your case."

Jhonate broke in, "Why was Justan told to come here tonight? The test results have not even been announced yet. The new students won't be able to enter the Academy until next week." Justan looked at his father expectantly, but Faldon shrugged.

"I don't know. I have my suspicions, but I was asked to leave before it became clear. Tonight I am here as Justan's father, not as a council member. I will learn what is going on when you do."

This didn't sound good to Justan, but he straightened his back and stood proud. If he was going to be rejected from any chance of entering the Academy, this was the way to go. He had the most brilliant fight of his life at his back and good friends at his side. Whatever the council wanted to tell him, Justan was determined to accept it bravely.

Chapter Twelve

Justan entered the Council Hall with his chin up, but his jaw dropped as he saw the man in the white robe standing on the raised dais with the Battle Academy Council.

"Father," he whispered. "Who is that man? I have been seeing him everywhere."

"That is Ambassador Valtrek from the Mage School," Faldon explained, a slight tremor in his voice. His face was filled with anger. "I don't like this."

Tad the Cunning stood. "Justan, son of Faldon the Fierce, step forward."

Justan complied.

"As dictated by your contract, we meet tonight to discuss the direction your life is to take." Tad lifted up a familiar stack of papers.

"But sir," Justan said. "The test results have not been posted yet."

Tad shook his head. "We know the results, Justan. We were all there. Each of us was amazed by your improvement. Believe me, all of us wish that he could have shown that kind of skill at your age." The official tone of his voice slipped for a moment. But it returned. "Justan, there is no doubt in our minds that you deserved five points today, though your official total will be four."

Justan's heart leaped in his chest. He was going to be accepted into the Battle Academy!

"However, since you have been in the Training School longer than any trainee in recent memory, we are holding you to higher standards than usual. I am afraid that fifteen points is not going to be enough for us to let you enter the Academy at this time."

Justan's heart dropped to his feet.

Faldon let out an angry shout. "This is an outrage!"

"Faldon, do not interrupt me again, or I will have you removed!" Tad said, though he knew making Faldon leave against his will would be a hard task indeed. "Please do not make this harder than it needs to be."

Faldon glared at the other members of the council but none of them would look him in the eye. Justan swayed with the shattering revelation.

Tad cleared his throat. "Once again, your contract states unequivocally that when your third year in the training school is completed your life will take the direction the council sees fit. So, even though we will announce your graduation from Training School with flying colors, you will not be allowed to enter the Academy . . . yet." The entire council looked uncomfortable with the announcement.

Tad was quick to add, "Justan, don't misunderstand me. You are indeed being accepted into the Battle Academy. But you must wait for two years."

"Two years, sir?" Justan wondered through a shocked haze. "Why? What must I do for those two years?"

"Tomorrow morning you will leave the Training School with Ambassador Valtrek. For the next two years, you are to train at the Mage School."

This was a blow he had not seen coming. "Mage School?" Justan's head was spinning.

"A wizard came on a tour of our school some time ago. He watched you in the strategy midterms your first year and, after seeing your performance, decided that you had great magical potential. Ambassador Valtrek attended the final exams today, and he too agreed. They believe you have it in you to become a powerful wizard."

Jhonate gasped and put both hands to her mouth.

Tad continued, "The Mage School came to us and asked for us to let you go. Your father didn't think that you would go willingly, so we struck a deal. We decided to let you try again for a third year. If you did not pass the exams to our satisfaction, we would bind you by contract to the Mage School." Tad saw the devastation on Justan's face and had to add. "Justan, you must understand. We are doing this for you. We are helping you to reach your highest potential."

Justan's father could sit idle no more. "At what price? Tell him what the Academy is getting in return."

"That's enough from you Faldon! Guards, escort him out of here."

Faldon looked at the two bulking guards that took hesitant steps forward. "Don't make me break you." The guards stopped and looked at Tad pleadingly.

"Tell him, Tad!" Faldon demanded. "He deserves to know!"

Tad sighed. "As part of a contract, we will exchange teachers. The Mage School will send scholars to help teach our students history and moral philosophy and the like, and we will send some instructors to teach self-defense to their students." Faldon stared at him and he finally said, "Alright, it's a very large contract. But that is not the main reason we are sending you there. Justan, we really do feel it is what's best for you."

Faldon threw his hands up in disgust and started pacing.

Justan felt some strength returning to him. "But this is unfair. I passed the tests! I would have passed with an even higher number of points if Kenn Dollie and Benjo Plunk had not waylaid me! I put my heart and soul into this year. I worked harder than ever before and I did it!"

"I was afraid it would come to this," Tad said. "Ambassador Valtrek would you tell him what you told us earlier?" Silence ensued as the ambassador stepped forward.

The ambassador smiled down at him. Justan wanted to punch the smile right off his face. "Justan, you don't know me, but I have been watching you on and off for a while now."

"I've seen you," Justan said with a glare.

"I was there in the arena today. What happened was no fluke. I can't explain how you did it, but you were pulling magical energy from the crowd until you glowed like a beacon." Justan and his father were stunned. Jhonate nodded.

Valtrek continued, "Think about it, Justan. You know as well as anyone that you fought beyond your ability today. It wasn't a miracle of skill. It was a miracle of magic. You need to develop this. If you don't, not only will you fall short of what you could become, but it is possible that you could hurt yourself or others by wielding this power unaided. What you are now is a child playing on a catapult loaded with burning pitch."

The man had such authority in his voice that even though Justan didn't like what was being said, he found himself listening.

"I have seen your work ethic and dedication. You have vast abilities. If you develop them, you could become something great!"

Justan was over his initial shock now. He thought over what he had been told. He remembered the feeling in the arena, and even further back during the distance weapons test. What the man in the white robe said explained a lot. But this was not what he wanted for himself. They were trying to force him into becoming something he did not want to be. Justan fought to control his anger.

He looked Tad the Cunning in the eye and forced his voice to remain calm. "Is there any other way?"

Tad shook his head.

"Very well," Justan pronounced. "I see that I have no choice. I will go to the Mage School and I will learn whatever it is I have to know to get out of there. But mark my words, I will come back two years from now and enter the Academy. This is but one more stepping stone on my way."

Faldon gripped Justan's shoulders. "Are you sure about this, son?"

"After everything that I have gone through, what's another two years?"

The rest of the night flew by. Ambassador Valtrek already had the two year contract with him, and Justan signed it right there. At his father's request, Justan was allowed to spend the night with his parents. He would meet Jhonate at the Training School in the morning to pick up his things and then he would go.

Faldon invited Jhonate to dinner with them. She declined the invitation at first, but Justan pleaded with her until she acquiesced. During the trip home, none of them spoke. Justan had things he wanted to say to Jhonate, but not while his father was listening. Instead, Justan found himself thinking of one person he had not allowed himself to think of in a long time. Darlan Begazzi, his mother.

While Faldon the Fierce was the master on the battlefield, Darlan was the master in the home. Justan had heard his father call her 'Darlan the Fierce' behind her back.

She had never liked the life that Faldon had chosen to live. She resented the fact that Faldon had been off to war so much throughout the years. She hated the months of worry, knowing that at any moment, someone could show up at her door to tell her that her husband was dead. Things were much better since Faldon joined the Academy Council and was gone less. But when Justan chose the warrior path as well, it nearly destroyed her.

Darlan had aged very quickly in the past few years as Justan went through Training School. Part of him was afraid to see her now. During the last year, he had not been able to make any contact with her at all, and he almost expected to open the door and see an old woman, prematurely aged and bent down with worry.

As they neared the old house, Faldon stopped as they neared the door.

"Justan, do me a favor. Please don't tell your mother about your plans to return to the Academy. When she hears that you are going to the Mage School, she is going to be so happy. I don't want to spoil that moment for her."

"Of course father. I understand."

When Justan opened the door to his childhood home, he was instantly assailed by the aromas of his mother's cooking on the hearth. It brought back such warm memories that tears started to well up in his eyes. Then she walked into the room.

She didn't look as he had expected at all. Perhaps it was his own guilt that had made her look so frail the last time he saw her, because when she walked into the room, he saw a vibrant, handsome woman, with a youthful smile that ran from ear to ear. She embraced him and they both cried.

Justan introduced Jhonate and his mother greeted her with a smile. Darlan had cooked up a storm. She wanted a feast fit for a king to celebrate her son's triumphant return.

She sat them down and loaded the table. Jhonate looked at

the feast with trepidation. Justan's mouth watered. His mother was an excellent cook, and after eating Training School food for over a year, it was a welcome sight.

As the family devoured the magnificent meal, Darlan pummeled Justan with questions. She had heard a lot of talk about her son's achievements over the past few days. The whole city had been abuzz with it and she was so proud that she nearly burst. She demanded that he tell her all about it; except for what had happened with the Scralag, he told her everything.

When he revealed that he was going to study at the Mage School for two years, she was thrilled at first. Then she became saddened as she realized that it meant he would be gone for another two years. But all in all, it was a wonderful evening. Jhonate arrived uncomfortable, but Darlan's mood was infectious and soon it was as if she was part of the family.

After the meal, Jhonate told them she had to go. She thanked his parents and said goodbye but Justan met her at the door.

"Jhonate, wait. I need to speak with you."

"It is alright, Justan. I will see you in the morning. Enjoy this night in your childhood home." She squeezed his hand and smiled. "It was . . . nice tonight. It reminded me of nights with my own family. I have not seen them in a very long time. Good night, Justan."

"Good night."

Justan rejoined his parents and for a short time, he was able to forget about his grown-up fears. For one last night, he was just a child laughing with his parents.

Justan went to his old bedroom that night feeling very content in spite of everything. As he lay in his own bed for the first time in a year, he remembered how carefree his life had been in that house. His mother had taken care of every need and he had always felt safe with his father around as protector.

As he tried to sleep, his mind began to wander. The events of the last few days collapsed in on him. The stunning weight of the week's revelations threatened to take him into despair. Justan could not believe how much had happened in such a small period of time. He had been learning so fast, and doing so well. He had become stronger and passed the tests. It was everything he had hoped for. Now the council tells him that he has magical powers?

That part burned in his mind most of all. Him, a wizard? There was nothing that they could have told him that would have been more destructive. Did this mean that his progress this week had been a lie? Had he been using magic during all the tests to supplement his abilities? Had he been cheating?

No. He wouldn't let himself believe that. He had worked too hard for it to be that way. There had to be some kind of mistake. He wasn't a wizard; he was a warrior. They would see. He would get to the Mage School, and they would scratch their heads, realize what fools they had been, and send him back. This thought brought him some satisfaction until he thought of his battle with Qenzic, and the power that had rushed through him. Then he wondered who was really being the fool.

The next morning when his mother came to wake him, Justan was sitting on the bed, ready to go. He hadn't slept at all that night. His mind had been loaded with too many questions.

Darlan smiled. "Ah, you are already up. Good morning, Justan."

Justan smiled back at her. "Good morning mother. I'll be in the kitchen in just a minute."

"Actually, I would like to talk to you for a moment." Justan motioned to the bed beside him and she sat down. "There is something I need to give you." She pulled something out of a large pocket in her apron.

"Grandpa's box! Wait, are you finally going to let me see what's in it?"

It was a small square box made of dark wood that had been polished until it shined. Justan had been trying to figure out what was in the box since he was a child. He had discovered it when he was six years old, but he hadn't been able to open it. His mother caught him and took it away. Ever since then, it became a game.

His mother would tell him that he wasn't old enough for what was inside, and hide it. Then Justan would search the house over for it when she wasn't looking. Every time Justan found the box, his mother would appear and take it away. She would hide it and Justan would go looking again. There was some trick to opening the box, but he had never discovered it. He had found it a dozen times over the years, but Darlan always caught him before he was able to figure it out.

Darlan smirked at the look on his face. "Oh how it must burn at you, Justan, this little mystery. And here I am again, taunting you with it. Maybe I'll give it to you, maybe I won't." She started to put it back into her pocket. "Maybe I should hold onto it for a while longer. At least it would give you a reason to come home."

"Mom!"

Darlan laughed and her eyes sparkled. "Your father and I talked about it last night. I have always told you that you needed to wait until you were older, and I suppose that now you are. Besides you might have a use for what's inside now." She handed it to him.

Justan looked at it for a moment and twisted it about. "How does it open?"

She chuckled. "It is a puzzle box that my father received on his travels. It's quite simple, really. Once you know how to do it, that is." She picked up the box and twisted the lid to the left, then pushed up from the bottom of the box and the lid sprung open.

Darlan held the opened box over Justan's hand and emptied its contents. Two rings fell into his palm. One was a rather plain silver band with a single line of gold that ran around the edge. The other was a copper color and had an intricate design carved into it.

"These rings are very special," Darlan said. She pointed to the copper colored ring. "This is your great grandfather's journey ring. He was a great traveler. He took it with him everywhere. Unfortunately it is all that our family has left from him. When my father was young, your great grandfather disappeared. Months later, a messenger brought father this box. We still don't know what happened to him."

"This other ring," she pointed to the silver one, "a wizard gave to me as a gift a long time ago. It has a protective spell on it. While wearing this ring, it will be much harder for a foe's blade to pierce your skin. I tried to get your father to wear it, but he never would. He says that it 'takes the sport' out of battle." She frowned. "The fool. Hopefully you will find it more useful."

She raised one eyebrow. "Perhaps you will lose less fingers that way."

Justan winced. "You saw that?"

"Through my fingers." She held her hands over her eyes and peeked out from between them. "If your father had not promised me that those mages would be able to put them back on, I would have marched down there and throttled that boy myself."

"Thank you, mother."

He placed his great grandfather's ring on the forefinger of his left hand. The silver ring would only fit on the small finger of his right hand. He didn't know what to expect, but he didn't feel any different when he put it on.

"This is a priceless gift," he said.

"You've earned it after all those years of trying to steal them from me."

Darlan had fixed a royal breakfast for their family. After they had eaten, teary goodbyes were exchanged. She promised to send letters to Justan whenever a student traveled to the Mage School. He promised to write her back. After he gave his mother one more embrace, he left his childhood home to head out into the adult world.

Faldon accompanied him to the training grounds. He was already heading that direction on council business, or so he said. The true goodbyes had already taken place, so they clasped hands. Faldon left his son with one last piece of advice.

"Justan, there is a saying an old teacher of mine told me. 'Whenever you are forced off of your chosen path, it's time to forge a new one.'"

"Sure . . . uh, thanks father."

"Yeah, I know. He wasn't very good at coming up with sayings. What I'm trying to say is I know that this is not the direction you would choose, son. But the Mage School is a marvelous place. I am sure that if you make the most of your time there, you can have an experience you will always treasure."

Justan filed the thought away, but didn't really pay much heed to it. Faldon was always saying things like that. Justan's goal was to get those two years over with so that he could come back and enter the Academy.

Jhonate was waiting for him at his room near the barracks. When Justan saw her, he felt a pain well up in his chest. He was leaving his best friend behind, and he might not see her again. A lot of things can take place in two years. Who knew how long she would stay in the Academy?

Jhonate nodded in greeting. Without saying a word, she opened the door to his room. The place was bare, but for a few bundles on the bed. She had evidently packed up his things for him so that he wouldn't be delayed.

He was a little disappointed. He had looked forward to packing the bags, thinking that it would allow him to spend more time with her. Then he noticed how spotless the room was and realized that she must have spent quite some time cleaning it. Perhaps he wasn't the only one who hadn't gotten much sleep that night.

"I, um . . ." He tried to think of something appropriate to say. "Thank you."

The tension in the room was thick. As Justan nervously lifted up one of the bundles, an apple fell out and rolled across the floor. When he bent over to pick it up, he smacked his head on the side of the closet door. Justan rubbed his head. Jhonate barked out a laugh in spite of herself. Then both of them were laughing. The tension drained from the air as if it had never been there in the first place.

"I have something for you," Jhonate said with a smile. She reached in the corner and pulled out a familiar package tied with a golden string. "You are ready now." As she handed it to him, she added, "I think it is ready for you, too."

As it neared his hands, Justan nodded. He could feel it pulling at him. The Jharro bow, an amazing weapon designed to fit him alone. He untied the golden string and was about to let it drop to the floor, but Jhonate stopped him.

"This is no ordinary string. It is a gift almost as great as that of the bow. This is a dragon hair bow string. It will lend extra strength to every arrow you fire. Do not lose it. They are hard to come by."

He carefully placed the string in his pocket and grasped the bow. Warmth flooded into his hand. He stared at the precious gift for a moment and looked at his friend.

"Jhonate, you have-" he began. Then he shook his head and started again, "As great as these gifts are, they pale besides the other gifts that you have given me."

"What gifts?"

"The training, the companionship, forcing me to grow. There are so many." Justan swallowed at his boldness. "But I haven't even mentioned the greatest gift."

"Oh? What is that?"

"The right to use your name," he replied without hesitation.

She embraced him. "You are wise," she whispered into his ear. Her voice carried a sultry note that sent a warm shiver down Justan's back. Then she released him and was all business again.

"Come, it is time for you to meet your traveling companions." They gathered his things and left his room for the last time.

As they walked towards the city, Justan stopped her. "Wait, you have given me so much over these last six months, and yet I have given you nothing."

"That is not true, Justan. The time I have spent with you has taught me much."

Justan wrestled with his hand and pulled the small silver ring off of his finger. "Here, this is a gift that you can remember me by."

She stared at it without an expression on her face. Suddenly, he felt foolish. Here he was giving her a ring like she was his betrothed or something.

"It once belonged to my mother. It is a ring that means a lot to me. I . . . would be honored if you would accept it." He didn't tell her about the ring's supposed protective powers, worried that she might refuse it.

Jhonate solemnly held out her hand. He placed it on her index finger where it fit perfectly. "A worthy gift. I will treasure it, Justan, son of Faldon the Fierce."

No more was said as they walked to the Battle Academy main entrance. As they waited for the other travelers to arrive, Justan could not get rid of the deep sadness within himself. He was leaving so much behind. Too soon all were there and it was time to leave. After he had placed his belongings on one of the wagons, he turned to her one last time. A tear ran down his cheek and his voice was thick with emotion.

"Jhonate, I can't bear the thought that I will never see you again."

She shook her head. "Worry not, Justan. I know that we will meet again."

"How can you be so sure?" he pressed.

"I asked the stars," she replied and pressed a kiss on his cheek. With that she walked away. Justan's eyes followed her until she stepped out of view.

He hoped that she was right.

Chapter Thirteen

In spring, the stunted and gnarled trees of the Trafalgan Mountains are bursting with colorful birds. It is the time of year for breeding and this day the excitement of these birds filled the air with maddening chatter. Then came the distant clomping of heavy feet. The chatter stopped. The birds held their tongues, for an ogre hunting party was approaching.

The ogres were large, powerful, ugly beasts with flat, sloping foreheads, bulbous noses, and thick jaws accustomed to tearing through flesh and bone. Their torsos were covered in coarse hair. Their massive arms were so long, their knuckles often touched their knees. Ogres are ferocious warriors and much feared among the smaller races. The only thing that kept them from being a major force in the developing world was their lack of intelligence.

They live primitive lives. Sometimes they build crude shelters, but usually they sleep in caves or under the stars. Their weapons are rudimentary, consisting mostly of clubs and the occasional spear. Any clothing that they wear comes from the skins of the animals they hunt.

Fist grunted as he looked back at his fellow hunters. They were grumbling about their lousy luck again. It had been a mediocre hunt. They had killed two goats and one rock boar, but that wasn't enough. They wanted something big, something that would bring them higher status within the tribe.

He growled at the others and motioned for silence, reminding them that the hunt wasn't over until they reached their home territory. They frowned, but quieted. Fist had led them on enough successful hunts in the past that they trusted his instincts. Fist had built quite a reputation among his people with his brute strength and fighting skill, but his intelligence was what made him a leader in the tribe.

He examined the trail as they walked, hoping for a sign that something had crossed it recently. Finally he saw it. A wide grin split his face. He led the other ogres off of the trail and up a rocky incline. At the top of the slope the ground leveled off into a stand of pine trees.

There between the trees stood a mountain mammoth.

The beast towered above the ogres, the top of its head half again as tall as any of them. Its back was turned towards them. Luckily, the wind hadn't carried their scent to it yet. It reached a long hairy trunk into the top of a nearby tree to pull a large bunch of pine needles down to its triangular mouth.

Fist motioned for the other ogres to stay back. A plan to take the beast down formed in his mind. The other ogres charged ahead, ignoring their leader's signals. They were young and cocky, eager for the honor such a kill would bring.

The Mammoth didn't notice them until they were upon it.

The three hunters ran in close and beat at its sides with their clubs, hoping to stay out of the rage of its deadly tusks. The mammoth cried out. It was startled, but not badly hurt. The ogre's club attacks weren't very effective through its thick fur.

The beast swung its head around, trying to spear them. When it couldn't reach them with its tusks, it tried to grab the ogres with its long trunk. The young ogres dodged out of the way. One of them jumped and clung to the beast's hair, trying to climb up onto its back. The mammoth snared the ogre's ankle with its trunk and hurled him into the trees.

The beast began turning and stomping. Soon the two remaining hunters were in trouble. Those huge feet could crush a full-grown ogre. Fortunately for them, their leader saw the beast's weakness.

Fist waited until the creature was turned away from him before he rushed it. Large, even by ogre standards, Fists's chest and arms bulged with muscles. With a mighty swing, he bashed the side of the mammoth's knee with his club. The beast roared.

"Bash the knees!" he shouted at the others and pounded the knee again. The joint gave with a crunch.

Now the mammoth was the one in trouble. It was

unbalanced, swinging about frantically trying to protect its injured leg. The other ogres were still too busy avoiding the creature's flailing attacks, so Fist was forced to attack the front leg by himself. He waited until the beast was again occupied by the other ogres, then bashed away at the leg. The mammoth swung at him. Fist dove out of the way and the tusk missed his face by inches.

He continued, darting in when his companions distracted his prey, then retreating when its heavy head turned to him. Soon, with one last bash, this leg gave in as well and the creature toppled over. Finally, with the mammoth unable to defend itself, the ogres were able to leap upon it and bash at its thick skull until it gave way.

While the other three ogres howled and shouted praises to their own prowess, Fist looked down on the beast with respect. If he hadn't been there, the other ogres wouldn't have been able to take it down; in fact, some of them would have died. He quietly gave thanks to the spirit of the beast. Its meat would feed his tribe well, and its fur would keep them warm.

When the ogres finished celebrating, Fist pointed out a new problem. The Mammoth was much too heavy for them to carry. The others wanted to drag their kill along the ground for the many miles back to their tribe, but Fist disagreed. This would destroy much of the furry pelt and possibly a lot of good meat. Instead, he instructed the ogres to knock a couple of trees over. Then they rolled the creature on top of the trunks and lashed it down with strips of leather. This way they could pick up the front end of the impromptu litter and drag it along the ground without damaging the carcass.

As they pulled their kill along the long miles of mountain terrain to their territory, the three younger hunters boasted that the women would not dare refuse them that night. Fist's thoughts ran in different directions. A kill of this magnitude would bring him much prestige in the tribe. They would be given a heroes' welcome and the feast would be great. With a few more hunts as successful as this, Fist's ranking might surpass even Old Falog.

Fist's tribe was the Thunder People. It was fairly large with over a hundred warriors, and twice that number in women and children. Fist's status had grown over the years so that he was basically third in command in his tribe. The only ogres higher in prestige were Old Falog and Fist's father, Crag.

Crag was the chieftain of Fist's tribe. His skills in battle were legendary among his people. With Crag in command, the tribe had grown in strength until The Thunder People had become one of the most feared Ogre tribes in the Trafalgan Mountains.

Old Falog's high status, on the other hand, came from the fact that he was the oldest ogre in the tribe. He boasted constantly and told tales of his prowess to the young ones, but in Fist's opinion, it was selfishness in battle more than his fighting prowess or his wisdom that had kept Falog alive for so long.

Fist wanted to surpass Falog so he could become chieftain when his father died. It wasn't because he wanted his father to die, or that he even wanted to be chieftain, but he did not trust Old Falog. If Falog ever became the chieftain, he felt the tribe would suffer. The old ogre would put his own needs before those of his people.

The hunters expected fanfare upon their arrival but were disappointed when there wasn't anyone to greet them at the territory border. To Fist's surprise, there wasn't even a guard posted. Grumbling, they continued to drag their prize along the trail towards the main tribal camp.

Finally, a voice called out to them, telling them to stop. When they saw who it was, the hunters grimaced. It was a rather unattractive ogre female that every one called Marg the Gutter. She was the woman in the tribe who cleaned and divided the kills brought in by the hunters. This wasn't a prestigious job like cooking, or tanning the hides to clothe the tribe, but it was necessary. The males didn't like her because she always stank from her job. Marg was constantly harassed by the other ogres and Fist tried to say a kind word to her whenever possible regardless of her stench.

"Big one." Marg looked up in awe at the huge carcass. The hunters waited as she stood there staring at it with her mouth open. Finally Fist nudged her and she showed them where she wanted the mammoth placed. She didn't look happy about the task of cleaning this one out.

"Get a little one next," she remarked, frowning at the hunters.

They rolled the beast on to a clean slab of rock. Marg used her teeth to cut the leather straps that tied the creature to the litter. The three other hunters wandered off to find company, but Fist stayed behind.

"Where is everyone?"

"They all in big cave." She shrugged. "They say Tralg is here."

"Tralg?" Fist scowled. Tralg was an ogre mage. Ogre mages were rare; most ogres born with magical talent eventually blew themselves up. The mages didn't belong to one particular tribe and usually kept to themselves. That one was here in their territory was not good to Fist's thinking.

The problem was Tralg had such high status that everyone deferred to him. He could be there for any reason. He might want to take some of their females for his harem, or perhaps it could mean a war was being started. Either way, Fist knew that Tralg did not have the Thunder People's interests in mind.

Fist hurried to the tribal cave. As he approached, he could hear ogre voices cheering.

The entire tribe was in the cave that night. The light from their torches set the whole place glittering from the crystalline specks in the rock. The place was sacred to his people. To take this cave for their own, the Thunder People had rooted out a tribe of over two hundred goblins. It was one of their proudest moments.

Fist pushed his way through the other ogres to the front of the hall. There stood Tralg, the ogre mage. He was addressing Crag and Old Falog, but it was clear that he was talking to the entire tribe.

"There will be much honor!" Tralg roared. "Much battles and much killings! The puny folks will run from the tribes and the Thunder People will be in front, chasing them. Then we will have all the treasures and all the foods!" The crowd roared and Fist's father was nodding his head. Old Falog was the only one not excited and he was probably just wondering how he could stay out of the fight.

"What is this?" Fist shouted.

Crag responded with enthusiasm. "Fist is back!" The tribe roared. "There is big honor to have! Tralg the mage has gathered together many tribes to kill the little peoples out of the mountains!" Tralg nodded and the people howled.

To the ogres, all of the little peoples (elves, dwarves, gnomes, and humans) were enemies. Fist had never seen the other races as a problem. Their lands were far from the Thunder People's territory. In Fist's mind, the only reasons that the tribe should go to battle were for women or food.

"Why do we care?" Fist asked. "They don't taste good to us!"

Tralg stepped forward. "We will kill them and take their foods! This is our mountains. They can not stay here!"

Fist did not understand. "We do not need little people's food! I killed big meat today! We have food for us, and furs. Who cares about little peoples?" The tribe looked happy at the mention of big meat, but Crag was frowning and Tralg was definitely not amused. "There are too many humans and short ones over there. How do we kill them all?"

Tralg smiled. "All the tribes will kill them and the Barldag will help!" There was a hush among the tribe. Despite being superstitious, the Thunder People did not worship a god. But if there was a godlike being acknowledged, it was the Barldag, the being known by the civilized world as the Dark Prophet. "The Barldag stirs and he sent a messenger! A magic one! He came to me in dreams. He brings big armies to join us!"

"Yes!" Crag threw his arms and head back and roared with glee, the battle lust already filling his veins. There were legends of the Barldag bringing ogres to great power in the past, but they were driven back by the little peoples of the land. At that time, the ogres had fought along with the rest of the Dark Prophet's army of monsters.

Fist didn't believe in the Barldag, but he remembered the tales. While most of his people gloried in the killing and destruction of war, the stories had never excited him. He enjoyed a good battle, but not without a purpose. Where was the glory in killing the little peoples unless they attacked the tribe? There was something else that bothered him. The tales of the Barldag spoke of more than just killing the little ones.

"Will we fight with goblins and Slimy ones too?" Fist

yelled.

Tralg looked like he didn't want to talk about that point. Goblins were lower than dirt to the ogres. To the Thunder People, they were like rats, a nuisance. They were not even good eating. Trolls were even worse. They were dangerous and they stank. "We will kill little peoples like in the stories. We will make the goblins kill them too!"

Fist snarled at the thought of allying with goblins and was about to speak again, when Crag jumped in. "Hear me, Fist! There is great glory to have in the little one's blood. The Barldag will lead us, and the Thunder People will own the mountains like we did back then."

"What of the Stone People?" Fist shouted. "Do we ally with ogres who stole our women? And the goblins that took our food? We should kill them first! There is no glory in fighting with them! We built our honor killing them!

"The little peoples don't chase us! The other tribes and the Slimy ones do!" The downsides of this war were building in Fist's mind.

"Stop, Fist!" Crag shouted. Crag's face had turned red. Fist was stepping over a line. Not only was he arguing with the Tribal Chief and an ogre mage, but he was also talking back to his father.

"If the warriors leave to kill the little peoples, what will happen to our land?" Fist was beginning to win over some members of the tribe.

"Stop now!

"What of our women?"

"Sit down, little one!" The sharp reprimand and insult was meant to remind Fist of his status in the tribe and to force him to back down. The crowd went silent. This was growing too heated. In an ogre meeting, that was never a good thing.

"No!" Fist knew he should back down, but this was too important. "The Thunder People don't give up their land! We don't play with goblins and leave our women for the Stone People to take!"

Now he just made the ogre equivalent of a line in the sand. His arguments were getting through to more of the ogres in the cave. Many of them were nodding now, including Old Falog.

Crag was forced into a hard place. Fist had just rebelled against his authority as tribal chief. If he backed down, the Thunder People would not go to war with the other tribes. They would miss out on all the glory. To get what he wanted Crag had no choice, but in his rage he went too far.

"Go to bed, child!" he roared, his face purple with anger. "You do not speak for Thunder People! I do! We go to glory with Tralg and the Barldag!"

The tribe howled. Crag had just given Fist one of the worst insults one ogre could make to another. Ogre children were not given names. They were just called 'child'. An ogre boy had to earn his name with deeds. Once his name was given, he was never to be called child again. If he was, he either had to take that 'child' status upon himself again, or fight for the honor of his name.

Fist didn't know what to do. His manhood had just been insulted in front of the entire tribe. If he backed down now his high status would be gone and in the eyes of many he would be seen as half a man. Crag instantly recognized what he had done. He would have taken back his words if he could, but it was too late.

Fist rose up to his full height, taller than any other ogre in the tribe and raised one giant arm into the air. "I am Fist! I am no child! I say we stay!"

Events were out of control. By rejecting his father's insult, Fist was a hair's breadth away from challenging his status as chief. Once an ogre chieftain was challenged, he had to fight to the death to keep his position as leader. Most likely that battle would have been avoided, but Tralg saw his chance.

"He challenges you, Crag! Do you fight for glory with the Barldag, or does Fist rule the Thunder People now?"

"I am chief," Crag said. There was no shouting this time. He knew what this meant. A large wicked grin split Tralg's face.

"They fight to the death!" He proclaimed. Tralg knew of Crag's prowess in battle and figured this to be an easy win for his side of the argument. Crag would kill Fist and the ogre would hinder his plans no more.

The Thunder People roared and left the cave to prepare the place of combat. Tralg beamed in anticipation, while Old Falog just shook his head. Crag stood with his head down in sorrow. Fist had brought so many honors to their blood with his prowess. Now Crag would have to kill him.

Chapter Fourteen

Far to the east of the ogre territories, among towering dunes, Deathclaw was in his element. This was a hotter day than usual in the desert. Deathclaw took point as the pack hunted along the cracked earth that appeared here and there between the dunes.

He was a raptoid. About the height and weight of a large human, a raptoid's head was like that of a reptile, with two hawk-like eyes on either side, and a large mouth filled with razor sharp teeth. Their skin was a patchwork of small, hard scales. Their legs were longer and much more muscular than their arms and each limb ended in a set of nasty claws. They had a long thick tail that ended in a cruel barb and walked hunched forward with the tail reaching straight behind them for balance.

Deathclaw hissed in irritation. He sensed nothing. No prey to be found. This stretch of their territory was one of the most choice in this part of the desert. There was moisture not too far down into the earth and it was the best place to find burrowing prey, but they had been unsuccessful all morning. He considered the prospect of leaving their territory to hunt in the canyon to the south. The stench of the enormous red dragon that lived there gave him pause though.

Deathclaw was more of a title than a real name. It referred to a leader's position in the hunting pack. He directed the movements of the other raptoids during the hunt and when the prey was surrounded, he was usually the one to strike the deathblow.

Deathclaw's pack was a close-knit group consisting of three males and two females. The pack used to be much larger, but not long ago, his pack had been decimated by two fire breathing red dragons much like the one to the south, a hunting pair. One day, they would rebuild by taking in stragglers from other packs, but for now they just struggled to survive.

It looked as though the pack would go hungry. Then the wind changed.

Deathclaw stopped abruptly, his tongue tasting the air. He chirped a quick command and the pack spread out in formation before darting over a large dune to the east. A large flat rock jutted out from the ground on the other side. The group of dragon spawn Deathclaw had sensed were hiding in the shade underneath.

Dragon spawn were three-foot-tall lizards that basically looked like smaller versions of the raptoids, except for the curved horns that protruded from their foreheads. Spawn were adept at catching insects and other smaller denizens of the desert and bred like rabbits in the sands.

Quickly, the pack had the rock surrounded. The raptoids hissed, and poked and prodded, but once under such a tight space, the spawn were difficult to root out. Deathclaw leaped onto the rock and started tilting it back and forth with his weight until one of the spawn was crushed. The rest of the spawn darted out from under their shelter. As soon as the creatures left their hiding place, the other raptoids attacked.

Like everything else in the desert, dragon spawn could fight back. There were ten of the creatures compared to the five members of Deathclaw's pack, and though they were half the size, they grouped together in bunches, hissing and spitting at the larger predators.

Three of the spawn leaped onto one of the male raptors, biting and clawing. Deathclaw darted into another group of three. As his tail spike skewered one through the heart, he caught another spawn's head in his mouth and jerked it so quickly that its little neck snapped. Deathclaw dropped the lifeless lizard from his mouth and kicked out with his left hind leg, his claws ripping open the side of another one that was speeding away.

As the other raptoids chased down individual prey, Deathclaw, dripping in gore and with the first spawn he killed still impaled on his tail, jumped over to aid the raptoid that had three spawns clinging to it. It didn't look good for that member of his pack. One of the lizards had managed to slash its throat pretty wickedly and the raptoid's lifeblood was pumping out quickly as it tried to defend itself.

As Deathclaw sliced the tail off of one of the spawn with his razor sharp claws, a buzzing noise filled the air above the battling creature's heads. Time seemed to slow to a crawl. Deathclaw could feel his every muscle stiffen. Soon all movement in the area came to a complete stop. Every creature was frozen in place. The only things still moving were their beating hearts and their breathing lungs.

Above the wide rock, the air began to shimmer. Two large heavily-armored humans stepped out of this shimmering portal onto the top of the rock. A thin oily-haired man dressed in ornate garments followed. The three men raised their arms, shielding their eyes from the glare.

"My, my is it hot!" Ewzad Vriil said. He held a glowing scepter gingerly in one strange hand whose fingers seemed to move bonelessly of their own volition. "This, men, is the Whitebridge Desert, destroyer of countless lives!"

He put his arm down and through eyes still squinting, leered at the dunes that surrounded them. "This is carnivore country. There's not enough moisture for most forms of plant life to live, and the plants that do grow have their own wicked forms of protection. Take care, every living thing is deadly from the smallest insect to the biggest dragon. Yes, you see for killing is a way of life in this place where the easiest way to get moisture is from the blood of another creature."

The two large men shivered despite the heat and Ewzad cackled at their discomfort. "Frightening isn't it? Yes, you know they say that the sand that covers this place is not truly sand at all, but just the crumbled bones of the dead. It is a ridiculous statement, of course. Surely bones only make up a quarter or maybe half-."

His eyes caught the frozen forms of the raptoids that surrounded the rock. He brought his strangely moving hands to his mouth and squealed.

"Oh yes, they are perfect!"

Ewzad thrust the scepter back at the larger of the two men behind him. The man took it from him with hesitant hands, careful to avoid touching the squirming fingers of his master.

"Come-come! Hold this, Hamford, and don't drop it, you

fool. I don't wish to have to fight this bunch of dragons. Do you?" He noted the quizzical expression on the large man's face. "Yes-yes, Hamford I said dragons! Of course, they are a smaller species. The scholars call them raptoids."

Ewzad grinned an evil grin and jumped off the rock. The two men stood stone faced, not daring to move, but the greasy man wasn't frightened. He walked to the nearest raptoid, a female that had been chasing after two of the spawn. He ran writhing fingers along the raptoid's muscled side, feeling the hard scales that covered her skin. He closed his eyes and sent magical energy into the dragon's lithe body for a moment before taking a step back.

"Raptoids! A silly name, I know, but oh are they fine! Look at them, men! Fast, powerful, and smart! Not too smart, mind you, but just smart enough to work together. To follow orders, yes! Working together, a pack like this one can take down any creature in the desert. And after my modifications . . ." He trailed off, deep in thought and sent his magical energies into the raptoid's body once more.

"Yes, these will make fine soldiers, don't you think? They will need some changes, though. Smart as they are, they have too little brain for my liking. I will need them to do more than run in formation." He cupped his hands around the raptoid's fierce head and after a moment, turned to the two men. "My, this is exciting. I had heard that these dragons have a different body make-up than other creatures, but I'd never have guessed that there was so much . . . power available."

He lovingly caressed the raptoid's wicked teeth. Then Ewzad seized its skull and murmured under his breath. His fingers writhed and magical energies flowed into the creature's head, manipulating its tissues.

The raptoid didn't understand why she couldn't kill this soft skinned creature that had touched her. She only knew the intense pain that focused in her head, and no matter how hard she tried, her frozen body could do nothing about it.

The raptoid's skull began to swell oddly, and the wizard's brow furrowed in concentration. Suddenly, its head exploded, showering the wizard with gore. He staggered back, spitting flesh out of his mouth. An evil chuckle escaped his red stained lips. "My, my. How unpleasant."

Ewzad wiped his face with the sleeve of his robe. "I think I'll stand back next time." He turned to the next raptoid, this one a male, and studied it for a moment. "Let's start with the rest of the body first this time, don't you think?"

The two men were still staring at the first test subject. It stood frozen in the same position it had taken when they entered through the portal, but most of its head was missing.

The wizard had his full attention on the next raptoid. He reached out and waved his fingers at it, mumbling oddly. Magical energies entered the unwilling subject and began changing its tissues at their most basic level.

The raptoid's arms lengthened and became more muscular, though the skin split in several places from the strain. The dragon's bones crackled as they grew and split and reformed. Its body straightened and it started to take a more humanoid shape. Then the wizard concentrated even harder, his fingers blurring, and its skull started to bulge until the back of its head blew out with a loud popping noise. The deformed creature stayed frozen in that position, very much dead.

"Oh, bother! I shall have to study this further." Ewzad Vriil turned to the two huge men who were now looking a little green in the face. "Dragons must be different in more ways than I thought. I have never had this problem before." The evil wizard frowned. "At least not in a while."

"Dear-dear, I will be very displeased if this whole trip is wasted," he mumbled to himself. He turned to Hamford, who was holding the glowing scepter uneasily because its light was starting to waver. "Do you know why a dragon would make a far more superior guard than say, a lizard man?"

Hamford shook his head.

"For one, they are warm-blooded," Ewzad lectured. "They can guard a man in any climate, whereas a lizard man would be useless if it got too cold. Not only that, but dragons regenerate. Yes, even if you cut an arm off, given enough time, it will grow back."

The two big men looked suspiciously at the bodies of the two dead raptors frozen in the air. "Oh, they can't regenerate just anything. They can die. For instance, look at that one." He pointed to the raptoid with the three spawn clinging to it. Its wound was no longer pumping blood. "That one is quite dead. Loss of blood, you see. Don't worry, you will learn these things eventually."

He looked at the two headless dragons and laughed. "Oh, yes. Right! It seems that I am still learning too. Hee-hee! Well, no better time to learn than the present, I always say."

Deathclaw was still immobilized like the others, but his mind was working, and at full speed. For a being whose whole life was rooted in freedom of movement, this imprisonment was maddening. He had seen the lives of three of his pack extinguished, and his instincts were crying for retreat.

He watched the wizard, who constantly made strange noises at the other two humans, point at the only other member of his pack left alive. It was Deathclaw's sister, the only other egg from his brood that had hatched. She was perhaps the most useful member of the pack. By sticking with him, she had stayed alive all these years.

The oily man waggled his fingers again in that strange way, and Deathclaw was forced to watch as his sister's form was mutated and misshapen into the resemblance of a female humanoid. Raptoids aren't exactly tightly knit families, but like most pack animals, they do care for the other members of their group. Deathclaw did not think of his brood mate as a sister in the traditional sense, but he knew her by scent and she was a very valuable member of his pack. If she died, it would be a very unpleasant experience for him.

Ewzad Vriil stopped the transformation before he got to her head. "Blast!" the wizard swore. "This is puzzling. Isn't it Hamford?"

Hamford didn't reply. He knew that Ewzad didn't really expect him to answer.

"Well, well." Ewzad snapped his fingers as if just realizing something "Perhaps if I alter the bone structure of the head by itself, first? Then I can grow the brain to fill it without any more eruptions, you think? The brain is always the most delicate organ to change. I will have to alter my spell to adjust for the different make up of those sensitive tissues." He scratched his head and turned back to Deathclaw's transformed sibling. "It is up to you, my dear. Let us see."

He thrust his arms at her once again. He muttered and waved his fingers in his twisted way and her long muzzle shortened. Then her skull began to swell and her eyes nearly popped out of their sockets as they moved from the sides of her head around to assume a more human position in the front of her head. The wizard stopped and smiled.

"So pretty." Then he waved his fingers once again, and though Deathclaw could not see what was being done, the wizard seemed satisfied. "The results on this one are much better. We will take it back to the keep where I can finish working on it."

The man beside Hamford leapt down from the rock and tried to pick up the changed raptoid. He strained, but it was too heavy for him. Ewzad cast a quick spell to help the man lift the raptoid and move it to the portal.

Ewzad looked at the scepter in Hamford's hand. The glow was pulsing now. "The paralysis spell is starting to waver, but we've time for this last one, don't you think?" the greasy man mused. He turned to Deathclaw. Ewzad pointed his wavy fingers and muttered his arcane phrases.

Deathclaw could feel a strange vibration in his body.

"Oh, My! How wonderful," the wizard crooned. "This one is perfect. Synapses so perfectly timed . . . I have seen none like it. Oh yes, he shall be my masterpiece!"

Deathclaw felt a sudden excruciating pain as his body began to alter. His bones crackled as his spine straightened and his posture changed. His shoulders broadened and his arms elongated. His hands grew. His muscles bulged. As his body was forced into this new shape, his skin split in several places. Hundreds of tiny scales fell to the desert sand.

Then the maddening pain focused on his head. He could feel his muzzle shorten, and his eyeballs bulged as his sockets moved forward on his head. His skull bulged out to form a humanoid cranium.

Deathclaw's altered body was vibrating with magical energy. He hurt all over and his primitive mind was frantic with thoughts of escape. With all of his powerful will and the utter physical control he had of himself, he resisted the spell holding him in place, but his body was being altered so much that he couldn't get a grip on it. The only part of his physique that had not yet been altered in some way was his muscular tail. By sheer force of mind, Deathclaw fought to seize control of it.

The wizard smiled and clapped his hands excitedly. “There! I am getting the hang of this! The cells are still a bit unstable, but let’s see if we can expand its brain.”

The wizard pointed a finger at him and the inside of Deathclaw’s head was on fire. He frantically pushed against the spell holding him and something finally gave. His tail was free!

Deathclaw flung the dragon spawn that was still impaled on his tail spike. The dead creature flew through the air towards the man holding the source of the spell that kept Deathclaw immobilized. Hamford put his hands up in a defensive gesture and the body of the lizard struck him in the arms, knocking the scepter from his hands. It fell to the ground and with a loud pop, the spell ended.

Deathclaw was free. He lunged and hissed at the startled wizard. The man jerked his arms back and the enchantment broke. Deathclaw’s mind was no longer on fire. He thrashed about. His body had changed too much for him to control it. He couldn’t even control his vision. The only coherent thought left to him was to flee. Deathclaw had no choice but to scamper off into the desert leaving his sister behind.

At the same time, his sister had also been released from the spell. She had no more control over her altered body than her sibling, but she struck out at the man trying to bring her through the portal. Her claws cut ragged gashes across his face, but before she could do more damage, she was hit by another spell that froze her in place.

“Blast! That was close!” The wizard's face was beet red, but he recovered his composure quickly. Ewzad scrambled back onto the rock. “It worked! It worked gentlemen!” He looked to the large man clutching his bleeding face. “Oh, don’t cry about that minor wound, Rudfen. We’ll take care of it on the other side. Now stop moping and get that dragon through the portal!”

Ewzad Vriil turned his gaze onto Hamford, who was numbly trying to wipe the dragon spawn’s blood off of his shirt.

"Pardon me, you fool! Do you have any idea what you have done?" The wispy man's visage turned dark and horrible and there was terrible power in his voice. "You let that masterpiece get away! Do you have any idea what the value of each dragon soldier would be? Do you know how much power I had to use, how many favors I had to call in just to get here? It will take years before I can organize another trip such as this! I should burn you to dust for what you have done!"

The large man groveled and whimpered on the rock. "Please sir! It wasn't my fault, I -"

The wizard laughed and suddenly there was a kind tone to his voice. "It's alright, Hamford. I might not have to punish you."

Hamford looked up, not expecting this kind of mercy from his master. "Really, sir?"

"Why yes, yes of course. I have one positive result from this costly trip." He pointed to Deathclaw's sister. "Here is my promise. If you can get back to the keep alive, I will not kill you." He turned to the other man who had somehow ignored his ruined face long enough to push his master's prize through the shimmering doorway.

"Come, every moment here drains more of my energy." Just before they walked back through the portal, he added. "Leave Hamford a sword, will you? He may need it." The man did as asked and they vanished, taking the portal with them.

Hamford stared in disbelief at the place where they had been. He didn't have long to feel sorry for himself, for he heard a chirp behind him. He jumped in surprise.

The surviving dragon spawn circled the rock, staring at him hungrily.

Ewzad Vriil collapsed as the shimmering gateway vanished. It took all of his concentration to keep the holding spell on the dragon. These gateways took too much of his energy. He much preferred traveling by mirror. If only he had a working one.

"Rudfen, you must get that lovely creature down to the dungeon at once. Give her her own cell. We don't need her killing any of my other wonderful beasties, do we?" The guard nodded, blood still pouring from his torn face, and began to drag the beast down the corridor towards the stairs. "Oh dear! Wait, Rudfen."

Ewzad struggled to his feet and stumbled over to the guard. He leaned on the man's shoulder for balance. "My, what a garish wound. Would you like me to heal that for you?" He reached a squirming index finger towards the guard's face.

Rudfen flinched away, his disgust apparent. "No sir. It's nothing. I'll sew it up later myself."

Ewzad laughed at the man's discomfort. He shoved the guard toward the stairs and leaned against the wall. "Go then. Don't you harm her, now. She will be the jewel of my collection."

Ewzad made his way down the corridor towards his rooms, using the cool stone walls for support. It took some effort, but his energy was slowly returning. When he reached the gold inlaid door, he threw it open and stumbled into his study.

The room was a jumbled mess as usual. "Must clean this place sometime, don't you think?" he mumbled to himself. But he was too busy to do it himself. He toyed with the idea of having a maid come in, then looked at the piles of arcane objects scattered around the room and threw the thought away. "Oh no, no, no. What damage might a maid do to this place? It could be disastrous."

Ewzad fell into the chair by his enormous desk and sighed. A terrible headache often came when he overused the rings. He placed both hands against the pounding in his temples and found the way his fingers twisted and writhed against his scalp soothing.

The trip to the desert had come so close to failure. He cursed the fact that he hadn't been able to bring back all five of the raptoids. The one that they did retrieve however, she was perfect. Her transformation was unfinished, but as soon as he gathered his strength, he would fine tune her. He grew nearly giddy with anticipation.

After a moment, he leaned forward and tried to grasp the handle on one of the desk's many drawers. His fingers curled about each other refusing to obey. Ewzad sighed. They sometimes did this when he was in a weakened state. He slammed his fist against the desk top and wrested control of the rebellious fingers.

"Yes-yes, that's right. Listen to me."

He opened the drawer and pulled out a soft leather pouch. Inside was a petrified moonrat eye. It was a hard, spherical object about the size of an apple that looked like it was once perfectly round but had pruned a bit. It glowed faintly at his touch.

"Are you there?" Ewzad crooned.

"*Yes, Master*," the voice breathed. It was a female voice but low and terrible. It spoke in a sensuous whisper. "*You seem tired, Master. You should keep this treasure with you at all times. I cannot contact you if it isn't in your presence*."

"Oh, should I? Don't be ridiculous. Your little bauble is a constant drain on my powers. Besides, I don't need you listening in on all my doings, do I?"

"*Bauble? I sacrificed a child to give you that treasure. I-*"

"And how are those lovely little children of yours?" Ewzad interrupted.

The voice seemed to forget her displeasure. "*We grow. We multiply. The elves are quiet. We hide our strength until you are ready, Master*."

"What of our armies in the mountains?"

"*It begins, Master. I send the sensitive ones dreams. I tell them the Barldag is coming. They gather the tribes as we speak. Giants, ogres, orcs, gorcs, and goblins, they all begin to gather. Trolls will come too. They will be harder to control, but they will come*."

"Good, good, good. Will they know me when I arrive? That is imperative you know."

"*Yes, they will know you. As more of my treasures find their way among them, my ability to communicate grows. They will dream of you every night until you come*."

"Fine-fine! Yes, I cannot wait," Ewzad laughed.

"*We must not be hasty, Master. There are threats that must be dealt with*."

"Of course there are, my dear. Of course! I will deal with Dremald's army myself. The only other obstacles are the Battle Academy and the Mage School. They too will fall."

"*They are formidable. We must proceed with caution*," the voice warned.

"Yes, well I have no desire to attack them head on. No I

don't. What we need is information. With more knowledge of their weaknesses, we will know how to strike. You have planted some seeds in the Mage School, yes?"

"*Yes, but they are not ready to be pushed.*"

"Soon then. I have another beautiful idea, my friend. Yes, yes it will work nicely. The Training School tests have just been completed. A caravan will be journeying to the Mage School. They will be passing right by you in fact. Isn't that nice? All the information we need will be right there. There will be mages and Academy soldiers for the taking."

"*Yes, one of the seeds you spoke of is with that caravan.*"

"Good-good. And there is something else they carry with them that I desire. There is an . . . artifact that would make my travel much easier."

"*Of course, so that is why you are so tired. I will send my children to arrange an attack. There are many goblins in the hills near the road. If we send enough of them, capture is possible.*"

"Goblins? Yuck, that's all? Oh well, it will have to do. If they fail, there are other methods." Ewzad smacked his forehead. "Oh! I have another wonderful idea. Send Marckus to help. He is most useful at gathering information. He's not that far from the Mage School is he?"

"*The orc, Master?*"

"Yes, yes. He has been loyal to me for years. He is an excellent choice."

"*I do not like that one. He is too strong willed,*" she hissed.

"My dear, am I not your master? Hmmm?"

"*As long as the Dark Voice wills it, I obey.*"

"Very well. Do as I say then."

Ewzad dropped the moonrat eye back into the pouch and tucked it away in the drawer. She was a useful tool, but dangerous. She might turn on him if her power grew enough. He was glad she was trapped in those woods of hers.

Ewzad stood and stretched. He barely wobbled on his feet. Some of his strength had returned.

"Ah yes, that is better. A few short hours and I will be able to visit my new pet." Ewzad's mind clicked away feverishly. "Oh, what plans I have for her!"

Chapter Fifteen

Fist stood in the tribal battle circle and stared down at his hands. His huge hands. These hands had squeezed the life out of so many enemies. Now he would have to use them on his father.

Honor fights were common among ogres in order to settle about any issue. Common struggles were over the rights to a particular female, territory disputes, food disputes, and disputes over whose muscles were larger. In fact, any disagreement between two ogres was usually settled by a brawl. It was the main source of entertainment for the tribe. Sometimes when there was nothing else to do, they would start fights for the fun of it. These minor clashes were usually over when one ogre either gave in or was knocked unconscious.

There were not many reasons for members of the same tribe to fight to the death. Tonight's battle between Fist and Crag was different.

Fist looked up at Crag, who stood across the circle from him. Never had he seen such pure fury in Crag's eyes. He had never been a kind or loving father by any means. Ogre fathers rarely were. As a child, Fist had taken many a beating from his father for his willful behavior. But Crag was also the ogre that taught Fist how to survive in the mountains, trained him how to fight, and had saved his life countless times in battle. Fist still felt that he was right in trying to keep the Thunder People from joining Tralg's army, but now he wished that he hadn't made a stand.

The other tribal members had gathered in excitement to watch the battle and Fist could hear them debating the outcome of the fight. While Crag was one of the best warriors in all the tribes, Fist was younger and stronger. Most believed that Crag's battle experience more than made up for the difference in strength, but

Fist had his supporters as well. Even though they were father and son, it didn't occur to anyone that either ogre would back down. That was the Thunder People way.

Adding to the tribe's excitement was the fact that this conflict would determine whether they had a new leader. Fist had enough status in the tribe that if he won, Old Falog wouldn't be able to dispute the outcome. Fist would become the new Tribal chief.

Fist looked to the side of the circle to where a smug Tralg stood with a wicked grin. Fist growled. The appearance of the ogre mage had started the whole thing. He would have liked to choke the life out of Tralg then and there, but more urgent matters pressed. The tribe began the battle chant.

Being the ogre present with the most stature, Tralg was the one with the right to start the battle. While the combatants faced each other with conflicting emotions, Tralg had been trying to grasp hold of a spell to start the battle off. He was finally able to pull the power together and a gout of flame leapt from his hands to begin the match. Unfortunately, it also set his arm hair on fire and he missed the first blow of the fight trying to pat the flames out.

The flash blocked Fist's vision. He didn't see his father coming. Before he could set up a defensive stance, he felt a large foot crash into his gut. He was nearly doubled over by the force of the kick, but he responded quickly with an uppercut that caught his father underneath the chin and sent him several feet into the air. This blow would have killed a human, but Crag was made of tough material and wasn't fazed.

Crag landed squarely on his feet, and shouted. "Toompa! You strike like an orc!"

The insult hit Fist harder than his father's kick. Toompa was worse than being called a child. It was an insult given to a child. It was the ogre word for infant.

Fist snarled, put his shoulder down, and barreled into his father, knocking him to the ground. Fist leapt on top of him and threw a wicked punch that caught the side of Crag's face, slamming his head into the ground. Crag responded by bringing his legs up and kicking Fist off of him. Crag leapt to his feet.

"Toompa!" he screamed and threw a stunning right hook

into Fist's jaw. The battle went back and forth. The tribe jeered them on.

For most ogre fights, there was not much defense involved. Combatants would usually just take blow after blow until one went down. This battle was different. Fist was brighter than other ogres and his father was more experienced. So while Fist tried to block an attack whenever possible, his father knew how to take a hit in such a way as to minimize the damage.

They beat each other all across the circle. Eventually, the balance of power began to shift. Fist's strength and energy gave him the advantage as his father began to tire.

Crag realized what was happening and changed tactics. He placed a powerful kick into Fist's groin. When his son began to double over, Crag landed an uppercut into his face that set him up on his toes. Then he wrapped both arms around Fist's torso and lifted him off of the ground in a bear hug. The tribe roared. Surely it was over. No one got out of one of Crag's bear hugs alive.

Fist was so stunned by the vicious uppercut that when his father wrapped him up in the bear hug, he wasn't prepared. The power of the squeeze forced the air out of his lungs. Try as he might, he could not push out of Crag's grip. His father was too strong. Fist's muscles began to weaken. Blood pounded in his ears. He felt like giving up. He didn't want this fight anyway.

One thing broke through his haze. His father was shouting one word over and over again. "Toompa! Toompa! Toompa!"

Something inside of Fist snapped. The part of him that had been holding back during the fight was burned away in the sudden fury that overtook him.

With all the force he could muster, he buried his forehead into Crag's face, splattering his father's nose and loosening his teeth. Still, the grip did not lessen. Fist slammed his forehead down again. His vision was filling with pinpricks of light, and though his strength was failing him, he slammed his huge fists with extreme force on either side of his father's head. Finally, the grip lessened and he pushed Crag away, taking deep gasping breaths.

The Tribal Chief fell to his knees disoriented. Fist recovered quickly and leapt upon him flailing away with his fists. His mind was in a red haze. Fist had no idea his anger was so deep.

All of it was coming out. His bitterness toward stupid ogre customs, the fact that he did not feel a part of his people even with his high status, everything, every unfair situation in his life struck him at once.

Then he stopped. Something caught the corner of his eye. It was his fist. It was covered in blood. His father's blood. The world crashed back in on him with resounding force. The tribe was roaring, chanting for his father's death. Fist looked down at Crag. The tribal chief's face was swollen and bloody, but his eyes stared right at him. He mouthed something and Fist staggered to his feet.

"No!" he shouted. "It is over! I yield!" His shout was interrupted by the angry bellow of the tribe. They would not let it end. Their blood lust was raised. This was supposed to be a fight to the death and Crag was still breathing.

Fist shook his head and backed away. He didn't want to be the death of his father. He didn't want to lead the tribe.

Fist did the only thing left to him. He fled. He broke through the crowd of angry ogres and raced through the camp, chased by shouts of betrayal. But as Fist fled the territory of his people, the last word his father had mouthed to him reverberated in his mind.

"Toompa."

* * *

In the Whitebridge Desert, a strange figure tried to gain control of its new body. No longer a raptoid, but something else, Deathclaw blindly wandered through the white sands and cracked earth.

Deathclaw's body was healing itself. The tears in his skin were mending and the imperfections in the wizard's work were being corrected by the regenerating abilities of his dragon heritage.

He could not move like he had in the past. His body was too severely altered by the wizard's twisted spells. His larger upper body and muscled legs had changed his center of gravity so much that his tail seemed to be in the way. The only thing he could do was crawl.

Like a newborn human, he had to learn how to coordinate

his eyes together. In the past, with his eyes on the sides of his head, he had a wide range of vision. Now with his eyes in the front of his head, his vision overlapped itself. This would eventually be an advantage to him as he gained depth perception, but until that day came Deathclaw cursed this new eyesight.

His sense of smell was changed as well. The sensors in his new rounded tongue were weakened. He also found that strange sensations were coming in through the breathing holes on his shortened snout.

As his body exerted itself trying to heal, Deathclaw began to starve. He wasn't able to hunt. His two main tools, his sense of smell and his sight, were out of his control. If he was going to survive, he needed to learn to use this new body quickly.

Unbeknownst to Deathclaw, the wizard had enlarged his brain radically. Without realizing it, he began to rely less on instinct and more on reason. Faced with the options of adapting or starving, he did something that was new to him. He sat still and pondered his situation.

He was trying to learn too many things at once. All of the new sensations from the different parts of his body had overloaded his ability to sort them out. He decided to focus on one thing at a time.

Deathclaw raised one hand in front of his new face. He saw two hands. He closed one eye. Now he saw the hand. Strange . . . he had never really thought about his hand before. This new hand was bigger and more powerful than his old one. He closed that eye and opened the other one. He still was able to see the hand, but from a slightly different angle. He opened both eyes and after several minutes of struggling, was able to focus them both on the hand.

His mental capacity was expanding at a rapid rate. His body's natural properties were connecting synapses within his new brain tissue. As they did so, his instinctual ability to control his new body grew.

A new species was being born.

Chapter Sixteen

The Mage School caravan left the city of Reneul without fanfare. The journey hadn't been planned with any great secrecy, but Justan's presence hadn't been advertised either.

The group consisted of Justan, Ambassador Valtrek, several mages who had been on loan to the Battle Academy as healers for the tests, three horse-drawn wagons filled with supplies and gifts for the Mage School, and a duo of Battle Academy graduates hired to guard them on their way. Their journey would take two weeks with few stops along the way. Fortunately, there was a well-traveled road between the Battle Academy and the Mage School.

Justan looked back in the direction Jhonate had disappeared, not knowing how he should feel. They had become dear friends, that was for sure, and he would always see her as the best teacher that he ever had. But something new had started between them during the last two weeks. He worried that it might be lost forever. Even if they did see one another again as she had predicted, what circumstances would their lives be in then?

Justan had left the city of Reneul only a few times in his life. When he was a child, his father had taken him out into the plains from time to time to show him how to survive in the wild. Justan had always looked forward to those trips outside of the city. But this time it was different.

As they cleared the outer gates of the city, he felt very alone. This time he wasn't leaving the city because he wanted to. He had been ripped from his chosen path and thrust onto an uncertain road. For two years he would be put into a situation he had not prepared for. Two years was a long time for an eighteen year old who had come so close to reaching his dreams.

Justan did not wish to sit inside the first wagon with the

mages, so he sat on the top step at the rear of the wagon and dangled his feet over the side. He grew more despondent each mile the caravan traveled.

It was a beautiful morning with clear blue skies, but the cheery rays of the sun couldn't penetrate Justan's gloomy thoughts. His mind was numb as he watched the familiar landscape of rolling hills flow away. In just a few short hours he was further away from his home than he had ever been before.

As afternoon neared, the road swung out from the hills. The caravan entered a smooth grassy plain. Justan heard the cawing of crows in the distance. The waist high grass rippled in the soft cool breeze.

Ambassador Valtrek stayed in his wagon alone and none of the mages tried to speak with him. Evidently they all had their own concerns. Eventually he tired of the scenery and Justan found himself watching the people on this trip he identified with most.

The two warriors who traveled with the caravan as guards were, up to now, relatively untested graduates of the Academy who had yet to earn a name for themselves. They rode to either side of the three wagons on Academy warhorses. The horses were proud, alert beasts bred to be both powerful and full of stamina. Justan could only hope that he would one day have the honor of riding a horse of that caliber.

The two guards kept a wary eye on the landscape around the traveling caravan, and every once in a while, one of them would ride forward to scout out the road ahead. Of course, this close to the city of Reneul, the academy's border patrols kept the road safe from bandits or monsters. But the guards kept it up anyway, knowing that eventually they would get to more untamed places where such confrontations would be more likely to occur. They needed to be in top form for when that time came.

As he watched them, Justan had a hard time figuring out what his place should be on this journey. He supposed that he would be expected to socialize with the mages along the way. But he really didn't want to. They seemed so odd to him, with their pale skinny bodies and high way of talking. Justan was used to the gruffer talk of the Training School. Besides, all they did was sit in the wagons playing cards.

It didn't matter. He wasn't a student of the Mage School yet. He was pretty sure that his contract didn't go into effect until he actually entered the school. Surely he could do whatever he wanted until then.

Justan had an idea. He waited until one of the guards was looking his way and waived to him. The guard guided his horse to the rear of the wagon.

He was a large man with dark deep set eyes. He wore a breastplate over a sleeveless suit of chainmail that showed off his muscular arms and his head was topped by an open faced helmet. Justan could tell from his pointed beard that his hair was a fiery red.

"Er, hello." Justan did not know quite how to put it. "We haven't met before. My name is Justan-"

"You're Faldon the Fierce's son. Yeah, I know. They told us you were going to be on this trip," the guard said. "I saw your fight against Qenzic in the arena the other day. Whoo, what a battle! I suppose that none of us should have been surprised how good you were. I took your father's class at the Academy after all." He pulled the horse in closer and stuck out his hand. "The name's Riveren by the way."

Justan had to lean pretty far off of the back of the wagon in order to shake his hand. "Good to meet you, sir. Uh, listen, I was wondering if I could travel with you two. You know, help out with the guard duties."

He didn't know how his request would be received. In his past experience, he found that Academy graduates tended to look down on people who hadn't actually entered the academy yet.

Riveren laughed. "Really?"

"Sure. You see there's nothing for me to do on this trip. I really don't want to hang out in the wagon with the mages and I figure that I could be useful."

"Well I don't see why not. We don't have another horse for you to ride on or anything, but . . . I'll tell you what. If you wanted to perch up on top of the wagon, these grasses are pretty high and we could use a bird's eye view."

"Are you sure the other guard won't mind?"

"Zambon? Nah, he's been complaining that we needed one

more guy anyway. The Mage School sends a group out every year and bandits know we'll be coming through."

Justan thanked him and climbed up to the roof. The ride was much rougher up there. He scanned the plains, looking for anything out of the ordinary. It wasn't the most exciting of tasks, but it made him feel useful.

The caravan stopped late in the day to make camp and Justan asked the guards if they would be willing to spar with him on the journey. Riveren was willing as he intended to practice along the way anyway, but Zambon wasn't interested. He just sat on a nearby stump and whittled a piece of wood with a short knife.

Before it got too dark, Justan and Riveren walked a short distance away in an area clear of the tall prairie grass and drew their weapons. Riveren's chosen weapon was a heavy double-bladed battle-ax. Justan whistled at the sight of it. The ax looked large and unwieldy. When Riveren let him hold it, Justan was sure that he would tire after just a few swings.

"How do you fight with something so heavy?" he asked.

"Why don't you find out for yourself?" Riveren smiled.

Justan understood how the large ax could be a useful weapon if one were fighting against several foes or even one large beast. But a quick swordsman should be able to defeat a man with such a large slow weapon easily because of the huge openings that it left in the man's defenses.

Justan was wrong.

Riveren swiped the ax in large broad swings that kept Justan at a distance. When it seemed that there was finally an opening, Justan darted in for an attack, but Riveren widened the loop of his swing and very nearly hit him before he could escape.

It didn't take Justan long to figure out why Riveren didn't tire. It was all in his technique. Riveren was lifting and swinging a very weighty weapon, but he did it with efficiency. He didn't break momentum. Every swing led into the next.

Justan was caught off guard several times and cursed his disloyal body. The brilliant control he had shown the day before in the close combat test was gone. He was the same old Justan, shaky as ever.

"You alright, Justan?" Riveren asked.

"I don't know. Yesterday I fought better than I ever had in my life." He shook his head. "However I did it, it seems to be gone now." Justan was afraid that the guard would laugh at him, but Riveren just smiled, and patted him on the back.

"Hey, that's all right. Everyone has their off days. It's not gone forever."

Justan wasn't so sure.

Later that night, Justan sought answers. He was able to get one of the mages to quit playing his card game long enough to tell Justan that he could find Ambassador Valtrek in the middle wagon of the caravan. It was his quarters for the trip.

Justan knocked on the wagon door but there was no answer. He waited for a moment and knocked again. Just as he was about to leave, a glowing rune appeared upon the oaken surface of the wagon door.

The rune brightened and the ambassador's voice came through it. "Yes?"

Justan scratched his head. He wasn't used to this sort of thing. Was he supposed to talk into it? He stepped up on the first step and leaned toward the rune, not quite sure how close he had to be for the wizard to hear him. "Um, this is Justan."

"Yes, what is it?" The rune responded. It seemed to brighten with each syllable.

"Well, can I speak with you, sir? I have some questions." Justan asked, putting his lips closer to the glowing symbol. It was a little too close, evidently, for the door opened into his lips with a resounding smack. Justan fell off of the step and landed on his seat, jarring his tailbone.

"What?" Ambassador Valtrek's head poked around the door to see Justan sitting in the dirt with his hand over his mouth. "No wonder you sounded so loud. You shouldn't stand so close to a closed door you know." Valtrek came down the steps and Justan caught a whiff of some kind of sweet spice before the door shut behind him.

The ambassador held out a hand, which Justan accepted, and pulled him to his feet. "You are right. It is time we spoke. Come, walk with me."

They walked past the campfire where the mages were gathered, laughing and swapping stories while playing their game, and traveled through the tall grass until they were out of earshot. Valtrek turned to him. Justan steeled himself for the possible confrontation.

"Now, Justan, I have as many questions for you as I am sure you have for me. I can't promise that I can or will answer them in the way that you wish to hear, but I can promise you this. I will do my best to answer as honestly as possible if you promise to do the same."

Justan crossed his arms and digested what had been said. "Fair enough. May I begin?"

Valtrek nodded.

"Alright. I wish to travel alongside the guards until we reach the school. As far as I know, my responsibility to the Mage School doesn't begin until we arrive. Is that correct?"

Valtrek made a placating gesture. "Until we arrive at the school, you may do as you wish."

Justan relaxed his posture, satisfied.

"However," the wizard continued. "I do suggest that you get to know the other students. They are curious about you, and it would be best if you spoke with them and dispel some rumors. Besides, you may find some friends there. It couldn't hurt, as entering this new place will be difficult enough without being alone."

"Students? But they are mages already. I saw them healing at the training tests."

The ambassador smiled. "There are many levels of advancement in the Mage School. All of the beginning students start out as cadets. As soon as they are ready, they advance to the status of apprentice. The next step after that is mage. It takes many years after that for someone to become a full wizard and graduate from the school." Valtrek held out a hand and a glowing ball appeared, floating above it. "How far do you wish to go, Justan?"

Justan, entranced by the ball, took a moment to respond. Then he blinked and straightened his body.

"I have already announced my intentions. I will learn what I have to in order to keep these powers at bay, and after my contract is finished, I will head right back to the Battle Academy."

Valtrek blinked at the sight of Justan standing with his back straight and head thrown back proudly. The wizard laughed.

"Why? So that you can become a warrior?" He held his other hand out palm up and the glowing ball cracked open. Out popped two miniature fighters that stood glowing on the wizard's hands. They began fighting each other, slashing with little blades, dodging back and forth across his palms.

"Yes, warriors have their purpose. But Justan, you have a much greater potential." Suddenly the scene above the wizards hands expanded so that Justan could see that the two men weren't fighting alone, but were part of a much larger battle; a bloody war, with hundreds of little figures fighting and dying on both sides.

Valtrek continued. "See what effect that one small warrior has in the scheme of things? He is but one tiny element, not really able to affect the battle one way or another." Little man after little man died just to be replaced by another. Then in the midst of the battling armies appeared one solitary man in a deep blue robe holding a staff. The scene focused in and Justan saw his own face on the man.

"This is the effect a powerful wizard could have on such a conflict." Valtrek said.

Justan saw himself shout out and thrust the butt of his staff deep into the earth. A pillar of flame shot up around him and then spread out in all directions, engulfing men in a blaze of heat that melted their armor and turned their flesh to ashes. The flames spread in waves like an ocean of fire until all of the warriors had been burned away. As the flames died down, the only man left standing was Justan with a grim expression wiping his brow with the sleeve of his robe, untouched. Then the wizard version of Justan smiled.

As suddenly as it had started, the vision vanished.

Justan found that both of his hands were clenched in anger. To see himself kill hundreds filled him with horror. He looked up at Valtrek's face and saw the sheer energy restrained in the man's eyes. He now seemed not a frail man, but a being of great power.

Valtrek spoke in a voice that filled Justan's ears with thunder. "Do you see what you could become? There is that much power in you! Now do you understand how insignificant your other skills are?"

Justan blanched. The thought of such devastation in his hands, all of the melted twisted bodies, all that life extinguished, sickened him.

"No!" He spit out. "I would never wish to have that kind of horror come through my hands! I reject your foul vision!"

The man's eyes softened.

"That is good." He smiled. "You have passed the first test." He placed one hand gently on Justan's shoulder. "This is why we wrested you from the Battle Academy."

Justan was filled with confusion. "What do you mean, it was a test?" He stammered. "It wasn't real. It was all just an illusion, right?"

"Of course." Valtrek smiled.

"Then this is not my future?"

"No, not at all. I don't know your future. I'm not the Prophet." The wizard chuckled at the visible relief in the young man. "Now don't misunderstand me. You do have that kind of raw power within you."

"I could make huge waves of flame?" Justan asked.

"Not necessarily. Wizards have strengths in many different areas. I have been watching you on and off all year to see what form your powers would take and I still don't know. But it is different from any that I have seen before. I knew that when I watched you at the Arena yesterday."

He brought his voice down to an excited whisper. "I have never seen such a thing like that in all my days. The amount of power you brought in was astounding; and yet when you released it, there was no shock, no recoil. Believe me, there are many at the Mage School who will wish to study you to determine the extent of your powers."

"I wish to know, myself," Justan replied, though the idea of a bunch of skinny old men studying him was unsettling. He didn't know how he felt about the whole situation. "Tell me. Why did you show me that . . . test?"

The man grew serious again. "We must be careful. The world does not need power hungry wizards with your potential about. At the Mage School, we do our best to make sure that such a being does not rise within our ranks. A full wizard with evil intent would be a terrible thing to unleash. Someone like that could upset the balance of the world horribly."

"Then what would have happened if I had failed this test?" Justan asked warily.

The wizard inclined his head and four of the student mages stood up in the tall grass not far from them. Justan hadn't even sensed their presence.

"It might be better if I did not answer that question." Valtrek replied. He gestured and the mages left back toward the campfire. "You passed the test. That is all that matters. Now let us return to the camp. It's getting late. Though there is much I still wish to know, we will have many nights to discuss it."

The man in the white robe turned and started back to the camp. It took Justan a minute to follow. Suddenly the depth of the responsibility that would accompany his new powers seemed daunting.

Chapter Seventeen

The next morning he awoke to the brightening of the dawn before everyone else. In an effort to shake the events of the night before from his mind, Justan took out his gifts from Jhonate, the Jharro bow and golden bowstring. He strode a short distance from the camp in order to find a suitable target. He hunted through the grasses and soon saw a plump rabbit gnawing at some tender grass near a tree a fair distance away. It would make a fine breakfast.

He felt a thrill as he notched an arrow on the string. He had been itching for a chance to try out his new weapon. The bow felt just right in his hands. He knew that it belonged to him as surely as his own arm.

Slowly, as not to scare the rabbit, he brought the bow up and pulled the string back to his ear. He could feel the arrow throbbing with power as he sighted in on the small creature. Justan deepened his gaze and felt that familiar sense of focus. He knew that the arrow would find the target.

When he let go, the arrow shot out so quickly that he was barely able to make out its flight. The arrow passed through the creature's body and disappeared into the ground behind. The rabbit exploded into tiny pieces. Justan gulped.

"Dear gods!"

Justan jumped at the unexpected voice and turned to see Riveren standing behind him. The guard's mouth was agape in surprise.

"How did you do that?"

"It's the bow." Justan hastily unstrung the weapon, shaken by its power. He put the golden bowstring away. "It's the first time I used it. I-I didn't know it would do that."

"Well it definitely won't be of much use when hunting," Riveren laughed. "Where'd you get it?"

"It was a gift," he explained. "From my teacher."

"Oh, so it came from the daughter of Xedrion then. That figures. She caused quite a stir in the academy with her fighting style and that staff of hers."

"You know her?"

"Well, I have seen her fight in the academy classes, and she is amazing. Mean though. I once asked her name and nearly got punched in the nose for my efforts."

Justan laughed. It felt good to speak with someone who knew Jhonate. "I know the feeling."

"You are lucky to have been trained by her." Riveren smiled and pulled a longbow from his back. "As long as you're shooting, would you like some competition?"

Justan was a bit wary of the weapon after the last shot, but he nodded. This time, he strung the bow with a regular bowstring instead of the golden one. They selected a knot on a large tree as a target and began shooting.

Justan found with relief that the Jharro bow did not quite have the same explosive effect when strung with a normal line, though the pure precision and strength that he was able to achieve was still quite astounding. The arrows often struck so far into the wood of the tree that he was unable to retrieve them.

They shot for almost half an hour until the smell of cooking bacon roused them to return to the camp. Justan handily bested Riveren with the bow. As they ate breakfast, he felt a little better about how badly he had fared while sparring with the guard the day before.

The caravan left while it was still early. Justan decided to keep some sort of workout schedule while on the road, so he jogged along behind the last wagon for the first several hours of the day. Then when he was finished, he sat down on the roof of the wagon and whittled arrow shafts with his carving knife. He needed to replace the ones he lost while practicing.

When they stopped for the midday meal, Justan realized that he had not seen Ambassador Valtrek all day. In fact, when he thought about it, the man had stayed inside the entire day before as well. What did the man do cooped up in that wagon? His curiosity piqued, he knocked on the wizard's door. He leaned in towards the rune, cautiously this time, and announced himself. The rune stayed dark, and no sounds issued from within.

He was about to knock again when he heard a shout. With a pounding of hooves, Zambon galloped toward the wagons. He had been scouting ahead.

"Goblins!" he yelled. "About a score of them lying in wait a mile ahead!"

Riveren ran from the far side of the wagons and received details. Then Zambon charged over to the mages who were arguing excitedly by the first wagon. Justan rushed in to speak with Riveren.

"How can I help?" he asked.

"You could be of best use to us with your bow," Riveren replied while checking his armor and weapons to make sure all was ready. "We can't go around the beasts. The wagons would never make it through the uneven terrain. We may have no choice but to fight them. Twenty goblins are probably too many for the three of us to handle alone, but we have eight mages with us. Hopefully some of them will have some experience with battle spells."

"Do you have any extra arrows? I started making some earlier this morning, but I don't have any arrowheads."

"They should be in the back of the last wagon by the door. We are taking along some extra stock to replenish the guards at the Mage School, so there should be plenty."

"Thanks." Justan strung his bow with the golden bowstring and ran to retrieve some arrows. Twenty goblins . . . Justan was curious as to what a score of those nasty little creatures were doing this close to Reneul. The road was protected by the Academy Border Patrols.

Goblins were small hairless monsters ranging from three to four feet tall with long pointed ears and wicked mouths full of sharp teeth. Their skin had a yellow hue and their fingers were tipped with pointed claws. They were not the most cunning of creatures, but they knew how to fight with sword and bow. If enough of them attacked together, they could be dangerous. Luckily they had not come out in force since the war of the Dark Prophet hundreds of years ago.

Zambon ran back to them with four young mages in tow. Justan was pretty sure that they were the same four that had been hiding in the grass the night before.

"These four should be of some help in the fight," Zambon said.

One of the mages stepped forward and addressed Riveren. Justan's eyes widened. This mage was a beautiful woman. Justan had heard that there was a woman healer at the tests this year. She had caused quite a stir with the students. Some trainees bragged that they had allowed themselves to be wounded on purpose, just so that she would tend to them.

"My name is Vannya," she said. "This is Fingre, Arcon, and Pympol. These three have some skill with fire, and I can handle a lightning bolt or two." She didn't appear worried about the upcoming confrontation at all, but spoke with confidence and flashed a dazzling smile that put everyone at ease.

Riveren quickly sketched out a plan. The guards would fan out on either side of the road, flushing out the ambushers before the wagons were in reach. Zambon wanted to charge into the fields with their war-horses and stomp the things out, but Riveren overruled him. They would leave the horses tied up with the wagons, so that they could sneak up on the creatures silently in the tall grass. Justan was to perch on top of the first wagon with his bow and pick off goblins as he could, while the mages with battle magic were to stay in front of the caravan and take out any goblins that headed for the wagons with fire and lightning. The drivers and the rest of the mages were to hole up in the first wagon until the battle was over.

It was a decent plan in some ways, but Justan found a few things lacking. He agreed with Zambon that the guards should charge through the field on the warhorses and scatter the beasts. Then he would have the mages placed atop the wagons where they could wipe out whole swaths of goblins in the grass. The odds were that the creatures would flee if they lost the element of surprise. However, he had never fought a group of goblins before so he kept his mouth shut.

Justan turned to Vannya. "What about the Ambassador?"

"Professor Valtrek? Oh he will come if he is needed. Don't

you worry," she said and took a seat on the front of the first wagon. Justan shrugged and climbed on top of the wagon with an arrow notched, ready to fire at a moment's notice.

They rolled closer and closer to the ambush at a steady pace. The two guards sped off to either side of the road with weapon in hand. The caravan continued past a large tree on the plain, and Justan's wary eye caught a glimpse of movement in its branches. He pivoted and trained his bow on the movement. The power buzzed in his ear and when he let loose, the tree shook with the impact. A red vapor floated to the ground, followed by a dying goblin scout. The arrow had penetrated its hip, blowing the creatures leg off.

Justan recoiled. Though he had seen drawings, it was the first time that Justan had caught a glimpse of a goblin. It was an ugly sight. He was about to see a lot more.

Justan put another arrow to his string. He pulled back, searching for another target. The grass rustled on either side of the road where the two human guards traveled to flush out the waiting goblins, but he couldn't see where the beasts were hiding.

Justan could feel his palms begin to sweat against the warm wood of his bow. This was his first real battle and there were twenty of those ugly little monsters lying in wait. He grew determined not to freeze up.

It started suddenly.

Goblins popped up on both sides of the road ahead of the wagons. Justan's brow furrowed. He could only see their heads above the waving grass, but by his count there were more than the twenty Zambon had estimated.

He pulled the string back but hesitated before firing. He still couldn't see exactly where Zambon and Riveren were and didn't want to shoot them accidentally. This problem was solved quickly, for just a moment after the creatures showed themselves, grass went flying. The two guards leapt from their concealment and began slaying goblins with mighty swipes of battle-ax and broadsword.

The creatures charged the caravan. Three goblin archers stood on rocks to get high enough to see over the grass. They began firing crude arrows at the wagons. Justan took a bead on one and let loose. The unfortunate creature's head disappeared in a puff of red.

As it toppled from the rock with a spray of blood, seven goblins came out of the grass and charged straight down the center of the road towards the first wagons. Justan trusted the mages to be able to take care of those. He aimed at the next archer. His arrow blew a hole in its chest, sending it cart-wheeling into the tall grasses.

The seven goblins attacking from the road didn't get very far. Fingre and Pympol sent fireballs down the center of the road. The trailing edges of the spells lit the grass on either side of the road ablaze. The fireballs incinerated the leading goblins and exploded into the rest, scattering them all over the road. While some rolled back and forth, trying to put out the flames, others ran into the grass leaving a trail of fire in their wake until they collapsed.

Justan aimed at the third archer, but it squealed and ran hunched-over into the grass. From his high vantage point, Justan was still able to follow its movement. He fired. With a thud, the surrounding grass was covered in a scarlet spray.

Riveren and Zambon were having a harder time. The tall grass blocked their view and they were forced to swing their weapons wildly, hoping they hit something. Though this worked great in the first moments of the battle as little limbs and body parts flew through the air, their foes quickly realized their advantage in the prairie and kept low.

This wasn't so difficult for Riveren who could just swing his mighty axe back and forth like a scythe, keeping them from being able to sneak up on him. But Zambon was stabbed in the back twice. Though the goblin blades didn't pierce his armor, he realized that he was in trouble. He headed back towards the road.

The fires started by the mage's fireballs spread swiftly in the prairie grass. Justan could see that the flames were beginning to surround Zambon. He shouted out in warning, but Justan's cry was cut short as an arrow whizzed by his head, nicking his ear.

Justan whirled around to see a goblin perched on the top of the third wagon behind him, fumbling another arrow onto its bow. Justan quickly drew back and fired, taking the evil thing in the chest and sending it hurtling through the air to land on the road in a heap.

Justan ran to the back of his wagon and looked down to see ten of the little beasts sneaking around the rear of the caravan. Zambon hadn't been very accurate in his estimate of the goblin's numbers.

"Goblins in the rear!" He yelled, and sent an arrow blasting through the head of one of them. The rest came in a rush toward the startled mages in front of the wagons. Justan swore under his breath. He couldn't hit the one directly below him. He laid the bow over his shoulder, drew his swords and jumped off the wagon roof onto one of the beasts.

They went to the ground with a crash and Justan felt the crunch of the goblin's bones beneath him. He quickly got back to his feet and skewered another creature through the lung. Justan felt a little lightheaded, but he didn't have time to recover. There were still seven goblins about. Most were on the other side of the wagon, but two of them had seen him take out their companions and attacked.

Zambon swung about wildly with his sword, keeping goblins at bay. The wind was blowing smoke his way. It was getting hard for him to breathe and tears streamed down his face from the fumes. Being shorter, the goblins weren't as affected by the smoke. They saw Zambon's distress and grew bolder. He found himself fending off several attacks at once.

Zambon needed to escape. He ran blindly into the flames, the edges of his clothes catching fire. When he finally burst onto the road, he fell to the ground and rolled through the dirt to extinguish the flames. Unfortunately for two goblins that followed him, they did not have the same wisdom and ran screaming until they fell, crackling and burning in the rough dirt.

Vannya looked around the side of the wagon to see five goblins approaching from the rear of the caravan. When they saw the mage, they started running toward her. Vannya yelped and scampered back, hastily preparing a lightning spell.

The two remaining goblins facing Justan didn't charge in blindly, but led a coordinated attack, both of them striking in concert. This was a time when Justan's two-blade style came in handy and he was able to fend off both attackers at once. If they had been better warriors, Justan wouldn't have had a chance, but goblins rarely put any time into training and these two were no exception.

Justan fought defensively at first, but he knew that there were five other goblins heading toward the mages. He shifted into his attack forms and was able to bat the attacking swords away and score several hits on the two beasts, lopping one goblin's hand off at the wrist. Justan was ready to finish them when, out of the clear blue sky came a blinding flash.

Vannya's lightning strike had been aimed at the goblins on the other side of the wagon, but the electrical charge flowed a distance across the ground as well. Justan and both goblins fell to the ground, their bodies jerking spasmodically.

Riveren cleaved the goblin he had been chasing in two and realized that he had strayed too far away from the wagons. He cursed himself for not thinking far enough ahead. He had hoped that the goblins would flee as soon as they realized what they were up against. Riveren had battled goblins before and they were notoriously cowardly, but for some reason, the beasts weren't giving up. The situation was quickly getting out of hand.

Riveren started back in time to see the lightning strike and the grassfires blazing out of control. A heavy weight fell on his shoulders. The caravan was his responsibility, and he had left them to fend for themselves. He ran back to the wagons, nearly tripping over the bodies of goblins he had slain.

Vannya, unaffected by the closeness of the lightning bolt, surveyed her handiwork. The strike had landed directly into the attacking group. Two of the nasty beasts had been hit directly and were no more than blackened husks, while two more lay on the ground with wisps of smoke rising from their bodies. One of them, still twitching, rose to its knees. Before it could get to its feet, Vannya strode over and launched a kick into its face. The hard heel of her boot sent goblin teeth flying, delivering the creature into unconsciousness.

As she turned back towards the front of the wagon, Vannya saw Fingre and Pympol gathered around Arcon. She ran quickly to see if she could help. The mage had a mean looking arrow sticking out of his chest.

She sent her magical energies into the mage's chest, probing the wound. The arrow tip had nicked his heart and it was coated in a wicked poison. It took all of her concentration to carefully remove the arrow while the other two mages kept the poison at bay.

The mages were so concentrated on their task that they didn't notice the ten goblins that came out of the grass and crept steadily towards them.

Justan, his muscles still misfiring from the lightening bolt, rose to his feet. The two goblins beside him were weaker than he was and still jittered about on the ground. He heard Vannya cry out and turned to see the last advancing goblins.

Justan couldn't afford to have the two monsters at his feet attack from behind, so he quickly dispatched them with swift strokes of his swords. There was no honor in killing them that way, but he didn't have time for anything else.

He reached the front of the wagon at the same time as the first of the goblins. He leaned into a double thrust that put two holes in the beast's hairless yellow chest. He kicked it off of his swords and waded into the rest of the things, slicing wildly in an attempt to draw the attention away from the defenseless mages.

A shout rang out as Riveren finally arrived at the scene. He burst through the wall of fire enveloping his side of the road and cut two of the creatures cleanly in half with one powerful stroke of his heavy axe. Zambon rushed in as well, his clothes still smoldering.

The next few minutes were a blur to Justan. The little monsters had surrounded him, attacking from all sides. He understood that Riveren and Zambon had joined the fight, but he was too busy trying to stay alive to coordinate any kind of attack.

The three warriors fought valiantly until the odds were evened with only three of the goblins left. Just when it seemed as though the battle was almost over, an arrow soared in from beyond the fires and caught Zambon in the shoulder.

The guard was able to strike down the goblin in front of him before he fell, the poison from the arrow sapping his strength.

"There are still more goblins in the grass!" Justan shouted, and skewered the goblin in front of him with a double thrust of his swords. Where were they all coming from? And where was Valtrek? Why hadn't he come to their aid?

Riveren swept his axe high, taking off the last creature's head from the nose up. "We misread their numbers," he said.

"You think so?" said Justan, the sarcasm coming out before he could stop himself. He had just realized that the only thing that had saved them from being overwhelmed by the goblin's sheer numbers were the fires burning on either side of the road. "We need to get Zambon back to the mages."

A group of seven more goblins darted onto the road ahead and charged, howling fiercely as they ran. Justan and Riveren stepped in front of Zambon and exchanged weary glances. They didn't have time.

A terrible roar rang out from behind the goblins. Justan saw one of the vicious creatures flying oddly through the air, launched out of the tall grass beyond the fires. It soon became evident that these particular goblins weren't charging down the road to attack the caravan after all. They were running away from something.

Their pursuer leapt out of the grass after them. It was a dwarf.

He looked about five feet tall, which was tall for a dwarf. He also seemed to be almost as broad as he was tall, with a huge chest and bulging arms that reached nearly to the ground. The sturdy fellow held what looked like a huge hammer over his head.

As Justan watched in astonishment, the dwarf swung the brutal weapon into the back of a fleeing goblin with an audible thud. The creature soared an unnaturally long distance before landing on top of two of its brethren, knocking them to the ground. As the dwarf stopped to finish the two that had fallen, the first of the remaining creatures reached Riveren and Justan.

They had no choice but to meet their charge head on. Justan knocked the leading sword of the beast away with his left blade and followed the swing through with the right, slicing deep into the creature's abdomen. He kicked the creature away and thrust his left arm forward, again spearing the next goblin through the ribs. Riveren ripped through others with long sweeps of his mighty axe, sending goblin chunks arcing into the air.

Soon the dwarf caught up with them and they finished the

remaining goblins together. As the dwarf's hammer turned the last monster's ribcage into a bag of jelly, there was a mighty clap of thunder. The land darkened.

To Justan's amazement the sky above them was suddenly filled with dark clouds. Rain poured down. Justan turned back to the caravan and saw Valtrek standing with his arms raised into the air, a glowing staff in one hand.

"Did I miss anything?" the wizard asked.

Chapter Eighteen

The sudden downpour extinguished the rampant fires and then the sky was clear again. The wounded were tended to: The mage, Arcon, had been wounded the most severely, but because of the quick action of his fellow mages, he was on the road to recovery. Zambon had been hit several times and was weakened from the ash in his lungs, but his burns were not severe. The arrow in his shoulder, though poisoned, had not struck any major artery.

Justan had several small cuts himself, which he felt were of no importance. He refused to be healed until the others were taken care of. He took his perch back up on the top of the wagon with his bow drawn, looking for any straggling goblins.

He was furious at Valtrek for sitting in his wagon while his students were in danger. What had he been doing in there anyway? Some of them might have died.

Vannya called up to Justan several times offering to heal him, but he refused, preferring to keep his vigilant post looking out for danger. Justan stayed on top of the wagon until the caravan stopped for camp late that afternoon. It was only then as he stretched out his aching back from his protective watch on the moving wagon that he let her heal him. She grumbled the entire time she was looking over his cuts and bruises.

"I can't believe how foolish you men can be. Do you feel like it makes you some big hero to refuse to be healed when there is no reason that you couldn't just stop for a few minutes? Everyone saw you up there bleeding and trying to look gallant. I hope you know that it just made you look like a stupid little boy!"

Justan blushed. Her remarks weren't too far off the mark. His first great battle had been fought that day and he had felt like the proud warrior he had always dreamed of being wounded, but standing vigilant. Now he felt a little sheepish, realizing how silly he must have looked.

"Well I was only making sure that no goblins came back." he explained lamely. She just snorted in reply and focused in on healing his wounds. He felt more than a little uncomfortable having this charming young woman running her hands over him. He understood why she had caused such a ruckus at the Training School.

Justan was relieved when she finished. Jhonate would have found his discomfort quite amusing.

"Anyway," Vannya said. "I suppose I should be thanking you. We-" She motioned towards the other mages, "really haven't been in such a battle before, and we froze up. We would have been in dire straights if you hadn't charged right in the midst of those things." She smiled at him. "You should come join us in the wagon some time. It might be fun. After all, we will be seeing each other at the Mage School and it can't be a bad idea to have friends in a new place."

As she left him, Justan felt a lot better. He had been so focused on his new role as protector that he hadn't realized how much discomfort the wounds were causing. Justan also felt more than a little bit chastened by her comments. She was right. It would be smart for him to try to make friends with the other Mage School students. But Justan had never been very good at making friends. He looked over at the mages with their weak bodies hiding mysterious powers and decided that he couldn't make himself do it quite yet.

He was startled from his musings by the sound of a gruff voice. The dwarf that had come to their aid had decided to accompany the caravan to the dwarven town of Wobble, which was the next village on their journey. Justan was so caught up in his own feelings of heroism that he had all but forgotten about him.

Justan walked past the main campfire where the mages were talking and playing their cards. The dwarf was standing in front of a cook pot, stirring a strange brown substance. For the first time, Justan realized how out of the ordinary the dwarf looked.

He was big for a dwarf, and he didn't wear long hair and a beard, as was the norm. His thick brown hair was cropped short and he was clean-shaven, but for a large handlebar mustache that curled up on the ends. It looked to be immaculately kept. As Justan approached, the dwarf looked up and grinned. His broad smile revealed a few missing teeth.

The dwarf's voice was loud and coarse. "Well, there you are, boy!" he said in an accent that Justan couldn't quite place. "I wondered when you was gonna come down from yer 'heroic pose' and join us! Did the smell of this here grub get to ya?"

"Actually, I just wanted to come and thank you for the help earlier." Justan felt quite embarrassed. Had everyone really noticed? He stretched out his hand. "I am Justan, son of Faldon the Fierce."

"Fightin' goblins is always a pleasure!" the dwarf exclaimed. "Slappin' them things around is more fun than rollin' a barrel full of hogtrops!" The massive dwarf guffawed, and slapped Justan on the back with enough force to send him stumbling forward a few steps.

Justan felt himself laughing too despite his stinging back. The dwarf's attitude was infectious. "How did you find us?" he asked.

"I've been stayin' in Wobble the last couple of days, visitin' some kin of mine. It gets borin' real quick around town and I got restless. So I went out into the prairie lookin' fer trouble. I saw some smoke and when I came runnin', I ran right into them goblins. I figured anyone being attacked by them smelly things is a friend of mine!" He laughed again, and Justan joined in. He liked this dwarf.

"Say, how would you like to try my special recipe pepper-bean stew?" The beefy dwarf didn't wait for an answer, but quickly ladled a bowl of the stuff and handed it to him. Justan looked back toward the main fire and noticed that no one else had taken the dwarf up on his offer.

Justan sniffed the stew. It had a pungent smell that stung his eyes and made his mouth water.

"What is it made of?" he asked.

"Why, dried pepper-beans, of course! I grew them fellers myself. It's a delicacy." Justan looked into the bowl with uncertainty. "Come on, boy! It ain't no good cold."

The dwarf looked on the verge of being upset so Justan

took a quick bite. His mouth was filled with pleasant spicy flavors.

"It's very good!" he exclaimed, and took several more bites, almost finishing the bowl. The flavors were so intense that it was almost overwhelming. Then the heat hit him.

Justan gasped. His mouth felt like it was literally on fire! He choked that bite down and stared at the bowl as if expecting to see little fire demons dancing in the sludge. His eyes were watering so bad that tears were streaming down his face.

"Well I'll be," the dwarf whispered. "I know it's good, but there's no need to be cryin'! Hell, I thought it'd be a little too mild!" He took the bowl from Justan and took a slurp. He eyed him quizzically. "Hmm, well it ain't as good as last time, but I'm glad you like it." He thrust out his meaty hand. "Name's Lenui."

Justan barely saw the hand through his blurry eyes, but he shook it anyway. "Lenny?" he coughed.

"Lenui," the dwarf corrected, but Justan didn't really hear him. He was too busy looking frantically for some water. "Wait just one minute!" Lenui suddenly bellowed. "You know Sir Hilt?"

"Yes. Do you know him?" Justan, whose mouth was now feeling more numb than hot, responded. He was wondering if he would ever get feeling back in his tongue.

"Well, hoppin' rock lizards! Of course I do. I made them swords yer wearin'."

"You made them?"

The dwarf smiled in pride, and puffed out his already bulging chest. "Yer lookin' at Lenui Firegobbler, the best smithy this side of the Whitebridge!" He scooped a bowl of the stew for himself and sat down on a tree stump. "Here, son, let me take a look see at them swords." Justan handed them over.

"So Lenny," Justan said. The dwarf raised one eyebrow at his pronunciation, but let it slide. "How do you know Sir Hilt?" His mouth was clear of that burning sensation now and to his surprise, he even entertained the thought of another bowl.

"I met the man a long time ago. We was both in the city of Dremald at the time, and I was lookin' to start a name fer myself in Dremaldria." The dwarf paused every once in a while to blow a whistle through one of his missing teeth between bites of the stew.

"You can have more if you want, son. Don't be shy." To

his amazement, Justan found himself doing just that. "Let's see. Where was I? Oh, yes. Well I bought this little shop on smithy row and Hilt was one of my first customers. That weren't his name back then, you know. It was somethin' like . . . George? Yeah, George I suppose. But he was in a hurry and I made these swords for him."

Lenui swung the swords a few times and though he looked kind of silly waving those slender swords with his beefy arms, Justan could see that the dwarf knew how to use them. "These were kind of a rush job, you know."

Justan was surprised. "You must be joking. They are the most perfectly balanced swords I have ever run across."

Lenui grinned his gap-toothed grin, "Why, that's a mighty nice complement, son, but it ain't deserved." He chuckled and handed the swords back to Justan. "Anyway, Sir Hilt insisted on payin' me far more than they was worth. When I tried to give some of it back, he told me to consider it a down payment on somethin' else one day.

"Well, years later when I was into my name as a smithy, he came back. Let me tell you somethin', boy. The man had a fire in his eyes and he asked me to make him the best pair of swords I could forge. He was gettin' ready to go to the Mage School and get named. He needed some namin' swords. Well I had been savin' some special ore that my brother gave me for just such an occasion." Lenui paused for a moment and reached inside his pack to pull out a waterskin full of something that definitely wasn't water because he gasped and whistled through his missing tooth again after he drank it.

"Come on, boy, eat! If you wanna keep the kiddies up tonight, you gotta fill-er up!" Justan didn't know what the dwarf was talking about, but he attacked the stew with gusto. Lenui chuckled again. The others in the camp gave the two of them puzzled looks. The stew tasted wonderful, but soon Justan was on fire again and Lenui handed the waterskin over.

Justan had never drank alcohol before. It never interested him. He always thought it strange that people would want to impair themselves. Besides, the students in the Battle Academy were not allowed to drink and Justan tried to live by academy rules even though he hadn't made it there yet. But at that moment he was caught off guard and he was willing to drink anything that would ease the pain in his mouth.

It was a mistake. This liquid washed away the heat of the stew like a lava flow might smother a campfire. He sputtered and spat, half expecting blood to come pouring out of his mouth. For a moment, Justan thought he would die.

"That's right, son, drink up! Pepper-beans make a right fine wine when fermented just right. The elves call it 'Firewater.'" He slapped Justan on the back with gusto. "Now back to my story. You see, I made two of the most purty swords you ever did see. Sir Hilt paid me well for 'em too. The next time I saw him, his name weren't George no more, no sir! He was Hilt, through and through. He had the rune on his hand, and on the two swords I made him." The dwarf sighed. "Some of my best work, they was."

Even through the fiery pain, Justan was fascinated by the story of his mysterious mentor. The gulp of the firewater he had taken had loosened his weary muscles and ignited something inside of him.

"This is what a dragon must feel like," he muttered.

Justan thanked the dwarf for the story and left to find his bed. He was sweating profusely. His belly ached. For a moment he was afraid that the food might eat its way out of him, but when he put his hand to his stomach, his skin felt cool.

Justan started for his bedroll to get some sleep, but halfway there he changed his mind. The dwarven meal had started a fire in his belly, but it had also ignited anger in his mind. He turned and headed towards Valtrek's wagon. The wizard had re-entered the wagon as soon as the caravan had departed the scene of the battle with the goblins and hadn't come back out. Justan decided to have it out with him then and there.

He strode a little unsteadily to the door and up the first step. "Hey, Ambassador!" He pounded on the door, and the rune glowed brightly. He leaned in until his lips almost touched it. "I need to talk to you!" he yelled. The doorknob turned and he stumbled off of the step, waiting.

The door opened and the wizard slipped out, holding both hands to his ears. As the door shut behind him, an aromatic smoke wafted out. "I told you before, you don't need to speak so loud.

This rune is a delicate instrument!" He looked down at Justan and saw the young man swaying red faced, with fists clenched. "Goodness boy, are you drunk?"

"I never drink," Justan replied, his voice slurred. "Listen Valtrek, I have a couple things I need to say to y-," He never had a chance to finish. The wizard gestured and froze him in place with a holding spell.

Valtrek paced around Justan as he spoke.

"Now you may not be officially under contract to the school as of yet, young Justan. But there are some rules that you will follow for the rest of this journey."

He paused and put his hands on either side of Justan's head. The wizard mumbled under his breath and the fire in Justan's belly was extinguished. His head cleared. Justan hadn't realized how clouded his thinking had been. The wizard stepped back and raised one eyebrow.

"Interesting. We will have to talk about that frost rune on your chest later, but as I was saying, there are rules I will hold you to." Valtrek stood in front of the immobilized man and spoke commandingly with both hands on his hips. "First of all, you will not drink liquor anymore. That is conduct unbecoming a Mage School cadet. Secondly, you will not call me simply Valtrek. I wish you to address me as Professor Valtrek, do you understand?" Justan couldn't move to respond. "Very well. You may move again."

Justan felt the spell lifted. He was embarrassed. As soon as the wizard had pulled the effects of the liquor from his mind, he realized how foolishly he had acted.

"I apologize for my actions. My mind was clouded." He explained. Still, he was not happy with the man. "Professor, I do have some questions for you."

"But of course." The wizard smiled. "As I said to you earlier, we both have much to learn from each other. But let's get away where we can talk in private."

They walked from the camp a short ways before Riveren stepped out of the shadows in front of them.

"Good evening, Ambassador. Hello, Justan." They both nodded in greeting. "If you have to hold council in the grass, please keep your wits about you. This close to the town of Wobble the chances are slim that you could be attacked by any more goblins, but I'm not convinced that they are all gone."

The wizard smiled. "Thank you for your concern, sir. We will take that under advisement." The guard nodded and walked away, his eyes darting about, searching for danger. Valtrek turned to Justan. "I must admit, the academy turns out a fine warrior. I can understand why you would want to graduate from there."

Justan was surprised to hear those words come out of the man's mouth. It set him off kilter. Every time he intended to confront Valtrek, the wizard seemed to disarm him. Even though he had come to Valtrek's wagon intending to shout at him, he now found himself taking a far more respectful stance.

"Uh, Professor, sir. I am puzzled by today's events. Why is it that you spend so much time locked up in that wagon?"

The wizard shrugged. "I understand your concern, Justan. I am afraid that I have much work to do, and I am not able to spend as much time as I would like in the presence of my students."

Justan couldn't accept that excuse. "But what could you be doing in your wagon that is possibly as important as your students getting attacked by a horde of goblins?" Justan was expecting an angry denial, but once again, the wizard surprised him.

Valtrek sighed and his shoulders slumped. He looked in to Justan's eyes with a weary expression. "Unfortunately, my boy, I am afraid that I will not be able to give you the true answer. The work that I do is very important, and I was only able to get away from it when I could truly help."

It still didn't sit well with Justan. "Surely you could have helped earlier. A wizard with your power could have stopped the fight before it began, couldn't you?"

Valtrek smiled a sad smile and shook his head. "I am afraid not. Though I do indeed have vast powers, they are not in the realms of offensive magic. The one time that I could help was in putting out the fires that my students so stupidly started. I know that it doesn't sound like a very good reason on the surface, but I must ask you to trust me. I would have done more if I could."

"I see, sir." Justan still wasn't convinced, but he evidently wasn't going to get any more out of the man, so he let it go.

Another thing had been plaguing his mind. "You mentioned the frost rune on my chest earlier. Can you tell me anything about it?"

"First you must tell me how you got the rune." Valtrek's expression turned to one of curiosity. "Tell me everything you can remember about it, no matter how insignificant it might seem."

Justan related the story of the Scralag and how it had touched him. The wizard's brow was furrowed in concentration and he never interrupted. When Justan finished, Valtrek looked just as confused as he was.

"This is quite a mystery. A spirit would not mark you without reason. It must have a very pressing need to keep it waiting around in those hills all these years. I cannot tell you much more than you already know about this, but there is a wizard at the school who might be able to help you. His name is Locksher, and he has the most brilliant deductive mind I have ever seen. This sounds like a puzzle that would strike his fancy. Yes, you should see him as soon as you get to the school."

"Do you think he can get rid of the rune?" Justan was very eager to get the symbol off of his body. He hadn't allowed himself to dwell on it, but it bothered him to have a ghostly rune imprinted on his chest. It was creepy.

"I do not know. But if anyone can help you, he can." The wizard put a hand on Justan's shoulder and led him back to the camp. Against his will, Justan found that he was starting to like the man in the white robe.

Later that evening as he lay in bed, Justan's abdomen began to cramp up. He soon learned what the dwarf had meant when he said "keeping the kiddies awake." He also learned that the pepper-beans hadn't stopped burning when his mouth did.

Justan did not get much sleep that night.

Chapter Nineteen

"Wake up, Justan. We're ready to go," Riveren said, nudging Justan with his boot.

"Wha . . . ? Okay." Justan sat up with some effort. He felt like his body had been turned inside out. His head pounded. His tongue seemed to have had swelled to twice its normal size and stuck to the roof of his mouth.

The air was getting colder as the winter season approached, and he had to rub his arms to keep down the goose bumps as he stumbled over to get a drink of water. Luckily no one teased him about his condition for he was not in the mood. Justan wondered if Professor Valtrek had intensified his body's reaction to the firewater just to teach him a lesson. Well if that was the case, it was one lesson that Justan considered learned. He could not think of anything that could get him to drink again.

The caravan started moving. Though his body screamed in protest, Justan stubbornly pulled his gear together and jogged behind the rear wagon for the first several hours of the morning. The dwarf, Lenui (whom Justan still thought of as Lenny) sat on the rear step of the wagon and chatted with him. Justan couldn't understand how the dwarf could have drunk so much more than him and still be so cheerful in the morning.

The jog was invigorating and helped Justan to beat back the aching in his body. Later, as Justan joined Lenny on the back step, he felt much better. He relaxed and watched the scenery go by as the dwarf told him about the town of Wobble where they would stop later that day.

Wobble was located on the very fringe of the stretch of hills that started at the base of the Trafalgan Mountains and ran for miles in every direction. The Scralag hills by the city of Reneul were an extension of these hills. The town had been built there by opportunistic dwarves years ago when the Battle Academy started expanding and the need for quality weapons grew.

"It all started with Old Stangrove Leatherbend. I believe he's kin of mine from somewhere down the line. Anyways, he lived up in the Trafalgan Mountains and he heard about yer Battle Academy and packed up all the weapons he could carry and took 'em down to the main road, here. The border patrol caught up to him and he sold his stuff so durn fast that he decided to make the trip again.

"Well, as you'd imagine, ever'body else saw how quick he got back and how full his purse was and they pried the story out of him. The next time Old Stangrove took the trip, half the village followed him. Well, son, with all the gold they got from that trip, they took a shine to that there place. Hell, some of 'em never left.

"Next thing you know, there was a whole new village right on that spot. First, they called it Stangrove, but there are so many quakes in those hills that they started callin' it Wobble. And that's the name that stuck."

While Lenny told him the story, Justan watched the scenery change once again as hills and boulders began to rise out of the prairie grass. They were surely nearing the town, for Justan could see trails of smoke rising from behind the hills ahead. Riveren and Zambon soon rode back to talk with them.

"We're almost there, Justan." Riveren said. "The town of Wobble, where a man can find the best weapons in Dremaldria! They may be a bit expensive, but they are well worth it!"

Lenny snorted. "Don't be foolin' yerself. They ain't the best around. Sure, them weapons are good if yer just a soldier. But if you plan on bein' a true warrior, or gettin' a name fer yerself, there are lots of better places to find real weapons."

Riveren seemed slightly offended. "Don't listen to him, Justan. This is where I got my axe and I believe that Zambon got his sword from here, too. The work these dwarves do is excellent." He turned to his fellow academy graduate. "Am I right?" Zambon nodded in agreement.

Lenny hopped down from his perch on the back step. "Lemme see yer oh so fine axe then." Riveren smiled and handed it over. The dwarf twirled it through the air with ease and whistled through his missing tooth.

"Yeah this is right fine . . . if you need to chop wood! One day, you come to my forge in Dremald and I'll make you a battle-axe so fine, it'll sing on the battlefield!"

"Sing?" asked Zambon, skeptically.

"Hell yes!" Replied the dwarf. "I'll show you what I mean." He walked to the side of the road where a dying tree stood. He swung the axe with one powerful stroke and drove it halfway through the tree's thick trunk. He stood back. "Okay, this is a sturdy weapon, I'll give you that." Then he pulled his hammer from the straps on his back. It was shaped like a sledgehammer with blunted striking ends on both sides of the head. The shaft was about three feet long and thick, also made of metal. The weapon was blackened by years of use at the forge and its head was covered in Dwarven runes.

"This is Buster. It was made by my great granddaddy, and it's been passed down through the family for years. This thing's been used to make more fine weapons than I can count. Now watch this." He turned to a granite boulder that stood as tall and thick as he was. "See that rock?"

Lenny spat on his hands, leaned back, and swung the weapon with all the force he could muster. When the hammer hit the boulder, there was a sound like thunder. Pieces of rock flew everywhere, pelting Justan and the guards. When the dust cleared, nothing but a pile of small rocks remained where the boulder had once stood.

Lenny grinned, his face covered in rock powder. He lifted the powerful hammer and kissed it, leaving a film of black dust on his lips. "Now that's a weapon that sings!"

No one could disagree. While Riveren was trying to tug his axe free of the tree trunk, Justan had to ask Lenny a question.

"How did your hammer do that?" He knew the dwarf was strong, but there was no way he was *that* strong.

"Why the durn thing's magic of course!" The dwarf explained. He lifted the head of the hammer up so Justan could see it better and pointed at the symbols. "See them runes? Thisun's the weapon's name." He pointed to what looked like a broken line. Next he pointed to one that looked like two circles crossing each other with wavy lines through them. "This is the one that gives it the power. Whenever I hit somethin' with Buster, it makes twice the impact. The rest of these squiggly lines are just fer show."

Justan was puzzled.

"I thought that dwarves don't have magic powers." Dwarves were known as having no affinity for magic. In fact it is said that even wizard's spells don't have much affect on them.

Lenny shrugged in response.

"Well if you don't, then how did your great grandfather make a magic hammer like that?"

"Don't need to have any dag-blasted magic powers of my own, to shape what's already there," Lenny explained. "Look here, son. Dwarves are the best there is at forgin' metal. But even the best-made weapon's just nothin' but a piece of scrap if it ain't got magic in it." Lenny leaned in close to whisper in his ear. "So what the Firegobbler family's always done is mine the best ore we can find and then have it magicked. With magic ore, I can make a weapon to do whatever I want."

Justan's eyes widened a little and he reached back to finger the hilt of one of his swords. "Are these . . .?"

"What in tarnation? Of course not! Do they seem magic?"

"Well, no."

"There's no way I could make every weapon I make magical. That ore's way too expensive. If it were that easy ever'body'd have one. Now the second set of swords I made fer Sir Hilt, them's magic. No, I only forge them kinds on rare occasions. I only make things that special for friends."

While they were talking, the caravan had continued on ahead of them. As soon as they were able to work the axe out of the tree, Riveren and Zambon rushed back to flank the wagons.

As Justan and Lenny hurried to catch up to them, Justan was amazed by the difference in these hills and the ones by his home. While the Scralag Hills were made of brittle shale, these were made of hard granite and had been weathered into rounded shapes by the wind.

With all of the earthquakes in the region, many of the hills had cracked and split. The ground between them was littered with boulders of all sizes. Some of them were so big that when the road was built, instead of moving the boulders to go through the hills in a straight route, the road wrapped around them. Vegetation was fairly sparse in the area. Nothing grew in the granite dust but a few tufts of grass here and there.

They caught up to the wagons just as the town of Wobble came into view. Justan was in awe. He had never heard of a town like this before. Most human settlements were made of brick or wood, while in this place every building was made with huge granite slabs.

"Lenny, why are all the homes built that way?"

"Well, boy, if they made em' out of bricks, the quakes'd tear em' right down. As it is, they's gotta be real careful how they put em' together so they don't break apart. Even inside the house, you gotta bolt everthin' down or else you'd always be pickin' yer junk up off the floor."

"Then why live here with all the earthquakes? Why not move closer to Reneul?"

"Where? In the plains? Nah too much open space. 'Sides, stuck between the hills like this, you could defend the town from an army."

Dwarves were determined people. They could take any inhospitable land and make it their home. Here in these hills of solid rock, they must have moved at least two or three entire hills of granite to clear the flat land that the town occupied. Wobble wasn't huge. There were only thirty or forty dwarves living there. But they had landscaped the place so that it had a pleasant, homey feel. The dwarves had even found a way to plow the rocky ground and bring in soil from the plains for several small gardens. Even though the place wasn't as big or fancy as some of the human cities, Justan was amazed at the simple hard work that had made this town a home for these hardy folk.

The place was made all the more cheerful by the singing of the dwarves as they labored. They were short, ranging anywhere from three and a half to four feet tall, and built like the rocks they lived in, with barrel-like chests and rough, chiseled features.

Dwarves were by nature a tough, sturdy people. They could live up to three hundred years without slowing down. They were resistant to most poisons and magic, and could survive about anywhere. A dwarf could take a grievous wound that would kill a lesser creature and keep fighting. But even though they loved a good battle, the dwarves preferred to keep to themselves. They rarely get involved in such things as war. Except for supplying the weapons, of course. However, if they ever were pressed into a war, they stuck together. A dwarven army was a powerful force indeed.

As Justan and Lenny came further into the town, they were assaulted by a rather portly looking dwarf with a full beard that hung to his shoes, wearing a wide brimmed hat. He had a necklace made of what looked like goblin teeth hanging around his neck.

"Lenui! Lenui!" The dwarf yelled in a deep voice. "You confounded son of a rock monkey! You took yer gall-durn time gettin' back here didn't you?"

Lenny scowled. "Chugk! You should keep yer dag-blamed nose out of my business!" They frowned at each other a moment longer, then both burst out laughing. Lenny put his arm around the portly dwarf's shoulders and turned to Justan. "Boy, this is my fat baby brother. Chugk, this is my new friend Justan from Reneul."

Chugk grinned showing that he was missing more teeth than his older sibling. Justan wondered if some of the teeth on the necklace were his.

Justan thrust out his hand. "I am glad to meet you Chuck!" Chugk shook his hand tentatively, but decided it wasn't worth the hassle to correct the mispronunciation of his name. "I must say that I am impressed with your fine town," Justan continued.

"Yeah! Fine town all right!" Chugk laughed. "Fine town if you like eatin' rocks fer dinner and pickin' yer teeth with goblins! We should all move out and settle somewhere in the mountains where life is easy! Of course, you sure can sell some goods here, though." The dwarf slapped Justan on the shoulder and turned to Lenny. "Speakin' of goods. Yer ore is here, Lenui."

The dwarf's face lit up.

"It's about durn time!" He turned to Justan. "That's the real reason I'm here, son. I've been waitin' on this new batch of magical ore fer weeks!" He took Justan's hand and shook it with gusto.

"I guess I'll be takin' my leave now. It's a plum shame I can't be travelin' with you the rest of the way, but I need to finish up some business 'round here. If you ever come to Dremald, come see me. I might even make you a real weapon, if you pay the right price." He slapped Justan on the back one more time for good measure, and then both brothers scurried off.

Justan smiled and shook his head as he watched them speed down a side street. He would miss the energetic dwarf. He decided that if he ever had a chance, he just might take the dwarf up on his offer.

Justan rejoined the rest of the caravan as they stopped for provisions. Everyone except Valtrek was searching for needed items in the small town marketplace. Justan found Vannya and Pympol haggling with a dwarven lady over the water prices. They just finished the deal as he walked up. Vannya noticed him first and smiled. When Pympol saw Justan, he rolled his eyes and pointed at the dwarf.

"Hello, Justan." Vannya said. "Nice of you to join us. This is Miss Hegla," she said, gesturing to the dwarven woman.

Dwarven females were built much like the males, with stocky but tough bodies, chiseled features, and even beards. It was said that, to a male dwarf, the thicker the beard on a woman the better. The dwarven woman grinned and waved while she walked over to a curve metal tube that was sticking out above the ground.

"She is giving us a most fair deal on our new water supply," Vannya continued.

While the dwarf's back was turned, Pympol leaned over to Justan and whispered, "These dwarven women are repulsive. Couldn't tell that one from a man." He broke into laughter. Vannya shot the man a withering glare.

Justan didn't join in the laughter. Even with the beard, the dwarf had . . . womanly attributes. It struck Justan as quite rude for the mage to make fun of a woman who he didn't even know. He walked over to where she was busily cleaning out the curved end of the pipe.

"Hello, miss. My name is Justan from Reneul," he said. She smiled and nodded at him. "Where do we go to get the water?" he asked the dwarf. There was no well that he could see, and there surely wasn't a stream nearby. When she responded, Justan was taken aback by the difference in her accent from Lenny and

Chuck's. She actually sounded quite normal.

"You get it right here," she replied. Justan looked puzzled, so she explained further, "this is a pump." Hegla tapped the curved pipe. "There is an entire river of water under these rocks, but it is too far down through solid granite for a proper well." Justan had never heard of such a thing as a pump, but he couldn't see how they would be able to force water up out of that tiny pipe. When he asked her for more explanation, she showed him. She led him to a crank that was set in the ground nearby, and explained that, as it was turned, the water was sucked up the pipe until it was blown out of the curved end.

Justan was skeptical, but Hegla talked him into turning the crank. It was hard work, and it took a while, but she encouraged him and finally to Justan's amazement, a stream of water began to pour out of the tube. Pympol and Vannya held some water bags and buckets under the end of the metal pipe.

Justan continued cranking until all the bags were filled. His arms and back ached from the strain. By the time they were finished, he felt like he might as well have dug a hole down to the water and carried it back up by himself. Still, he was impressed with the dwarves' ingenuity. The complexity of making all the parts to get such a thing to work had him shaking his head with amazement. These dwarves could truly build anything.

When they were done, Justan waved a goodbye to Hegla. As they headed back to the wagons, laden with water, he realized that Pympol was laughing at him. Vannya was shaking her head.

"What is so funny?" he asked.

"She totally came out on top in that one," Vannya explained. "She made us pay a good sum to get that water because it was going to be such hard work for her, and then you came along and did the work!" She started to giggle.

Justan couldn't help but join in. The dwarf had truly had her way with him. He wasn't upset, though. The pump had given him some interesting ideas. He felt that the lesson learned had been well worth the aching muscles.

The caravan wasn't going to stay long. The group had only been on the road for three days and they didn't need that many supplies. The mages bought a few baubles while the two guards bought some knives and such.

To Justan's surprise he found Riveren drooling over some heavy axes. There were some nice ones on display and Lenny's comment must have shaken some of the man's confidence in his own weapon. Justan took the opportunity to buy a quiver of good steel arrows and some extra granite heads just in case he had to make some more of his own down the road.

When they left the village of Wobble, Justan wondered if he would ever get the chance to meet Lenny again. He had truly enjoyed the dwarf's company. But with the way that his life kept changing directions, it didn't look likely. Justan sighed. It seemed like there wasn't much that he had any control of lately.

He was mulling this over when he heard a shout from the direction of the town. He looked up and could see a figure running up the road toward them carrying a large pack. It was Lenny, panting and trying to catch up, his short, thick legs pumping with the effort. Justan reached out and with a great deal of effort, pulled the dwarf up beside him.

"What made you decide to join us?" Justan asked with a smile.

"This ore's too dag-blamed heavy to go carryin' it all the way to Dremald by myself. I figger I'll stay on with you 'till we get to the crossroads down in Sampo across the river," he explained through deep breaths. He pulled the pack off his back and set it beside him with an audible thud. "'Sides, with you around, I think the trip will be a lot less borin'!"

Chapter Twenty

The road didn't stay long in the granite hills but turned southward again through the tall grassy plains. Justan spent the next couple of days having an enjoyable time with his new friends. He spent a lot of time during the day with Lenny and the two academy guards, trading stories and practicing combat.

Every once in awhile, Vannya would even come out and join the four warriors. Her cheerful smile and ready wit made her a welcome presence. Not to mention, Justan and the guards agreed, she wasn't too hard to look at. Lenny did say however that she could use a little more hair about the face. When the others looked at the dwarf with bewildered expressions, he didn't press the issue.

While the days were filled with camaraderie, the nights were a time for deeper contemplation. This was the time when Justan's thoughts turned inward. He found himself re-examining his thoughts and feelings. He thought about his life before, how it would change in the future, but mostly he thought about Jhonate.

Every evening, Justan made it a point to stop by the wizard's door and call to him through the glowing rune. Valtrek still stayed in the wagon all day. Justan was getting more and more curious about what kind of work kept the man locked inside that place.

Each night the professor answered his knock and would come out to visit with Justan for a short time. The second night after leaving Wobble, Justan brought out the book given to him by the Scralag. He hadn't mentioned it to the Professor before because he hadn't trusted him, but these last few days he had developed a respect for the man.

He asked the wizard to read it, hoping that he would get some answers.Valtrek's eyes lit up when he saw the torn cover.

"Yes, Justan, now this might give us some answers." The

wizard opened the book and started to read. One hand stroked his neat beard. His eyes widened, then squinted. “Hmm, this is interesting.”

“What is it?” Justan asked, hoping that he would finally get some answers. The day that he had met the Scralag seemed almost like a dream now, but he was reminded of it every time he saw the glittering rune on his chest.

The wizard’s brow furrowed again and he waved his fingers above the page. For a brief moment, Justan thought he saw intricate glowing flows of energy pass from the man’s fingers to the book. Valtrek blinked a couple of times and focused on the book even further. After a few seconds his mouth twisted and he bent over and retched. Valtrek closed the book and sat on the ground, his head in his hands.

Justan’s heart fluttered. This didn’t look good. “What did you see? Are you okay?”

The Professor composed himself for a moment and answered, “I’m fine, I’m fine.” He took a deep breath. “But this book is unreadable.”

“What?” Justan asked. The sight of the powerful wizard on the ground looking green in the face was unnerving. Then he remembered the disorientation that he had felt when he tried to read the thing and he understood why the wizard had the reaction.

“The text is warded by a powerful spell. I tried to counter it, but it is quite clever,” the wizard explained. His eyes widened and he retched again. “Whoo! I’d like to learn that one for some of my books.”

He grimaced. “I’m sorry but again I am going to have to suggest that you contact Professor Locksher at the school. He will know what to do.” Valtrek reached out his hand and Justan helped him to his feet.

Justan didn’t see the wizard the next night, for the rune on his door was dark and he didn’t answer any knocks. Justan was again tempted to force his way in and find out what went on in there, but he decided to respect the man’s privacy and walked back to the campfire.

He found the mages sitting and playing their card game. Vannya invited him to join in, but he wasn’t interested. Card games were silly. There were much better ways to spend one's time. He walked to the cook pot where Lenny was once again cooking his fire sludge. Justan quickly refused a bowl.

"Lenny, I've been curious-" he began, but the dwarf interrupted.

"Dag-blamed son of a . . . Look, boy, could you use my confounded name right for once?" The dwarf froze. He cocked his head, then raised his hand before Justan could answer. Lenny put a finger to his lips. "Shh! Do you hear that?"

"What?"

He waived Justan silent and put a hand to his ear. "Follow me." The dwarf pulled out his hammer, and crept away from the campfire. He stopped near the edge of the tall grass and leaned into the night.

Justan waited silently and tried to listen for anything unusual. He didn't hear anything at first, but then it came, an eerie chittering moan. The hair on the back of his neck stood on end. The noise was like all of the creepy sounds of Justan's nightmares rolled into one.

"Moonrats!" the dwarf spat. "I hate those damned things!"

Justan frowned. He hated rats. When he was a child, the things had gotten into the family's storeroom. The rats had eaten into their grain and spoiled it with their little droppings. His father had given him a shovel and made him hunt the things down. They were vicious, nasty little creatures that had tried to attack him when he had them cornered. Justan had finally killed the rats, but not until after he was bitten. It wasn't a pleasant memory.

Justan pulled his swords from their sheaths on his back. "Are they dangerous?" he asked. The eerie sound was sending shivers down his spine. Before Lenny could answer, a tall misshapen figure stood from within the grass. Lenny raised back his hammer as the being walked onto the road.

"Whoa, hold it. Put your weapons down, it's me." It was Zambon and he had something big and weird on his shoulder. They walked back toward the campfire until they could see better and he threw his burden on the ground.

Lenny spat on it. "See? I told you. Moonrats. Filthy things!"

Whatever it was definitely had the head of a rat. But it was huge. It must have been four feet long, and thick around the middle. It was covered in greasy gray fur and it had what looked like an extra set of arms growing out of its back. This was bizarre, but what was even stranger to Justan was the hand-like appendage at the end of its tail. The beast had a garish sword wound in its side, and oddly shaped organs were spilling out of it.

Lenny snarled. "What the hell are they doin' out of the forest?"

Zambon shrugged. "I hear that they come out once a year in the fall to mate in the plains. These moonrats seemed pretty preoccupied and I doubt that they will attack. I only ran into this one because I stumbled over it in the dark. I killed it before it had the chance to strike me."

Justan looked a little white faced and Zambon put a hand on his shoulder.

"Don't worry, they are out of their element on the plains. Riveren is out shadowing them right now. Moonrats don't really get dangerous until deep in the forest, and the Mage School has the road warded through that part of the woods to protect travelers."

Justan felt a little better until something grabbed his ankle.

He looked down just as the creature they had thought was dead opened its eyes and snarled. The grasping appendage on its tail squeezed Justan's ankle with wicked claws. Its abnormally large eyes were without pupils and glowed with an unnatural light.

Buster exploded into its head, extinguishing the renewed signs of life. One of the beast's glowing eyes rolled across the ground to stare up at Justan until the light flickered and winked out.

"Ugh!" Lenny snarled. "Zambon, you dag-burned nugget eater! Next time make sure the digustin' thing's dead 'fore you show it to people!"

Justan gulped. The moonrat's eye, now so dark that it looked like it was all pupil, sat there like an evil beacon looking up at him.

Justan wasn't used to the fear of anything but failure, but that night he couldn't sleep. He just stayed awake listening to the haunting chitter of the moonrats in the grass, and shivered.

The next morning Justan was out practicing sword forms before the sunlight lightened the horizon. Except for the guard on watch, everyone else was asleep.

Justan was shaken by the amount of fear he had felt at the sound of the moonrats. Sure, in the past he had felt afraid during battle, but his father had told him that all good warriors did. "Fear is a motivating emotion. It activates a warrior's senses," he had said. Justan found that statement to be true, as long as he was still able to think the battle through. But the night before, his fear had been nearly paralyzing. This was unacceptable to the young man who so craved control. So he was desperately trying to recreate the fluidity of motion he had achieved in the close combat test. Justan went at the sword forms with a fury. So focused was he in achieving this goal that he didn't notice someone coming up behind him.

"Excuse me," the voice said, and Justan was so focused on his sword work that he almost cut the person down before he realized that it was Vannya. His left sword stopped three inches from her slender neck. She yelped before she could stop herself.

Justan stared at her, still breathing heavy with exertion from his exercise.

"Never walk up on someone who is practicing with a sword!" he exclaimed.

She shrugged sheepishly. "Sorry."

He put his weapons away. "What do you want?" Justan asked, somewhat rudely. He wasn't in the mood to talk to anyone at that moment, especially a disturbingly beautiful young woman that would distract him from his focus.

"Well, I didn't get much sleep last night," she said. "I just couldn't close my eyes, what with all of that horrible howling. I hate moonrats! It gets a lot worse when we go through the dark part of the forest, you know. Those things are moaning at you the whole way and watching you with their disgusting glowing eyeballs! Anyway, I saw you out here and thought you might want some company."

Justan's eyes were wide. He did not like the thought of going through the middle of a dark place with those things about.

"Yeah well I didn't sleep much either," he replied. "Um . . . What do you mean when you say the dark part of the forest?"

"Well half of the entire trip from the Mage School to the Battle Academy is through the Tinny Woods. It can take almost a week to get from end to end. When we traveled up for the training tests this year was the first time I had been through it. First we went through the elvish wood where the Silvertree Sect lives-"

"Silvertree Sect?" he asked. There was too much about this journey that he hadn't been told.

"Yes, there is a small group of elves that live in the forest between the dark wood and the river. They are pretty secretive and they don't bother people who stay on the road. They pretty much just keep their dealings with the wizards." She took a deep breath. "Anyway, then we went through the Dark Woods. There is one stretch that takes almost a day to get through where the trees have grown so close together that it is almost pitch black. Professor Valtrek says that's where the moonrats come from."

"And we will have to go through this on the way there?" Justan asked uneasily.

"Of course," Vannya replied. "Unfortunately there is only one road through the woods that is protected. You see, the mages placed magical wards on that road long ago that keep the wildlife off of it. That includes the moonrats. You are safe as long as you just stay on the road. On the way to the tests, Pandros stepped one foot off of the path and got bit by a poisonous snake. He was lucky that we were there. It took four of us to heal him."

Justan was suddenly not looking forward to the rest of the trip. Vannya saw the expression on his face. She stepped unnervingly close to him and put her hand on his arm. "Are you scared of those things, too?" she asked.

Justan wanted to shout out in denial. He didn't want to look the fool in front of this alluring woman. But he couldn't really deny it. It was the truth.

"Those things give me the shivers," he said. "I have hated rats ever since I was a kid, and these things are the most disgusting, big, nasty rats I've ever seen. So yes. Yes, I'm scared of them," Justan said, refusing to be embarrassed.

"Will you promise me one thing?" She threw her head back

and raised the back of one hand to her brow. "When we go through that awful part of the woods, will you stay by my side and protect me? I might faint with all those scary beasts about! It would make me feel *so* much better to have a gallant knight such as yourself around."

It took Justan a moment to realize she was joking. He bowed to her and exclaimed in grandiose fashion. "Why, it would be an honor to protect a woman as refined as you, most fair maiden! No snakes or bugs or spiders or rats or creepy crawlies will dare harm a single hair on your head as long as I am around, my lady!" He lowered his voice and added with a wry smile, "However, I can't promise anything as far as the rest of you is concerned. They may be hungry."

She punched him in the arm and they both laughed. Justan felt better. Laughing about it helped. As they walked back to the caravan, he realized what a good thing it was to have friends around.

For the next two days, the caravan journeyed slowly through the plains until they reached the town of Pinewood on the edge of the Tinny Forest. Justan passed the hours practicing his skills, spending time with Lenny and the guards, and even occasionally, Vannya.

The wizard Valtrek did not answer his door at all during this time and Justan didn't know what to do about it. The guards didn't think it mattered and Lenny just said that wizards were peculiar sorts. The mages weren't even worried. They explained that he had only come out of his wagon once during the entire journey to the academy.

Despite what the others said, Justan became concerned. The man had been absent for long stretches before, but never for two entire days. Professor Valtrek was supposed to be the leader of this trip and surely no matter how busy he was, he wouldn't just abandon everyone. Perhaps he was sick or hurt or even dead. No one would ever know. Justan was the only one who even checked on him.

He tried to entertain himself with his friends, sparring with Riveren or talking about blacksmithing with Lenny. But the darkened rune on the wizard's door stayed in the back of his mind.

The town of Pinewood was situated on the border of the plains and the Tinny Forest. Though it was mainly a logging town, Pinewood stood as the last place to stop for supplies for anyone traveling through the woods. The place was built like a fort with tall wooden walls surrounding the entire town. Massive gates were watched over by alert guards to make sure that nothing unsavory got in.

The caravan arrived in the evening as the light was dimming. With Valtrek still in hiding, the guards made the decision to stay just outside of the town gates for the night. In the morning they would go into Pinewood for supplies and then be on their way. Everyone was eager to get through the forest as quickly as possible, especially the mages. They had been away from their home for a long time.

As they stopped, Justan got his first glimpse of the forest. He had imagined a dark, twisted place, but it didn't look forbidding at all. In fact it looked pleasant. The fall weather had turned the leaves on the trees into a myriad of colors and though some of the branches were bare, their leaves having long since floated to the ground, the view was resplendent, reminding Justan of comfortable fall outings in the woods to the east of Reneul. With that memory in mind, his fear of the next part of the journey dissipated and he found himself looking forward to it.

As the night deepened and his friends were talking at the fire, Justan was drawn once again to the wagon of the man in the white robe. It had become almost a ritual to him now as he walked up to the door, stepped up on the first step and touched the rune. He called out to the wizard.

"Professor Valtrek, this is Justan. Can I speak with you?" There was no answer. "I was hoping that you might help me with some questions." Still there was no response from the wizard. But then, for a brief moment, Justan thought he saw the rune flicker. "Sir, can you hear me? Are you alright?" Another flicker. Justan began to worry even more. He continued to try, but the rune remained dark after that.

He left the wagon and went to his bedroll to sleep. Justan lay there for a few hours and then gave up. His curiosity was getting the best of him. The familiar questions still burned in his mind. What went on in that wagon? What did the man do while shut in that small room all day? Justan had to do something. Besides, he had to make sure that the man wasn't hurt, didn't he? He wasn't sure, but the excuse was enough for him to justify giving in to those urges.

He snuck over to the wagon again.

"Professor," he whispered into the rune, and when there was a slight flicker of light, he grasped the door handle. Instantly, he was hit with a shock that jolted him and singed his hand.

"Oww!" he gasped. His curiosity was turning into anger at the wizard.

Justan was determined to get into the wagon now. He flexed his aching hand and wrapped it in a handkerchief. He grasped the handle once more and was shocked again, but the cloth muted it. He tried to twist the knob, but the door was locked. There was a greater shock this time as he twisted the handle. His hair stood on end.

"This is it, professor! Let me in!" The rune didn't flicker this time, but he put his shoulder down and drove his weight into the door. The wood around the lock splintered and Justan sprawled inside.

He quickly sat up. A glowing light came from a pedestal in the corner of the room, stinging his eyes, but his vision soon adjusted from the darkness outside. The wizard wasn't there. There was a small neatly made bed and a chair that had dust on the seat. It looked to Justan as if no one had been there in weeks. The place even smelled empty, as if it had been sucked dry of all scents.

Justan's eyes were drawn to the one object in the room that stood out. Along the rear wall of the wagon was a large full-body mirror. Its surface shone as if just recently polished. The mirror had a silver inlaid frame covered in runes and symbols in a way that was almost as hypnotic as it was beautiful. It wasn't bolted to the floor and Justan wondered how it could have stood upright on all of the bumpy parts of the road.

As he gazed at the exquisite frame, Justan was compelled to reach out and touch it. Without thinking, he raised his arm and stretched his fingers towards the glass. Suddenly, the mirror's face changed from his reflection into something cloudier. Justan felt compelled to touch the mirror. No, not just touch it. He wanted to enter it.

His vision shifted for a moment and he saw tendrils of energy reaching out from the thing to grasp at him. He shook his head and pulled back. He didn't like that compulsory feeling.

Evidently the wizard had used that mirror to go travel somewhere. He looked back at the door and winced at the damage. He wondered if there was a way for him to repair it before Valtrek got back. As he went to examine it closer, he noticed something on a small table beside the door. He looked closer. His heart shot into his throat.

Suddenly many questions were answered.

A gust of wind blew out of the mirror, bringing with it the sweet spicy smell that Justan had smelled on his previous visits with the wizard. Justan quickly swept the object from the small table and turned in time to see the man in the white robe emerge from within the silver mirror. He trailed a cloud of aromatic spicy mist behind him. The wizard's features were laced with anger.

"Justan! How dare you enter my personal quarters without my permission? This is unconscionable conduct from a student who-" He stopped when he saw what Justan had clenched in his hand.

"You!" Justan snarled, rage burning in his eyes. "You . . . you villain! How dare you accuse anyone of unconscionable conduct?" He held out the object he had taken from the table. It was a vial of sleeping potion just like the one Kenn had used to kidnap Jhonate. "You put Kenn and Benjo up to it, didn't you! It was all a ploy to keep me from entering the academy."

Justan trembled with the betrayal. Not only had the wizard tried to keep Justan from achieving his dreams, but his dearest friend could have been seriously hurt. "What do you want from me? What do I possess that you would stoop this low to get?"

The wizard's arms fell to his sides. His features slumped. He did not deny Justan's accusations.

"I am not proud of what I have done," he began. "It is true that I gave the potions to that weasely little man. But I did not know the depth of the anger he held toward you. I had hoped that by delaying you in the exams, that I might have a better chance of convincing you to come along, but it was not for any personal gain, I assure you."

"Then why? Tell Me!" Justan shouted.

"For you. I did it for you, Justan. You must believe me. I have seen the sheer depth of the power that you could have, and I could not leave it be. If I could see your potential, then so could others. I couldn't leave you on that path knowing that someone could come along and corrupt that power. You need to learn about that magic. You need to be able to control it. If not, much harm could come to those around you!"

"You lie!" Justan snapped, and threw the bottle at the wizard's feet. It shattered into pieces, pelting Valtrek with potion. The wizard swooned and fell to the floor, a victim of his own magic.

Justan fled from the wagon. He didn't know what to do. He was too blinded by his pain to think straight. His world had been upended once again. He had even begun to look forward to the new experiences awaiting him at the Mage School. Now he could not imagine going to that place and trying to learn from the very people who he knew had plotted against him.

He looked up the road. He couldn't go back to the academy either. They wouldn't take him if he breached his contract. It seemed to him that the doors to his future had been shut in his face and now he was left out in the cold. Justan gathered his belongings and fled into the one place that seemed at all familiar to him. The Tinny Woods.

Chapter Twenty One

The man in the white robe awoke in a pile of shattered glass. A single shard caught his eye as it sparkled on the floor by his face. After much effort, he was able to rise to his feet and brush the glass out of his white hair and neatly trimmed dark beard. His ears rang and his head felt like it had been stuffed with cotton. That poor fool boy, he thought.

Valtrek had told the truth when he said that he was not proud of what he had done to get Justan in the Mage School. In fact, he knew that he had deserved the treatment he received when the young man found out. The whole situation had gotten out of hand.

In the beginning, he had thought young Kenn Dollie to be not much more than a little prankster who had a dislike for Justan. But the slimy little man had been more dangerous than he had expected. It was only much later when he found out what had almost occurred because of his sleeping potions that he realized his mistake.

Even so, he reminded himself that the boy would have never learned of his shady deed if he had just been more careful. The boy's progression was the important thing. He had let himself be distracted by work that he believed required his personal touch. A war was brewing and there were so many tasks to complete.

Throughout the journey, Valtrek had used the mirror to travel to the Kingdom of Benador where he was lobbying the king to strengthen his force on the border of the Trafalgan Mountains. Valtrek had been forced to leave in the middle of an important dinner function to answer the alarm sent to him by his wards on the door to his wagon. No doubt the king was wondering where he had gone. These talks were crucial, but he now realized that it would have been better if he had asked one of his colleagues to handle it.

Instead, his absence from the caravan had spurred the already angry young man into irresponsible action.

Valtrek ran one hand through his white hair and sighed. Life in his position was always so complicated. What he wouldn't do for some time off, perhaps a few weeks at the wizard colony on the island of Troi. But that was a luxury he didn't have. He needed to find Justan and make things right. It would not be an easy task, but the boy's potential was just too great to ignore.

The professor opened the door into the morning sunlight. How long had he lain asleep on the floor? He grumbled under his breath as he rushed down the steps and across the camp. He had so much to do. Well, the king would have to wait until he could straighten things out with Justan.

The students were chatting amiably as they climbed into the wagons. Valtrek realized that they had already been in the town gathering supplies and everyone was putting everything away so that they could be on the move. Valtrek searched around past the surprised stares of his students, but he could not find Justan.

"Vannya!" he called.

"Yes!" she chirped from right behind him.

Valtrek swung around. "Ah, yes. You have befriended Justan?"

"Uh, yes sir."

"Good. Where is the boy?"

"I don't know professor. I haven't seen him since last night." She looked worried.

"Blast! Young lady, you were supposed to keep track of him!" The wizard spun away, his mind moving at blurring speeds. He didn't have time to send out a search party for the boy. He stomped his foot in frustration.

Vannya watched the Professor pace back and forth, stroking his neat beard ferociously. Then he stopped and closed his eyes. He murmured under his breath and snapped his fingers.

To her surprise, the Professor's body went limp and fell to the ground. Vannya rushed over with the other students to check him. She tried to send her magical energies into the wizard's body to discover what was wrong, but they were jolted back into her with so much force that she was physically thrown back a few steps. Evidently his body was warded against such intrusion. She felt his pulse and when she saw that his heart was still beating, she sighed and had the others carry the wizard back to his wagon. Stranger things had happened where Valtrek was concerned.

Valtrek's essence soared along the winds, looking for the missing Justan. Leaving ones body this way was very risky. Normally he would have prepared a lot better before attempting it, but he had no time to waste. His body would be safe among his students. Even so, he still couldn't keep himself from looking back at the thin stream of energy that connected his spirit with his body every once in a while to make sure that all was well.

He flew along the ground at a furious speed searching for Justan, but he was no tracker. The area Justan could have traveled during the night was huge. Where had the boy gone? Did he head back to the academy even though nothing was there for him, or would he have gone into the town of Pinewood to hole up and think of his options?

Valtrek did not know where he would go if in Justan's position, but he realized that he could not have traveled that far. He checked the road back towards Reneul first and saw nothing but a small horde of goblins skulking about the hills. He would have to inform the town about that before they left. The wizard searched the town and the plains until the only place he had not checked was the most unlikely place that Justan would have headed into.

Valtrek looked into the Tinny Woods and realized that there was nothing he could do if the boy had gone in there. With a sigh that was carried along the wind, he retreated to his body. As always, there was so much work to do.

Justan stumbled through the trees, anger boiling in his mind. He tried to take some comfort in the pleasant forest smells and peaceful sounds of night birds and crickets. Where could he go now? He certainly wasn't going to go back and join the caravan after all that had occurred. He lurched blindly forward in the darkness, obsessing over the disaster his life had become.

He wandered throughout the night, railing at his fate, cursing, and sometimes even crying as he thought of all he had lost. What were his options now? He supposed that he could go back to Reneul. The academy wouldn't take him in, but his parents wouldn't turn him away. What would he do there, though? Sit on his hands? He didn't want to be a burden on his parents. He would need to make money. But where would he work?

Justan stopped and sat on the trunk of a fallen tree. He had graduated from Training School after all. That was enough prestige to get a job in just about any army he wanted. He could go to Dremald and join the king's army. Over time he could work his way through the ranks and make a name for himself.

Justan's shoulders slumped. That wasn't what he wanted. He wanted to enter the academy and there was only one path that would take him there. He had to go to the Mage School. Justan frowned. That would just be playing into Valtrek's hands. He refused to let that man control his life.

One thought came unbidden to his mind. What would Jhonate say? He imagined himself showing up in Reneul, having abandoned his goals. He would go up to Jhonate and say . . . what? "I give up?"

He shuddered at the thought of what she would do to him then. No, he would say, "I am sorry Jhonate, even though it cost me the academy, I just couldn't let them-" . . . Let them what? Justan didn't really know what their plans were for him. He imagined standing before her, telling her what Valtrek had done and she would say . . .

She would say, "Do not tell me you ran away, boy. You stood in front of the man trying to keep you from your dreams and you did not fight? Just when you had him on the defensive you ran? Have you forgotten everything I taught you?"

The terrifying thought strengthened him. She would be right to respond that way. She wouldn't let him give up. That's for sure. He tried to think of what he could do that would make her proud.

Justan gritted his teeth. He would take control. He didn't have to let the knowledge of Valtrek's betrayal destroy his goal. This was only another obstacle in his way. In the past whenever fate had thrust something on him that was beyond his control, it had only served to strengthen him. He couldn't let this time be any different.

No longer would he burden himself down with things he could not control. He would continue to the Mage School, and he would conquer it. He would choose to learn all that he could. He would make the best of these two years and come out triumphant.

But he would not trust Valtrek again. Of that he was certain.

He let out a deep breath. His confusion had dissipated, replaced instead with a new sense of purpose. Justan took a sip from his water bag and looked around. The woods were coated in a thick mist, but even though he could not see the sunrise through the trees, it was bright enough that he could tell that it was morning. He had walked all night. As he gazed around at the endless stretch of trees, Justan realized the new predicament he was in.

He was lost.

For the first time since he entered the Tinny Woods, Justan felt a pang of fear. Suddenly, instead of a place that reminded him of pleasant childhood memories, he saw himself in an unfamiliar and dangerous place. The mist obscured much of his view and he could not see past two or three trees in any direction. The ground was slippery and treacherous with its covering of wet, decaying leaves. The bare branches of the trees seemed to reach for him.

His heart was racing. Justan took a deep breath and tried to take control of his fear. He drew his swords for comfort and walked around trying to see if he could retrace his steps and find his way back to the caravan. Unfortunately, Justan had not paid enough attention in the tracking classes at the Training School and this was not one of his strengths.

He tried to think about it logically. He needed to get back to the road. Now he was sure that he hadn't crossed over the road in the night. He had entered the forest to the east of the road, so he knew that the road had to be to the west. But which way was west?

Justan remembered his father telling him that moss was only supposed to grow on the north side of the trees because it did not like the sunlight. He checked the trees and soon found that this rule evidently didn't apply everywhere because moss seemed to cover every inch of the tree trunks in this forest. He looked up at the bright blob that was the sun rising above the mist. He knew that the sun always rose in the east. If he kept the sun at his back, he would travel to the west until he reached the road.

So with a lighter step, he plowed along through the forest using the sun as his guide. As noon came, he realized that it was not so easy to follow the sun when it was right overhead. He was exhausted and knew that it was going to be easy for him to get lost again if he didn't know the direction he was traveling.

He stopped and took a deep drink from his waterskin. His stomach rumbled. In his haste, Justan hadn't packed away much to eat. He had a few dried strips of meat and a hard roll, which he devoured quickly. He sat while he ate and his eyes grew heavy. Justan decided to take a short nap and continue on when the sun was further on its way across the sky. He sat with his back to a tree and closed his eyes.

Justan awoke abruptly as something slithered across his neck. With a yelp, he jumped to his feet. He looked around with his hand to his neck, but could not see what it was that had wakened him. He shivered as he stared at the ground. The leaves could hold any number of surprises.

He looked up to see that the sun was way past its zenith. Justan knew that it must be late afternoon. He had slept far longer than planned. Fortunately the mist was gone, evaporated in the noonday sun. But in a way, now that he could see farther ahead it was even worse. The tall leafless trees seemed to stretch forever. There was no road in sight.

Justan plowed with haste toward the sun on its western path, deciding that he could not be too far from the road. Surely he couldn't have traveled that far during the night. He moved along, and the trees became taller and the leaves got deeper as he progressed until at times they were knee deep.

He trudged through these places ignoring the thought of what could be hiding in those depths, but the struggle sapped his energy. He also noticed that the further he traveled, the quieter it got. There were less bird chirps, less insect buzzing, until finally when the sun descended below the horizon, it was dead silent. Justan tried to whistle to clear some of the silence, but his whistling sounded uncomfortably loud in his ears and he feared that he might attract the attention of something he did not want to meet.

In the dusk, he picked up his pace and scrambled faster through the leaves. He really wanted to reach the road before it got dark again. As he hurried along, the trees grew closer together and dead brown plants appeared to clog the space between the trees. In places it was thick enough that Justan had to use his swords to chop his way through. The ground was also softer here and it seemed to suck at his feet through the dead leaves at his every step.

Justan started to panic. The road couldn't be this far to the west. Maybe he had crossed it at some point without knowing.

Justan was at an impasse again. Should he retrace his steps and circle through the less forbidding part of the forest, or should he continue along this clotted path? He didn't have time to wait around and think about it. Justan decided that his earlier logic had to be correct. He just needed to calm down and continue on the path that he had chosen. He would come onto the road sooner or later.

Night fell.

It became so dark that Justan couldn't see his hand in front of his face. There was no moon that night and the trees had grown so thick together at this point that even the sparse starlight couldn't penetrate the blackness. After hitting his head on a low branch, he decided that he couldn't travel any farther in these conditions. He would likely hurt himself or get even more lost than he already was. So he reached in front of him and grabbed a tree. He knelt at its base.

He couldn't think of anything better to do but cover himself in leaves and try to get some rest. He dug down and his hand touched something slimy. He remembered the thing that had slithered across his neck earlier. The story that Vannya had told about the mage who had been bitten by the poisonous snake made his skin crawl. Justan knew that he wouldn't be able to sleep.

He stood with his back to the tree and drew his swords, waiting for the smallest sound. He wouldn't lie down and didn't dare to try climbing the tree. Strange creatures could live in a tree, too.

His mind could not keep up this panicked state for long. His fear began to dissipate. After a while he fell into a half-awake trancelike state. The hours slowly marched by. He started to see imaginary swirlings in the blackness, glowing faces and ghoulish apparitions. He shook his head and then he heard a sound that made his blood run cold. It was far off, but he heard it as distinctly as if it was beside him. A chittering moan.

Moonrats.

Justan clenched his fists around his sword hilts and waited with his blood pounding in his ears. He had never felt so helpless or been so terrified in his life. The moan was joined by another, and yet another until the night that had seemed so silent before was now like a cacophonous madhouse of chatter.

Justan stood as still as possible, not daring to make a sound. He didn't see how they would be able to hear him over the noises that they were making, but he didn't know anything about the beasts. How sensitive was their hearing? Would they be able to smell him? Would he know that they were coming or would he just be rushed quickly from behind?

The forest started to brighten. Justan realized that morning must be coming. He started to be able to make out more details of his surroundings. Then suddenly Justan saw pairs of glowing lights in the distance. The chittering sounds grew louder as the moonrats approached.

Justan knew he would not be able to flee. Where would he flee to? He took the only advantage he had. He climbed the tree. In the dim light, he could just make out a limb overhead. He was barely able to reach the lowest limb by jumping with all of his strength. From there he climbed up until he was sure that they would not be able to reach him.

Justan watched the glowing eyes come closer, bobbing up and down with the creatures steps. His horror was mounting. Even with the brightening of the forest, Justan could not see the creatures yet, just their pupil-less eyes. Several sets of those glowing orbs gathered under his tree and Justan could not tell whether they were looking up at him or not. Then the moaning abruptly stopped.

They just sat still, eyes glowing in the dim light. He quietly slid the Jharro bow off of his back and notched one of his new steel arrows to it. The moonrats kept their patient vigil for a few moments longer. Justan pulled the string back and waited for any reason to shoot. He was nearly petrified with fear and the only thing that kept him sane was the warmth of the bow in his hand and the throbbing power in the string as it was humming by his ear.

He began to be able to make out their forms in the weak light and it didn't make things any better. They were frightening beyond all belief with their extra sets of hands wiggling about and their glowing orbs staring silently. One of them came up to the tree and put its front paws up on the trunk. It stood there sniffing up at him and gave a sharp yelp. Justan was so startled that he almost fired his arrow right into the dirt.

He heard a chitter behind him. He turned to see another moonrat in the tree next to his, hanging from a branch by the arms that grew out of its back. Its luminous eyes seemed to stare straight through him and it snarled.

With a cry, Justan shot the arrow right between those glowing orbs. The power of the shot sent them shooting out of the monster's head in opposite directions. The dead creature fell to the ground and the beasts that milled around beneath him went mad. Three of them fell over the remains of the one he had slain, gnawing and gorging. The rest swarmed around his tree and started climbing it. Justan pulled another arrow as fast as he could and fired down with such force that his missile burst through two of the beasts before burying itself in the ground. More frenzied creatures started to devour these dying moonrats, but the awful calls were answered in the distance with a swarming fury.

He looked around him and he saw more of the creatures using their extra arms and the appendage on their tail to swing through the branches toward him. He fired as quickly as he could with his new steel arrows and blew the beasts apart. He knew that he would run out of ammunition soon but he didn't have time to think.

He shot another monstrosity swinging towards him and pinned it to a tree, its back broken. More moonrats leapt from the branches above it to feed. He was lucky that they were happy to eat each other because that distraction was the only thing keeping him alive.

Soon, Justan must have killed over a dozen of them. He only had five arrows left in his quiver, when he felt wet drool land on his head. He looked up just in time to see a moonrat hanging from a branch right above him by its tail, its four front arms were open and grasping while its mouth was open about to snap at him.

Justan couldn't get his bow up in time and the beast fell upon him, knocking him off of the branch. They fell several feet to hit the ground with a thud. Justan landed on his back with the creature on top of him. He tried to push it off of him while gasping for air. He knew that the others would be on him right away.

Suddenly a deafening roar ripped from the darkness. A huge maw full of sharp teeth closed about the head of the rat on top of him and flung the beast away. Justan caught a glimpse of a reptilian head and brown fur. Then it was standing over him.

Whatever the giant creature was, it stood above him on four long, partially scaled legs. It roared in defiance at the smaller creatures. The moonrats hissed in reply and the giant creature leapt at them, biting with sharp teeth and rending with its front claws.

Justan grabbed up his bow and ran. He did not know what it was that had just saved his life, but he wasn't going to wait and find out. He ran until he realized that he wasn't being pursued and then stopped. He could hear the battle raging on behind him.

Justan knew that he should keep running, but there was something about that beast that had rescued him that made him pause. Why had it saved him? Most likely it just wanted a less hairy dinner, but something in his heart said otherwise. He had not felt any malevolence from the creature.

Despite his logic screaming at him to run away, Justan notched an arrow and found himself heading back towards the fight.

The forest had lightened enough at this point that he could make out the struggle. The large beast that had saved him looked like a slapped together patchwork mix between a reptile and a horse, with the head of a lizard, yet the ears and mane of a horse reaching down a long neck to a broadly muscled back that was covered in an equine pelt. It had a long sloping lizard-like tail that it was using to bat the moonrats away, and its legs and abdomen were covered in scales. It was using the sharp claws on the end of all four legs to slash away at any beast that got close to it. Despite the awkwardness of the mix, the monster didn't move like a lizard or a horse, but more like a cat.

Even with its deadly defenses, the creature was surrounded from all sides and above by the chittering moonrats. Justan knew that there was no way that it could win the fight. This creature would die if he didn't do something. He had to help. Justan crept forward until he was positioned behind a tree where he wouldn't be seen. The rats rushed the beast.

Just as he put an arrow on the string, Justan heard a loud cry for help enter his mind. Sharp pain ripped through his brain. His vision blurred and it was as if he was seeing the battle in two perspectives. He saw the fight with his own eyes from behind the tree, but he also seemed to see the battle from the beast's point of view.

No, not a beast. A name came into his mind. *Gwyrtha*. Her name was Gwyrtha. A flood of images and scents assaulted him that were alien to his mind. He seemed to be sensing this creature's thoughts and it, no . . . *she* thought in different terms than him.

Justan didn't have time to think, just react. He muted these new thoughts down in his mind and focused in. A moonrat had dropped from the tree and was biting Gwyrtha on the back of the neck. Justan's arrow sent it sailing several yards before it landed into a pile of other moonrats who were feasting on their other dead brethren. Just four arrows left. He used them to clear a path for the creature, blowing the moonrats to pieces.

"*Run!*" He shouted at her with both voice and mind and she did. Straight for *him*.

As she barreled toward him, Justan's instincts were to run screaming, but in his heart, he knew that her intentions were benevolent. Somehow, through the jumble of images in his mind, Justan knew that she wanted him to climb on her back. She paused beside him. He grabbed her thick mane and swung his leg over her back. She took off.

She ran with the leaping bounds of a jungle cat. Justan had to hold on with all his might just to keep from being thrown off. The moonrats were howling and moaning in frustration behind them and Justan knew that they were still being pursued. However at this point, he was more afraid of being thrown off than being caught by the evil things.

The trees streaked by. As they entered a small clearing, he

discovered that the moonrats hadn't just been chasing them. They were also calling ahead. They were surrounded by moonrats on the ground and hanging in the trees, all moaning and chittering at them madly.

Gwyrtha wasn't frightened by this development. She was ready for another fight. Justan had no choice but to draw his swords and slide off of her back. They would have to battle their way out together.

It didn't look likely that they would survive. But Justan found that, even though he had been sorely afraid of these creatures just moments before, the fear was gone. With his new ally there as support, Justan decided to go down in a way that Jhonate would be proud of. He would kill as many moonrats as he could before he fell.

Justan and Gwyrtha prepared mentally for the coming attack. Their minds remained linked, and though Justan could not completely understand all the thoughts she was sending to him, he did understand the goodness of this strange creature. They had only known each other for mere minutes and yet there was already a strong bond between them. Justan felt a strength flow into him from that bond and his tired muscles filled with energy. He felt like he could fight forever. *And we might have to,* he thought, for the horde of moonrats attacked.

Justan and Gwyrtha worked together in concert. That is to say that they didn't get in each other's way. Their fighting styles were different enough that it was hard for them to mesh as a coherent unit, but through the mental bond between them, they could both tell what to do to best help the other.

Justan spun from left to right, attacking with both swords independently. With one sword, he pierced the glowing eye of a creature while his second weapon slashed open another beast's throat. He began to feel like he had not felt since that day in the arena when all of his reflexes were working together in harmony. The strength that he had received from Gwyrtha not only gave him stamina, but a newfound agility that he put to good use.

Gwyrtha bit one of the filthy things nearly in half and spat it aside. Oh how she hated the taste of these creatures. She spun and knocked a moonrat across the clearing with her tail. She also felt different since gaining this connection with the young human.

Things seemed a little sharper and her mind was able to focus more. His thoughts were hard for her to follow, but she did understand his determination and it steadied her.

The glowing eyes of the beasts were easy targets because of the way they stood out. Justan worked his swords with a frenzy, putting out one light after another.

They fought valiantly. Soon the clearing was filled with thrashing moonrats feasting on the bodies of their dead. But the moonrats that had been following them from the earlier battle arrived from the rear. The two companions began to tire. They were both covered in scratches and bites from the dirty beasts and the odds were overwhelming.

Suddenly above the chittering din of the moonrats, Justan heard a rhythmic pounding. A jolt of pure fear struck him through the bond. Something new was approaching. Something that scared Gwyrtha much more than the horde of moonrats.

Chapter Twenty Two

The jolt of fear coming from Gwyrtha hit Justan's mind with paralyzing force. A moonrat got through his defenses and bit deeply into his calf. Justan howled in pain. He lopped the top of the moonrat's head off with a mighty swipe, then spun and kicked another in the snout, knocking it away. The pain in his leg was searing. He had been bitten earlier in the night, but never this deep.

Justan knew he had to be careful. The emotions coming from Gwyrtha made it hard to distinguish her thoughts from his own. He could not afford that kind of distraction in the heat of battle. The only thing that had saved him in the fight so far was the fact that she thought in such different terms than him. He wrestled with the chaos of thoughts plunging through his mind. Somehow, he was able to grasp the foreign thoughts and mute them, pushing the feeling of fear away.

The rhythmic pounding from the unknown threat was getting louder, and soon Justan and Gwyrtha weren't the only ones to notice. Several of the moonrats scurried off toward the beating sound.

"What is it?" Justan shouted at Gwyrtha as he ran another beast through with a quick thrust. In response, a rush of information came through their bond and Justan was flooded with images that came so fast that they were hard to follow. He saw menacing figures with massive arms and hairy faces roaring and clubbing others of Gwyrtha's kind. These images were interlaced with feelings of fear and sorrow. The visions became unbearably intense and he had to force them away as several more of the moonrats attacked.

The menace came closer and Gwyrtha was frozen with intense terror. As she stood immobilized, several moonrats swarmed over her, biting and clawing. The pain jolted her out of her fear and she rolled over, crushing the creatures that clung to her back. Gwyrtha tore into the remaining ones with teeth and claw, killing them quickly. More moonrats came out of the shadows to take their place, and she backed away growling.

Justan swung his swords in curving arcs that kept the creatures at bay. The newfound control over his body allowed him to dance about the beasts, giving him the extra room needed to make successful attacks. Without that extra bit of control he would most likely have died several times over. A new problem was arising. His calf was stiffening up. The nasty beast must have bitten deep into his muscle.

Justan turned briefly to see Gwyrtha roll about and crush several moonrats. The pounding sound was closer yet. He could sense that she was beginning to panic. If he didn't do something quickly, she was going to flee and he would be left alone.

Justan burst his sword though one moonrat's glowing eye and into its brain. As the beast squirmed in its death throes, he picked it up over his head. Ignoring the damage inflicted on him by its flailing limbs, he threw the creature into the milling mass of moonrats attacking Gwyrtha. The others pounced on the new meat and fought each other for it.

He reached Gwyrtha's side just as she was about to run and grasped her head in his hands. He didn't know what this connection between them was or how it worked, but he figured that if she could send thoughts and emotions to him, he could do the same to her. She nearly snapped at him in her fear, but he sent soothing emotions through to her from the bond they shared. She whimpered and tried to pull away. The rhythmic pounding of the new threat was almost upon them and the moonrats would not be distracted for long. Justan threw his heart into it.

"It will be okay," Justan said aloud and sent to her through the bond, "*Whatever this is, I will help you defeat it.*" He tried to send as much calm and assurance with those words as possible, and it seemed to have some effect because she stopped struggling. It was just in time, too, for the new presence let itself be known.

The oncoming creature roared. Though Justan could not see it through the trees, he heard a concussive thud and a moonrat flew threw the air in a misshapen tangle as if its bones were pulverized. Suddenly Justan's forced calm was replaced by sheer elation, for he recognized the roar of this beast.

"Lenny!" he shouted. In response there was a loud thud followed by another flying moonrat and a stream of obscure curses. He turned to Gwyrtha and sent a stream of encouraging images. This new arrival was not a threat, but a friend. She snarled as the dwarf came into sight and Justan was forced to stand by her, holding her head and stroking her mane, trying to calm her. He did not want to see either of his new friends hurt by each other.

Lenny fought with precision, shaping his enemies as if they were but hot metal at the forge, every strike crushing bones and rupturing organs. Buster hummed and each hit brought an explosion of concussive power. The dwarf saw Justan standing there with the large beast and cursed up a foul storm, using obscenities so strange that Justan was sure that he made them up on the spot.

"Garlfriggin', hoopskirtin', son of a . . ." He sputtered. "Boy! Get your dag-flamed hind end over here! You think I'm gonna kill all these damned things by myself?"

At that moment, even more chittering moans and yelps erupted from the forest around them and a score more moonrats attacked from out of the trees. Some of them leaped on the carcasses of their fallen brothers, while others attacked the three strangers to their world. Justan found himself laughing despite the overwhelming odds. With Lenny there, he grew excited about the fight. Justan quickly sent another burst of comfort to reassure Gwyrtha that his friend would not hurt her. Then he released her head and leapt into the fray.

Justan had so much that he wanted to ask the dwarf, but the fighting was too fierce for Justan and Lenny to communicate. He could sense that Gwyrtha joined in the battle as well. She leaped into the air, ripping moonrats out of the trees, while Justan danced amongst the crazed beasts, putting eyes out and slicing open throats with his blades. Lenny's fighting style was more direct. He just cursed and beat the evil moonrats into pieces.

Even with his new burst of stamina that came through the bond, Justan grew weary. His moves became less precise. Fortunately for the friends, as the sun grew higher in the sky, the moonrats seemed to lose their taste for the fight. Some just scurried away, while others, engorged from feasting on their dead, simply lay on the ground panting, too bloated to move.

The fight wound down until Justan dispatched the last persistent moonrat with a skull splitting chop. His sword was wedged into the bone and he had to kick at the convulsing beast several time in order to wrench the blade loose. Justan turned to his friends but didn't have time to celebrate. Another struggle was brewing.

Lenny and Gwyrtha had locked eyes. Gwyrtha growled a deep sound that came from the back of her throat. She swung into offensive posture, as if about to pounce. The dwarf, on the other hand, was staring at her with open admiration. He made no move to defend himself.

"Son, do you got any idea what this thing is?"

Justan kept a wary eye on Gwyrtha and answered. "No, Lenny, I don't. But don't make any sudden moves. She doesn't seem to like you very much."

"I can't say as I blame it," he remarked absently. "Sonny, that there is a rogue horse. It's a beauty at tha-" He didn't get to finish his sentence because at that moment, Gwyrtha attacked.

She knocked the dwarf off his feet and pinned him to the ground with her considerable weight, digging into his chest with her claws. Lenny sputtered a few curses. She bit down on his head.

"*NO*!" Justan shouted with all his might and Gwyrtha stopped just shy of breaking the dwarf's neck. She froze, and looked at him with her large intelligent eyes. Lenny was wisely silent. Justan send her mental images as he spoke. "*Gwyrtha, he is a friend.*"

Justan pulled up memories of Lenny fighting along side of him and laughing with him over the fire. She resisted and without knowing how he was doing it, Justan pushed all of his feelings of goodwill and admiration for the dwarf over to her through their bond. She struggled against the feelings at first. Then with reluctance, Gwyrtha released Lenny's head from her powerful jaws and sauntered away. She left grudgingly, but accepted Justan's feelings. She would wait and see. If the dwarf was found untrustworthy, she would kill it later.

Justan sighed in relief and went to check on his friend. Lenny's head was surrounded in wounds from Gwyrtha's sharp teeth and they were bleeding profusely. The dwarf didn't seem to notice, though. He sat up and gazed at Justan in wonderment.

"Well, I'll be. I don't know how you dun it, boy, but thanks fer stoppin' the beast." A row of nasty punctures traveled from his jaw up onto the side of his head. "It's amazin'. I didn't know there was any of em' left."

"'It' is a she. Her name is Gwyrtha." Justan explained, while checking his friend's wounds. Somehow calling her an 'it' didn't feel right. He examined his friend's bleeding chest and was troubled. "Lenny, you don't look so good. Are you ok?"

Under all the blood, Lenny looked at him quizzically. "I'm standin' ain't I?"

"No. You're not. You're sitting. We have got to get out of here. The moonrats aren't attacking right now, but I don't know how long that will last."

He reached out and helped the dwarf to his feet. Lenny was pale and he didn't look steady at all. Justan noticed many wounds on his friend that he hadn't seen before. The dwarf had been fighting for a long time to reach this place. He must have lost a lot of blood even before Gwyrtha bit him.

There were many questions that Justan wanted to ask. How did the dwarf find him? Where was the rest of the caravan? Were they out looking for him? Justan was also concerned about Gwyrtha and what her bond with him meant for their future. But he didn't have time for asking questions. The engorged moonrats were starting to stir and he didn't know where the others had gone.

He picked up Lenny's hammer and strapped it to the dwarf's back. Lenny didn't even protest. He just stood there swaying.

"Can you walk?" Justan asked.

In response, the dwarf's eyes rolled up in his head and he fell over unconscious. Justan quickly bent to try and pick his friend up. A nearby moonrat roused itself enough to hiss and snap at him. Justan paused and lopped the beast's head off, then again tried to pick Lenny up. The dwarf was far too heavy for him to sling over his shoulder. It was like trying to pick up a boulder. Justan grunted in frustration. He couldn't carry his friend. There was only one choice left and he wasn't looking forward to the confrontation.

"*Gwyrtha, I need your help.*" He sent her mental pictures of what he needed her to do. She glared at the unconscious dwarf. She would rather leave it and let the moonrats feast on it than carry it on her back. Again Justan loaded her with his feelings for the dwarf and tried to include an understanding of the situation they were in. "*Please.*" She reluctantly plodded over to the dwarf, hissing in disgust the whole way.

Justan tried to pick Lenny up so that he could throw him over her back, but for some reason the dwarf wouldn't budge. He tugged again and saw that Gwyrtha was resting one foot on Lenny's back.

"*Gwyrtha . . .*" Justan rebuked.

She snorted and moved her foot away, presenting her backside to him. It was a struggle, but Justan was able to hoist the dwarf over Gwyrtha's back. Luckily, the dwarf had rope in his pack and Justan was able to tie him down.

Several of the moonrats were over their grogginess by now and while some of them crept away, others were snarling and chittering at him. Justan slashed any that got too close with quick slices of his twin blades and bade Gwyrtha to move out.

The forest was still teeming with danger. He knew that they would make much better time if he weren't walking. Justan asked Gwyrtha if she could bear the weight and got an affirmative grunt. He leapt onto her back and leaned over the dwarf to hold on to her mane.

She knew what to do. Gwyrtha moved forward quickly, but carefully, aware of the riders on her back. She didn't like carrying the dwarf and let Justan know about it too. She sent sulky emotions over to him repeatedly through their bond, but it didn't slow her down. Gwyrtha seemed to know where she was going, so Justan just concentrated on holding on and looking out for danger. He felt vulnerable on her back. He had to use both hands to hold on to Gwyrtha's mane and he wished he could have at least one weapon on hand ready for use.

As they traveled, the tops of the trees grew closer together and Justan realized that they were heading deeper into the dark wood. The light dimmed more and more as the tangle of tree branches blocked the sun's rays. Gwyrtha's agility saved them many times over in the dark. She was miraculously able to avoid most obstacles, but several times Justan had to duck under low branches and once he was knocked off her back and had to climb back on.

The chittering moan of moonrats was a constant presence in this place. Even though Justan was extremely tired after the long night and fierce battle, those calls still pumped enough adrenaline in his veins that he remained wide awake.

The further they traveled the more dangerous their surroundings became. Pairs of glowing eyes were scattered through the darkness. Justan could also make out all kinds of brightly colored snakes and spiny-looking beasts gathered in the dark woods. Justan sent many questioning messages to Gwyrtha about their chosen path, but she seemed so sure of her direction that he finally let it be and trusted her sense of direction. Whenever he could free a hand, Justan reached down and felt Lenny's leathery neck for a pulse. It was there, but faint.

The forest grew fouler and darker until eventually they reached a place where the darkness was complete. The air reeked of mold and death with fumes that seemed to clog their throats. Skeletons of various animals littered the forest floor and there was a gooey substance on the ground that sucked at Gwyrtha's feet with every step. She sensed the danger and picked up speed, surging out of that part of the forest as fast as they could.

As soon as they left the foul place behind, a glimmer of daylight pierced the darkness. Justan took a deep breath, grateful for the fresh air. Though they had escaped from the source of the rot, he could still smell it on his clothes and it felt as if it coated his lungs.

They journeyed in this manner for hours. Justan grew used to the movements that Gwyrtha made as they traveled and was able to adjust his body accordingly. Even so, he ached all over from the past day's activities. His skin itched and chafed from the many tiny scrapes and bites, his calf throbbed stiffly, and his spine ached with every movement from the stress of getting used to Gwyrtha's strangely feline gait.

As the immediate danger subsided, Justan's exhaustion caught up to him. The stress of the day, along with his body's tired condition, led him into a half-awake state where, though his body automatically shifted with Gwyrtha's movements, his mind went in alternate directions. It was in this state that something strange happened to him. It started out as just a blurring of his vision. Then, though his eyes were open, he started to dream.

These dreams started out as faint visions and then they came with startling clarity. He saw moonrats tearing each other into pieces while Jhonate ran through the forest shouting his name.

The scene blurred and shifted to the caravan. Valtrek was standing by Vannya, pulling her pretty face off like a mask to reveal another face that was obscured by blowing hair.

The scene shifted.

Justan could sense that somewhere two monsters were out hunting for him but they didn't know it.

The scene shifted.

There was a puny stick of a man that stood above the known kingdoms and plunged a wicked knife into the earth. Where the knife penetrated the rock, a wound appeared and monsters poured out by the hundreds until the land was swarming with them.

The scene shifted.

A tiny figure was being chased by hellish creatures. It landed on Justan's shoulder and refused to leave.

The scene shifted.

The Scralag stood before him and cradled him like a parent would. But everywhere it touched him it left an icy scar.

The scene shifted.

Justan confronted an evil being so vast that it filled the world. It reached one clawed hand into his soul and ripped all of his strengths away, leaving him puny, naked, and alone.

–Blur-

Justan's father was standing in front of him. With a sad expression on his face, Faldon raised his famous sword, the Monarch, and stabbed it into Justan's ear.

The searing pain was so real, it jolted Justan awake. He heard a chittering hiss fade behind him. Justan reached up to find that his ear had been torn open.

Gwyrtha wasn't running as smoothly as before. Justan sensed an urgency in her thoughts. The path was shrinking and she was tiring. Her breathing was rough and the equine portions of her pelt were lathered up. Justan was amazed that she had been able to keep up this mad pace for so long.

He looked around and realized that they were through the dark part of the forest, but the moonrats were once again lying in wait. The chittering creatures were all around them, staring with their luminous eyes, and moaning their awful moan.

Gwyrtha dodged between the trees, avoiding clumps of moonrats and trampling any individuals that got in her way, but soon the creatures were so thick in the air and on the ground that there were not many places left for her to go. It seemed as if the squirming mass of chittering beasts could simply cave in on the companions and kill them with the sheer weight of their thrashing bodies.

Gwyrtha had to stop. There was no escape. They were cut off and it seemed as if their doom was assured. Hundreds of moonrats gathered around them. The cacophony generated by their chitters was unbearable. Justan slid off of Gwyrtha's back and drew his swords. He shouted out in defiance at the swarm of beasts.

Moonrats came hurtling down out of the branches like possessed bees. It wasn't until he saw that the other moonrats immediately began to feed on them that Justan realized the falling creatures were dead. The ground was quickly heaped with a writhing mob of evil creatures in a feeding frenzy. Some attacked the companions but Justan and Gwyrtha made short work of them with claw and sword.

Suddenly, the forest was a buzz with a flurry of arrows. Dozens more moonrats fell to the ground and the milling mass on the ground consumed them. With that signal, Gwyrtha let out a roar of joy and Justan knew that help had arrived.

The fall leaves on the ground suddenly seemed to come alive and glide into the midst of the swirling battle. Justan numbly felt the leaves grabbing his arm and leading him through the chaos. It all seemed like a surreal dream. He wondered if he wasn't awake, but still dreaming on Gwyrtha's back, fleeing through the forest.

He dimly realized that his surroundings were changing as he traveled guided by these unseen hands, and the air around him brightened. He blinked the weariness from his eyes and saw that the late afternoon sunlight was bursting through the trees overhead. He looked down to see that the beings holding him up and guiding him were not made of leaves after all.

They were elves.

Chapter Twenty Three

The elvish people were a beautiful race. From the way they carried themselves to the places they chose for their homes, everything about them was shrouded in splendor. They possessed a lithe, slender body type that looked frail on the surface, but hid wiry strength.

Elves lived long lives. It was said that there were a few elves still around who had lived for over a thousand years, though that is debatable since few would speak of their age. Their race was a secretive one.

They had learned that open relations with other races eventually led to war, and war meant death. For the elves, this was an unacceptable thing. Though they lived long lives, their numbers were small compared to the other races. It was very hard for an elven female to get pregnant, and when she did, the gestation period of the child lasted almost three times as long as that of a human child. To an elf, every life was of immeasurable value. Therefore there were not many things that an elf would fight to the death to defend. About the only thing they saw worth fighting for was their homes.

The homeland of an elven clan was sacred to them because it was imbued with the very life force of the elves that lived there. Every flake of skin, every drop of sweat, every hair of an elf, even their waste contained a small portion of their immeasurable life force. The longer they lived in an area, the more of it was absorbed into the environment. The trees, the grass, and even the animals partook of this substance and kept a small amount of this energy with them. An elven homeland would stay lush and green the year through for even the harshest temperatures could not kill these plants. Developing such a wondrous place was not easy. This is a process that takes decades, even centuries to complete.

With the wonderful blessings of such a home also came a great curse. The fruits from the trees of elves were highly prized for their curative properties and so were all of the things that their lands produced. Who wouldn't want a home made with wood that would never warp or crack or weather? Who wouldn't want seeds for a garden of immortal flowers that would bloom all year round?

For those things many atrocities had occurred. Elven lands had been raided, elven possessions stolen. Elves had been kept as slaves, forced to tend the gardens of the rich and powerful. And some forests have been burned to the ground just out of the fear of such unnatural beauty. At one time there was even a plague of humans who became addicted to feeding on the immortal blood of the elves to extend their lives beyond their normal limits.

Because of events like these, the elves grew very mistrustful of others. Most clans stayed hidden from the view of other races, making their homes in obscure places. Some were so intent on isolation that they would kill any non-elves that ventured into their home, even if the person entered by mistake.

There were also clans that were more trusting of the other races and had developed trade with them. There were even elves that chose to forsake the ways of their people and lived in the exciting world of the humanoid races.

The Blotland elves had always been one of the most mistrustful elven clans. They guarded their borders fiercely and their open hostility towards the other races had borne heavily on some of the younger elves until they protested the strict policies of their elders. This rebel group called themselves the Silvertree sect. They named themselves after a tree in the Blotted Forest with a silver hue that took the extra nutrients gathered from its roots and spread them out among the other nearby trees resulting in a joined root network that benefited the other trees equally.

Eventually there was a break within the clan and the Silvertree sect split off to find a new home. With only fifty elven warriors, they had traveled to Dremaldria to meet with the wizards of the Mage School. The wise wizards saw an opportunity to use this situation to help them with another threat. They guided the sect to the Tinny Forest.

A great rot had settled within the bowels of this place. This was the origin of the evil moonrats. The elves and wizards joined forces and together they destroyed much of the evil and were able to establish a warded road for travelers.

After the heat of battle waned and the moonrats had been pushed back to the darkest places of the forest, the Silvertree elves made a pact with the Mage School for their mutual benefit. The elves were given possession of the forest between its dark heart and the river of Fandine that bordered it. In return the elves promised to keep the evil from spreading again.

The wizards also promised that if the dark heart of the forest was ever destroyed, the elves could claim it all for their own. In gratitude, the elves granted exclusive trade status to the school. This was a huge boon for the wizards because there were many spell implements that require things that only an elf could provide.

Not long ago, the elves' battle with the darkness of the forest and the moonrats had been fought to a standstill. Two of their number were killed in the last great battle. The elves retreated to mourn. The mourning rituals were still going on. A period of rest from battle was to last all year, but something had roused the elves to action. It was not coincidence that the elves had been out in force to save Justan and his companions.

Justan awoke to a bright sunny morning with the welcoming sounds of birds and cicadas in the air. He couldn't remember what happened to him at first. Then it all came rushing back, the betrayal, the battles, the rescue. But where was he now?

He looked around to find that he was still in the forest, but in a cheerful place. There was a green tree or two settled among the leafless ones, and instead of the foul moldy smell of the dark forest, he was delighted with a pleasant fall breeze. Justan sat up to find that he was naked beneath a clean soft cotton blanket. At first he was alarmed, but he turned to see that his clothes and pouches were folded in a neat pile nearby, clean and stitched. Somehow, his benefactors had even managed to get out the bloodstains. He lifted up the pile to find with relief that his weapons were there too.

Justan reached up to his ear to find it bandaged. His other major wounds including his calf were also dressed, while most of the cuts and scrapes and bruises had some sort of salve on them and were healing nicely. He wondered how long he had been asleep.

After looking around to make sure that no one was watching, he stood up and hurriedly donned his garments. He then strapped on his swords and swung his bow over his shoulder.

If he was okay, then where were his friends? He closed his eyes and looked inside himself to find that his connection with Gwyrtha was still very much intact. She was somewhere cool, content, and sleeping, though her dreams were a whirl of foreign images that he couldn't decipher.

With his mind put at ease about Gwyrtha, he just needed to find Lenny. He was about to call out to the dwarf when he felt a tap on his shoulder.

Justan jumped and swung around with a fist cocked but stopped when he saw that it was a thin female elf staring at him with curiosity. She was dressed all in fall colors and her clothes were a patchwork of sewn cotton and silk. This was why he had only seen swirling leaves during his rescue. The elves were dressed in camouflage.

He smiled at the elf and bowed. She just looked at him wide-eyed in return. Her hair was a golden yellow color and it was cut short, exposing her pointed ears. Her face was narrow and pretty with large expressive eyes, a button nose and a small petite mouth.

"Hello, my name is Justan, son of Faldon the fierce," he greeted and stuck out his hand. When she didn't shake it, he continued, "Okay. Well I must thank you for coming to my rescue. My friends and I were doomed until you showed up." She smiled slightly. "Do you know where I might find my friends?"

She still didn't respond. Instead, she reached inside of her cloak and produced an apple. The elf held it out to him. Justan realized that he was famished. He hadn't eaten in almost two days. He took the apple with gratitude and consumed it greedily.

Justan wasn't normally fond of apples. He enjoyed the sweet meat inside but disliked the flavorless peel. This apple was different. It had such a pungent, smooth texture that he didn't even notice the peel as he devoured it. The juice seemed alive. It quenched his thirst as well as his hunger and he felt life and energy enter his body. He felt as though he could continue in his journey right away.

He looked to the elf in gratitude.

"Thank you, that was wonderful." She smiled and nodded. "Can you please let me know where I can find my friends?" he pressed.

In response, the elf bent over and picked up a small rock. With a fluid motion, she hurled it into a nearby pile of fall leaves.

The rock sank in with a thud and the pile of leaves exploded in the fury of the naked dwarf that had been buried underneath them. Lenny came up cursing.

"What the hell? Dag-blast it, who hit me?" He looked quite ridiculous with his hair full of leaves and his normally immaculate mustache sticking out in all directions. "Where in the galldurn world am I?" He saw Justan standing by a very amused elf. "An elf? What in the pisseatin' . . .? Of all the damndest things!"

Justan ran over to his friend and clapped him on the shoulder, happy to see him alive. The dwarf's body was covered in poultices and bandages. His wounds had been pretty severe. The lithe female elf held out an apple for the dwarf. He accepted hungrily.

Lenny devoured it quickly and licked his lips, seeming unsatisfied. He sighed, and oblivious to his nakedness, bent over and rummaged through his belongings which had been tossed in a pile. They weren't folded as neatly as Justan's had been.

Justan looked away in embarrassment. The elf just giggled. Lenny came up with a familiar waterskin and gulped down several swallows. He coughed and belched.

"Now that makes a dwarf feel better!" he exclaimed. Still naked, Lenny turned to the lithe female elf whose face was starting to look a little rosy. "Please accept this gift of firewater from a thankful dwarf." He handed the flask to her. "The name's Lenui."

She smiled in gratitude and clasped the waterskin to her chest. "Thank you, Lenui." Her voice had an airy, almost musical sound. "We haven't had any of this in ages." Justan didn't know why the elf had suddenly decided to talk. Perhaps when he met her he had used improper etiquette.

"May I ask yer name milady?" Lenny asked. Justan was surprised at his uncharacteristic behavior.

"I am Antyni Blynt, and thank you for asking so kindly, Sir Lenui."

Justan chuckled and shook his head. Lenny looked at him crossly.

"What's wrong with you, boy?"

"I'm the only one that seems to get your name right," Justan replied.

Lenny's face went red but before he could say anything, the elf interrupted.

"Please, get yourselves ready and I will take you to the others." Antyni walked over to a nearby tree and leaned against it.

Lenny glared at Justan and seemed about to say something, but threw up his hands in disgust and gave up. The dwarf bent back over his pile of belongings. Justan didn't know what he was upset about. He was just glad that Lenny was finally getting dressed.

As Lenny pulled on his trousers, careful not to dislodge any bandages, Justan had some questions. "Lenny?" The dwarf grunted in response. "How did you know to find me in the forest?"

"Valtrek said that that was the way you was headed," Lenny replied absently, rummaging through his things. "The wizard wouldn't let Riveren or Zambon go 'cause they was under contract or some such thing, and since no one else had the rocks to go after you, I said I'd do it." He looked over his shoulder at Justan. "What the hell was you thinkin' anyway, runnin' off like that?"

Justan explained what Valtrek had done.

"That dirty crabsnatcher! Well, whaddya you expect from an old crafty wizard like him anyways?"

Justan agreed with the sentiment. "But how did you find me? I was hopelessly lost."

Lenny snorted. "You only left a trail a mile wide. If yer ever wantin' to be a great warrior, you need to get back to that academy and take one of them forestry courses. A drunken ogre could've found yer trail. The plan was fer me to catch up to you and get you down to the road. When I found you, you wasn't that far away from it, you know, only a couple hunnerd feet."

Justan fumed. He had been so close! If only he had pushed on. Well, then he wouldn't have met Gwyrtha, would he?

The dwarf finally found what he was looking for: a small mirror. He gasped at his reflection and pulled a small comb and a ball of soft wax out of a pouch. The dwarf began shaping his thick handlebar mustache.

"Anyways, I just followed yer trail 'till I heard all that yappin' and saw lots of dead moonrats. Then I knew you was in trouble. Yer lucky you wasn't killed in the first ten minutes in that forest." He stopped for a moment to look at Justan curiously. "Say, how did we get out of there anyway? We wasn't even in the bad part yet."

"Gwyrtha carried us almost all the way out," Justan explained. "Then the elves came and saved us. After that I don't know any more than you."

"That rogue horse carried me out?" Lenny asked with a surprised expression. "Well don't that beat all. I'd a never thunk she'd let the likes of me on her back."

Justan chuckled. "Believe me, it wasn't easy to get her to do it. Why does she mistrust you so?"

Lenny sighed and shook his head. He had all the leaves combed out of his hair by now and was buttoning his shirt. "Son, it's a long story and one I'd rather not get into. There's lots of things in my past I ain't proud of, and that's one of 'em. Just know that I'm not the one responsible for what's botherin' her." He tucked his shirttails into his pants and started strapping on his gear. "Where'd you find her anyway?"

Antyni's ears perked up at that question and she came closer to listen.

"I don't know. I fell out of a tree almost covered in moonrats and she just appeared out of nowhere to save me. I got away, but I couldn't just leave her there surrounded, so I helped." Justan's brow furrowed as he tried to figure out just what had occurred. The more he thought about it, the more excited he became.

"Lenny, the strangest thing happened then. It was like our minds reached out to each other and linked. I know it sounds crazy, but I could hear her thoughts and she could hear mine. Only she doesn't think like you and me. She thinks in pictures and smells and sounds and . . ." Justan struggled to find the words, but threw his hands up in frustration. "It's complicated." Lenny looked like he didn't understand a thing Justan had just said, but he continued anyway.

"It's not just that. Since we've had this connection, I've changed. Lenny, I can fight. I mean I've always known how to fight, but I've never been able to get my body to do it. But back in the forest I could. It was like I gained some of her strengths. I had control. I had energy. Do you have any idea what I'm saying?"

Lenny slowly shook his head. "I can't say as I do, but I've seen stranger things happen." The elf followed every word.

Justan looked to the south. "I can feel it now, Lenny. That, that . . . bond. Yes, that's it, a bond. Gwyrtha's right over there." He pointed through some trees and Lenny and the elf looked, though they couldn't see anything. "She just woke up and some elves are patting her down and saying hello. She doesn't understand everything they are saying, but it makes her feel good. Oh! She knows I'm watching. Here she comes."

A moment later, Gwyrtha padded out from behind a tree. Justan ran up to her. She looked at Lenny with a wary eye, but nuzzled her head up against Justan.

"Hello, girl. How are you?" He paused as if listening. "Good." He turned to Antyni. "Do you have another one of those apples?" She threw one to him and he gave it to Gwyrtha. She munched it happily.

"Well I'll be barnshuffled." Lenny said with wonder. "He's got her tamed."

The elf shook her head. "No, not tamed. Never that. It's something else." She thought for a moment. "Come, everyone, we must meet with the council."

Lenny finished pulling his gear together and they started to leave. As they walked by the place where Justan had slept, Lenny saw the clean white blanket.

"How come he got the blanket and I got the galldurn pile of leaves?" Lenny asked irritably.

The elf shrugged. "You also had a blanket at first," she explained. "Then Gwyrtha took it away and buried you." Justan and Antyni had a laugh at that and soon Lenny joined in.

Chapter Twenty Four

Again Justan was surprised to see that scattered among the trees full of fall colors were trees bursting with green leaves as if it were spring. The further they walked, the more common these became until they entered a grove where every leaf was a brilliant green. The lush grove truly seemed out of place and it was disorienting to Justan when the light breeze blew autumn leaves across the ground in this small piece of spring.

"How do you get these green trees to grow in the middle of the fall?" Justan asked Antyni.

"These trees are imbued with our essence," she explained. "In a hundred years, this entire forest will be green. This is a young grove yet, so only some of the land truly lives." That gave Justan even more questions, but she raised a hand. "Shh. The council comes."

A gust of wind filled the space between the trees with flying leaves, obscuring Justan's vision. As the leaves settled, he saw seven elves dressed like Antyni. Lenny bowed to the council and Justan followed suit. The dwarf seemed to know things about elf etiquette that he didn't.

"I am Lenui Firegobbler and this is Justan, Son of Faldon the Fierce. Thank you fer lettin' us enter yer homeland. We promise to leave in peace and not to divulge the location to anyone," Lenny intoned with his head still bowed low.

One of the elves stepped forward. He had piercing blue eyes and short red hair. He didn't look any older than the others, but his eyes held a certain wisdom that spoke of long years, and Justan had no doubt about the elf's authority. This one was their leader.

"We accept the intent in which your promise is given, but it isn't truly necessary. One of our own has already spoken for you.

Well, not you specifically, but him." The elf pointed to Justan. "Will you vouch for the dwarf?" he asked.

Justan was surprised. Who had spoken for him?

"Uh, yeah. Yes I will," he responded. "He is an honorable person." *At least as far as I know*, he had to admit to himself. Gwyrtha's mistrust of the dwarf was a little unnerving, but he pushed the doubt away. He had to trust his friend.

"Very well," the elf pronounced. "You may both stay with us as long as it takes for your wounds to heal."

"I'm sorry, but we won't be able to stay fer that long," the dwarf said. "We got a caravan waitin' fer us in Sampo."

"What?" Justan asked.

"Valtrek said he'd be able to tell if you was killed. As long as he knows yer alive, they're waitin'." Lenny paused. "Yer still going to the Mage School ain't you?"

Justan thought for a moment. He had decided that he would go to the school, but his situation had changed. What about his bond with Gwyrtha? Was it something that would just go away? What were his responsibilities now? If he had to, he could travel elsewhere, but . . . no. He had his direction set. He would finish his two years and return to the academy.

"Yes, I'm still going."

The leader of the elves interrupted. "You are a student at the school?"

Justan sighed. "Not yet, but I have signed a contract and will be inducted as soon as I arrive."

"Hmm." The leader mused. "It looks as though things have changed. There will be a different plan." Then he turned to the council. They began whispering among each other so quietly that Justan could not hear. He was puzzled. What plan was the elf talking about?

While they waited for the council's decision, Lenny turned to Antyni and whispered, "Pardon me fer askin' but, I gots to ask. How come you all got short hair?" Justan looked at the council members and realized that they all wore their hair short just like Antyni. All of the other elves he had ever seen wore their hair long.

She whispered back, "We must seed the ground with our

essence to be able to grow our homeland." She fingered the ends of her short hair. "It's a beginning."

The leader stepped away from the other council members and faced them again. He spoke in a formal tone.

"I am Elder Toinyt, spokesman for the Silvertree Council. Young human, our paths have crossed in a way that demands our attention. What you do next is of importance to us. Before you can go we need some answers to very important questions."

Justan straightened his back. "I will answer as well as I can." He had no idea what was going on, but had no reason to balk at their demands.

"First we must know what brought the two of you so deep into the forest."

"Sir, I was traveling with the caravan to the Mage School and I had a disagreement with the wizard in charge." He left out the details. He still wasn't too sure about their relationship with the Mage School and didn't know how they would react to his story of Valtrek's betrayal. "I ran into the woods to think and I got lost."

"An impulsive decision," one of the council members said.

"I ended up surrounded by moonrats and Gwyrtha saved me."

He described as best he could what had happened between him and Gwyrtha. Their eyes were all completely focused on him and they devoured every word. When he completed the story, he had to ask them a question of his own.

"Why do you all seem to know Gwyrtha so well?"

Elder Toinyt answered. "Gwyrtha has lived with us for the last ten years. A very powerful wizard who was a personal friend of mine brought her and left her with us for safekeeping. She has become one of us you might say. When she left the other day, we searched for her everywhere. We had promised my friend that she would not come to harm. We had no idea just how far she had strayed until we found you surrounded by the foul moonrats. We are in your debt for rescuing her."

"No, it is I who am in debt to her. She saved my life several times over. If it wasn't for her speed and agility, we would have never made it out of there." He looked at Gwyrtha and smiled. "She is grateful to be back."

The elder frowned in deep thought. "Do you know why she left us to travel in the Dark Forest in the first place?"

Justan concentrated through the bond and tried to ask her in as simple of terms as he could.

"I don't know. She doesn't know. She just felt drawn to the place. Gwyrtha knew where she was going the entire time, but didn't know why."

Toinyt looked crestfallen at that statement.

"I see. Well, he told me that this would eventually happen. I supposed that we had all just hoped that it wouldn't." When he saw the question in Justan's eyes, he added, "The wizard told us that eventually, someone would come for her and that she would know when the time came for her to leave us. Perhaps that time is at hand." None of the elves present looked pleased with that statement. Justan began to understand how much Gwyrtha meant to their people.

"But there is more. He also told me that we must not let her presence be known to any other wizards. He was afraid that they would want to study her and she would never be truly free. If you are going to the school, we cannot let you take her with you. She cannot leave us until you are ready to bring her with you."

Justan's heart sank. He had become excited to have Gwyrtha around and explore this new relationship. But the elder was right. After all, if Valtrek couldn't be trusted, how could he trust any of the other wizards in the school?

"Before you leave this wood, I must have a solemn promise from both of you that you will not mention Gwyrtha's existence to anyone until you have left the Mage School and Justan is able to take her with him."

Justan and Lenny both agreed without reservation.

With the major business done, one member of the council hesitantly stepped forward. "Justan, son of Faldon, may I examine your bow?"

"Penytri! This is not an appropriate thing to ask of a Jharro wielder!" the elder protested.

"No, it's alright. I'm not offended." He held out the bow to the elf.

Penytri ran his fingers lovingly over the carved wood. He

focused his attention on a small marking that Justan had not noticed before. The elf's jaw dropped.

"This was carved by Yntri Yni himself!" The other elves gasped. "And it has a dragon hair string! If I may ask, young human, how did you come to possess such an exquisite weapon?"

"It was a gift from a good friend," Justan explained, intrigued with the elves reactions.

"Truly a great friend he must have been. This must have cost a king's ransom. Yntri Yni is a master of weapons, but he does not carve one of Jharro wood for just anyone." Penytri beamed as he handed it back to Justan as if it was an honor just to have touched it.

Justan's heart skipped a beat. He was aware that the Jharro bow was a very precious gift, but he had not known just how special it was. How had Jhonate been able to get it made for him? How would she have come across the great amount of money necessary? A grin stole across his lips. One would not give such a gift to just any friend.

Lenny didn't understand. "What makes this bow so galldurn unique? I know it's got magic and ever'thin', but there's lots of bows like that."

Penytri explained, "This weapon was made from the wood of a Jharro tree. They only exist in the heart of the oldest elf homelands. They are ancient trees that have come to possess a certain intelligence. They are so full of life that no weapon or tool can harm them. One cannot simply cut a piece of wood from one of them. It must be given by the tree itself. There are but a few Jharro weapon makers in the known world. One must be truly in tune with the spirit of the forest to convince a Jharro tree to give of itself like this.

"The weapon that Justan wields has a tiny part of the life-force of thousands of elves within it. It is said that the spirits of those elves grant the weapon its power. These weapons were once so coveted by greedy humans, that people did terrible things to get them.

"To keep Jharro weapons from getting into the hands of those with ill intent, Yntri Yni gathered the Jharro weapon masters together. They decided not to make another Jharro weapon unless it was attuned to a single individual. You see, Justan's bow is attuned to him. To anyone else, it would be just a normal bow. There is no reason for someone to try to steal it."

Lenny's face lit up. "Now that's an idear! I can't believe I never thunk of that before. That would solve so many of my problems. Now how'd I go about doin' it?"

He pulled a sheet of parchment and a small piece of lead from a pouch on his belt. He took a small pair of round-lensed spectacles out of a pocket in his vest, put them on the bridge of his nose and began to jot down some notes. He noticed everyone staring at him and sputtered, "What? My eyes are fine. I only need em' fer readin'!"

That evening, they were treated to a large feast of succulent fruits and vegetables and tender meats. It was a meal unlike any Justan had eaten. Each bite of food brought rejuvenating energy. He could actually feel his wounds tingling as they healed.

Lenny made some of his famous pepper-bean stew. The elves were overjoyed to try it. They weren't able to stand the heat any more than Justan was, but they kept coming back for more. With the combination of dwarven food and drink, the elves were in fine spirits. They danced long after dark before leaving bent over, holding their stomachs.

In the morning, Justan and Lenny gathered their gear together. Their plan was to travel through the woods until they reached the river, follow it up to the bridge and cross into the city of Sampo.

Two of the elves, Antyni and Penytri, chose to accompany them to the bank of the river. The council allowed Gwyrtha to come along as well. Once they reached the river, she would have to come back and stay with the elves until Justan was ready to leave the Mage School.

It was a pleasant two days. Justan and the elves amused themselves with shooting contests and betting on which curse words Lenny would utter next. The dwarf seemed to have an unending supply of them and the elves soon gave up.

Justan spent as much time as possible with Gwyrtha during the journey, riding on her back much of the way. Their bond grew stronger every hour and Justan was able to pick up more thoughts and understand more about this marvelous creature.

Gwyrtha's attitude towards Lenny didn't change one bit. Even though the dwarf went out of his way to be kind to her, she was constantly tipping him over or rummaging through his things. Once she even stole Buster and ran around for quite a while with it in her mouth while the dwarf cursed and chased her about. To Justan's surprise, Lenny took it all in stride.

The time went by far too fast for Justan. Soon they arrived at the river. The elves took their leave with a smile and a bow. Even Lenny seemed sad to see them go. When Justan said goodbye to Gwyrtha, he wasn't sad. Justan didn't know how their bond would change with distance or time, but he knew that she would be there with him all the same.

It was strange to him, as he looked into her intelligent eyes. This beast should, in normal circumstances, frighten him with her very appearance. But this creature of nightmares had a noble heart. Justan scratched her behind the ears and was surprised to think that after all his years of single-minded solitude such an intimate bond would bring him comfort. When she left with the elves, he could feel that she didn't want to leave him, though she too seemed to understand that they weren't truly parting.

Lenny watched them go and scratched his head. "Well, son. You sure done lead a strange life." He clapped Justan on the shoulder. "It's time to get goin'. If we hurry, we'll reach Sampo by nightfall." They traveled along with Lenny doing most of the talking, telling Justan stories about the great Fandine River. The entire time they walked, Justan could feel Gwyrtha's warm presence in his mind.

Chapter Twenty Five

The Fandine River started out in the peaks of the Trafalgan Mountains, where Lenny claimed that it was mostly troll piss. The stream was fed by springs and melting snow along the way as it traveled for miles down the mountains until it reached the hills. There it meandered around, carving deep canyons as it went. By the time the river got to the city of Sampo, it was wide and deep, with swift currents that were too fast for a ferry system.

When the road to the Battle Academy was built, a long bridge was erected across the river. It was called the Sampo Bridge and it was wide enough for two wagons to pass each other. The city of Sampo was built on the west side of the bridge around the crossroads. To the north, was the capital city of Dremald and to the south was the Mage School.

They reached the bridge before the sun met the horizon on its downward path. The bridge was carved with intricate murals depicting trade and battles and river scenes. The bridge curved up and over the river. When they reached the highest point, Justan could see the city in all its splendor.

The place was huge, sprawling over several miles. It was the largest city Justan had ever seen. The streets were crawling with every race of people from human to gnome and was lined with every kind of building he could think of, from shacks to palaces.

"Lenny, how are we ever going to find the caravan in this place?" he asked.

"They said that they'd meet us at the Winkin' Maiden. It ain't the best place in town, but they have space fer someone to leave their wagons. You know that Valtrek ain't stayin' in the inn." Lenny continued down the slope of the bridge.

Justan realized something. "Lenny, one thing," Justan said

as he caught up to the dwarf. "Please don't say anything about Gwyrtha."

The dwarf scowled. "I heard what the elves said."

"I know, but you can't tell anyone. Not even Riveren or Zambon. The less people that know, the better."

"Alright, alright. Keep yer galldurn britches on. I won't say nothin'," Lenny replied and led Justan into the city.

The streets were bustling with people. Justan noticed that everyone was carrying a weapon openly. Lenny loosened the straps holding Buster on his back. He grabbed Justan's shirt and pulled him down so that he could whisper without being overheard.

"Look here, son. In this town there's a law that says ever'body's got to be carryin' some sort of weapon." Justan saw two old women haggling over some food. Both of them had large daggers strapped to their waists.

"Why would they want to do something like that?" Justan asked.

"It's done to stop crime, and it works too. At one time, this place was crookeder than a troll's teeth. But most thief's ain't willin' to risk their life fer a couple of coins. And now there's hardly ever any crime here. You just got to be careful 'cause sometimes accidents happen."

Justan gripped the hilt of one of his swords loosely and watched as everyone went by. Indeed there was a sort of carefree feeling. People showed their wealth openly here. One fancily dressed man walked by twirling a gold pocketwatch on a chain. No one would have dared to do that in Reneul. Sure they had great guards trained by the Battle School itself, but one still had to be careful.

"You know, I once thought about settin' up shop here," Lenny continued. "You'd think it'd be good business fer a smithy, but I found out that ever'body here's so gall-durn cheap that the good stuff just won't sell."

They turned down several streets until they reached a road lined with inns and pubs. The signs were garish and sometimes vulgar. Evidently some of the places sold more than just beds. Justan's face turned red with embarrassment. Here was another place that wouldn't have lasted long in Reneul. There were laws against that kind of thing there.

Lenny stopped and yanked his arm. "There she is!"

The Winking Maiden was a slightly dingy establishment with a sign out front that was painted with a smiling, scantily clad young lady holding out a foaming mug and winking exaggeratedly. Inside, the place was clean but a little rough around the edges.

It was a two-story building and the bottom floor was the common room. This served as both a pub and a restaurant. There were several tables filled with people, a bar and a serving area. An older woman who looked like she had been pretty in her younger days was on a small stage in the corner singing bawdy songs. The men were laughing and eating while a few barmaids served them. It was too early for anyone to be too drunk.

Justan was surprised to see that a wizard who was so staunch about his students drinking had decided to stay in this place. He was about to ask Lenny about it, but the dwarf was already at the bar ordering a plate of meat and a tankard of ale. Justan didn't know where to go until he heard an excited squeal coming from up the stairs. Vannya came running down and pulled him in for a quick hug.

"Justan, you're alive, I can't believe it! We were all pretty tense, but the Professor said that you were still okay. Wait until the others find out you're here." She grabbed his hand and pulled him up the stairs and down a hall. She reached a room and threw open the door. She dragged him inside to the open stares of all seven of the other mages who had taken the journey. Pympol dropped his cards on the floor. Evidently Vannya wasn't the only one who had thought him long gone.

"Look, everyone, the professor was right. He's here!"

Justan was surprised to see that most of them actually seemed pleased about the news except for Pympol, who mumbled as he picked up his cards. Everyone wanted to ask him questions about his adventure.

Justan chose his words carefully. He told them that he had an argument with the professor and took a walk to calm down. Then he told about how he got lost and his harrowing battle with the moonrats, but left out the part about Gwyrtha.

They were all delighted by his recounting of the tale and

very interested about his encounter with the elves. They all wanted to hear more, but Vannya saved him by telling the mages that she had to take him to see Professor Valtrek.

When they left the room, she stopped him with a questioning gaze. "You didn't tell the whole story in there, did you?"

Had he been that transparent? "Well, let's just say that when you deal with elves, there are just some things you can't talk about."

Vannya seemed to want to ask more, but Justan had given a reasonable excuse. Everyone knew that elves were very particular about their secrets. She led him out of the back of the inn to the place where the horses were stabled and the wagons were stored.

"How long have you been here waiting for me?" he asked

"Oh, we just arrived here yesterday. It hasn't been too long a wait, but everyone is ready to get back to the school." They walked around to the wizard's wagon.

"Here we are," Vannya said. "But before you talk to him, there are some things you should know. After you left, the Professor went crazy looking for you. He sent his spirit out of his body to search for you and that is a very risky thing to do. He did things differently after you left. He would come out every couple of hours to check to see if you had come back. After the dwarf volunteered to go after you, he told us to go ahead and travel through the forest in hope that you would catch up to us.

"Then one night, it got real creepy going through the dark forest. We could hear the moonrats going berserk. We were scared. They were hanging in the trees all around us, making that awful noise and staring at us with those glowing eyes and Professor Valtrek came out again. He cast a blanket of silence around the wagon so that we couldn't hear them, and then he brought us to the edge of the ward and gave us an anatomy lesson on the things." She saw that Justan wasn't impressed and frowned.

"Justan, he tried to comfort us! What I'm trying to say is that something you said made him change."

Justan just looked at her.

"And I'm supposed to love the man now?"

For some reason, his remark must have stung her, for she flinched.

"Look, I don't know what he did to you that makes you feel this way, but whatever it was, I am sure he regrets it. You should give him a chance to explain."

He didn't get it. Why was she defending the man?

"Hey, I'm sorry, but after what he did to me, it's going to be very hard for him to earn my trust again."

"Then what did he do?"

Justan looked at the wagon. "I can't explain now, Vannya, but I promise to tell you all about it later." She glared at him, spun away and stormed back into the inn.

Part of him felt like he should go after her, but whatever was bothering Vannya would have to wait. He stared at the wagon door, steeling himself for the likely confrontation. He stepped up the first step and knocked on the door. The rune glowed almost immediately and Justan spoke into it.

"Professor, it's Justan. I'm back."

After a moment, there was a response. The rune flared with each syllable the wizard spoke. "Please come in."

Justan gingerly grasped the knob of the door, half expecting to be shocked, but when he felt the cool metal and nothing happened, he opened the door. The wagon was as empty as the first time he had entered and it was brightly lit inside. As Justan shut the door behind him, the large silver mirror swirled with cloudiness and that familiar spicy-smelling mist poured out of it, filling the room.

The wizard's head poked out of the mist and he squeezed through the mirror into the room. As soon as he exited, the mirror shimmered and turned back into its normal reflective state. The mist dissipated into the air and was soon gone.

The man in the white robe took a seat on a nearby chair and gestured for Justan to sit on the bed. Valtrek sat calmly with his hands folded in his lap.

Justan was surprised by the wizard's demeanor. He had expected an outburst. He thought he would be yelled at and punished for the way he had left, and was willing to put up with it in order to reach his goals. He found himself sitting down on the bed as invited.

"Justan, I am glad to see that you made it out of the forest alive," Valtrek said. "I must begin by offering you an apology. I don't expect you to accept it, but all the same, I am sorry for what I did. I truly had no business interfering with your tests and I am aware that I put your friend's life in danger. If it were possible, I would apologize to her too."

This was far more than Justan had expected. Once again, the wizard was disarming him before the fight began. It irritated him that it was so hard to stay angry at the man.

"I appreciate your apology, but it doesn't make things right. I am still being forced into this situation against my will."

"I know. There is nothing that either of us can do about that now. You have this magic gift. If you don't learn to use it, the result could be a disaster. I must ask you to trust me-"

"Trust you?" Justan interrupted. "I don't think that's possible. You have already shown me that it is your own agenda that is most important to you, not mine. I have something that you want, that's what I think. You didn't sell the potion to Kenn for *my* sake."

The wizard ignored the young man's outburst and replied with a smooth tone, not letting the conversation get out of hand. "Whether you trust me or not, you have a decision to make. What are you going to do Justan?"

"I . . ." Justan wanted to shout at the man again, but Valtrek was so calm that his heart just wasn't in it. He sighed. "I have already made a decision. I am going to attend your school for the two years and be done with it."

"That is not the decision I was talking about, Justan. I had no doubt that you would attend. The question is what do you plan to do when you get to the school? Are you going to sit and bide your time until it is over and waste two years of your life?" Now there was passion coming into Valtrek's voice.

"No, I'll tell you exactly what I'm going to do. I'm going to go in there and do what I have to do in order to get this power under control. I am going to learn every drop of information I can. In fact, I will probably be the best student you have. And when these years are over, I will go back to the academy and be what I am meant to be. A warrior." Justan stood up. "Is there anything else you wish to know?"

The wizard chuckled wearily and shook his head. "I suppose I should have expected nothing less from the son of Faldon the Fierce. Very well, so you don't plan to trust me. I can live with that for now and so can you. Just know that there may come a time when you may have to trust me for both our sakes. When that time comes, please remember this. Though my actions were wrong, my intentions were pure." Valtrek stood to face Justan.

"Now go, get some sleep. We leave in the morning." Justan turned to leave and the wizard stopped him. "One more thing. Don't go running off again." He patted Justan on the shoulder. "It isn't worth it."

Justan stormed out and headed for the inn. He reached out to Gwyrtha through the bond. With days of travel between them, her thoughts seemed a bit muted, but Justan could still feel her presence in his heart. The man in the white robe didn't need to know how wrong he was. This time, running away had been well worth it indeed.

Justan re-entered the Winking Maiden and headed for the common room. He didn't feel like talking to the mages again at that moment. As he walked through the door, he saw Riveren and Zambon sitting by Lenny at a table. The dwarf was being quite loud and boisterous. He had three empty plates and four empty tankards in front of him.

"Justan!" The two guards shouted out, and gestured for him to sit down.

"It is great to see you alive!" Riveren exclaimed. "Lenny told us all about your amazing battle with the moonrats. You sure are lucky, my friend!" He gave an apologetic grin. "Hey, listen. We really wanted to go after you, but our contract states that we have to stay with the wagons."

"I understand." Justan assured him and looked at Lenny who was busy downing another drink. "Do you think it's wise to let him keep drinking like that? He's just going to keep getting louder until someone throws him out."

Zambon laughed. “You think we could stop him?”

Lenny put the tankard down and smiled mischievously at Justan through his mustache.

“Besides,” Riveren said. “He’s a dwarf. It’s going to take more than a half a dozen tankards of this weak stuff to get him drunk. I think he’s just being loud for show.”

Zambon laughed. “Riveren’s the one to know. He likes to do it so that he can get away with harassing the barmaids.”

“I have no idea what you’re talking about,” Riveren said as he pinched the behind of an attractive young woman who slid by. She twirled around and glared at him. He feigned innocence and pointed to Justan. The girl growled at Justan and stormed away.

The evening passed by in such a fashion, and indeed the dwarf did get louder, but not enough to get them thrown out. Justan stayed a little later than he should have because he knew that Lenny would leave in the morning and the guards would go their separate ways at the Mage School.

It was late when he finally trudged up the stairs to the room that he and Lenny were to share. Even though the bed was lumpy, it was the first bed he had slept in since leaving the Training School. It felt so good that he was asleep almost instantly. He didn’t even hear Lenny come in until the dwarf shook him awake.

“Wha . . .?” Justan croaked, squinting his eyes against the light of the candles the dwarf had lit.

“Wake up, son. I’m takin’ my leave,” the dwarf pronounced. He dragged a chair over to the bed so that he could talk to Justan face-to-face.

Justan sat up and rubbed his eyes. He had hoped that this moment could be delayed. Other than Jhonate, Lenny had become the best friend he had. “Why must you leave now? Why not come along with us? Surely there is some business for you at the Mage School. It would be helpful to have a face there I could trust.”

The dwarf sighed. “Sorry, boy. I done been away from my own forge far too long. The orders are probly pilin’ up and my durn fool apprentice nephew just don’t quite got the touch yet.”

“I’m sad to see you go.”

“Please, son. Don’t go all teary on me. This is just somethin’ that has to be. ‘Sides, knowin’ you, it won’t take long fer you to find somebody else to trust." Lenny reached out and dragged his pack over to his chair. Evidently he had retrieved it from the wagon. It was bulging with the precious magical ore he had brought.

"Look, before we left Wobble, I grabbed somethin'." The dwarf turned and rummaged through the pack. He pulled out a velvet-covered bundle. "My brother had started makin' this for a strange old man who come into town. But weeks went by and the man never come back in with a deposit so he didn't finish it. I was bored when I first got there and the shipment of my ore was delayed, so I finished it."

He unwrapped the velvet package and inside Justan saw a dagger in an ornate sheath. The dwarf handed it to Justan. "I figgered I could sell it to one of them mages in the caravan, but I couldn't get myself to part with it."

Justan turned it over. The handle was unusually wide and carved of some kind of bone that was inlaid with silver etchings. The sheath was also much wider than with a normal dagger, and made with a mix of silver and some other metal that Justan couldn't place. It was so well polished that it gleamed in the candlelight. "Wow, Lenny, I don't know what to say."

"Go ahead, boy. Pull it," prodded the dwarf.

Justan whistled. He had never seen its like. It had two blades coming out of the hilt so that it almost looked like one wide blade that had been split down the middle. One blade was a simple carving blade with a wicked edge, while the other one had a jagged edge that looked like a saw blade. Justan hefted it and found that it was exquisitely crafted with perfect balance and it was made of the same metal that the sheath was. "What is it for?" Justan asked.

"The old man that brung the drawin's to Chugk said it was a ceremonial dagger. I don't know. I've made lots of them kinds of daggers and ain't never seen one like this. But I figger you might be able to use it. At the very least you'll make the other cadets greener than a week old steak."

"Lenny is this magic?" Justan asked.

His friend smiled. "It don't got any magic in it yet. The stranger that brought the drawin's fer the dagger also brought some unique ore that has the potential and Chugk mixed it with silver.

When I finished it up with Buster, I used the right process; so it's set up with the correct pathways to be magicked. Maybe you'll learn how to charge it up some day. Who knows?"

Justan found a lump in his throat.

"It is a fine gift, Lenny. Thank you." He reached into his shirt pocket. "Last time I left a friend I was unprepared." He pulled out a bowstring necklace that was threaded with several sharp teeth. He had put it together as they traveled with the elves in the forest.

"Moonrat teeth. I pulled them out of my boot heel. I figured it would give you a start to your collection so that you can one day match your brother." He handed it over to the dwarf. "Oh, and here's another one I found stuck in one of my pouches. Maybe Chuck can use it."

Lenny solemnly tied the string around his neck. "My brother always did start the dag-blamed trends."

They sat there for a moment in silence. Neither one knew what to say. Then Lenny pulled his stuff together and stood to leave.

"Now listen, son. When you get out of that durn school and yer ready to make yer own name, come see me in Dremald. I'll make you some swords that sing!"

"Yeah, if I ever do get out of there. I really don't know what's going to happen. Maybe a warrior is not what I'm meant to be," Justan said. With Lenny's departure it seemed like everything was crashing in.

"What in the cowpickin' dust are you talkin' 'bout? Let me tell you somethin' and you listen good. I been watchin' you and you got the warrior blood. I seen you fightin' them moonrats in a situation that would have had most men crappin' their britches, but you kept a level head. That's the true mettle of a warrior and don't you forget it. If you don't come to me fer them swords in a few years, I'll be comin' after you with Buster! You hear me?"

Justan smiled. "Yes sir." He saluted.

The dwarf nodded. "That's right."

Then he left. As Justan sat alone in the dark, turning the dwarf's gift over in his hands, his world seemed a little emptier.

Chapter Twenty Six

Fist fled his tribe's territory, his mind in chaos. The vision of his father's swollen face as he lay beaten nearly to death, echoed in his thoughts. His father's visage mouthed one word over and over again. "Toompa."

The events of the day had started out so well with his marvelous hunt. When he had come home to see the folly of the war his father was about to lead the tribe into, he had done what he had felt was necessary for the good of his people. His good intentions had degenerated into a huge mess.

Now he was out in the wilderness, truly alone for the first time in his life. And he was scared. The fact that he was afraid was humiliating to the ogre who had become the strongest warrior in his tribe.

He had been so sure that he was right. Joining the tribe with their bitterest enemies in a war against the smaller races didn't make sense to him. But now he was an outcast. A rogue ogre. Fist had been brought up to despise ogres like that. An ogre was only cast out if he was bad for the tribe, and an ogre that was bad for his tribe was of no worth to anyone.

Fist blindly ran along unfamiliar mountain trails. Eventually as the night deepened, Fist collapsed with exhaustion under a stunted tree and slept. This was not a smart thing for him to do in this harsh place, but he was lucky and the morning dawned without incident. When Fist awoke, his body was sore and his head ached from the beating his father had given him.

He slowly sat up. He didn't know what to do. Fist leaned back against the tree, put his head in his hands, and cried. This was the low point of his life. Here he was, a grown ogre crying and alone. When he was a child, his father had beaten him when he cried. His life might as well be over. He felt like dying.

Fist's self pity was interrupted by a mocking, chattering sound. He looked up to see a rock squirrel on the ground nearby. The creature had gray fur, large eyes, and a big bushy tail. It stood there watching him and chattering madly, almost as if laughing at him.

Fist was outraged that any creature had seen him in such a pitiful state. He leaned forward and unleashed his rage in a mighty roar. The wind from his breath ruffled the tiny creature's fur, but it didn't run away. The squirrel cocked its head and chattered at him again.

Fist snarled and rose to his full height, towering over the creature. As he stood, he cracked his head on a branch overhead and a scattering of seeds fell to the ground. Fist reached up to rub his head and watched as the little creature ran about his feet without fear, gathering up the seeds and stuffing them into its cheeks.

Fist raised his foot and considered stomping on the creature. How dare it not be afraid of him? He was an ogre, a big one too. It just looked up at the heavy foot hovering over its head and calmly gnawed on a seed.

Fist grunted in frustration, but instead of flattening it like it deserved, he found himself reaching into one of the seed laden branches and pilling a handful loose. He was getting hungry. Out of curiosity, he poured some of the tiny seeds into his mouth and chewed. Instantly his mouth was filled with a vile, bitter powder that seemed to suck the moisture from his mouth. He coughed and hacked and spit the nasty things out.

Fist looked back at the squirrel again tempted to squash it, but instead he reached down and poured the rest of the seeds beside the little thing. The squirrel looked up and chattered at him questioningly. The amount of seeds left by the ogre's huge hand made quite a large pile from a squirrel's perspective.

As the little creature went to stuffing its cheeks, Fist sighed and pondered his situation. He did not know where he should go. He knew the mountain land to the north because his tribe had been in so many battles up there. Fist grimaced. The north was full of other ogre tribes. His instincts told him to head that way, but Fist couldn't make himself do it. He didn't want to spend the rest of his life going from tribe to tribe begging for acceptance.

If a tribe ever took a rogue ogre in, that ogre had no prestige. He was even below the women. This meant that he started out as the grunt, the laborer. Even the children would make him do chores. For proud Fist, this was not an option. No, there was nothing for him to the north.

So what was left? There were jagged cliffs to the west and troll country to the east. The southern stretch of the mountains was unknown to him. He didn't know what to expect there, but where else would he go? Fist decided to head south. He would either find a way to make a life without his tribe, or he would die. At that moment, he really didn't care which.

The chatter of the little gray rock squirrel accompanied Fist as he began his journey south. It followed him, scampering around the rocks. Every once in a while Fist would turn to it and growl, but the thing would just cock its head at him with its cheeks stuffed with seeds and chatter at him questioningly.

Fist finally just ignored the little creature and continued his journey. He knew which direction he was headed, but didn't know what he was looking for. As he hiked along the rugged trail, a swift wind chilled his skin. He had fled from his tribe so quickly, that he had left his prized skins behind. The only clothing he wore was his fur boots and waist wraps. The higher in the mountains he went, the colder it became.

When night fell, Fist knew that he would have to find a good kill soon, but he was exhausted and decided it would have to wait until morning. He found a crevice where he was shielded from the wind, curled into a tight ball, and fell asleep.

Fist awoke the next morning cold everywhere but a small spot on his chest where there was a pocket of warmth. The warmth came from a bundle of fur that was snuggled up against him. He looked at the sleeping squirrel with irritation. Why wouldn't it leave him alone? He picked it up by its tail, startling it awake, and tossed it to the side. It landed on all fours a few feet away and scolded him for waking it up.

"Go away!" Fist growled at it.

When Fist sat up, a small pile of seeds fell out of his armpit. The ogre snarled at the squirrel in aggravation as he brushed any remaining seeds out of his hair. He stood up and stretched. The morning air was cold and dry. It chilled him to the bone and he was reminded that he needed to find some good fur right away. As he started walking he kept an eye out for game, but mostly he was looking for something he could use as a weapon.

The thunder people had fought goblins on many occasions and though the creatures were weak and small, they used much more sophisticated weapons. Fist had kept a few of those weapons and examined them, trying to figure out how to make them for an ogre. However, in his tribe, Fist's ideas had always been stifled. The others had thought his innovations untraditional. An ogre did not carry any weapon but a club or rock.

Now he was free to pursue his ideas. Fist found a tree with a promising branch that he broke off to use as a handle. Then he reached behind his waist to pull something from his waist wraps. It was his secret treasure. He infolded the leather bundle to reveal a goblin dagger.

A year before his tribe had attacked a nearby goblin clan in order to expand their territory borders. Fist had killed ten of the little things himself and after the fight, he had pulled this dagger out of his thigh and decided to keep it. Over that year, he experimented with it when he was able to find a place alone and found its sharpness and durability useful.

Fist used the dagger to shave the bark off of the branch and shape it into something easy to grasp. Then he found a suitable shaped rock and threw it on the ground, breaking it in two. He cut some leather strips off of his waist furs and used them to strap the rock halves to the end of his branch. It took several tries for him to figure out how to tie it right so that the rock wouldn't fall off of the end.

He hefted the weapon. The weight felt good in his hands. He was proud of himself. In just two days away from his tribe he had already began his new life by creating something new. Now it was time to hunt.

He walked for a few miles and found a little stream of water. Fist bent to drink and his reflection caught his eye. For a brief moment, he was disgusted and horrified by his appearance. His hairy face, wide mouth, and big nose looked alien to him. It was like that face didn't belong.

Fist slammed one hand into the water, destroying the reflection. He leaned back, his heart beating madly. Slowly, the feeling passed. He leaned forward again. His reflection hadn't changed, but it looked familiar again. Fist shrugged off his unease and drank thirstily, feeling very unogrelike.

The squirrel came to the stream beside him and drank. Out of irritation, Fist reached out one finger and pushed it in. The creature swam out on the other side of the stream, shook itself dry, and scolded him mercilessly with its chatter, pointing one tiny accusing paw.

Fist continued on his way. Around the bend, he came upon a small cave. He ducked behind an outcropping of rock and peered around the edge. By the scattered bones and the wisp of webbing around the cave, he knew that it was the lair of a giant spider. Fist examined the area to make sure that there were no other dangers and considered attacking the arachnid.

Giant spiders were very hairy and if they were properly skinned, an ogre could make a good wrap to protect himself from the cold. The skin on its legs also made great leather straps. Fist licked his lips. He hadn’t eaten in over two days and was quite hungry. He remembered with fondness, the last time he had eaten giant spider.

Such a spider had killed one of the women in his tribe when it had come out of its hiding place in the Thunder People’s great tribal hall. The goblins that lived there before the ogres drove them out had worshipped the thing as a god and made sacrifices to it. When the Thunder People had been there for a month, the spider struck out in anger because it had not been fed. Fist had enjoyed the sweet meat that came from its legs.

This made his mind up for him; he needed this kill. Fist thought for a moment. The first thing he needed to do was lure the thing out of its cave. He looked around for the squirrel, but it was nowhere in sight. Perhaps it had finally decided to leave him alone. He would have to be the bait.

Fist lifted a small boulder from the rocky ground and kept it in the crook of his left arm. Then he hefted his new weapon in his right. He walked down and stood at the entrance of the cave, steeling himself for the strike, but nothing happened. He waited a few moments. Just as he was thinking about going into the cave after it, the spider attacked.

The small size of the cave was deceptive, for when the spider squeezed out its hairy bulk, it was three times the size that Fist had expected. It leapt at him so fast that Fist barely had time to bring the boulder up before its poisonous fangs were upon him.

He shoved the boulder into its maw so that the fang-tipped front jaws couldn't reach him. This must have been a female giant spider because it was much larger than the one his tribe had killed. Fist was having second thoughts about this course of action, but it was too late to change his mind now.

The spider grabbed at him with its front legs. Fist swung his new stone mace at its head. The weapon struck one of its many eyes, bursting it. The spider jerked back and released the boulder from its mouth. Now Fist was really in trouble.

The spider leapt forward and clutched him with its front legs, pulling him in so that its fangs could reach him. In desperation, Fist dropped his weapon and grabbed the spider's jaws just above the fangs. It took nearly all of his considerable strength to keep them from piercing his skin.

The spider drove him to the ground, trying to sink its fangs in. Fist squeezed with his mighty hands until venom squirted from the fangs. He felt it spatter on his legs.

Though he hadn't been concerned about living earlier in the day, he had no desire to be eaten by a spider now. He pulled the jaws apart with all his might. The ogre strained until his face turned red and his muscles bulged to the breaking point.

With a pop, one of the fang tipped appendages ripped free of the spider's jaws. Venom and fluids poured out of the hole where it had been. The spider hissed in pain and pulled away from him, but Fist held on to the remaining fang and refused to let go. He punched the joining point of the fang and jaw over and over again.

The spider reared back, lifting Fist off of the ground and slammed him down onto his back again. It pushed forward with all its weight, trying to pierce his skin with the remaining fang. Fist now grasped the fang with both hands. He held the spider back far enough that he could get one leg up. He pressed his foot against the spider's jaw and pulled until the second fang ripped free.

The spider was now without a form of attack. It pulled back and turned around, trying to escape to its cave. Fist leapt forward and grabbed it by the back legs. He wasn't going to let the creature get away now. The spider hissed madly.

With one spider leg in each hand, Fist put a foot up on its abdomen. He pulled and pulled until with another popping sound the legs came off. It tried to drag itself away, but Fist grabbed his stone mace from the ground and tackled the thing. He bashed its head repeatedly, bursting eyes and cracking chitin. The spider thrashed around until its head was nothing but a slimy ruin.

Fist stood above his kill breathing heavily and gave a prayer to the spirit of the spider in thanks for this source of food. He heard a familiar chattering sound and turned to see the rock squirrel sitting nearby calmly chewing on a seed. Fist sighed. If the thing wasn't going to leave now with the body of a giant spider nearby, he supposed that it was going to stick with him for good. To his surprise, the idea didn't bother him as much as it had the day before.

Now he had to find some wood so that he could start a fire to cook his meal. The rock squirrel followed him and chattered, and Fist found himself talking back. He told it about how to make a fire and which wood was the best to use. It felt good to talk to something. Ogres weren't the most vocal race, but it made him feel like he wasn't so alone.

He told the little creature all of the things about his tribe that had so frustrated him. Fist couldn't think of an appropriate name to call the creature so he just called it "Squirrel". He found a small dead tree a short distance away. With a bit of twisting and pulling, he was able to pull it free of the rocky ground.

As he headed back to the spider's cave, he told the squirrel what had happened to drive him out away from his people. Squirrel scampered along beside him, pausing every so often in the way that squirrels do. There was no way that the creature could have understood, but that wasn't important. It was a relief to share that burden, but it was also a depressing reminder of his current state.

When he neared the cave, Fist saw a trail of slime leading toward the place where he had left the spider's carcass.

"Trolls!" he growled.

Fist rushed up the trail to find two of the foul beasts tearing into the abdomen of the spider he had killed. He eyed the two trolls with open hatred. After all of his hard work, he was not about to let these things take his food away.

Trolls were a bastard race. Among the scholars their origins were constantly debated. Some said that they were one of the giant races, as evidenced by their height and strength. Others said that they were a goblin hybrid with their sharp, nasty teeth and long dirty claws. Not much was really known about their origins for no one had ever actually seen a troll child. The only thing agreed upon was that they are unpleasant.

The average troll was between seven to ten feet tall and covered in a grey skin that excreted a foul slimy substance that dripped behind them wherever they went. Their arms were long and lanky and ended in hands tipped with sharp claws. Their heads were hideous with beady red eyes, a mop of dirty hair and a mouth full of rows of jagged teeth.

Trolls were scavengers more than hunters. A troll's intelligence was so low that they weren't motivated by thoughts or even instincts, just urges, mostly hunger. They would eat almost anything.

For centuries the humans called them ghouls for the way that they sometimes robbed graves for a meal. But the thing that made them most feared and despised was the fact that they were so hard to kill. Trolls regenerated, and they did it with alarming speed. Many a landowner had thought he had killed a troll just to have it come back again. The only way to completely make sure that a troll was dead was to burn it. The slimy substance that their skin excreted was flammable and they went up like torches.

Unfortunately, Fist had no fire with him. He had always hated the slimy things. They were mean and nasty and had no respect for an ogre's territory. One of the biggest problems his tribe had to deal with was destroying the trolls that constantly invaded their territory. He picked up a medium sized boulder.

These trolls were so preoccupied with their meal, they didn't notice Fist's presence until the boulder struck one of them in the leg, breaking it and pinning the beast to the ground. The other one immediately turned and attacked.

Fist met the thing head on with a mighty swing of his rock mace. The weapon smashed into the troll's face, sending teeth and slime flying. Even with its broken jaw and face, the troll continued its attack. It slashed out with its wicked claws and sliced at Fist's arm. The claws made long deep furrows in his skin. Fist howled. He kicked the beast away and followed through with another devastating blow of his weapon that crushed the troll's skull and snapped its neck. The beast fell to the ground and flailed about.

Fist readied himself to strike again, but the other troll tore its crushed leg free from the boulder. It scampered along the ground and leapt onto the ogre's back. The troll bit deep into Fist's shoulder and began clawing at his chest from behind. Fist roared and dropped his weapon.

He reached back and grabbed the thing's head with both of his hands and squeezed with all of the strength he could muster. The troll's head was so slippery that it was hard for Fist to grasp. It howled and continued to bite down on his shoulder and rake his skin with its slimy claws. He grunted with the pain of the beast's attacks and pushed his thumbs into its eyes until they popped with a rush of fluid. Still it continued thrashing at him. The troll's hunger was so absolute that the pain didn't even register. What was important was the food. It would heal later.

Fist was beginning to panic, his wounds were deep and trolls were so filthy that the wounds they left would become infected. He pushed his thumbs in deeper and deeper and squeezed with his powerful fingers until with a crack, the troll's head came open. Now its thrashing was uncontrolled. Fist pulled the beast off of his back and threw it to the ground. The other troll was starting to move again and he stomped on its head until it stopped.

Fist dragged the trolls a short ways away from the remains of the spider and pulled them into a pile with the small tree he had uprooted. He knew that he needed to work quickly before they recovered enough to strike back at him. Ignoring the pain from his injuries, he pulled two small black stones from within his waist wrappings. Fist furiously struck them together until sparks started to fall into the pile of wood and trolls. Finally, a spark hit one of the slimy creatures and its skin was rapidly engulfed with flame.

Soon both trolls were ablaze and their bodies thrashed about again. The weight of the tree held the bodies down and Fist had to stand back because of the heat of the fire. He groaned. Blood was dripping from his many cuts and abrasions and he was covered in troll slime.

Fist walked over to his hard won kill and examined what was left. Luckily the trolls, who were no connoisseurs, had only eaten the bulbous abdomen of the spider, which was the only part Fist had not intended to eat. He pulled out his goblin dagger and began to skin the remains of the spider.

Giant spiders had a thick furry skin over their chitinous skeleton and this was what Fist intended to make his winter wrap out of. The trolls had damaged some of it, but since the spider was so much bigger than he had expected, Fist had plenty to work with. As he peeled the skin from his prize, he felt a flush of heat come over him and knew that his wounds were going bad quick.

Normally an ogre his size could take a hit from a troll and not even be fazed. But the sheer amount of cuts and the fact that Fist had not eaten in two days led to a fierce fever. Squirrel appeared again and sat next to him as he worked, chattering in a concerned manner.

Fist laughed. He had a new tribe now, composed of an ogre and a squirrel. He would call it “The Big and Little People”.

Fist chuckled as he completed the skinning of the animal and pulled the spider’s legs over to the fire to toss them into the coals. The chitinous shell would protect the meat from burning while in the coals. The flesh of a spider was slimy in consistency and was nasty to eat raw. While cooking, the meat firmed up. The end result was quite tasty.

While the spider legs were cooking, Fist scraped the inside of the skins clean and laid them out to dry. His fever was getting stronger and he was weakening. Fist instinctively knew that to fight off the infection, he needed to eat and give his body some energy.

He pulled the legs out of the coals to let them cool for a moment. His shoulder ached, and his other scrapes and cuts burned like fire. He didn’t know anything about healing herbs or how to best cleanse his wounds. These were things that an ogre warrior never learned about. The women did that.

Normally after battle, a wounded ogre would go to the

women to be massaged and tended and have their wounds treated. He had no experience with anything but the most rudimentary of healing techniques. He pulled a couple of troll teeth out of his shoulder and threw them into the fire. The skin was swollen and red around the punctures, but the bleeding had stopped.

"Do you know how to fix me Squirrel?" he asked. His little friend cocked its head and pulled a seed out of its cheek to eat. Fist would have to depend on the strength of his body to pull him through.

Fist cracked open the charred shell of the spider legs segment by segment and pulled the sweet steaming meat out. He devoured it hungrily. The legs were so large that after eating half of them, he was completely stuffed. Fist popped the remaining segments apart and placed them on top of one of the dried sections of spider skin to save for a later meal.

By this time, it was nearly dark and the wind was picking up. The cold felt good on his hot forehead, but his body was chilled and he knew that he had to shelter himself soon. The squirrel chattered at him from the entrance to the small spider cave. Fist picked up the spider pelts and stumbled over to the cave. He crept inside, pushing away the piles of bones that littered the place. His fever had grown so hot that he knew that he wouldn't be able to tend the fire. Even though they had not completely dried, he pulled the spider furs over him and shivered.

The contamination from the troll scratches moved through his system and as his body fought against the intruders, Fist became delirious. As the night wore on, he began shouting out to his father and vowing to kill Tralg. He tossed and turned and moaned. Through it all, the rock squirrel stayed by his side.

When the fever reached its peak, the contaminations in his body were winning the fight. Fist grew very still and dreamed. The squirrel curled up on his chest and watched over him.

Ever since fleeing from his tribe, Fist had been battling an inner war about his future. Part of him did not want to continue on. Now at the height of his fever, he had to make a choice. It would be so easy to give up. Then he wouldn't have to face the great world alone. Another part of him was hungry for change. It was a part that had long been pushed down by the traditions and lifestyle of his people. This part wanted to leap into his new existence and make a life for himself where he wouldn't be held back by others, but grow and become something . . . new.

The comforting feeling of his new friend lying on his chest was the final piece that made him decide. He had already started on the path to a new existence. Though unconscious, he pushed his body to fight back and win.

Fist lived.

*   *   *

"Where is the artifact, my dear? Where is the mirror I wanted?" Ewzad Vriil asked, communicating with her for the first time in over a week.

"*I could have told you long ago, if you had just kept my treasure with you, as I have requested!*"

"Enough, enough. Where is it, dear?" Ewzad was not in the mood for insolence. She would have to disappoint him.

"*Well . . . The goblins failed us, Master,*" the female voice said. Oh how she had hoped he would forget about the caravan.

"Blast! Those goblins are worthless little beasts, aren't they?" Ewzad fumed "Yes, yes they are."

"*The academy guards were well trained and they had some help, Master. The goblin tribe had but few survivors.*"

"Hmph! Of course they couldn't succeed. Why, oh why did I let you take control of the mission? It is a good thing we sent Marckus. He has never failed me, no-no."

Ewzad was testing her. While he held the eye of her child, she had partial access to his mind and could tell that he didn't think she had followed his instructions. Of course she hadn't. Why send an orc that so willfully resisted her commands?

"*Unfortunately we suffered a much worse setback than the loss of a goblin tribe,*" she said.

"Oh, is that so? And what was it, my dear?" The wizard's anger was stirring.

"*While the caravan was passing through the protected road, my sweet children were attacked by an unknown force.*" In truth, she had recognized the man and the dwarf from the caravan immediately. They were now on her revenge list. The rogue horse and the elves had been an annoyance for years. *"We were caught by surprise and half of my poor babies were murdered!"*

"Half? Half of your moonrats destroyed? Oh my! How could you be so careless? Make more! Make more then! I need them ready when my army marches. I-," Ewzad stopped as he made a realization. "Wait, are you telling me that Marckus did not attack the caravan?"

"They came so close to me, right at my doorstep. If only they had been a bit closer and my babies hadn't all been chasing them, I could have reached out and crushed them myself . . ."

"Answer me! Where is Marckus, dear thing?" Ewzad's rage was barely restrained. She sensed the arrival of the painful headache that accompanied his tantrums and took pleasure from it.

"He is in the area, but even if I tell him that they are coming now, he won't have time to set up a proper ambush."

"Why, why . . . How dare you not send the orc as I commanded?" His head was pounding now. "The Dark Voice promised your fealty and he has given me ways, oh yes, ways to ensure it. Send Marckus now! It is time you stopped acting like a foolish woman, don't you think?" Ewzad paused a moment, before adding something he knew would anger her. "Ah, well that is if you really are female. Hmm, sometimes I wonder if you are not simply a twisted thing that pretends to be a woman. Oh yes-yes, quite an interesting theory, don't you think?"

"Perhaps one day you will get to meet me and see just how much of a woman I am, oh Master," she crooned, sending as much allure and sensuality as she could through their limited connection. It was enough to give him the image she wanted him to see. She sensed Ewzad's irritation at his body's response and her mood lightened a bit.

"Just send Marckus!" Ewzad shouted as their connection ended.

She knew that he had thrown her precious gift across the room of his foul little study. She could feel it impact against the wall. The fool! A snarl ripped through her mind. He was lucky the treasure was undamaged. If he had broken it, she would have found a way to make him pay, perhaps rip out his mind and make him dance like a puppet. She considered doing so anyway, but she knew the Dark Voice wouldn't allow it.

Instead, she sighed and contacted the orc as she had been commanded.

Chapter Twenty Seven

Justan dreamt that he was alone in the lightless bowels of the Dark Forest. It was the foulest part, where the ground was covered in a sticky substance and the air was so fetid that it was hard to breathe. He trudged slowly through the dead leaves and noxious slime until his feet were stuck. Justan tugged and tugged, but they would not come free. He sensed something approaching behind him. Panic rose in his throat. The world slowed down. Then he heard the chittering moan of a moonrat.

Justan leapt out of bed and swung his fist around, clipping a surprised Pympol on the head. The bony man was knocked to the ground

"Oww!" the mage complained. He glared up at Justan from the floor, holding the side of his head.

Arcon, who had been standing in the doorway, laughed. "I told you not to wake him up with your moonrat impersonation."

"Shut up! It's not funny," Pympol snarled. He turned over and rose shakily to his feet. Justan had hit him right beside the eye. It was already red and starting to swell.

Justan yawned and sat back down on the bed. He wasn't amused. He didn't get much sleep after Lenny left and was still very tired. The mage had deserved what he'd got.

"He's right, Pympol. You're lucky I didn't have a sword or knife with me." Pympol frowned and shot him a glare, still massaging his sore head. Justan didn't feel like looking at the man any longer. He turned to Arcon. "What's going on?"

"We're getting ready to leave. The caravan is waiting outside and Vannya asked me to come up and get you," Arcon explained. "Also, Pympol and I heard that you were wounded by moonrats and those types of wounds can get infected. We were wondering if you would let us check your bandages."

Justan looked at him curiously. Arcon was quick to add, "The elves use different healing techniques than we do and it would be an interesting exercise to see how they tended the wounds."

Justan shrugged. He was pretty sure that all of his minor wounds had been healed by the time he got to the city. The Elven food and salves seemed to have worked wonders. He sat patiently while the two wizards unwrapped the bandages on his arms and back, all of his scratches and bruises were completely healed and it didn't give them anything to study. Justan put his hand up to his ear to find that it was completely healed as well.

The mages muttered as they realized that there wasn't going to be much to learn from. The only truly serious wound had been the one in his calf, but he had been walking on it with only a little stiffness. When Arcon unwrapped the bandage on that leg, they began whispering excitedly. There were some healing herbs still tucked into the wrappings.

Justan flexed the leg. There was a pink scar where he had been bitten, but there wasn't any soreness left in it. Even though the mages could have healed him faster, the fact that he was as good as new in three days was amazing. He let the mages keep the herbs and bandages and asked them to leave so that he could get ready.

It didn't take Justan very long to put his things together. He never had the chance to unpack in the first place. He was a little frustrated that he didn't have the time to take a bath, though. The elves had somehow cleaned his wounds when he first arrived with them, but it had been two weeks since he had been able to sit and soak in a hot tub of water. Hopefully there would be ample opportunity for such things at the Mage School. He quickly washed as best as he could in the washbasin and changed into his cleanest set of clothes.

As he began to strap his pouches on, he debated whether or not to wear his swords into the school. He was entering a new chapter in his life, and he had a feeling that such weapons would not be looked upon with approval there. It didn't matter. He wanted to enter that school as the warrior he was. He wasn't going to change that just for them.

After belting his swords on, he turned the silver inlaid dagger that Lenny had given him over in his hands. He really didn't know what to do with it. It was an obviously expensive item that would get people wondering about him if they saw it. Justan considered strapping it on under his jacket, but changed his mind. He would wear the dagger proudly. It was a gift from his friend. It didn't feel right to hide such a thing. Besides, an extra weapon would just make people think all the more.

He strapped on the dagger and restrung his bow with a regular string instead of the golden one. That string was a little too dangerous to wear just for looks. He tucked the golden string into one of his belt pouches.

Justan examined himself in the room's only mirror and decided he liked the look. Armed to the teeth. It would be a reminder to the wizards and the rest of the students that he was the one in control of his life.

He hurried down the stairs and joined the rest of the caravan just as they were about to leave. The caravan would reach the school by late afternoon and the students were a little surprised to see Justan come out of the inn wearing full warrior regalia. Riveren just smiled.

The caravan traveled out of the main gate. From his perch on the back of the last wagon Justan watched the magnificent city of Sampo fade over the horizon. It reminded him of when he had sat in this same spot and watched Reneul fade away. He wondered what Jhonate was doing. Did she miss him?

After a little while Vannya came out of the wagon and sat beside him.

"Hey," she said.

"Hello, Vannya." Justan leaned back against the wooden door of the wagon. Seeing her didn't help him sort out his feelings about Jhonate.

"Justan, I'm sorry about last night. You have the right to feel however you want to about the professor."

He sighed. "Do you really want to know why I feel this way about him? Because it might change your feelings about him if you do." She nodded. Justan told her about his life at the

Training School, how hard he had worked, and how Valtrek had sabotaged him to force him to go to the Mage School.

Vannya winced as he told her of how the wizard had lobbied against his being able to enter the academy. Her jaw dropped when he told her what Kenn had done with the potion Valtrek gave him and what he had tried to do to Jhonate.

"I can't believe he . . . I-I guess I don't blame you for how you feel." Justan nodded in satisfaction. She continued, "So what do you think would have happened if he hadn't sold the potion to that . . . that guy?"

"Chances are that if Kenn hadn't kept me from competing in that test, I would have scored highly and the council would have had no choice but to let me enter the academy." Justan stated. However he had to admit, "But then again, who knows? They might have still made me go."

"What if they had given you a choice?"

"What?"

"What if they had brought you in and let Professor Valtrek make his case? With the knowledge that this power of yours could be dangerous, would you have made the decision to go to the Mage School voluntarily?"

Justan thought on it a moment. "Probably not. At least not at first. Maybe after some thought and discussing it with my family . . . The point is that I'll never know. I didn't get the chance. Valtrek took that choice away from me."

Vannya sighed and put her head in her hands. She looked at him through her fingers. "I'm sorry about what happened. I understand how you feel now. How are you supposed to trust him if he doesn't trust you?" She grasped his forearm. "That is one thing you always need to remember about wizards, Justan. They become so used to knowing more than everyone else, that they start to believe they are the only ones that can do anything right. It's one of the things that irritate me about being a mage. The wizards feel like they have to hold your hand the whole way!"

Justan was looking at her with one eyebrow raised. "Sounds like a fun place I'm going to." She smiled in response. His eyes brightened. "How about we don't go there at all?"

She lifted her head up out of her hands and looked at him

questioningly. "What do you mean?"

He continued with a completely straight face. "What do you say we jump off this wagon and run off together?" She looked at him wide-eyed. He couldn't help but smile. "We could spend our whole lives out in the wilderness. Think of it. You, me, a couple of kids . . ."

Vannya laughed and punched him in the arm.

"Well I'm insulted." He pouted exaggeratedly.

"Be serious for a moment," Vannya said. "There are some things to watch out for while at the Mage School, like the politics of the place. It's good not to step on anyone's toes. This is important for a cadet especially. If you make the wrong wizard mad, you may find yourself given extra kitchen duty. Believe me. Scrubbing pots all day is no fun."

It all sounded childish to Justan at first, but when he thought about it, that was what it was like at the academy too. Except it was more likely you'd get stuck digging ditches than scrubbing pots.

"Is there a good side to this place?" he asked.

"Of course, Justan!" She became animated, waving her hands as she spoke, "Just wait until you see it. The best of science and technology are represented at the Mage School. Especially in the Rune Tower. Everything there is magnificent! Our library is the biggest in the known world. If there is anything you want to know, you can find it there."

"Hmm." The idea of all that knowledge just waiting there for him did sound intriguing. "But what do I do when I get there? I really don't know what to expect."

"Well you haven't exactly been going out of your way to find out, have you?" Vannya admonished.

Justan had to admit that she was right. He had been so interested in getting past his time at the Mage School that he hadn't given much thought to what he would do while he was there.

Vannya continued, "Normally what would happen is that you would go through orientation for the first couple of days with the rest of your starting class. But you have come in at the end of the year. It is a few months before the other cadets will arrive. I asked the Professor what they would have you do until the new year begins and he already had plans. He has picked out a student to show you around."

"You?" Justan asked.

"No, not me. I'm going to be busy catching up on all the work I've missed over the last month that I've been gone. Oh my! Year-end tests will be here in no time! I doubt I will be getting much sleep for a while," Vannya said, her mind elsewhere. She wasn't looking nearly as excited about going back as she had before. "No, he has someone else picked out for you."

"Who then?" Justan wondered. Going into this new situation was daunting. He had always felt at home in the Training School. Now with him entering this new place, he felt out of his element. He wondered if he would be allowed to spar with the academy-trained guards while he was there.

"I have no idea who he's chosen for you, but it will probably be someone who has reached the level of mage. He said that he planned on having you tutored until the new year started. That way you can start off with some more advanced classes in the spring." She smiled. "Evidently he wants you to make the most of these next two years."

"Well it doesn't matter. I had decided to do that anyway," he replied. "Is Valtrek going to be watching me the entire time?" It had been hard enough to endure his father's watchful eye at the Training School and that was a man that he loved. He didn't want to have to bear being under the finger of the man in the white robe.

"Oh, no. The *Professor* is much too busy." She emphasized the word 'professor' to remind him of proper protocol. "He has arranged for your early arrival and everything, but he spends most of his time away from the school. I doubt if you'll see him much at all."

"Good," Justan stated. That suited him just fine. He jumped off the step and started walking along behind the wagon. The conversation was making him antsy and he couldn't sit still anymore. Vannya saw the stubborn look coming back into his eyes and took this as a hint for her to leave. She started to get up, but Justan spoke out. "Wait, I wasn't asking you to go. Please, tell me more about what to expect. What does a cadet do?"

Vannya sat back down. It seemed weird to her to be talking

to a man walking behind the wagon. She hadn't ever met a man like him, someone who would actually enjoy walking or exerting himself instead of sitting. The bizarre thing was that something inside of her liked it.

They didn't really get to talk much more about life in the Mage School before the door to the wagon opened and Pympol stuck his head out. The swollen spot on the side of his eye had started to turn purple.

Justan couldn't help but needle the man a little. "Ooh, you need to get that looked at."

Pympol made it a point to ignore him. "Vannya, come in, we need to talk with you." She nodded and waved at Justan before she went in. Pympol sneered at him as he shut the door.

Justan shook his head. He had known for a while that Pympol didn't like him. Justan had sensed it from the first and didn't understand why. What was it about him that caused some people to dislike him so?

Vannya was a puzzle. He felt like he had developed a friendship of sorts with her. At least they both seemed to enjoy each other's company. But he didn't fit in with her crowd and she didn't really feel comfortable with his. When she had come to sit with him and the guards, Justan had always known that she was there to see him.

It was odd to Justan that a girl so amazingly beautiful would want to spend so much time with him. Was it that she was trying to be nice by befriending the new student? Then again, she always did defend the professor. A mistrustful side of him wondered if Valtrek had something to do with her being so nice. He didn't like the notion of Vannya being in league with that man.

After several miles Justan decided that walking behind the wagons just wasn't enough. He ran back and forth along the length of the wagons for a while, but he needed more. The cool fall air and the feeling that the freedom he had enjoyed on this journey was coming to an end made him want to push himself.

He ran faster, passing the first wagon to the stares of the students that were driving. He sensed that he could go faster still. His legs pumped and Justan really took up speed. He was surprised at the amount of energy blossoming within him. He would never have been able to run this fast before bonding with Gwyrtha. Perhaps the changes in him would be permanent. It was a nice thought. Oh what a surprise they would have when he returned to the academy.

Riveren was scouting a grove of trees about a mile ahead of the wagons on his horse when he saw Justan pounding down the road as if there were a horde of orcs after him. Riveren pulled his battle-axe from its sheath on his back, wondering what could be chasing the man. But as Justan got closer, Riveren could see a wide smile on his face.

"What's into you?" he shouted. Justan slowed as he neared the guard. He wasn't even breathing heavy.

"I have no idea. I just felt like running, I guess." He had been meaning to speak with Riveren before they arrived at the school anyway, so this was an opportune moment. "So this is it. After we get to the school, the journey's over. Where are you going to go?"

Riveren raised his eyebrows. "Didn't you know? Zambon and I are going to take a guard shift at the Mage School." Justan looked surprised and Riveren explained. "Not that we want to. We had actually hoped to go back through the forest to Pinewood as soon as we were done escorting the caravan.

"You see, after you disappeared, Valtrek told the town that there were a lot more goblins coming out of the hills. The people of Pinewood were putting together a task force as we left. We figured we'd see if they needed any help and offer our services. But Valtrek wouldn't let us. He said that he wanted us to come down to the school and relieve some of the guards."

"He has the authority to make you do that?" Justan asked.

"That's exactly what I asked him. But he brought out a document signed by the academy that said that we were to follow his orders exactly."

"Surely you don't have to keep to that letter after your arrival at the school." Justan suggested, once again irritated at the wizard. Why did he have to act like he ruled everyone's life?

Riveren shook his head. "That isn't the way it works, Justan. The contract he was given doesn't have an ending date on it. We could be forced to stay there for years, I don't know. But when we get to the school, I am going to send an official complaint back to the council. Surely they didn't leave the contract open-ended like that on purpose."

"Well, I'm sorry that this happened to you, but at the same time I'm glad to have you there. It'll be nice to have someone to spar with," Justan said. Then his shoulders drooped. "That is if they'll let me."

"Hey, sure. It will be nice to see you around." Riveren smiled. "You know, staying there really isn't such a big deal to me. I've always wanted to see the Mage School. I hear it's a pretty impressive place. A lot of important things have happened there. The only thing I'm worried about is that the guarding assignment could get boring. I've never been on one of those before." He realized that he still had the axe in his hand. He had forgotten why he had drawn it in the first place. "But let me tell you, Zambon was really angry when Valtrek told us."

"I would have been." Justan paused, then asked something he'd been wondering for some time. "Riveren, I hope you don't mind me asking, but what is it with you and Zambon? You seem to be friends, but . . . I mean, I don't really have anything against him, but you two are completely different."

Riveren shrugged. "We were both in Training School at the same time and got to be friends there. He's actually a real good guy with a noble heart. He's just been acting strange lately." Concern wrinkled his brow. "Justan, I don't know what has been into him. He used to be a lot more fun to be around, but recently he's been, oh I don't know . . . different. I have no idea what it's about. He was on a guard assignment at Dremald Castle for six months and when he got back, he wouldn't talk very much. He seemed, well, hard."

He shifted in his saddle as he put his axe back in its sheath. The sheath was made so that it was easy to take the axe out, but it was a pain to put it back in. "Anyway, any time I ask him about it, he just changes the subject or something. For instance, today he said that he would guard the rear and he's just stayed back there all morning, so far back that no one's seen him. It's weird."

Justan nodded in agreement. "All I know is that he has always seemed like he was distant or something. Like he didn't want to be here with the rest of us. I guess I can't blame him for that. I never really wanted to be here either."

He hadn't given much thought to it, but he hadn't really liked Zambon very much from the start. It wasn't that he had disliked him. He just hadn't hit it off with the quiet man. It seemed like Zambon was there during meals and sometimes around the fire when the friends were joking around and telling stories, but at the same time Justan couldn't remember him joining in except for the night before at the inn.

"Yeah, I figure he'll get over it," Riveren suggested. "Maybe he just met a girl or something."

At that point they could hear the sound of the caravan catching up. "I hope so," Justan said, and changed the subject. What Zambon did was none of his business. "in case I don't get the chance to tell you later, I want to thank you."

"For what?"

"I needed someone on this trip that I could feel comfortable around. The mages seemed so weird to me when we left Reneul, and I felt completely out of place. You didn't ignore me like the other academy graduates I've met. You helped me get over the fact that I am actually going to have to see this through." Justan felt a little weird talking to another warrior like this. "Besides, you saved my life during the goblin attack, so again, thank you."

"Hey, we saved each other's lives, okay?" Riveren seemed a bit uncomfortable too. "I have a feeling that the Mage School will be easy for you."

"That's the plan," Justan said and shook Riveren's hand. "Tell Zambon that I said thanks to him as well. I hope that he feels better."

"Yeah, I guess I'd better go check on him."

The wagons finally caught up. As they passed the two men, Justan hopped back on to his familiar perch on the back step.

"Justan!" Riveren yelled. "You had better go back to the academy when these two years are over!" He turned his horse and rode back up the road to check on Zambon.

Justan planned on it.

Chapter Twenty Eight

The caravan made good progress and they arrived at the Mage School in the mid afternoon. They came over a tall hill and Justan heard the students shout out as the school came into view. He climbed to the top of the wagon so that he could see the place where he would spend the next two years of his life.

At first, all he saw was a single spire rising over the horizon, disappearing into the clouds above. He realized that it was the tip of a gigantic tower. Justan marveled at the skill of the engineers that had built such a thing. The tower rose up higher than any structure he had ever seen. More and more of the structure came into view until Justan could see that a huge wall surrounded the tower.

"It's a fortress," he gasped.

Justan had always thought of the Battle Academy as the example of a perfect fortress, but this one dwarfed it completely. Justan's strategic mind quickly counted the benefits of a wall such as this.

The wall surrounding the tower was easily fifty-feet-tall and curved outward towards the top. Justan imagined that for a besieging army, staring up at the towering wall that curved overhead would be very imposing. It would look like any moment it could fall on top of you.

As the caravan got closer, he could see that the wall was so smooth that it looked like it was carved out of a single sheet of rock. At least there were no seams as far as he could see. This would make it difficult for any enemy to scale, and the way that it was curved outward made it very easy for a person to defend. Even if the enemy was able to construct sturdy enough 50-foot ladders to climb it, a single guard could easily topple the ladders before anyone could scale that height.

There was no city surrounding the Mage School, so he figured that the wizards were pretty self-sufficient. Whenever they were in need of supplies, they probably just sent a caravan out to Sampo to pick some up. This meant that there was no outer perimeter for the school to defend. If an army wanted to overtake the school, they would have no choice but to besiege it. Justan would not envy an army trying to besiege a school full of wizards in such an easily defended fortress. He could just imagine a powerful army being whittled away to nothing by fireballs and lightning strikes, and who knows what other kinds of spells, being hurled from atop this mighty wall.

Vannya came out of the wagon and saw Justan standing there slack jawed, staring up at the imposing structure. She climbed up and joined him. "That's the Rune Tower. It's pretty amazing isn't it? It's been around about as far back as the records go."

Justan didn't even turn his head to look at her. "It's not the tower I'm looking at. Why would a school for wizards need such a huge wall?"

She smiled, thrilled that Justan showed so much interest in the place she was so fond of. "The wall dates back to the war of the Dark Prophet. The School learned of the oncoming armies far in advance of their arrival. They realized the threat to the civilizations of the world if the knowledge contained in the library was lost. So they commissioned a group of architects, strategists and wizards to develop an impenetrable defense around the School. After the designs were complete, the most powerful black wizards in the known lands joined together and pulled the rock up directly from the ground around the school. The people molded them into what you see."

"Wow," was all Justan could say.

"They created a fortress that could never fall."

"Oh, it could fall." Justan smiled. Ideas were forming in his head.

Vannya snorted. "It has stood all these years through battles and sieges by armies so vast you couldn't see an end to them and it has never fallen. No one has even come close."

"Hmm, I see some possibilities." Justan was sure that some

of his ideas might work. He just needed to see more of the structure first. "Give me some time and I could draw you up a plan to conquer this place," he promised.

"Oh, well you've got a deal, you big showoff!" She laughed. "Come on. It looks much better from inside." As the wagons neared the giant wall, a portcullis was raised so that they could enter. Justan and Vannya climbed down from their perch.

The opening was large enough that two of the wagons could have entered side by side. The caravan crawled through that opening and Justan and Vannya followed on foot. The wall surrounding the school was so thick that it was like passing through a tunnel. When they broke through, Justan was surprised. The inside of this place was like nothing he would have expected.

The wall enclosed a huge area half again the size of the Battle Academy, and the tower only occupied part of that space. From the appearance of the outside of the school, Justan had envisioned anti-siege equipment and dark, tough, buildings. But on the inside, the place was completely different.

Near the entrance, the land was covered in manicured grass and bushes. It was a bright, sunny day and the place almost glowed with the life of bright green color. Meandering through this area were crisscrossing paths with benches along them. There were several students strolling on these paths. A few of them stopped to wave at the passing wagons.

The final quarter-mile of the caravan's journey was along the major road that passed through the center of the school grounds. The road was paved with white brick and on either side of it stood large buildings. Students in many different colored robes flowed in and out of those buildings loaded down with books and talking animatedly with each other. Only a few of them that passed by the wagons stopped to take notice of the returning group.

As he walked down the road with Vannya, Justan admired the place. There were trees and bushes planted along the road for shade and aesthetics, and every building was a thing of beauty or a marvel of craftsmanship.

"Vannya, it's nothing like I expected," Justan admitted.

"Oh?" she replied while waving at some of the students. "What did you think it would be like?"

"I don't know. I guess I had thought that it would be a little more dismal."

She laughed. "It's definitely not a dungeon." Justan shrugged and she pressed her point. "You need to realize that even though you, the heroic warrior, didn't want to come to this school, there are many who would give almost anything to have the opportunity to study here. In most parts of the world wizards are truly treated with respect."

"Hey, I always respected wizards," Justan retorted.

"Yeah right, I bet you respected the power of magic, but you always saw it as 'cheating'. You fighter types always think of things relative to how you can affect them physically. Magic is intangible to you, so you see anyone wielding it as not fighting fairly."

Justan had to admit that she had a point. But to his relief, before he could voice it, the wagons stopped. Their journey had come to an end.

They had come to the center of the school grounds. The main road ended in front of the Mage School center square. The square was lined with eight fluttering fountains that spouted water into the air in interesting patterns. In the middle of the square, surrounded by those fountains, was a thirty-foot tall miniature of the Rune Tower gilded in gold. It was a starling contrast to the real tower, which loomed far overhead. At the top of this replica tower was a large square box with four huge clocks on it, one facing each direction. He imagined that this clock tower could be seen from anywhere on the grounds.

Vannya confirmed this as she stood beside him. "They had to commission over a hundred clock makers to make the clocks for the school. Time is very important here, so everyone is supposed to keep track of it. Every class is exactly timed and the students are only given a short amount of time to get from one class to another. In fact, we have a clock in every building. There is no excuse for being late at the Mage School."

The concept appealed to the logical side of Justan. Structure was how he had pushed himself so far. He preferred things this way. In the Training School, classes had been kept on a bell schedule. Only the Training Council had a clock and a member rang a bell when it was time for a class change. His father had told him that they had more clocks in the academy where classes were kept on more of a strict schedule.

The Mages piled out of the wagons in front of the fountains and unloaded their belongings. Justan had all of his important things with him already. His clothes were neatly bundled and placed inside his pack, his weapons were strapped on, and the Scralag's book lay nestled safely in one of the pouches around his waist. So with nothing else to do, he helped them unload all but Valtrek's wagon. This one, no one was allowed to touch. Vannya had already activated the door rune and let the wizard know that they had arrived.

When they were finished unloading, the wagons were led away by a stableman and a few students. Vannya explained to Justan that the school only employed the one stableman, Jeffrey. All of his assistants were either students who had either 'volunteered' to work there, or were being punished. In the Mage School each student was required to have at least one job taking care of the grounds. They called this 'volunteer' work even though it was mandatory.

After the wagons were gone, all of the mages except for Vannya went their separate ways. At that point, Justan noticed that Riveren and Zambon had not come into the school with the caravan. In fact, he didn't recall seeing either of them after he had spoken with Riveren, and that was over an hour ago. He thought that strange, but he dismissed it from his mind. As far as he knew, this was standard procedure for the guards at the school.

He turned to Vannya. "So, where do I go from here?"

"The professor told me that when we arrived, I should take you into the library and have you wait until he had someone come for you." She smiled. "I can't wait for you to see it, Justan! I have been here most of my life and I am still amazed every time I go in there."

They walked along a paved path that curved around on either side of the clock tower. He looked for the library building, but Vannya led him straight towards the tower and Justan realized that the library must be contained inside.

The Rune Tower covered over a quarter of the grounds of

the school. It was made of huge blocks of gray stone inscribed with thousands of magic symbols. As he stood there gaping up at it, Justan still had no idea just exactly how tall it was.

The base of the tower was surrounded by a wide swirling moat spanned by a massive drawbridge. Huge chains attached the end of the bridge to holes farther up into the tower so that the mages could pull it up and use the tower for a fallback position in the unlikely event that the outer wall was breached.

Justan walked to the edge of the moat and looked in. The waters were flowing rapidly clockwise around the structure and Justan was pretty sure that he saw many small dark shapes swimming in the water, keeping pace with the current. “Hey, what’s in the water?” he asked, leaning over for a better look.

Vannya rushed over and pulled him away from the edge. “What ever you do, don’t even think about touching the water. Those things you see are called the Perloi. The High Council supposedly has control over them so they don’t attack anyone except for in times of war, but I still don’t trust the little monsters.”

“Why?” he asked, still entranced by the movements of the things.

“Because I have seen them fed. The wizards bring in a live goat every once in a while and toss it in. As soon as it hits, the water thrashes around and in seconds, the thing is gone. Nothing’s left, not even the bones. It’s a creepy thing to watch.” She shivered. “Anyway, let’s go inside. There are far more interesting things to see.”

Vannya walked onto the wide drawbridge leading into the tower and Justan followed her. But he couldn’t keep his eyes off of the deadly shapes that darted about under the water.

The doors to the tower were thrown open wide and they entered into a large corridor. There were torches set in the wall every so often for lighting, and the walls were lined with elaborate tapestries depicting the folklore and culture of the lands. As they walked by, Justan wanted to examine each one, but Vannya tugged him after her.

“Come on!” she said. “You have two years to see all this stuff. You can even sign up for tapestry cleaning duty if you want.”

On either side of the hallway, there were stairways

branching up and down. Justan wondered where they led. If the tower were this tall, how far into the ground did it extend? Vannya didn't take any of these doors or give Justan an opportunity to explore. She continued straight until the end of the corridor where a pair of large ornate doors stood.

"Here we are," she said. "All the knowledge in the world is kept in here." They opened the doors and stepped inside.

Justan gasped as they entered. The library was huge. It was five stories high with ladders and stairways to the different levels sprouting everywhere, but the center of the room was open and the ceiling arched far overhead, painted with fantastic murals. The bottom section of the library was covered in tables filled with students who had their noses in different volumes. The carpeting was a deep red color. Since all of the furnishings were a dull brown, it made a startling contrast.

"It's magnificent, isn't it?" Vannya whispered to Justan, but he didn't even hear her. He was too busy absorbing everything.

"It's wonderful," he mumbled, more to himself than to Vannya. His mind was a whirl with the possibilities waiting in this one large room. Previously, the most books he had ever seen in one place had been in the small Training School library. They had about a hundred books on warfare and such subjects and he had read every one during his years there. Now he could see thousands upon thousands. As he looked around the library, two years suddenly did not seem like such a long time. He had a feeling that he would be spending much of his time right in this room.

He dimly realized that Vannya was tugging on his arm. "Justan!" she whispered. "Hey!"

He turned his head and looked at her. "Sorry. What were you saying?"

"Shh!" she whispered, putting a finger to her lips, and Justan realized how quiet it was in the room. All he heard was the ruffle of pages, the soft sounds of padded footsteps and the low murmurs of whispering students.

"We can't just stand in the doorway. Come let me introduce you to Vincent. He has been the head librarian here for over two hundred years." As she led him across the floor, Justan wondered how a wizard had managed to live that long. When they arrived at the main desk, he understood. Vincent was a gnome.

Gnomes were an extremely intelligent people with an unnatural thirst for knowledge. They were also notoriously absent-minded. It was said that the gnomes had both learned and forgotten more than all of the other races combined. It was because of this that not a whole lot was known about them even though they were fairly common. No one even knew for sure how old a gnome could become, for if you asked one how old it was, it most likely wouldn't be able to remember. Despite their downfalls, most of the major scientific discoveries and inventions in current history came from the gnomes.

They were a very tall and thin race as a whole marked by their long hooked noses and dog-like ears that drooped down to their chins. The average gnome measured between seven and eight feet in height yet they usually weighed very little. No one was sure if this was the way their bodies were supposed to look or if they just constantly forgot to eat.

Gnomes were one of the less populous races. Some say that it was because they were so frail that it was hard for them to carry a baby. Others believed that they were so wrapped up in the pursuit of knowledge that they let such diversions as parenting go by the wayside. But when a gnome survived childhood, they lived for a long time. It was often said that if they hadn't been so long lived, the gnomes might have died out long ago.

Vincent was a good example of an average gnome. The tops of his ears were long and droopy. He had a long pointed nose that he had a habit of tugging on whenever he was thinking hard, and a pencil-thin mustache that barely touched the top of his lips. He was about seven feet tall and was so wispy thin that he looked skeletal, almost as insubstantial as a ghost. Vincent had kind eyes, though, and that erased any trace of menace in his appearance.

"Oh, hello Miss Vannya," he said and bowed. His ears flopped in the breeze caused by the sudden movement, and the spectacles perched on his forehead clattered to the ground. He quickly picked them up and set them back on the top of his head. "It is so good to see you. Why, surely it has been over a week. You haven't been neglecting your studies have you?"

"Actually Vincent, I have been gone for over a month," she replied with a grin.

"Ah. Well. How time flies." The gnome looked over at Justan. "Who is your unsightly friend?"

"Oh! This is Justan. He is going to be a student here. Justan, this is Vincent. I'm afraid that we don't know his last name."

"It will come back to me some day soon, my dear," Vincent said as if a little insulted. "Why just this morning I had several of my assistants go and search the archives for it." He paused for a moment, tugging on the end of his pointed nose. "That's funny. They haven't come back yet." He shifted his attention to Justan. "Well, Justan is it? Hmm, I'll file that away." He bent over with a feathered pen and scribbled something down in a large bound book. Vincent looked back up to Justan. "That won't do, though."

"What?" Justan asked.

"I am afraid that you can't be allowed to trounce around in this library with so many weapons. It's against school policy." He cocked his head and yanked on his long nose. "Or at least I think it is. I'll have my assistants look it up. In the mean time, would you please leave them behind the counter with me? I will let you take them with you when you leave."

Justan reluctantly removed his bow and unstrung it. He unbuckled his sword straps and handed them over, and the thin gnome tucked them away behind the desk. Justan started to hand over the knife but Vannya stopped him.

"That's okay. It's customary for most of the students to carry a ceremonial knife around. The rest of the weapons you'll probably want to keep in your room," she whispered.

Justan didn't want to leave them in his room. He wanted everyone to know just who he was. "What is the actual rule?" he asked.

"I'm not sure." She turned to the gnome. "Vincent, can you show Justan to the school rule book? He wishes to know the laws on carrying weapons on the grounds."

"But of course. Follow me, sir."

Vannya grabbed Justan's arm. "Listen, I have to go. Don't worry, someone will come for you soon. I'll see you later."

"Sure, no problem." Justan replied, simply excited to see more of the library. Still, he couldn't help but add, "I won't miss you at all. I have Vincent here to keep me company." He smiled at her sweetly and followed the gnome.

Vannya shook her head and smiled as she walked away.

Chapter Twenty Nine

Vincent moved through the aisles with a precision and grace that belied his gawky frame. Justan, on the other hand, had to constantly bob and weave, dodging students that were moving about. The gnome stopped in front of a large bookcase and took out a wide bound book. It was gilded in gold.

The gnome handed it to Justan. “Here you are, the Mage School constitution, complete with updated amendments and relevant bills. The part that will interest you is in the Cadet Rules, page one thousand one hundred and forty two, section b, paragraph two, on the second line, I believe. Peruse it at your leisure. Just make sure to return it to me or one of my assistants at the front desk when you are done. I can’t have you putting it back on the wrong shelf.” He pulled a card out of his pocket and started to write a note on it. “Now where are my spectacles?” The gnome mumbled as he patted his pockets and vest.

“Vincent, I believe that they are on your head,” Justan said.

The gnome reached up on his head and found them. He pulled them onto his nose. “Very kind of you, very kind of you. Mister . . .” Vincent looked up at him from the card he was writing on.

“Justan, son of Faldon the Fierce.”

The gnome stopped scribbling and beamed. He pushed his glasses back to the top of his head. “Faldon the Fierce? My, well this is wonderful! I met him years ago when he was just building his fame. If I remember correctly, he asked me about several books regarding the naming ceremony.”

“The naming ceremony?” Justan asked, surprised. His father had never mentioned looking into being named himself.

“Why yes! He was very interested. He came every day for a week. Aisle one hundred and fifty-four, section eight, volumes three through four. Yes what a joy to meet his son, uh, Mister . . ."

Justan laughed. "Justan."

"Ah yes, Justan." Vincent chuckled. "Silly me! I'm always forgetting such things." He started patting his vest again. "Now where are those glasses?"

"On your head, Vincent."

He found them. "Oh. Thank you. Well, young man. Don't worry. If you are lucky, you too may one day meet Faldon the Fierce or perhaps even someone just as famous." He finished scribbling on the card and put it in his vest pocket. "Off with you now. Shoo, study." He turned and walked back towards the front desk, tugging his nose as he went.

Justan carried the bulky book to a table in the center of the room and opened it. There were so many questions he wanted answered. He flipped through the pages of cadet rules, and addendums to the rules, and addendums to the addendums and had to stop. There was no way he was going to make sense of this in one sitting. There were hundreds of pages and it was just too complicated. He decided to start with the rules on carrying weapons in the school. Everything else would have to wait until someone explained it in simpler terms.

What page had the gnome said it would be on? There was an index in the back of the book that was over a hundred pages long by itself. It took some effort, but he eventually found what he was looking for and turned to the relevant chapter.

There was a lot of grandiose sounding talk of the dangers of having unstable students running around with swords. Justan snorted. As far as he was concerned, it was a load of nonsense.

Justan searched further. There was a lot of talk about swords and other bladed weapons being dangerous. There were laws banning the carrying of such arms in any area of the school grounds except for the walls and guard training area. There were many other small provisions and loopholes including the one that allowed the carrying of ceremonial daggers.

Justan smiled. There was no mention of bows or arrows. He would have to keep his swords put away in his room unless he was sparring with the guards in the training area, but he could bring his bow and quiver with him everywhere. He nodded. That was exactly what he would do. It would be his form of protest for having been brought to the school by deceptive means.

As he sat there gloating, a musical voice intoned, "You have got to be the first student I have ever seen smiling at the pages of that book."

Justan turned and saw a thin student with long dark braided hair wearing black robes with red accents. Justan's eyebrows shot up as he noticed the student's pointed ears. He was an elf.

The student held out his hand in greeting. "I am Qyxal. The professors have asked me to show you around." Justan shook the offered hand.

"Nice to meet you, Qyxal. I'm Justan." The elf's grip was firm despite his slender frame. "As to why I was smiling at this book, it all seems so silly."

"Oh?" The elf took a seat across from him at the table.

"Like this section here. It details the many ways that students could harm themselves with swords. They get pretty creative here, talking about students accidentally putting their eye out or falling on their own blades." Justan snickered. "If you ask me, the most dangerous thing that wizards could possibly carry around is their own magic. If they are truly afraid of the students hurting one another, they should make you walk around with your brains removed."

Qyxal smiled and shook his head. "Just be careful who you talk like that around. Sarcasm isn't smiled upon by most of the professors. They take the rules very seriously."

Justan lifted the enormous book. "What? Don't you find these rules funny?"

"The rules themselves, no. They make perfect sense when you think about it. But I can see the humor in the process the wizards use to come about these laws. The political posturing and maneuvering that goes on to bring them about is quite humorous."

Justan leaned back in his chair with his hands behind his head. "I must admit, I am quite surprised to see an elf here as a student. I thought that only humans could use magic."

Magic interacted differently with each race. It flowed through every fiber of the elves. Justan had recently found that the dwarves also had some form of it flow through their veins as well.

But with these races, the use of magic seemed to be all internal. Humans didn't have any of that inner magic, but every once in a while, they were born with the ability to control magic with their minds. This outward manifestation, which was used by the wizards, was rare in the other races.

"You are right," the elf responded. "However, every once in a great while, a human and an elf marry. Such it was with my great grandparents. When I was born, my sect realized that I had inherited this power inside of me. I guess it was one of the factors that led them to live near this place." He leaned forward. "I hear that you visited with my people on the way here."

"You are from the Silvertree Sect?"

"Yes, and I have got to ask. How did you get so far off of the road as to run into my people?" The two of them chatted for a little while about Justan's journey and how the sect was doing, though Justan didn't mention Gwyrtha.

Justan found himself liking the elf. Qyxal wasn't arrogant at all. He didn't even act removed like the rest of his sect that Justan had met. He talked like he was just another human. Perhaps that was something he had needed to do to fit in at the school. Justan doubted that the wizards would put up with arrogance

"Justan, I for one will be very interested to see how your power develops," Qyxal said. A bell rang in the distance. Though it sounded muffled in the library, everyone noted it and many of the students cleared out. The elf smiled. "That means it's time to eat. Are you hungry?"

Justan nodded. "I'm famished. We didn't even stop for lunch today."

"Good. I didn't eat lunch either. Follow me." The elf stood and started for the door.

Justan stopped him. "Wait, I am going to need to go by my room first. I have some things to drop off. Do you know where I am staying?" Qyxal nodded.

Justan ran across the library floor to the front desk. Vincent gave Justan a lecture about running in the library, but handed over his weapons.

Qyxal led the way out of the Rune Tower and across the grounds to a many storied brick building with a sign carved above the doorway. It read “Cadet House” in fancy lettering. They entered the building and walked down a hallway.

“Here we are.” Qyxal said. He pulled a key out of his robes and handed it to Justan. “Cadet House, room seven. Just put your things away and change, I am starving.”

Justan opened the door to a small room with two beds, two closets, two desks, and one tiny window. One of the beds was disheveled and clothes and books and shoes were scattered all over the place. He looked back at the elf. “I didn’t know I was going to share a room.”

“Everyone does,” the elf explained.

Justan supposed he shouldn’t have been surprised. They normally didn’t get their own room in the academy either. “Okay then, who’s my companion?”

Qyxal grinned. “That one’s a jewel. His name is Piledon, and he’s a third-year cadet. Normally people make it to apprentice by the second year. Let’s just hope that he likes you, because if he doesn’t, your life won’t be too much fun. I hear he’s somewhat of a prankster.”

Justan groaned. That was the last thing he needed.

The closet on his side of the room was empty but for one set of clean grey robes. Justan put his pack inside and considered changing into the robes. They were light and looked pretty comfortable, with many concealing pockets, but he wasn’t quite ready to don them yet.

To Qyxal’s surprise, Justan began strapping on his swords. “What are you doing?”

Justan smiled. “This is the first time that most of the students will see me and I want to make a good impression.” He bent the Jharro Bow and started stringing it.

“Yes, but Justan, it isn’t going to be just students in there. The wizards eat with us too. Everyone will be there,” Qyxal emphasized. “Besides, it’s against the rules for a student to carry swords on the grounds.”

“Ha!” Justan said, while checking all the straps. “I just checked the rules. I am not a student yet. I haven’t been sworn in or signed anything but a letter of intent. For now, I’m just a guest, and there are provisions for allowing guests to wear their weapons.

That's why the guards can go wherever they want and still wear them." He pushed past Qyxal and into the hall.

"Well at the very least, it's rude," the elf pronounced.

Justan smiled and bowed to the elf. "I won't change who I am. This will just be a reminder to everyone who sees me. I'm a warrior first. Now where's the food?"

Qyxal sighed. "This way."

They crossed the grounds and passed the clock tower to a large building. Even from outside, Justan could smell food cooking and hear hundreds of plates clanking and people talking. They opened the doors to a cacophony of sounds and smells. There were over a hundred tables in this enormous room, and students were eating and chatting amiably. Justan noticed that most of the time, the students with similar colored robes sat together. He made a mental note to find out what the colors meant.

As Qyxal led him in, the noise died and everyone stared at the new arrival. It was not normal for a man to enter the dining hall dressed for battle. The guards ate at their own part of the grounds and guests were usually shown to a quieter place to eat.

Justan was a little uncomfortable about the sudden silence, but figured if he had gone this far, why not go all the way? He smiled at everyone and waved, while Qyxal looked down in embarrassment. After a few awkward moments, the students went back to their dinner. Qyxal grabbed Justan's arm and led him to the serving area.

The cooks loaded their plates with stew and bread. Justan's mouth watered. This food looked much better than the stuff they ate at the Training School. Qyxal tried to lead him to a small empty table, but Justan ignored the elf and headed for a large table where eight students were already sitting. There were two empty chairs.

Qyxal groaned as Justan took a seat. The other students at the table just stared at him with open mouths.

"Good evening," Justan said. "Do you mind if my friend and I join you?" He didn't wait for a response, but pulled out a chair for the elf, which Qyxal reluctantly sat in.

Justan dipped some bread into the stew and was about to eat it, when he felt a hand on his shoulder. When he saw the way that the other students were smiling, he had a pretty good idea who it was.

"Justan, what do you think you are doing?" Vannya asked. She winked at the other students at the table. "Hello, boys." They stammered hellos back at her.

Justan looked up at her, frustrated. "I think that I am trying to eat this delicious looking stew. Would you like to join us?" The other students at the table jumped up and offered their seats.

"No, it's okay guys," she said to the students. "Justan. We have bigger things to worry about," she whispered to him urgently.

Something in her tone made Justan's smile fade. "What?"

"Riveren and Zambon are still missing."

Justan shrugged. "Well, they really didn't want to come here in the first place. Maybe they just decided not to."

She shook her head and with a deadly serious tone that darkened her pretty face, said, "Their horses just arrived without them."

Justan stood up. "Sorry, gentlemen. We'll have to get to know each other another time." He grabbed Qyxal's arm and pulled him to his feet.

"Hey, what?" the elf complained, having only taken one bite of his food.

"I'm going to need your help," Justan said and ran for the door. Qyxal and Vannya hurried after him.

Chapter Thirty

Vannya led them across the grounds to the stables. They spoke as they walked. “Why didn’t the arrival of riderless horses raise an alarm?” Justan asked.

“The incident has been filed away with the clerk. A council session is scheduled in about two hours from now. It will be brought up there.”

Justan shook his head. He just found another hole in the school's defenses.

They arrived just as the stableman was leading the warhorses into the stable. They were still saddled up and bridled. Qyxal’s eyes lit up when he saw them.

“I know those horses,” the elf said. He quickly stopped the stableman. “Hello, Jeffrey,” he said.

“Why hello, Qyxal! What are you doing down here at this time of day?” The man asked. “You are not scheduled for work until tomorrow morning.”

“I know, Jeffrey, but my friends and I have some questions.”

“Sure Qyxal, what can I do to help?”

“When did Stanza and Albert come in?” Qyxal asked.

Jeffrey looked up at the clock tower. “They came in about half hour ago, I guess. They were just nibbling on the grass outside the front gate when one of the guards noticed them.”

“You know these horses?” Justan asked.

“Why of course he does.” The stableman answered in the elf’s behalf. “Qyxal has volunteered with me for years and Stanza and Albert are two of our finest horses. They go out with every caravan.” He scratched one of them fondly behind the ear. “They were a gift to the school from the Battle Academy years ago, and the guards love them.”

Qyxal was examining the saddle of one of the horses. "They know the road to the school as well as anyone by now. That's how they knew to come here." The elf whispered comforting words to the horse and ran his hands over its flanks, examining it. "There's a cut along Albert's side. It looks like an arrow grazed him."

"That's the horse that Zambon was riding," Justan pointed out.

"Oh!" Vannya was examining Stanza. "This one has blood on it." She put her hands over the spot and sent flows of magical energies into it. "That's human blood, and . . . goblin blood. There's goblin blood too!"

"Oh my!" the stableman gasped.

Justan took charge, "Vannya, please go and find some of the wizards, tell them that we are going to look for the missing guards."

"Wait, Justan," Qyxal interrupted. "I don't think it's a good idea."

"He's right, Justan," Vannya agreed. "We should go to the council first and tell them what we have found before you go running off."

Justan thought it over quickly. They had a point. In some ways this paralleled the situation when Kenn took Jhonate. He had made the wrong decision then. Was he repeating his mistake? Justan shook his head. No, this situation was different. He had only been in the school for a few hours and no one knew him well enough to listen. If Riveren and Zambon had been in a battle, time was of the essence.

"You can tell them, Vannya. We don't have the time to wait. What if Riveren and Zambon are still alive somewhere in need of rescue? We can't sit around until the council makes a decision. After reading that rulebook, I don't get the impression they'll come up with one quickly. Am I wrong?" Both of them shook their heads reluctantly. "I didn't think so. Come on Qyxal." Justan put his foot into Stanza's stirrup.

"Hey, why do you need me to go?" Qyxal protested. "Why don't you just get some guards?"

"Because we don't have time and you, being an elf, are

probably a better tracker than any of them. Now hurry and get on!" Justan commanded. The elf sighed and mounted Albert.

"Wait just a minute!" Vannya complained. "I'm going too. If they are injured, I'm a better healer than Qyxal!"

"Then who's going to tell the council?" Justan asked.

"Jeffrey will." She walked over to the man and gave him her most charming smile. "Jeffrey, would you please tell the council and the guards that we are going out to find the missing men?"

The man blushed and nodded.

"Thank you. Oh, and please also tell them that we need them to send some people to help, just in case, okay?" Without waiting for a response, she turned to Justan and lifted a hand.

With a wry grin, he helped her up behind him. "You are something else," he said.

The threesome galloped out of the school and up the road. Qyxal rode with fluidity, almost as if he and the horse were one. On the other hand, Justan didn't have as much experience on horses as he would have liked, and obviously neither did Vannya, for both of them bounced around madly. It would have made more sense for Vannya to ride with Qyxal, but they didn't have time to trade off. Besides, for some reason, Justan didn't want to see her riding behind the handsome elf.

The trip that had taken a couple of hours for the caravan was much quicker for the would-be rescuers galloping along at full speed. Still, to Justan it seemed as if it lasted forever. His legs and buttocks were bruised and battered and he knew he'd be sore in the morning. As they arrived at the grove of trees where Justan had last seen Riveren, the sun had almost reached the horizon. The light was quickly fading.

Qyxal pulled his horse close to Justan. "This is where you last saw him?" the elf asked.

"Yes, but Zambon had already been missing for most of the day. I have no idea how far back down the road Riveren went," Justan responded.

"I see. Well, we'll just have to move slowly up the road until I see some sign that the guards left it." Qyxal patted the horse's head and whispered some words into his ear. He looked back at Justan. "Albert should be of some help. I have a certain understanding with him. Remember, the horses know what happened even though we don't."

Justan looked back at Vannya who was wincing with every movement from the horse. "Have there been any reports of goblins in this area?" he asked.

She shook her head. "There haven't been monsters of any kind on this stretch of road for years. However, I've been gone for a month, so maybe things have changed."

They both looked to Qyxal who shrugged. "About a week ago, there was a traveler that came to the school, who swore that he had been chased along the road by something. The guards were sent out and nothing was found. If Vannya hadn't found goblin blood on the horse, I wouldn't have believed it possible myself."

They searched along the road at a slower pace, and as the light dimmed, Justan began to worry. When the horses had been discovered, he had been so sure of his course. But as he looked at his two companions, Justan had to wonder. Had he been stupid in taking off like this, accompanied by nothing but two mages? Anything that could have overcome two academy graduates surely would be more than a match for the three companions.

Perhaps the fact that he had fought his way out of a forest full of moonrats made him feel invincible. But what of these two who had come with him? What if something happened to one of them? He thought about what had almost happened to Jhonate the last time he had charged headlong into such a situation and shuddered. Just as he considered turning around and returning to the school, Qyxal motioned that he had found something.

Justan leapt down from the horse and ran over to him, feeling his sore muscles protest the whole way. Vannya grumbled and gingerly dismounted from Stanza, wincing and rubbing her lower back. Qyxal pointed to the east side of the road. The bushes were disheveled and when the elf tried to bring Albert that way, the horse refused.

Justan had Qyxal tie the horses on the side of the road out in the open. If help came from the school, this would let them know where they had gone. He suddenly realized that his companions had no weapons. He berated himself for not thinking that far ahead. He tried to give them his swords, but they both shook their heads and pointed to their temples. Magic would be their most effective form of attack.

Qyxal led them off of the road, for his elven eyesight was keen even in the dim light. Just past the disheveled bushes was a clearing. Justan didn't need to be a tracker to know that there had been quite a skirmish there. Plants were flattened and trampled and the elf found patches of blood, both goblinoid and human. There were no bodies, just one crudely made arrow.

At the sight of the arrow, Justan pulled the Jharro bow off of his back and restrung it with the golden dragon hair string. He had a quiver full of arrows and had a feeling he might need them. From the clearing, there was a trail of snapped branches and twigs that led them to the lip of a ravine. A glow came from deep within, and faint voices could be heard.

Justan and his friends laid down in the leaves by the ravine and peeked over the edge. The glow came from a campfire at the bottom. There were several large forms moving around the fire.

"Orcs!" Qyxal hissed.

Orcs looked much like goblins, but were much bigger, about the size of a human. They were mean brutes with beady yellow eyes and green mottled skin. Far more intelligent than their diminutive cousins, they carried many different types of weapons. The orcs weren't as plentiful as goblins, but often used the little beasts as slave labor.

Several goblins were tossing wood in to the fire from nearby trees and there were two hideous bodies being turned on a spit above the fire. At first Justan thought the worst, but then his nose caught a whiff of something that he had smelled all too recently. It was roasted goblin flesh. Justan figured that these were the bodies of goblins killed by the guards in the skirmish by the road. Orcs were known to eat their slaves.

Justan motioned and the three companions crept along the lip of the ravine to get a closer look. When they got closer to the fire, they laid down again. On the south side of the fire staked to the ground, were the two missing guards. At this distance, Justan could see Riveren struggling in his bonds. Zambon was unmoving, however. He looked around the campfire and counted five orcs and four goblins.

Justan's tactical mind started working. "Qyxal, what spells can you use to help?"

"Fireballs and earthquakes, but I don't dare try them from this distance. I might kill your friends. I do have a sleeping spell, but I would have to get up close to use it."

Justan turned to Vannya. "From personal experience I know that the effects from your lightning spell spreads out over the ground. If you strike on the opposite side of the fire from the guards, could it still harm them?" She nodded apologetically. Justan sighed. "Okay. Qyxal, can you fire a bow?"

Qyxal smiled. "I am an elf aren't I?"

"Good, then this is the plan. I'm going to take out as many of the orcs as I can with the bow before they know what's happening. Then I'm going to hand it over to you and go down there with my swords. The bow will not be as effective if I'm not using it, but with the dragon hair string you should be able to do some damage.

"Vannya, as soon as I hand the bow to Qyxal, send a lightning bolt as close as you dare without harming the guards. This should give me some time to get down there. Qyxal you cover me. I should be able to handle whatever is left when I arrive." He got to his knees. "Do you understand?"

They were staring at him open jawed, but managed to nod. Justan pulled the quiver off of his back and handed it to Qyxal who strapped it on. Justan took three arrows out of the quiver and stuck them point down into the ground in front of him within easy reach.

"Alright, this has to be perfectly timed. Are you ready?" They nodded again. "I know we can do this." He put an arrow to the string and pulled back, feeling the power vibrate. "Here we go."

Chapter Thirty One

Riveren was staked to the ground spread-eagled. The ropes tied to his wrists and ankles were stretched so tight that his back barely touched the ground. A goblin was sitting on his chest, giggling at his discomfort. The pain was excruciating. His sockets felt as if they might pop at any second.

Riveren was a strong man. His body was perfectly sculpted and he was in great shape, as one had to be in order to fight with his ax style, but with his extremities stretched to such lengths, he couldn't even begin to pull on his bindings. He was helpless.

He looked over at Zambon. His friend wasn't tied as tightly. His wounds were so serious that to stretch him like that would probably kill him. Riveren didn't see much chance of survival for his friend or himself at this point. The only glimmer of hope that he had was that it was goblin flesh being cooked instead of horse flesh, which was an orc's favorite meat. This told him that the horses had escaped and since they were regularly stabled at the school perhaps they would return there. At the very least it would give the wizards some warning because as far as he could tell, the orcs were planning some sort of attack.

The beasts had been torturing him for information for hours. One in particular, their leader, was named Marckus, and he was big and mean. He was an amazing fighter too. Riveren had watched the orc beat Zambon with ease.

Marckus demanded to know about the defenses of the school. He was prying for any kind of weakness. When he told Marckus that he had never been there, the orc didn't believe him. Riveren had been burned with coals until he had finally explained that he was from the Battle Academy and not the Mage School. Then all the orc wanted to know was about the academy.

Riveren hadn't told him anything. But through the pain, he

wondered what would happen if he did. He doubted that a group of eight orcs and four goblins would be able to do anything to harm either school. The only thing that kept him from talking was the sheer boldness of these orcs coming so close to the tower.

It was possible that these orcs were just a scouting party for a much larger army that was planning an invasion. Riveren kept his mouth shut and endured the pain. He could hear Zambon's breathing become ragged. The hope that his friend's suffering was coming to an end was comforting.

The goblin sitting on his chest spat on him to get his attention. "Hey, big man. You answer Marckus he maybe let you go, huh? Maybe we not eat your friend."

He spat back at the goblin, hitting it in the eye. The creature laughed and stood up on his chest. The nasty little creature began jumping up and down. Riveren's joints felt like they were on fire.

Then the goblin's head exploded.

The creature was jerked through the air in a hail of gore. Justan didn't wait for it to land, but fired at the orc standing closest to the guards. It was slack-jawed, wondering how the goblin had died until the arrow caught it in the chest. The powerful shot sent the heavy creature flying several yards to collide against the ravine wall with enough force to crack its bones.

The orc standing closest to it had the chance to let out a surprised shout before the next arrow tore its throat out. The force of the shot sent the orc flipping into the fire. The orc's macabre dinner fell off of the spits. As sparks flew, the remaining orcs and goblins in the camp cried out in alarm.

Justan quickly handed the bow to a stunned Qyxal who had never seen such a raw display of power from a weapon before. Justan patted the elf on the shoulder and jumped over the edge of the ravine. The drop from the lip they had been looking over was steep, but sloped at the bottom and Justan slid down the incline in a storm of dust and pebbles.

During his fall there was a blinding flash and Justan knew that Vannya's lightning bolt had struck. The bolt hit the orc furthest from the fire full on sending so many volts through him that his toes shot off. He was dead on contact. The shock traveled through the ground as well and killed one of the goblins closest to the orc, boiling its blood. Another orc was paralyzed and lay jittering on the ground.

Only one orc was left standing. It was the leader, Marckus. He had dived for cover behind a large rock as soon as the first goblin was hit.

When Justan came to a stop at the bottom of the ravine, he pulled his swords and ran towards the fire. The first enemy he came upon was a goblin that had been away from the fire, gathering firewood. The creature was still blinded by the flash and he didn't see Justan until it was too late. It put its hands up in defense as Justan came in. The first sword swipe took off its fingers. It didn't have a chance to register the pain before Justan twirled around and followed the first strike with a stab through its goblin's heart. It collapsed soundlessly.

Marckus watched from behind the rock until Justan wasn't looking directly in his direction. Then he took advantage of the opening and ran for the guards. The orc dove beside Riveren and put a knife to his throat. Justan was running after the last goblin when Marckus cried out.

"Stop, human! This man dies before you strike!"

Justan was startled to see an orc still moving and wondered why Qyxal hadn't put an arrow into it. By then the huge beast had wedged enough of its body under Riveren that an arrow might not kill it with the first strike. The guard cried out in pain with the extra strain placed on his arms and legs by the orc wedged underneath him.

Justan surveyed the situation. The last remaining goblin was hiding behind the same rock that the orc had taken cover behind previously. Zambon was white as a ghost and unconscious. His chest still rose up and down, but shallowly. Riveren was doing much better despite a painful looking series of burns on his body. Even with the orc's knife pressed against his throat, Riveren's eyes burned with an inner fire.

Justan spun his swords in his hands and looked at the orc leader, options circling through his head. He could offer to let the orc go in exchange for Riveren's life, but some things were starting to become obvious. Normally a band of orcs would have killed the guards at once. Why not this time? The burns on Riveren's body were the final clue. Justan understood that they were in the area scouting for information. If he let the leader go, then there was a chance that it would take that information to someone.

Justan supposed that he could deceive the orc into thinking he was letting it go and then chase it down and kill it. But that thought didn't sit well with him. Instead he walked over to the orc that had been paralyzed by the lightning bolt and put a sword to its throat.

"I have a better idea. Let the man go and I won't kill you or your friend, here. We'll just take you prisoner, instead."

The orc laughed. "Marckus does not surrender." To Justan's surprise, the orc released Riveren and got to its feet. It pointed the knife at Justan. "You will surrender, human."

Justan was taken aback. What made it think it had the advantage, and why wasn't Qyxal shooting it right now? He heard a noise on the other side of the fire and received the answers to both of his questions.

Justan frowned. He had miscounted. Three orcs that Justan hadn't known about stood there holding Vannya and Qyxal. The mages were gagged and bound with leather straps. The orcs must have been out scouting when Justan and his friends had arrived. One of the orcs tossed Justan's bow and quiver to the side with a clatter and several of the arrows spilled out into the dirt.

While bound and gagged, the mages couldn't cast any spells. Besides, fireballs or lightning strikes would be of no use in such close quarters anyway. Justan's plan had started out without a hitch, but now he was at the disadvantage.

The paralyzed orc at his feet was starting to move. Justan kicked it in the head to make it still again. He pressed the sword point deeper into its neck. "Let them go and I will let this one live," he pronounced grandly though he already knew the answer.

Marckus chuckled. "How brave you are, human, but no. You drop your weapons or all of you die."

Justan knew that he had no choice, but he was sure that if he laid his weapons down, they would all be killed anyway. The orcs weren't going to let them go. Perhaps if he attacked the orcs, he might be able to overcome them before all of his friends were killed, but the death of even one of his friends was not something he was willing to face.

"No!" he shouted, his mind searching for another option.

The leader grinned. The orcs raised their knives.

"Wait!" Justan yelled. In desperation, he appealed to the leader's vanity. "Marckus, are you a great fighter?"

The orc leader looked at him suspiciously, but one of the other orcs shouted out. "He could kill any ten men!"

"Very well, then," Justan pronounced and pointed one of his swords at their leader. "Prove it. Fight me one on one. If I beat you, my friends must be let go."

The orc snorted. "And what do I get when I win that I don't already have?"

Justan shrugged. "If you win then I will be dead." He kicked the orc lying beside his feet. "This orc will live, and you will prove to your men that you are not a coward!"

It was a gamble, but Justan was pretty sure that with his new found agility he could beat the orc.

Marckus growled, his mottled green skin turning pink with anger. The orc knew what Justan was trying to do and didn't particularly care to give in to the human's ploy. But the other orcs were watching him and he refused to let them think that his prowess could be challenged.

"Very, well, human. If you are that eager to die." The orc chuckled to himself. This might be fun, anyway.

Justan watched as the orc called out to the hiding goblin. The creature scrambled over to a corner of the camp and came back with a long-handled scythe. The weapon was heavy and the goblin struggled not to let either end drag on the ground, fearing the wrath of its master if the weapon got dirty. It was a magnificent weapon. The shaft was about five feet long, capped on one end by a sickle blade and on the other end by an iron ball.

Justan wondered why the weapon was made with that iron ball on the end. Normally with a scythe, or any similar weapon like an ax, only the attacking end was weighted, making it easier to maneuver the weapon during battle. If the handle were weighted, the weapon would become unnecessarily heavy and awkward.

Justan finally understood the purpose of the counterweight once the goblin had handed the scythe to the orc. Marckus twirled it over his head like a quarterstaff, which was a weapon that had to be weighted equally on both ends.

Marckus saw the unease on Justan's face and grinned. The orc leader spun the weapon through the air with both hands in complicated patterns, passing the blade dangerously close to his bulky body. He twirled faster and faster, letting the weight of the weapon lead the way, until he finished with one hand on the ball and the entire five-foot length extended straight out, his arm taking the strain of that extra weight with barely a quiver.

The orcs roared in approval of their leader's prowess. Justan had to force himself not to be impressed as well. For a moment, he pondered going into one of the more impressive dual sword forms, but then he thought of the absurdity of it all, showing off to a bunch of eager orcs. He didn't want to show his skill and make Marckus cautious. He wanted the orc angry.

Justan put on his most impetuous face, twirled his twin swords exaggeratedly with his wrists and stabbed the orc lying prone on the ground in the buttock with his right sword. The four standing orcs gasped. Justan looked down.

"Oops," he yawned and leaned on the pommel with his elbow. The orc awoke and howled. Justan kicked it in the head to silence it again, and looked at the leader. "Well I'm ready. Are you?"

Marckus snarled and gripped the shaft so hard that his knuckles turned white. He wasn't mad about the humiliation of his fellow orc, but at the arrogance of this young human, mocking his battle dance. The orc decided to take this opportunity to prove a point to his soldiers.

"You are going do die horribly," he promised.

Justan charged the orc, figuring that it would not expect the attack. In fact, the orc had also been about to charge, so Justan's offensive did catch it by surprise but the orc was experienced and swung the scythe end of his weapon to meet the human.

Justan saw the swing coming and flipped over it. As he landed on his feet, he whipped his sword out behind him, gashing the orc's outer thigh.

Marckus hissed with the pain, but continued the rotation of his swing, twisting its upper body to bring the ball-end of the staff in line with Justan's head. The human was already darting out of reach. The ball came close, but whizzed by harmlessly. Justan had claimed first blood.

The orc ignored the wound and struck back with a series of quick right and left strikes. Justan was able to block the attacks, but the orc was strong and his weapon heavy. Each block jarred Justan's arms to the bone and he knew that this sort of defense wasn't going to work. He would weaken too quickly and one blow from that weapon could kill him. He needed to find out the leader's weaknesses.

Justan was able to get Marckus back on defense with a couple of easily blocked jabs and then worked his swords with a fury, not trying to score an easy hit, but to keep the orc from striking back. He went through a blinding series of attacks, getting in closer and closer to the orc where it couldn't defend itself as easily. He was able to nick the orc a couple times about the hands, but the orc wasn't allowing an opening large enough for him to do any real damage.

Finally Marckus had had enough. With a roar he extended his weapon to full length, grabbing it by the ball, and swung it like a club. Justan saw the swipe coming and jumped, but was not quite quick enough. The scythe edge grazed his back, slicing through his sword straps and into his skin, leaving a long gash across his shoulder blades.

Justan didn't know if he could defeat this orc. His skills had improved greatly, but Marckus was a veteran of many battles, while Justan had only recently experienced serious combat. The orc was strong and fast. Justan desperately needed a new strategy.

He began to taunt the large orc and stay just out of its attack reach. When the orc lashed out, Justan would slice at its arms or elbow, or whatever he could hit and get out of reach again. Marckus countered by darting forward as he struck, hoping to catch the quicker human before he could jump out of the way.

Justan's back burned with the pain of the cut and the straps that had been sheared by the scythe whipped about maddeningly as he moved, irritating him. He broke away from the orc and managed to pull the sheaths off of his back. Instead of throwing them to the ground, he threw them at Marckus. The orc batted them away, never taking his eyes off of Justan.

Justan's eyes darted about, his mind searching for anything he could use to his advantage. Marcus wasn't giving him many opportunities to attack. The orc's aggressive fighting style kept Justan on his heels. Marckus was getting faster and faster in his movements, and Justan was running out of ways to evade him.

They battled about the fire until Justan was forced near the orcs holding his friends. He got too close and one of them kicked out at him, catching Justan in the hip and putting him off balance. He barely dodged a swing by the orc leader. In retaliation, Justan took a swipe at the orc who had kicked him, but the beast ducked the swipe, and the tip of his sword scored Qyxal's cheek instead.

"Sorry!" Justan yelped out and Marckus used the moment to his advantage. The orc twisted around and extended his weapon, grasping it near the blade of the scythe. Justan didn't see the orc extend the weapon because for that fraction of a second, the orc's back was to him. As Marckus twirled around, Justan was too close to jump out of the way of the incoming attack. Instead he lifted his left sword to block the weapon, but the strike landed too close to the hilt. It was a powerful blow, and with the effort of blocking it, Justan felt something in his left hand snap. Pain shot up his arm into his shoulder. The sword dropped from his fingers.

Everything slowed down for Justan. He knew that he was done for. He could never hope to defeat the skilled orc leader with only one sword and the intense pain in his hand distracting him. As he heard the low voices of the orcs shouting in triumph, he saw his last hope. Before Marckus could strike again, Justan dove for his bow and arrows that the orcs had discarded on the ground. He grabbed one of the fallen arrows with his right hand and reached for the bow with his left. Pain shot through his arm as his palm hit the weapon. He hoped that he could force his fingers to close around it.

Justan hit the ground and rolled, coming up to his knees. He twisted around and brought the bow up with his crippled left hand. He wasn't able to grasp it fully, but had it hooked between his thumb and forefinger.

Marckus bore down on him and was just a few feet away when he saw what the human was doing. Instinctively, the orc brought his weapon before him with both hands in a blocking gesture, but he underestimated the power of the Jharro bow. Justan smoothly drew back and fired.

The orc's block was amazingly accurate. The arrow hit the staff right between his hands and splintered it in two with concussive force. The arrow continued into Marckus' chest and lifted him five feet off of the ground. The orc arced through the air to land on his back just in front of the fire, the splintered remains of his powerful weapon still clutched in his fists.

Justan quickly fumbled for another arrow and turned to the orcs holding his friends, but they were on the ground asleep. Justan's slice across Qyxal's cheek had cut through the gag and the mage was able to release the sleep spell that he had been preparing.

Qyxal stood there, still bound tightly and hooted in joy. "Justan! Hurry and cut me free so that I can wake Vannya." She had succumbed to the spell as well.

Justan pulled his dagger with his good hand and sliced the bindings on the elf. Qyxal quickly scrambled to his fellow mage, muttered a few words and laid a single finger on her forehead. Her eyes opened.

As Qyxal woke Vannya, Justan used his sword to cut the straps holding Zambon's limbs to the stakes. The guard's face was very pale and his breathing was ragged and shallow. Dried blood was pooled on his chest and ichor oozed from an open wound in his belly.

"Vannya! Get over here quick. Zambon's about gone!" The mages rushed over and laid their hands upon the dying man. Justan cut Riveren free and helped the man to his feet. "Are you okay?"

Riveren didn't answer the question, but with a fixed glare at the sleeping orcs said, "Where's my axe?"

Justan shook his head. "No, Riveren. They are helpless. We'll take them prisoner, but we can't just kill them like that."

"Do you think that they would offer us the same courtesy?" the guard asked. Justan avoided having to answer the question.

Instead, he turned to Qyxal. "Will Zambon be alright?"

The mage ignored him, focused on the man's wicked wounds. Justan saw Riveren find his double bladed battle-axe. Trying to remind him of their duty, he asked the man to help him bind the sleeping orcs. The guard reluctantly joined him. As they were tying the hands of the third orc scout behind its back, Riveren shouted out in alarm.

Justan turned to see Marckus, the orc leader standing over him with the ball end of his splintered weapon raised over his head. The orc's face was twisted with rage. Blood was pouring out of the jagged wound in its chest and Justan could see the fletchings of his arrow barely poking out of it. With a roar that was mostly gurgle, Marckus swung the weapon at Justan.

He tried to dive out of the way, but the iron ball sank into his hip with a sickening crunch. Justan cried out in agony. He could feel bone grinding against bone deep within him and he knew his pelvis was broken, a crippling injury. The orc raised the ball for a killing blow, but Justan never saw it descend.

All went black.

Chapter Thirty Two

Fist journeyed with Squirrel for over a month before finding the place where he wanted to live. Along the way, he learned many new things. He learned to arrange his spider skin wrap much more efficiently to allow for freedom of movement. With the beasts he killed, he added to his clothing, making fur leggings and a cloak. Fist even developed a pouch for Squirrel to live in.

During the journey, Squirrel had become a true companion. The little creature now kept a perch on Fist's shoulder where it could chatter at him without interruption and he could talk to it and tell it what he was thinking. This was a new experience for Fist. He never had a confidant before. Sure, he had warrior companions and hunter friends, but ogre conversations were mainly in grunts and gestures and nobody shared their feelings. Even his father had rarely spoken of such things with him.

It was strange, but even though Fist was sure that the little creature didn't know what he was saying, it didn't matter. He now had someone to protect and care for. He found nuts and seeds for it whenever possible and he saved the little creature from predators many times. In fact, Squirrel's pouch was made from the skin of one of those predators. There was nothing that the little creature had to offer in return but companionship, but that was what Fist needed the most.

Fist continued to develop his weapons as well. He made a spear for long distance throwing, which he also used as a staff, and made a belt around his waist that he could tuck his mace into.

They kept a leisurely pace in their travels. There was really nothing urgent in their search, but along the way Fist did look for a spot where he would want to stay. Deep down he needed a place that he would be proud to defend and call home.

Spring passed and soon summer was well underway. He and Squirrel headed out of the higher ground of the peaks and searched among the less rugged areas in the lower elevations. There was a lot more life out here and it wasn't always the harsh, dangerous sort of life to be found in the upper regions. This southern range of the Trafalgan Mountains had leafy trees mixed in with the pines and there weren't any warring tribes of giants or goblinoids in the area.

One day Fist found what he was looking for. They entered a small peaceful grove of leafy trees where birds sang and insects chirped. From the moment he entered the grove, Fist couldn't help but smile. There were acorns everywhere and Squirrel leapt off of his shoulder into a nearby tree to scavenge.

He stopped to drink from a tiny spring that bubbled forth with fresh water. Nestled in the middle of this grove was a group of tall boulders. Fist neared the boulders and instantly felt a fondness for the place. He didn't know why the presence of the rocks made him feel that way. Perhaps it was because they looked so out of place in the grove and it reminded him of his life.

The positioning of these boulders gave him an idea. He needed a shelter and there was a nice large space in the middle cluster of boulders that was more than big enough for his purposes. All he needed was something to keep the water off of his head.

Fist scouted around the area and found some dead trees including a few that had been struck by lightning. It took some time, but with his brute strength and some ingenuity, he was able to drag them over to the boulders. He leaned the dead trees against the boulders and climbed up to the top.

He pulled the tree trunks on top of the boulders one by one until they covered the right amount of space and lashed them together with leather strips from the pelts that he had collected over his journey. He then cut down great pine bows and stacked them on top as tightly as possible before lashing them down as well.

The next day, Fist stood under his shelter with great pride as the first great rainstorm of the summer came. His roof leaked, but most of the water drained off of the roof. Fist was satisfied. He had started the new home of The Big and Little People.

Weeks went by in his new home and Fist enjoyed life. During the day, he was either trying to improve his shelter or hunt for food. Squirrel always went with him on these outings perched on his shoulder and chattered at him about this or scolded him about that. Fist spent the evenings thinking by the fire and sleeping in his rugged house. Squirrel had its own crawl space between two of the boulders where it kept its horde of food, but every morning Fist continued to awake with his little friend curled up in the crook of his arm.

He began to expand the borders of his little home bit by bit, marking his territory with piles of rocks. Several times he had to chase off a trespassing bear and once he killed a rabid wolf that wouldn't leave.

One day as he was wandering about a mile outside of his little territory walking along the edges of a small forest, he heard tiny voices. Fist peeked around a tree to see two little creatures playing by some rocks. At first he thought that they must be dwarves from the descriptions he had been given by his elders, but as he watched them play, he realized that they were children. Their ears weren't pointed so they weren't elves. This meant that they were human children.

Fist knew that he should have left as soon as he saw the things, but he couldn't make himself leave. He watched them for a while, entranced by their strange coverings and the carefree way they played. Any ogre children seen playing that loudly and not actually fighting would have been cuffed and berated.

The smaller of the two children wore one long piece of clothing that didn't look like fur. The larger one had two pieces of material that were similar in look, but different colors. One piece covered its chest, while another covered its waist and legs.

Their speech was similar to that of ogres in some ways and he could make out a few of the words they said. They were playing a game where the larger child was a mighty warrior of some sort and the smaller child was a female he was protecting. Fist could not understand why a child would want to pretend to be a female until he realized that it actually was a female.

That was something else startling to him. The male and

female child played together and the male didn't hit her. He didn't even ignore her, but treated her with courtesy and bowed to her before fighting his imaginary enemies.

The children laughed and played for a while until there was a ringing sound and Fist heard a deeper voice shout from a distance. The voice said something about food. The children screamed in delight and ran around the cluster of rocks.

Fist knew that he should get as far from this place as possible and never come back again, but his curiosity overcame him. He turned his head and spoke to his little friend that was perched on his shoulder.

"What you think, Squirrel? Should I find where they going?" The creature didn't respond, but pulled a nut out of its cheek pouch and began to nibble on it. "Me too," Fist replied. He crept over to where the children had been playing and looked around the rocks. His jaw dropped.

Beyond the cluster of rocks was a large stretch of ground covered in rows of tiny plants that looked like they had been placed there purposely. Beyond these rows of plants was a shelter. It was quite a bit larger than his and made entirely of logs except for a strange material on the roof.

Smoke poured out of a stack on top of this roof. At first Fist thought that the shelter must be on fire. But there was no screaming, and the children ran towards the house in a carefree manner. Perhaps they made a fire inside the shelter on purpose.

Fist caught a whiff of something that could only be food and his mouth watered with the texture of the smell. The humans were cooking in the house. When the children arrived at the door, a tall human that could only be their father scolded them for going beyond the property line but he didn't beat them.

Fist watched a little longer entranced by the way the humans had built their home, then shook his head and reluctantly headed back to his home territory. Along the way he described to Squirrel everything he had seen. The ogre had caught a glimpse into a completely different life than he had ever known. There were aspects of it that fascinated him.

Another thought occurred to him and Fist frowned. The human's territory was too close for comfort. What would they do if they found out about his presence? He would have to be careful.

Over the next several weeks he found himself often at the border of the human's territory, though he was careful never to put a foot inside it. Fist would watch the humans and their habits, trying to figure out how some of the things that they used worked. There were four-legged beasts that pulled something made of wood and metal. The tall male human would ride this thing and make deep furrows in the ground with it. Little plants grew out of the furrows.

Other times another human with clothing similar to the girl child would come and pick growths off of these plants. Fist realized that the humans ate these plants with their meat. It was a fascinating concept to him, growing one's own food. They even kept a small flock of birds that didn't use their wings. Why, they hardly had to go hunting at all.

Fist would often come home after such trips and lay awake thinking about ways to implement these interesting practices in his new tribe. He tried several things, but they didn't seem to work very well. He couldn't build a fire in his own home without filling it with smoke, and any birds he was able to capture simply flew away.

The thing about these trips to the human land that he most enjoyed was watching the play of the children. As time went on, he found that he could understand more and more of what their tiny voices said even though they used terms that he did not understand. The male child's name was Cedric and the girl child's name was Lina. Their father was Tamboor. He knew this because the boy child would refer to himself as Cedric, son of Tamboor.

The children's games were fanciful, often the female would take the part of a warrior too and they would spar with sticks as if they were swords. This was also intriguing to him because the male child did not think the idea of a female warrior strange at all.

Fist began to develop a fondness for these humans and even thought of them as extensions of his small tribe. There were several times that he saw the tracks of dangerous beasts on the border of the human territory. He hunted the beasts down so that the children would be safe.

Sometimes their father would accompany them while they

played and join along in the fun. Fist found such familiar interplay with their father fascinating. Tamboor hugged them and played along and laughed at their antics. But the father also kept a watchful eye on the surrounding area and Fist was very careful not to show himself. The man kept a rather long sword strapped across his back and Fist did not want to have to kill him in self-defense.

Fist also learned something else while on these risky forays. This one human home was actually just on the outskirts of a large community of humans. This worried him because he knew that if they ever found out that he was there they would hunt him down. At least that was what the Thunder People would have done if a human was found living on their border. He kept his distance from any human roads or houses, but he couldn't stay away from the family of Tamboor. He saw something in them that he wished he had for himself.

One day as Fist was in his usual place waiting for the children to come, he sensed that something was amiss. It was strangely quiet and Squirrel had disappeared. Squirrel usually stuck right by him unless Fist was going into battle.

The children's voices chimed out from behind the rocks like they normally did, yet something raised the hair on his neck. Fist sniffed and scanned around with his eyes but didn't see anything until he looked up into the branches of the trees above. There perched a large treecat. It was almost as big as he was. The beast was watching intently as the children came into view.

The female, Lina, was playing with a small stuffed rag, while the boy whacked rocks and trees as he walked along with a fake wooden sword. Fist watched in horror as the great cat shifted its weight in the branch and hunched its shoulders in preparation to attack. The children were coming closer and the cat was just waiting for the proper moment.

Fist knew that he should turn away and go back to his new home. If he intervened here, then the humans would discover his presence and find his new home. Fist grimaced. He would have to leave.

The children continued to blindly walk into the danger laughing. Fist could not stand it any more. He had to do something.

He hefted his spear and wondered if he could take the cat

out of the branches before it attacked. But he wasn't a very accurate shot. If he missed, then he would lose his spear in the fight. A spear was a necessity in a fight with something as quick as a treecat. Soon the children were almost directly under the tree where the huge cat was waiting to strike and he couldn't wait any longer. He ran out of the trees and onto the path where the children usually played.

"Run childs!" he shouted and waved his huge arms.

The children saw the ogre come out of the trees and screamed. As they ran back towards their house, the cat saw its dinner fleeing and jumped down after them. Fist was already running before the cat hit the ground. He tackled it before it could chase after the children.

The great beast roared. It was very strong and agile. It tried to scramble out from under him. Fist reached around and grabbed it under its front legs. He had to hold it back because the cat was far faster than any of them and could still catch the children with ease if it got away.

Fist was in grave danger himself. Tackling the cat wasn't the best way to attack it. The treecat's claws were long and sharp and its front teeth could rip out huge chunks of flesh leaving wounds that even an ogre as big as Fist couldn't recover from.

The cat quickly stopped trying to chase after its prey and turned on its attacker. It growled and thrashed. Fist held on tight and struggled to stay behind it and out of the way of its claws. The cat twisted its back end and clawed at him while its head whipped back, snapping at his face.

Fist was sliced by its rear claws several times as it tried to break free. In desperation, he wrapped his legs around the cat's lower body. He released the cat's arms and grabbed it by the neck. He pulled its head back and squeezed. The cat screamed and thrashed frantically. Ignoring the wounds from its frantically ripping claws, he twisted and twisted until, with a loud crack, the cat went limp.

Tamboor came home early from his patrolling that day. There had been a strange lack of monsters around the mountain border town of Jack's Rest lately and there had not been any reports to check up on. As he came on to his property, he sighed. When he was out doing his duty as part of the town patrol, it reminded him of his warrior days back in the Academy Sword Wielder's Guild. He had been called Tamboor the Fearless back then.

Sometimes he missed the thrill of battle, the slaying of evil beasts, and the knowledge that by the strength of his arm, he was saving lives. That had been his life for over twenty years. Then he met his wife.

Tamboor had met his wife, Efflina, while working for the academy guild. They had three children together while living in the city of Reneul. His oldest son followed his footsteps and graduated from the academy.

On that day, as his son took his place in one of the guilds, he had stayed up all night comforting his wife. She wept in his arms knowing that the two men in her life would be going into danger every day. Tamboor was crushed. Through all the years they were married, she had never let him see how she felt.

The next day he had announced his retirement from the guild. They begged him to stay even as a teacher, but he could not bear to live so close to the daily fight and not take part in it. So they had packed up their things and left Reneul. Tamboor had asked around and heard of a place that caught his fancy.

Jack's Rest was a rugged border town where danger was near, but the soil was good. They had lived in this place for over a year now. Though sometimes he had regrets about leaving his old life behind, as soon as he saw his homestead, he forgot about any misgivings.

Tamboor loved his new home. He bought the land with his own hard earned gold. He built this house and worked the fields with his own hands. It was hard work and he had hated it most of the time that he was building this place, but Cedric and Lina grew carefree and happy and his wife was in love with the small town.

As he walked up the stairs to his home he was completely at peace. He could spend the rest of his life here. Who needs battle anyway?

Those were his thoughts as he opened the door of his home. Five minutes later, he ran back out in a fury with his sword in hand. Evidently his retirement wasn't completely over.

Chapter Thirty Three

Fist trudged back to his new home with a heavy heart. Luckily the furs he wore took the brunt of the great cat's attacks and his wounds were only superficial. Squirrel reappeared right after he had killed the cat and now it sat on his shoulder, scolding him. He ignored his little friend, not really having a good explanation for what he had done.

He had never done anything like that before. Sure he had saved the lives of his fellow tribe members on countless occasions, but why had he risked his life and home over these humans? Fist looked down at the little rag doll that he had taken before he left the scene. It looked frail and tiny in his large hands. He couldn't really answer that question. All he knew was that he didn't regret it.

When Fist arrived at his new home in the grove of trees, he didn't want to leave. In the short time that he had lived there, this place had become more precious to him than the territory of the Thunder People had ever been.

When he entered his dwelling, he found that Squirrel wasn't eager to leave either. The little creature crawled into its little hole between the boulders and wouldn't come out. Fist tried to coax it out with acorns for a while before giving up. He started gathering his belongings together.

Large tears welled up in his eyes.

From the moment that he ran out of his home with sword drawn, Tamboor had been filled with a fury that he could barely restrain. His sense of well-being about his new home had been shattered. For the first time in his life, danger was touching his family directly and that was unacceptable. His children were off limits. Whatever had dared come near them was dead.

When his Cedric and Lina had first started to play out at the edges of his land, he had been afraid about them going this far from their home in this part of the borderlands. But then he had come with the children and scouted the land out to find that it was pretty quiet. Now that he thought about it, the forest had been too quiet in fact.

Actually his whole life had been too quiet. He had gotten complacent. He had known it too.

Tamboor had been itching for a fight for weeks. Now he had it. Tamboor also knew that he could not afford to let his emotions rule. He couldn't rush into a fight without knowing what he was fighting. He needed to shake the anger from his mind and track the beast from an impersonal point of view. He could not miss anything.

He had many questions about the incident. If a giant truly had gone after his children, and he had no cause to doubt them, then why had it yelled at them to run? Tamboor had some experience with giants and knew that they could be pretty cruel to their prey.

Perhaps it wanted to have some fun with the human children. It might have wanted to scare them before it ate them. But if it was taunting them, then why didn't it chase them all the way to their home? He had built a sturdy house, but none that would withstand the attack of a giant. The thought of a giant destroying his house angered him again. He had to make sure and kill the thing before it could come back.

When he came upon the enormous treecat with the broken neck, he stood with jaw agape. His anger turned into background noise and his training kicked in.

With his vast tracking and battle knowledge, he could tell certain things. The creature that had scared the children definitely was a giant or something akin to one, because it would have taken enormous strength to break the cat's thick neck. The presence of the cat explained the roaring sounds that his wife had heard, but what were the odds that a giant and a great cat would have a battle right on the edge of his land?

Another peculiar thing was that the giant had not taken the cat with it when it left. This didn't make sense unless it was too wounded to carry the beast. A giant always took its kills back to its lair to eat if not just for the fur. Tamboor searched, and though there was some blood on its claws, there was not enough to suggest that the giant was incapacitated.

A set of heavy footprints left the scene and entered the forest. From the depth and size of the footprints, this wasn't that big of a giant, maybe 600 to 700 pounds at the most. Tamboor nodded grimly. This was a foe that he could handle easily.

Tamboor searched the surrounding forest next and found many more tracks, enough for thirty giants or more. His emotions were kicking in again and outrage lined his thoughts. How had he lived in this place for a year and not known that a group of giants had lived so close to his land?

Tamboor considered going to the town and gathering a hunting party, but then he noticed that the tracks were all identical. No, it wasn't a large group of giants at all, perhaps only one. He examined the age of the tracks and shivered. This particular beast had haunted the edge of his land for weeks! His children played out here every day. The thought of a leering giant watching his children at play and planning its dinner caused his insides to squirm.

Tamboor tracked the trail of the giant and began to get a better picture of what he faced. But for every answer he found, several more questions were raised. He found several piles of rocks that he knew to be territorial markings. Only ogres used formations like that, but this beast wasn't acting like an ogre.

Ogres were stupider than giants and were possessed of more of a savage brutality than an evil cruelty. An ogre wouldn't have observed his children for weeks. It would have immediately killed them and brought them home for supper.

He continued his tracking and found that his fury was becoming tempered by curiosity about the creature. He knew he was getting closer to the beast's lair when he noticed several areas where deadwood had been chopped or pulled down and carried away. The ogre would need that for its fires.

Tamboor entered a tranquil grove of trees where birds were chirping and crickets sounding. This was strange because the presence of an ogre almost always scares off the local wildlife. The surrounding area was almost untouched except for the ogre's tracks. Tamboor had never been into an ogre territory where the land was not scarred by the ignorant beasts. When he finally came upon the ogre's home, he was stunned.

The beast had actually tried to build a house. There were several boulders grouped together with a makeshift roof on top and a bearhide flap for a door! Tamboor even saw what looked like an attempt at a chimney, though he didn't see how it could be functional. In front of the ogre's dwelling several furrows were dug into the ground with dead plants lined up in them. This didn't make sense. Ogres didn't have gardens.

It took a moment for Tamboor to finally realize what was going on. The pieces fell into place. The beast had been watching his land and trying to learn!

Tamboor stood in front of the dwelling and decided to call out to the ogre. Normally, he wouldn't have challenged the beast. His original plan had been to wait for it to leave its home and kill it quickly before it even knew he was there. But this one had him curious. He couldn't kill the thing without getting some questions answered. He was starting to have some suspicions about this beast and if they were true, he would know as soon as it stepped out of the door.

"Ogre! Come out and face me!" Tamboor shouted.

He heard sounds from inside and the bear hide flap stirred. His instinct was to pull out his sword and charge, but he held his ground and waited. A huge hand grabbed the bear hide and pulled it away from the entrance.

Out stepped the biggest ogre Tamboor had ever seen. The beast came out with back hunched, but immediately straightened its back and rose to full height. Tamboor reached for his sword, but stopped before grasping the hilt. The ogre didn't make any aggressive moves. It crossed its arms in front of its chest and waited, a frown on its wide mouth.

Tamboor didn't know how to react to the ogre's posture. Its stance exuded confidence, but there was worry in its eyes. He wouldn't allow himself to let his curiosity overcome his responsibility, though. He was about to demand that the ogre leave his land or face death, when the most peculiar thing happened.

A gray rock squirrel appeared on the ogre's shoulder, rummaged around in a small pouch hanging by the ogre's neck and calmly began chewing on a nut. The ogre didn't seem to register the little beast's presence at all, but continued to look down at Tamboor with its brow furrowed, saying nothing.

Tamboor wanted to shout out at the beast and charge it for coming anywhere near his children, but something in its demeanor halted the force of his anger. What came out instead was, "What are you doing here?"

Its voice was deep and throaty, "I live here."

Tamboor didn't know how to respond to that. Suddenly he felt like he was the intruder here. That unnerving feeling re-ignited some of his anger.

"What were you doing on my land?" Tamboor asked.

Now the ogre looked embarrassed. It unfolded its arms and scratched behind its ear. The squirrel on its shoulder was startled by the movement and dropped the seed it was chewing. The little creature scolded the ogre and pulled another seed out of the leather pouch.

"I was watching," the ogre said.

"Watching what?" Tamboor pressed, an edge in his voice.

"You," the ogre stated. "The humans."

Tamboor knew that there had to be more to it. Was this ogre a scout for a marauding tribe?

"Why?"

The ogre's brow furrowed and it shook its head as it tried to decide how to best answer the question. Finally it sighed. "I don't know."

The ogre's behavior was completely disarming. Tamboor growled in frustration. This was not how the meeting was supposed to go.

"What is your name, ogre?"

"Fist," it replied.

"Okay, Fist. Why did you kill that big cat on the edge of my land?"

The ogre hesitated and then replied, "it was going to eat Cedric and Lina."

"How do you know their names?" Tamboor had grabbed

the hilt of his sword without realizing it.

Fist grasped the head of the rock mace at his belt in response.

"I listen," the ogre said, watching Tamboor's sword hand. "The male is Cedric, the female is Lina. You are Tamboor, and the woman-" He pointed towards the human's land. "is mommy."

Tamboor couldn't accept what he had learned. This ogre had been watching his family for weeks and yet it had not disturbed them at all. It had even saved his children's lives today. Part of Tamboor supposed that he should be grateful, but he could not reconcile the fact that this was an ogre that stood before him. With a grunt, he put his sword away.

"Alright, Fist. I will make a pact with you. I promise not to tell the other humans about your presence here. But you must not ever step a foot near my property again. If I ever learn that you have come anywhere near my land again, I will bring all of the hunters in the town and kill you."

The ogre looked a bit confused at first as if puzzling out Tamboor's meaning. "I stay away from your land, humans leave me alone?"

"Yes."

"I agree to this." The ogre looked relieved.

"Very well." Tamboor said and left without another word. As he walked past the open flap, he caught a glimpse of what was inside the ogre's house and stumbled. It was stacked with animal hides. Tamboor now understood why the town patrols had been so quiet lately.

The next week passed by uneventfully. Fist grew frustrated with his projects. He couldn't seem to make anything work right. All of the ideas he had developed while watching the humans floundered. He didn't go back to the human's land. His sense of honor forbade it, but he often looked in that direction longingly, sure that if he could only spend a few more minutes studying the land, he would be able to figure out how to make his projects work.

He also missed the children, their laughter and playing. It was disconcerting how attached he had grown to the little humans, but there was nothing he could do about it. Their father had spoken.

One night it rained fiercely. His roof leaked more than normal and he shivered through the night, soaked. In the morning he awoke to the sound of footsteps outside of his dwelling. With a growl, he grabbed his mace and charged out.

Fist was startled by the sight of Tamboor pulling a loaded handcart.

"Good morning, Fist," the man said.

"Why you here?"

"My wife has decided that I have been acting unneighborly."

Tamboor pulled a large piece of oiled canvass off of the cart and shook the rain off of it. The cart was loaded with food and bags of seed. There was even a smoked ham and a small bag of sweetnuts for Squirrel.

"I am here to thank you for saving the lives of our children. I am also to thank you for keeping the beasts off of our land. Will you accept these gifts as thanks?"

Fist did not know what "unneighborly" was. He didn't even know what most of the things in the cart were. But the sight of the meat made his mouth water and he knew that the humans were showing him goodwill. It was something he had never experienced before.

Tamboor sensed that the ogre was at a loss for words. He took a look around. The ogre was soaked and a trail of water ran out from under his doorway. The ogre's home was in bad shape.

"Well, Fist, it looks like you had a rough night. Would you mind if I helped you with your roof?"

Fist smiled in response. A new friendship had begun.

Chapter Thirty Four

The leader of the raptoid pack was gorging on their fresh kill. The other members of the pack watched him eat, keening softly with hunger. They would not be allowed to feed until he was finished.

While they were preoccupied, Deathclaw approached the leader of the raptoid pack carefully, staying downwind of the others. This was a tricky thing to do because the dunes dispersed the wind between them in ways that were hard to predict. Deathclaw had lived in the dunes for so long that this was almost second nature to him, but with the changes in his body, nothing was quite the same.

For weeks he had wandered along the outskirts of the desert, slowly but steadily gaining control over his new body. At the beginning he had been an awkward mess, stumbling around and unable to see. Now he could run with ease and his eyes moved in concert. The world had a new depth to it and he could see greater distances.

These new senses made him a far better hunter. He learned to go to the top of a high dune and look over the desert for movement. The sensors in his tongue and nostrils were able to pick up more delicate scents than before. Once upon his prey, he had another new advantage. His arms had new mobility. He could reach further, and with the bulging muscles on his back and chest, they had great power.

Though he did not comprehend the enormity of it, his mind had changed as well. His thought processes were expanding and he was beginning to see things in a new light. He was starting to question things, something he had never done before. This is what had led him here, downwind from the deathclaw of a new raptoid pack.

Once Deathclaw had enough control over his body to hunt and survive, he had one last overriding instinct. He needed to build a pack to replace the one he lost. He searched until he found scent markers that told him he was near a small pack. He followed the pack for two days undetected and watched their movements.

There were six of them. Two females and four males. Their deathclaw was the largest male. As he watched the raptoids take down several kills, Deathclaw knew that he was stronger than any of them

Usually a lone raptoid had to enter a new pack as a submissive. It would need to start at the bottom, surviving off of the scraps the others left behind until it could work its way up through the pack. One day if the deathclaw of the pack was wounded or ill, he might be able to kill it and take its place as the new deathclaw.

This method was now unacceptable to Deathclaw. With the changes to his brain, his sense of self had altered too. In his mind, he was a distinct individual now. He had led his own pack for so long that deathclaw wasn't just his title anymore, it was who he was. He could not be content with groveling his way through the ranks of a pack for years, known apart from the others only by his scent.

There was only one acceptable way for him to join a new pack now. He had to kill the deathclaw and claim the pack as his own. He had done this before on previous occasions when he had led the largest pack in the desert. When a new pack entered his territory, he would surround the pack, kill their leader and absorb the surviving members into his own pack.

The only reason that this tactic had worked for him was because his own pack so outnumbered them, they didn't dare protect their deathclaw. This time he would need to do something different. If he attacked head on, they would all fight back. He had to use stealth and kill the leader before the rest of the pack could react.

Now was the time. The leader of the pack had sated himself on the kill and moved a short distance away to lay down. The rest of the pack tore onto the kill now that he was finished. Deathclaw saw his opportunity. He darted forward.

He pounced on the raptoid from behind, seizing its neck with his powerful jaws. It was sated from its meal and reacted a fraction more slowly than usual. This gave Deathlaw the time to grab its front arms with his own before it could slash at his eyes. He raked its back with his rear claws, tearing through muscle and into its kidneys.

The raptoid screeched and tried to get to its feet but his weight kept it down. It sent its tail barb at him, but he used his own tail to bat it aside. It screeched again. The other raptoids had looked up from their meal and came to their leader's aid.

Deathclaw was out of time. He grunted and clenched his jaws with all his might. He twisted his head, his muscles bulging beneath his scales. The raptiod's neck snapped with an audible crack.

He leapt off of the dead creature and faced the rest of the raptoids. Deathclaw screeched in triumph, claiming ownership of the pack. The five remaining members circled him warily.

He hissed an order at them. They paused for a moment, then continued to circle. Deathclaw did not understand. The leadership of the pack was his now. If one of them wanted to challenge his position, it had to bellow a challenge. He hissed another order, more forcefully this time, demanding that they back down. The pack cocked their head at him and several of them hissed back in defiance.

One of the males stepped out of the circle. It chirped an order. The rest of the pack obeyed, spreading out into an attack formation.

Deathclaw backed away slowly. They weren't seeing him as a contender for leadership. His commands had confused them at first, but now they had decided what to do with him. They were treating him as an attacking predator.

Deathclaw finally understood. To them, he was no longer a raptoid.

Their new leader leapt forward, leading with the talons on its powerful rear legs. Deathclaw darted to the side and sent his tail out as it passed by. His tail barb caught the raptoid's head mid flight and pierced through its eye into its brain. Its short career as leader ended as it convulsed in the sand.

The remaining four backed away. One of the females assumed leadership. It chirped an order and they entered into a different formation.

Deathclaw knew that order. The new leader understood that he was too great a threat for them to come at him one at a time. They would all rush him at once. He didn't have much choice. Deathclaw fled.

His new muscular legs caused him to run differently than he had in the past. He ran hunched over, occasionally using his arms to pull him more quickly through the sand. The raptoids paced him, but he didn't stop to fight. He slashed with tail or claw if one of them got to close. When he left the boundary of their territory, they slowed and stopped, screeching taunts at him.

Deathclaw continued to run, his mind awhirl with new feelings. They were right. He was not a raptoid any longer. What was he? Sadness tore through him along with self pity. What was he to do? He screeched in misery.

There was a startled yelp a few dunes away. Something had heard him. He came to a halt and listened. He heard frantic scampering and labored breathing.

He followed the sounds until he saw the tracks of a strange beast in the sand. The wind kept most of its scent from him, but he caught a faint trace from the tracks. He hissed. It was a human. The one creature in all the world that Deathclaw feared.

Deathclaw followed the tracks over two dunes. When he reached the crest of the last one, flattened his body to the sand and peered over.

The lone human trudged through the desert with no weapons but a sword. The man was bent by the heat and nearly dying of thirst. He recognized this human. It had been there the day that his body was changed. Deathclaw held his breath, afraid to give away his presence.

With his expanded mind had come another new experience. Deathclaw had dreams. Every night as he slept mostly buried in the sand, he relived the moment when the wizard had destroyed his pack and changed him forever. Sometimes in the dreams, his sister screeched pleadingly to him as she was dragged away. The wizard would approach him with its hideous wiggling fingers. His head would hurt and hurt until he awoke, disoriented and shaking.

Deathclaw quivered with a mix of fear and anticipation. This human was weak. Perhaps he could kill it. But what if it froze him like the time before? What would it do to him then?

He kept his distance, but continued to follow the man as it stumbled through the sand. Yes, it was very weak. He could attack at any time. It would die before it could freeze him. But something made him stay back. As a raptoid, Deathclaw would have simply killed the man and ate him. Now, a part of his brain that he had rarely used before was leading him. It was curiosity.

He followed the human to the edge of the desert. A green bush or two stuck up out of the sand, and he could smell a host of foreign smells. There was an abundance of water and vegetation this way. He could smell strange animals and insects.

The human seemed excited by this development. It laughed and shouted things into the air, though there were no other humans in the area. Deathclaw was startled by this outburst and followed from a further distance.

The dunes and cracked earth ended and were replaced by trees and grass and flowers. Deathclaw watched as the human disappeared into thick grasslands.

He stared at the grass in puzzlement for he had never seen anything like it before. He heard the human continue on its path through the grass and struggled with himself. His instincts said to leave the human and stay in the desert, but something prompted him to follow.

It wasn't just curiosity that nudged him forward. Deathclaw had learned that he was no longer a raptoid. He was something else. The desert was all he knew, but it no longer belonged to him. He entered the tall grass and left his desert home behind.

Deathclaw decided to find out just what he was.

Chapter Thirty Five

For an eternity Justan's mind soared through an empty and lonely darkness. Distantly he saw a misty source of light. He willed himself toward it. As he approached the light, he entered into a cloudy tunnel. The inside of the tunnel was bright and Justan was able to see his arms and legs. He had form. This surprised him for he had always imagined his spirit to be without substance. He flexed his left hand and felt a distant twinge. That was funny. Spirits weren't supposed to have pain.

The light within the cloud came from tiny swirling beacons that were dispersed equally within the mist. Justan stared at the lights, enjoying their hypnotic spinning. Out of curiosity, he reached out his hand and touched one.

With a jolt, he was looking out of someone else's eyes. The air was cold and dry. He was in a rocky wasteland and hunting for food. Justan had no control over the body he inhabited, but he could see, smell, and feel everything. He was conscious that the being he was in had immense weight and strength. This being was a warrior. A warrior, but also a hunter. As the being knelt beside a tiny stream for a drink of water and looked at its reflection, Justan was startled. His spirit fled. He left the bright cloud and sped back into the darkness. He had no desire to inhabit a monster.

Justan's eyes opened to complete whiteness. His hip ached with a dull pain. Justan lifted his left hand in front of his eyes. It was unbandaged. He attempted to make a fist. His fingers clenched without pain, though his tendons seemed a little stiff. He looked down and saw that his body was covered in a light blanket. He was in a bed.

Justan was in a white painted room filled with small beds, though few were occupied. The beds on either side of Justan's were empty, but a bed across the aisle held a familiar face. It was

Zambon. The guard was sleeping, but his cheeks were flushed with color and he breathed without struggle.

Justan smiled. They must be in the Mage School. His suspicion was confirmed when he heard a door open with a bang. Vannya smiled when she saw that he was awake and ran across the room. She sat on the empty bed beside him.

"Justan! How do you feel?"

"I guess that I'm fine, though my hip still hurts a little." He was happy to see her pretty face looking back at him. He had thought himself a dead man.

"Hmm," she murmured and reached across him to grab his blanket. She started to pull it down across his chest.

"Whoa!" Justan realized that he was naked underneath the thin blanket. He snatched the blanket back and pulled it up to his chin. "What are you doing?"

Vannya chuckled and her face turned a little red. "I am a healer, remember? I have to have contact to work properly. Trust me." Justan reluctantly released his death grip on the thin blanket and she brought it down to his waist. Vannya gasped, one hand shooting to her mouth.

"Justan! What is that? Does it hurt?" She stared at the frost rune glittering on his chest.

"Oh, I thought you knew." He briefly told her about his encounter with the Scralag.

"Fascinating," she said and traced the silvery scar with one finger. "It's still cold." Her faced turned red again. "Sorry."

Her hands moved down his sides to grasp him on the side of either hip. Justan wished he were anywhere else but there. He didn't know how to react having this unbelievably attractive woman touching his bare hips. Vannya closed her eyes and her brow furrowed as she concentrated.

Justan looked down and his vision shifted. He saw lightly colored flows of blue and gold energy leave from her hands into his waist. The twinge of pain in his pelvis stopped and she released him.

"See?" she said and pulled his blanket back up. "The break is pretty much healed, but when an injury of that magnitude is healed, even magically, it is going to take a while for your body to readjust. Your hip will protest for a while. To keep from aggravating it, you need to stay in bed for a week."

"A week?" Justan sputtered. "I don't think so!" He started to get out of bed until he remembered that he was still naked under the blanket.

"Yes, a week. By then your body will be fully adjusted. You will probably be as good as new." He glared at her until she acquiesced a little. "Okay, if you want to push it, you only have to stay in bed for two days. But you will be confined to the infirmary until the end of the week. That's it, no arguing."

Justan still wasn't happy with the idea, but he had a question or two. "Vannya, what happened? All I remember is being hit and that orc standing over me."

"As soon as you went down, Riveren split that orc's head like it was a ripe melon. It was really gross," she said, her petite little nose wrinkled. "After that, we dragged you and the three captured orcs to the top of the ravine."

"Three? What about the fourth one?" he asked

"The one you stabbed in the buttocks?" she asked with a slight grin.

Justan nodded his head and returned the grin. He wasn't exactly proud of the tactic. The creature had been lying there helpless after all, but he had done what he felt was necessary to goad Marckus into fighting him.

Vannya shrugged. "We don't know. In all the confusion, it must have limped away. One of the guards is out tracking it now."

"How did you get Zambon, me, and three orcs back to the Mage School?"

"Well, Zambon was in really bad shape. It took pretty much all of our magical strength just to fight off all of the infection in his wounds. Belly wounds are the toughest, you know. There are so many little cuts that need to be repaired on internal organs and veins and tissues. Anyway, we fixed him up as best as we could and I kept you unconscious so that you would sleep through the pain. As far as how we got out of there with you, we were forced to send Qyxal back to the school for help."

"But how did you and Riveren take care of two wounded men and three angry orc prisoners until he got back?" Justan asked.

"I took care of you two, while Riveren watched the prisoners." She frowned for a moment. "He wouldn't even let me touch those terrible burns on his body until help came. He was acting ridiculous. It wouldn't have taken much for me to at least relieve some of the pain."

Justan thought he understood why. Riveren was punishing himself for being captured and putting everyone in danger. Besides, he had just been through a very traumatic experience. Sometimes you needed a little pain to keep you focused.

"What he was doing wasn't that difficult," she continued. "All he did was wait until one of them fussed and hit it on the head with the flat of his axe. But we didn't have too keep it up for long anyway. Qyxal was less than half way there when he met up with a contingent of guards and wizards coming to our rescue."

Justan smiled. Evidently in the right situation, the council wouldn't wait for a meeting to decide something important. When the stable man told them what was happening, they must have organized the party right away.

"Anyway, when we got back here to the school, we were in big trouble."

"Why? What did you do wrong?" Justan wondered.

She took a deep breath and did her best impression of a stuffy old wizard. "Well, we 'left school grounds without permission, acted irresponsibly and in doing so, corrupted a younger student.' Yeah, I think that's what they said."

"You should have told them the truth." Justan felt bad about getting her and Qyxal in trouble. "I'm the one who dragged you both into it. Blame it on me. I don't care. They already punished me enough just by making me come here."

"Oh, please. You didn't make me do anything. Qyxal and I both knew we were breaking the rules when we went along with you. We were willing to face the consequences when we left." She leaned over conspiratorially. "Besides, it wasn't that bad. Each of the professors congratulated us privately when it was all over. We were pretty much given a token punishment so that the other students wouldn't think they were being soft on us."

"Let me guess, you got 'infirmary duty'."

"For a week."

He leaned back and put his hands behind his head. "So, is it hard work taking care of us sick people all day?"

"Actually, I'm cleaning floors. Oh! I need to get back to work before Miss Guernfeldt gets back." She stood up and for the first time Justan noticed that her robes were dirty and damp.

"Guernfeldt?"

"She's the matron of the infirmary. Very strict on working students. Also on patients, so don't think that you are getting out of bed before I said you could. I am going to inform her of your schedule." She turned and worked her way around some beds to get out of the room.

Justan called after her. "I saw it, you know."

"What?" she called back.

"The magic. When you were, uh, fixing my hip, just a minute ago. I saw the magic coming out of your fingers and into my hip."

She grinned and her eyes lit up. "Oh, that's wonderful! Usually it takes a cadet a week to figure out how to use his mage sight. I've got to tell Master Latva!" She ran out of the room.

"Latva?" Justan had no idea who that was. After Vannya left, he stared at the ceiling and thought about everything that had happened to him in the last few days. It was amazing to think that just a few short weeks ago he had been training for the Training School tests.

He closed his eyes and reached deep into his mind searching for Gwyrtha. He hadn't even had a chance to think about her with all of the things that had been going on. He found her warm presence in the corners of his mind. The bond was faint at this distance and he had to concentrate harder than he had in the past, but from the flashes of sights and sounds he was able to pull up, she was in the forest, frolicking and playing with some elven children. That was surprising because he hadn't seen a single child during his brief stay with the elves.

Gwyrtha noticed his intrusion and he felt a surge of affection and concern for his well being come from her. She had noticed his distress the night before, but the elves wouldn't let her leave. Justan grinned and concentrated on sending her an account of his harrowing battle the night before. Her response was happiness that he was okay and a feeling of regret for not being able to fight by his side. Justan wasn't sure, but somehow her responses seemed quite a bit more intelligent than they had been when he had first bonded with her.

Justan needed to learn more about what had caused this connection. Some of the wizards might be able to explain it, but he couldn't ask the wizards about it without letting them know of her existence. He would have to do some study in the library on his own and see if he could find an answer.

The door to the room slammed open, startling him from his reverie. In walked a rather large woman with a nasty mole on the side of her chin. Her hair was a dirty shade of brown and was tied back in a tight bun. Her features looked to be chiseled from stone and her arms were thick and powerful like they weren't arms at all, but tree trunks. She must be Miss Guernfeldt.

Following the massive woman was an old man with a crooked hat who walked slightly hunched over with the use of a staff. He was the perfect picture of an old wizard with a long white beard and voluminous blue robe. But his youthful blue eyes had a twinkle in them that made his age look like an act. Walking beside the old man was a gaunt gnome that Justan hadn't yet met, carrying a stack of papers and a large silver-bound book.

The old wizard took a seat on the empty bed beside Justan's. Once again, Justan was well aware that with these strangers in the room, he was naked but for a thin blanket. It made him feel, well, naked. The old man spoke and his voice sounded nothing like Justan would have expected. It was a voice full of life and energy.

"Greetings, Justan, son of Faldon the Fierce. First let me say that this is the first time I have given this speech to so small an audience. Usually I have at least twenty or thirty cadets at the same time." The old wizard coughed into his hand and cleared his throat, a raspy sound that conflicted with his clear speaking tone.

"I am Latva, so named at the Bowl of Souls in this school fifty years ago." The old man pulled the sleeve back on his left arm and opened his left hand so that Justan could see a rune emblazoned upon his palm, the mark of a named wizard.

The naming of wizards was a bit different than the naming

of warriors. A wizard's use of magic was dependent on his knowledge of himself and his abilities. A magic user who was truly at one with his own abilities could unleash much greater levels of magic. The naming of a wizard was a confirmation of this oneness. It was a mark of power.

Unlike warriors, a wizard could attempt the naming once a year throughout his life. This was done by completing the proper rituals and dipping the blade of one's ceremonial knife into the water of the Bowl of Souls. If he were found worthy, his true wizard name would be given to him.

Justan was in awe. He had never met a named wizard before. "Uh . . . nice to meet you, Master Latva."

The old master chuckled at the expression on Justan's face. Latva had seen the same expression on the faces of thousands of different people who met him for the first time.

"Calm down, young man. I am still just a man like you. The reason that I introduced myself so, is for you to understand the importance of what we are about to do."

"What is that?"

Both of the wizard's eyebrows shot up. "We are inducting you into the school as a cadet, of course."

"Here?" Justan asked in disbelief.

"Why of course. It's as good a place as any."

Justan looked at the matron who stood sternly with her arms crossed in front of her. "Shouldn't I be wearing more clothes or something?"

"Pah!" The master said, waving the idea away with one hand. "Were you not naked for your birth? That was a much more auspicious occasion than this." He leaned forward and with a twinkle in his eye, added, "in some cultures, one has to be naked for such a ceremony! For instance, in the Guataga people, a man must wear nothing but a-."

The gnome standing beside the bed grunted, and the wizard stopped what he was about to say. "Oh, yes, well, hand me the papers please, Alfred." The gnome complied and handed a small stack of documents to the master. "Thank you."

Latva pulled a pair of spectacles from within his robes. Justan thought that the glasses were for the wizard, but instead the old man handed them up to the gnome. "Here, Alfred, try not to lose them again. Now please turn to the proper page." While Alfred opened the silver tome, the wizard set the papers beside him on the bed. He looked back at Justan.

"Magic, is part of all life," the wizard began and extended his left hand. Above the rune on his hand appeared a flame. "It is in the elements."

The flame on his hand was blown out by a gust of wind and became a rock. A crack appeared in the rock and water poured out of it.

"The four elements make up all magic. Fire, air, earth, and water. We are all made up of these tiny little elements, or intelligences." The mage looked at Justan. "Raise your hand."

Justan raised his hand.

"No, higher. In front of your eyes." Justan complied and the wizard said, "Watch."

The air around Justan's hand shimmered and his vision zoomed in so that he could see it close up. His vision zoomed in closer.

"Do you see the elements?" The wizard asked. Justan shook his head. He saw all of the tiny ridges of his hand, but could see no little elements. "Look a little closer," the wizard bade.

The vision zoomed in even more. Justan could see a foreign landscape of flesh where little alien blobs and creatures with waving feelers moved about. He wrinkled his face in disgust. Were all those tiny things living on his hand?

"Look closer," the wizard said and the scene tightened again. Now Justan could make out tiny networks of structures clumped together. "This is as close as I can show you, but if you could look still closer, you would see that those little clusters are made of even tinier structures, which are made of even tinier structures and so on. The tiniest of the structures are the true elements, the tiny building blocks of all matter that we wizards call intelligences. At the Mage School, we learn to control these little intelligences. That is what we call magic."

Justan was stunned as the vision dissipated. How large the world seemed, when confronted by the smallest of things. Magic was starting to sound interesting.

The wizard smiled. "We have three mottos here at the Mage School: We search for knowledge. We reveal the truth. We advance that which is right." Justan nodded thoughtfully. The wizard handed him a sheet of parchment with the mottos written on it. "Remember them well."

Latva lifted the rest of the papers from beside him and held them out to Justan. The master spoke out in an official tone, "Justan, son of Faldon the Fierce, do you wish to enter the Mage School as a cadet?"

"Yes sir, I do." Justan replied, and for the first time he really meant it. If Valtrek had shown him like this, he might have been willing to come to the Mage School on his own.

"Very good. The rules for cadets are all here. This last sheet is your class schedule. It isn't quite like the normal schedule for first year cadets, but you are not like most first year cadets, so it will have to do. Your first class starts today after dinner with Professor Beehn."

He motioned to the gnome who held out the silver-bound book to an open page. Justan saw a long list of signatures. Master Latva handed him a pen. "Sign your name here. You will be held to a two year contract pursuant to all the rules and regulations thereof."

Justan didn't see a need to hesitate and signed right away. The Master lifted the book, examined his signature, and smiled. "Mage Vannya tells me that you have seen the flows of magic, is this true?"

Justan nodded, "I think I have, sir."

Latva turned the book back towards Justan. "Do you see it now?" Justan just saw lettering on the page. The old wizard shook his head.

"Concentrate," he said and touched Justan between the eyes with the tip of his finger.

It was if the man's finger had left an impression there. The spot he had touched vibrated. Justan looked at the page again and thought he saw a faint glow in the signatures. He focused in and like when Vannya had been treating his pelvis, his vision shifted. The signatures were swirling with colors, some brighter than others and some with a different hue altogether. Justan's shown the brightest. He couldn't make out the colors.

"Do you see?" Latva asked. "That is your potential. It says a lot of things about you."

"What does mine say about me?" Justan asked.

The master looked at the clock on the wall above Justan's bed and sighed. "I am sorry, we have no time to speak of it now, young Justan. Perhaps later."

Justan was disappointed. The things that the named wizard had revealed to him were so interesting. He wanted to know more.

Master Latva turned to Miss Guernfeldt. "Matron, please let the welcoming committee enter."

To Justan's horror, she opened the door to the room and a flood of people Justan didn't know poured in to congratulate him on being a new student. They all seemed very pleased to meet him. Evidently, word had gotten out about his rescue of the missing guards and he was becoming somewhat of a celebrity. All that Justan knew was that he was mostly naked shaking a bunch of stranger's hands.

After about half an hour of introductions, he was just beginning to get used to being in that uncomfortable state. Then Miss Guernfeldt entered the room carrying a large washbasin full of soapy water.

"Everybody out!" she shouted. "It is time for this patient's bath!" She reached into her apron and pulled out a large sponge. Justan felt like screaming.

So began his first day as a cadet in the Mage School.

Epilogue

"*Marckus has failed you, Master. It is just as I warned,*" she said.

"Oh, has he?" Ewzad's fist tightened around the eye and she worried once again that it might break. "Marckus? Fail me? No-no, he succeeds where the others fail."

"*The orc arrived late, Master. The caravan made it to the school unharmed. He captured two of the guards, but they were rescued.*" She tried her best to keep the sarcasm out of her tone for now. It would be much more delicious later.

"Blast him! I needed that mirror!" She knew that he was stomping around his office enraged and the thought pleased her. The vein in his forehead was pulsing again. "Get him here, you understand? Get him here right away? That would be best, don't you think? Yes, I think he needs to be taken on a tour of my dungeons and showed what failure means."

"*Unfortunately, he would fail you in that task as well, Master,*" she intoned.

"Oh? Fail me again? Fail me in what? Showing up?"

"*Well, yes. That would be difficult for him. You see, he is dead.*"

"Dead is he?" Ewzad seemed so disappointed.

"*Killed by one of the guards, Master.*" She didn't tell him about the involvement of the man that had killed her sweet children. She had her own plans for that one. "*And he allowed the other orcs to be captured. They are in the hands of the wizards as we speak.*"

"Idiot! That idiot!" Ewzad could feel his plans slipping through his fingers. "Blast him! What do they know? The orcs, that is. I cannot have them telling my secrets to the wizards before my forces are ready. No-no, that won't do!"

"*They know more than they should. Marckus was a loud creature and his lips were too loose for my liking. But worry not, Master. They are true believers in the Barldag and their minds are weak. I will not allow them to talk,*" she soothed and reached through their limited connection to drain his stress away. Oh how she hated fawning for the little man. But the dark voice demanded it and she could not disobey.

Her manipulations were working. Ewzad's tone softened and his pacing slowed. He was not ready to give up his concerns, though.

"Yes-yes, but still. Still, the wizards are crafty old men. Yes, the orcs could be made to talk."

"*They will not, dear Master. They will die before they talk. Worry not,*" she assured him and moved more of her presence through the connection and into his mind. She reached to the pleasure centers of his mind and stroked gently. He let out a sigh and more of his tension drained away. "*I will fulfill my duties, Master. I have plans in place to disrupt the schools while we build the army. When you are ready to strike they will be weakened. The Mage School in particular has some wicked surprises in store. You focus on your tasks and leave the rest to me, Master. I will not fail you.*"

He was vulnerable now. It would not take much to corrupt him, to change his perceptions of her. A bit more and she would be able to make him see her as she once was. The slimy little man would not be able to resist her then. She stroked the pleasure centers of his mind once again and reached just a bit further . . .

"Stop!"

Ewzad's mind seized her presence and squeezed. She tried to pull away, but he twisted until she cried out. In the dark center of the forest, her real body convulsed and flailed about.

"*Let go! Release me!*"

"Oh, should I? Never, dear servant. Never. Never. Never touch me so again." His anger was back, but along with it was pleasure at her pain. "Yes, stay out of my mind. Stay out unless I specifically request it. Do you understand? Do you?"

"*Of course, Master. I am sorry, Master. I meant no offense,*" she simpered and tried to pull out of his grip, but he wasn't letting go. She fumed at herself for forgetting how strong his will could be. The dark voice had chosen him for a reason. Somehow the wizard must have read her thoughts.

"Yes. Yes he did. Don't forget that, dear servant." He flexed his mind and she cried out in pain again. "If you stood here before me, I would have you on your knees begging not to be turned into a beast as ugly as those nasty little children of yours. Oh yes, you would make a marvelous pet, wouldn't you. Yes, oh the things I could make out of you . . ."

"*The Dark Voice would not like that, Master. He had you recruit me for a reason.*" The stupid man was trying her patience. His grip was so tight that the only way to get free was to break his mind altogether. She was getting to the point where the option was more than tempting. If he didn't let go soon, she didn't care what the Dark Voice would think.

"Perhaps you are right, yes?" His grip loosened and she withdrew from his mind, leaving only their vocal communication open. Ewzad laughed. "Yes, you go on and distract the Mage School and Battle Academy while we build our army. I go to solidify my position with the king soon and it will not be long until we are ready to strike. Oh yes. That moment will be so sweet. I can almost reach out and taste it."

"*Of course, Master. I go now to prepare*," she crooned, but inside she was seething. For the hundredth time, she vowed to take the wizard's life as soon as she was permitted. Ewzad was not aware of the enormity of her power. He did not know the things she knew. He wanted to rule the lands, but she had been given far greater promises. Yes, far greater promises indeed.

Don't Forget to check out:

HILT'S PRIDE

A novella that takes place right after Sir Hilt leaves Justan during Testing Week at the training school. Available Now

About the Author

Trevor H. Cooley was born in South Carolina and has lived all around the United states, including Utah, New Mexico, Michigan and Tennessee.

His love of reading started in the second grade with Lloyd Alexander's Chronicles of Prydain series. He couldn't get enough and continued with David Eddings, Tolkein, Robert Jordan, Stephen King, and many others. Since then, all he wanted was to become a published writer.

The characters and concepts that eventually became the Bowl of Souls series started in his teens. He wrote short stories, kept notebooks full of ideas, and generally dreamed about the world constantly. There were several attempts at starting a novel over the years.

Not long after he was married, his wife told him to stop talking about the story and write it down. Many years and rewrites and submissions and rejection letters later, he finally put the books on Amazon in May 2012. He sold over 15,000 copies of his books in the first year through Kindle.

He currently lives in Idaho with his wife and four children.

The following is a preview chapter from:

MESSENGER of the DARK PROPHET

The Bowl of Souls: Book Two
Now available

Fist awoke in a panic, sitting up so fast that Squirrel flew from his sleeping spot on the ogre's broad, hairy chest. It skittered to a stop on the floor, chattering angrily. Fist ignored his little companion and padded to the door, mace in hand. Something was wrong.

A lot had changed in Fist's life during the last year. His boulder-lined shelter was now truly a house, with a thatched roof and comfortable fur rugs lining the floor. Tamboor had taken many of the furs that Fist acquired and sold them, using the money to purchase Fist the things he needed for his home.

They had chiseled away the rough spots on the boulders and filled in the gaps so that cold air couldn't seep in. They built a chimney. Tamboor had even taught the ogre how to cook inside and bought him a pot to use.

Fist's life had grown comfortable. He got all the action he needed hunting the wild beasts that threatened the mountain town and in particular, Tamboor's family. He now had a fine spear and massive steel mace that Tamboor had procured for him.

He was content. Usually his sleep was deep and dreamless, but during the last night his sleep had been mixed with uneasiness. He had tossed and turned all night long.

Now, as he charged from his home, he was filled with dread. His hackles were raised and his heart pounded in his chest. He didn't know what was going on, but his instincts had him prepared for battle.

Fist's calm grove of trees seemed peaceful as usual, but something was amiss. He trotted around the grove a ways, then froze. He listened carefully and heard twigs snap. Holding his mace at the ready, Fist advanced towards the sound.

He heard voices. Orc voices. What were orcs doing on his newfound tribal land?

Soon he saw them through the trees. The invaders were two burly orcs and a gorc. All three were fully armed. The orcs wore leather hide armor with metal helms. Each carried a wicked long blade with serrated edges that looked more like saws than swords. The gorc was smaller than the orcs and had a patch over one eye. He carried a long sharp dagger and a bow with a crude arrow notched at the ready.

With a growl, Fist approached them. He stood in their path and rose to his full height with his arms crossed. At his full height, Fist was just over eight feet tall and weighed close to four hundred pounds, most of it muscle. The one-eyed gorc squealed in fear at the sight of the enormous ogre standing in their way. The orcs gulped. They hadn't seen many ogres quite so big.

"Stop!" Fist commanded in the ogre tongue, his deep voice booming. "Don't you see the markings? You are in territory of the Big and Little People tribe. Leave my land now or I kill you!"

Two of them looked eager to do exactly that, but one orc stood his ground. "We seen yer marks," the orc barked. "Our leader, Gerstag, sented us. He say to tell you we are big army of the Barldag. Your tribe joins us or dies like the humans!" The others seemed to gain courage from the orc's speech and straightened their spines, looking up at Fist defiantly.

Though he betrayed no emotion, the orc's words struck Fist a mighty blow. It had taken him so long to find a place where he belonged. Now that he finally had it, he could sense it falling through his fingers.

Fist had often wondered about the great army that the ogre mage had tried to raise back in high mountain wilds. Every time the thought had risen in his mind, he had ignored the threat. He hadn't even mentioned it to Tamboor, hoping that the ogre mage had been unsuccessful in his attempts to unite the goblinoids and giants.

"The Barldag's army is here now?" Fist asked. The goblinoids nodded.

His worst dreams were being realized. Now the only thought in his mind was to warn his human friends. Fist was trying to decide just how to kill the three goblinoids the fastest, when Squirrel appeared in a branch above them. Squirrel chattered fiercely, shaking one tiny fist at them and berating them for coming onto its land.

"Look what I sees. Little meats for breakfast." The one-eyed gorc smiled and brought up his bow. He began to pull the arrow back and didn't even see the metal head of the mace coming. Fist's new weapon plowed through its skull, leaving a ruined mess and the gorc dropped to the ground soundlessly.

Fist smacked the bloody head of the mace into his palm. "No one hurts my tribe!"

The orcs started to laugh, thinking the death of the gorc nothing but an ogre joke. Fist threw the mace at the first orc. Its laughter ended in a squeak as the round steel head thudded into its chest. The force of the strike knocked the orc off its feet, shattered its ribs, and pulverized the vital organs beneath.

The remaining orc backed up, "The Barldag commands that you join us!"

"If the Barldag comes, I will kill him too!" he promised and charged.

The orc desperately lashed out with its sword, scoring a minor hit along Fist's side. The ogre took the scratch with a slight wince and grabbed the orc's helmet between his giant hands. He squeezed and the metal screeched until there was a loud pop and the orc stopped thrashing.

Fist threw its crushed helmet to the ground and spat at the bodies of the goblinoids. He then picked up his mace and whistled. Squirrel jumped from the tree to his shoulders.

Fist stood in his quiet grove for a moment while Squirrel munched a seed and wondered how far away the army was. The orcs had said that Gerstag was their leader. That was an ogre name and it sounded familiar to Fist. Though he could not place where he had heard it, the name confirmed to him that at least some of the ogre tribes had joined the Barldag's army. This did not bode well at all.

He had to warn his human friends so that Tamboor could get word to the rest of the town. The Barldag's army would destroy everything in sight. He looked at his beautiful territory and felt like weeping. How much time did he have?

Fist sniffed the air and his heart sank even further. With squirrel safely in its pouch, the ogre ran to a nearby clearing and saw with his eyes what his nose was telling him. Smoke. Great columns of smoke were rising from the human town of Jack's Rest. He had no time at all.

Fist ran back to his house and retrieved the fine steel spear that Tamboor had purchased for him. The ogre took one last sorrowful look at his marvelous home and hurried through the woods. He couldn't save the land, but he had to at least save the only family he had left in the world.

Fist ran through the familiar trails of his woods, the smell of smoke thick in his nostrils. He felt a pang in his heart as he thought of the friendship that the humans had shown him. Right now in the village, people were fighting and dying at the hands of this evil army.

As Fist sprinted, he caught sight of a party of four goblin scouts slinking through the trees just inside of his territory. They were moving toward the home of his human friends. Once again, anger surged through the ogre.

The little goblins looked up in surprise just as Fist's spear took one of them in the belly. He followed with an underhand blow of his mace, caving in the pelvis and belly of another goblin, sending it soaring up through the air. Before the two remaining scouts could do anything more than squeal, he smashed their heads together with a wet crunch, his enormous strength ending their lives quickly.

Adrenaline surged through his massive body as he retrieved his weapons and raced recklessly through the forest. He didn't give much thought to what would happen once he found his friends. Maybe they could escape down to the towns in lower altitudes. He didn't have time to worry about how the humans in another town would receive him, his only concern was getting to Tamboor's family. They were his tribe now.

As he got closer to the house, he saw with relief that there wasn't any smoke coming from that direction. Perhaps he would get there in time. Squirrel crawled out of its pouch and curled up along the back of his neck as he ran, its furry warmth helping to comfort the ogre. Fist rounded the big rocks that lined the edge of Tamboor's property and sighed with relief. Everything seemed to be untouched.

When the ogre's presence had first been revealed, Tamboor hadn't let Fist have anything to do with his family. But as the friendship between the human and ogre had grown and his wife and children kept insisting, Tamboor had relented. Fist had become a regular visitor to their home.

The inside of the house was small for the ogre and he had

to hunch over more than usual to move inside the place, but he didn't mind. The children loved Fist and climbed all over him, including the ogre in their games. Fist pretended that he was putting up with the children's attention, but both Tamboor and his wife knew that he enjoyed the children's play just as much as they did. Their only problem had been keeping Fist's existence a secret to the town.

Tamboor had taken the credit for killing all of the monsters that Fist hunted. Though the ogre had not known it, he had even bought Fist's land from the mayor of Jack's Rest so that none of the townsfolk would go up there without his permission. It had worked so far. No one in the town even suspected the ogre's presence.

As Fist approached the house, Tamboor's wife Efflina opened the door. At first she smiled, but when she saw the state the ogre was in, she became worried. Blood was spattered on his arms and ran from the cut along his side.

"Fist! What's going on? Are you okay?" The two children, Cedric and Lina, darted out from behind her in the doorway and ran to the ogre, laughing and yelling "Fist! Fist!"

"No! Stay inside!" the ogre commanded. As the kids pouted and walked back, Fist looked to their mother. "Where is Tamboor?"

"Why he left a little while ago and told us we had to stay in the house. Evidently there is a big fire in the village or something because smoke is everywhere."

"Not just fire," Fist moaned. "Goblins and monsters is attacking the peoples in the town."

"How many goblins?" she asked. Every once in a while a troop of goblins would come too close to Jack's Rest. Usually the tough men of the town handled such raids easily.

"Too many," Fist said impatiently. He looked up the road that led to the town. The army could come down on them at any moment. "A army comes! We must take Cedric and Lina away. We must keep them safe!"

Efflina looked uncertainly at the pillars of smoke coming from Jack's Rest and then looked back at the ogre.

"Please," Fist begged. "Trust me."

Efflina bit her lip. She hated to leave her home; the home that Tamboor had built with his own hands. But she trusted the ogre. She turned to the children.

"Cedric, Lina, gather the 'run packs'. We are going with Fist for a while." Her husband had demanded they always keep emergency supplies for just such an occasion. Lina squealed with delight, but Cedric frowned. He knew what those packs meant even if Lina didn't. The children ran towards their rooms.

"What about Tamboor?" Efflina asked.

Fist had fought alongside the retired academy warrior several times during the last year against savage beasts and had great faith in his prowess. He could only hope that Tamboor would survive the attack.

"He will come. Hurry!"

Efflina ran back inside the house and Fist could hear her directing the children in the things they had to bring. Fist paced on the porch, knowing that every moment before they left was a moment wasted. Then he heard goblin voices. Bile rose in his throat. He crept to the edge of the porch and looked down the road.

He ran back to the house and yelled through the doorway, "Wait! Hide! They is here!"

The goblinoids streamed from the trees and headed up the hill towards the house. More than a score of them came, goblins, gorcs and orcs.

"Protect the tribe," he whispered and Squirrel left his shoulder to run into the house.

Fist did not know what to do. He doubted that he could defeat twenty of these creatures by himself, but if he failed, his tribe would be killed. He took a deep breath and steadied himself. He would not fail.

He walked off of the porch and stood in the road where the goblinoids would see him. The goblinoids seemed unconcerned about the appearance of an ogre. They stopped in front of Fist and one of the bigger orcs stepped forward.

"Ogre! I am Pintok, square leader. What you here alone for? Why you not killing mens at the village?"

Fist thought quickly and shouted back, "I followed mens to this house and killed them." He showed his bloody mace and forearms. The orc smiled evilly.

"You kill them all and leave none for us? Not even womens?" the orc asked.

Fist had to force a growl out of his throat. "No. I kill them all."

The goblinoids scowled in disappointment. The orc sighed. "Then we takes foods and burn the house."

"No!" Fist shouted, and tried to think of a good excuse.

"Why not?" The orc drew his wicked sword and sneered at the ogre.

Fist fumbled about for a bit, but finally found some words. "This house has been claimed by my tribe!"

Pintok clenched his teeth with anger. "What tribe is that?"

"The Rock People," Fist claimed, randomly picking an ogre tribe that he thought would have joined the army.

The orc pointed his sword at the ground. "Gerstag's tribe?"

Fist finally remembered who Gerstag was. He was mighty warrior of the Rock People tribe. Fist had fought him once years ago, when the Rock People had stolen some of the Thunder People's women. Fist had gained the upper hand and been about to kill him when the leaders of the tribe had stopped their fight.

"Yes," Fist said with new confidence. "Gerstag wants this house and the foods inside." He was beginning to think that this just might work. The orc didn't look too happy about Fist's declaration and appeared as if he was thinking about going in the house anyway, but finally he grunted and turned to the other goblinoids.

"Gerstag's claimed this house. We go down the road to find other foods!" The goblins started to leave and Fist was about to breathe a sigh of relief when a cry rang out by the road.

A small goblin ran up to the orc leader. "Human's coming!" it declared and Pintok grinned.

The orc directed the goblinoids to prepare themselves. Five archers stood just in front of their leader, while the rest ran into the trees on either side of the road that led up to the house from Jack's Rest.

Fist stood by the porch, waiting to act until he knew what was happening. From his higher vantage point, he saw who was approaching before the orc did. It was Tamboor, followed by two villagers that Fist knew on sight, a solid looking dwarf named Ryebald, who carried a heavy axe and a human named Petyr, with a long slender sword and a small shield. Both of them were retired academy graduates, just like Tamboor. They were running towards the house as fast as they could.

The orc leader saw their approach and grunted out a command. On cue, the goblinoid archers pulled back their arrows.

"Hold it," the orc whispered. "Wait, hold it . . . Fi-" Pintok stopped in mid-word and looked down at the bloody tip of Fist's spear that protruded from its chest. The archers didn't even hear their leader fall over. With one powerful swing of his mace, Fist sent two of the goblin archers to the ground crushed and bleeding.

"Tamboor! Goblins in the trees!" Fist bellowed and kicked another goblin in the face, caving it in, sending teeth and eyeballs flying.

Tamboor heard Fist yell, but didn't stop. He turned his head and shouted something to the two companions that were with him. The other two, simply nodded and followed Tamboor's lead. They were combat veterans, unafraid of goblinoid riffraff.

Fist crushed the head of another archer with his mace, but the fifth one, an orc, saw him coming. It shot an arrow from five feet away. The arrow struck Fist between the eyes. The tip of the arrow ricocheted off of his hard skull and burrowed upwards under his skin to protrude weirdly out the top of his scalp. The fletchings came to a stop right above his nose.

Fist's head snapped back and he stumbled a couple of feet, his head ringing from the blow. His vision blurred for a moment. He saw two orcs instead of one slowly reaching into a quiver behind their shoulders to pull out another arrow. But it was okay because as he raised his arm and stumbled forward, he saw that he had two maces.

Things didn't move that slowly for the orc archer, though. It hadn't expected the ogre to keep coming after it an arrow stuck in his head. The archer backpedaled as it tried to fit another arrow to its bow, but the ogre was faster.

The mace whipped across, breaking both of the orc's arms and knocking the bow away. The orc stood, vacantly staring at his arms which were bent in weird angles, as the ogre's giant mace came back around and connected with the side of its head.

As Tamboor and his two friends neared the house, the trees on either side of the road erupted in a flurry of motion. The remaining goblinoids rushed out of the foliage with weapons held high. The companions were lucky that the ogre had warned them, because if they hadn't been prepared for the strike, they likely would have died in the first few moments of the fight.

Fortunately all three of them knew how to fight against overwhelming odds. Ryebald, the dwarf, roared and plowed headfirst into the orcs that came rushing at him, surprising them with his fury. Tamboor and Petyr stood back to back and fought in concert, Tamboor's savagery and Petyr's style of calm, piercing attacks set the attackers off balance.

Fist stood over the body of the orc and shook his head. He was still dazed and blood began streaming into his eyes from his garish head wound. He could hear the fight between the goblinoids and the warriors, but he could not join the battle if he couldn't see.

Fist grasped the tip of the arrow that stuck out at the top of his scalp and broke the arrowhead off. Then he grasped the fletched end and pulled the arrow shaft out of the hole over his nose. The removal of the arrow brought a fresh rush of blood, but that was good. The blood would help clean the wound. The ogre wiped his eyes and rushed towards the battle.

Only moments had passed since the battle started and neither Tamboor nor Petyr had been severely injured. However, the humans hadn't taken much of a toll on the monsters either. So far, they had only killed two of them and those were just goblins. They were so busy defending attacks from several opponents at once, that it was hard to get an offensive strike in. The two humans made a great team, but both were tiring as they had been fighting all morning back at the village.

Ryebald, on the other hand, seemed to be tireless. His fighting style was much more straightforward, which was more effective in this case. The dwarf made great sweeps of his ax, aiming low to the ground, taking out legs and bellies of the creatures. So far, he had killed three and wounded several more. Unfortunately, this tactic left him open for attack. He had been struck several times, but each hit just seemed only to enrage him further.

As Fist reached the fight both Ryebald and Petyr saw him and cried out to Tamboor in warning.

"Don't worry about the ogre! He's a friend!" Tamboor shouted.

His words were confirmed a moment later, when Fist waded into the battle with his mace, sending dying goblinoids sprawling every which way. At this point, the momentum swung into the townsfolk's favor and the goblinoids began to flee. Soon, there were only six left and they only remained because they were too afraid to run.

It looked as though the fight was over, but no one saw the small ball that rolled across the ground from the trees. When it reached the center of the fight, a strange buzzing noise filled the air. All of the combatants froze in place.

CPSIA information can be obtained at www.ICGtesting.com
Printed in the USA
LVOW01s1504270415

436247LV00001B/158/P

9 781478 114048